Silver Victory

An *ISC Fleet* Novel

The third book
in the
Preeminent War
Series

Rock Whitehouse

Like I've said before, this is a work of fiction.
Fiction.
As in, everything in it is made up.
By me.
So,
Any similarity to actual persons living,
or dead,
or yet to be born,
or any actual event,
past, present, or future,
is still either pure coincidence
or blind dumb luck.

That's just how it is.

Dedication

I heard the voice of the Lord saying,
"Whom shall I send, and who will go for Us?"
Then said I, "Here am I. Send me!"
Isaiah 6:8

Therefore,
this work is dedicated to all those who
bravely go forth in this fallen world,
doing good in the battle
for truth,
for freedom,
for health,
for knowledge,
for wisdom,
or
for faith.

Author's Note

Well, here we are in the last installment of the war with the Preeminent. Thanks for coming along this far, and I hope you'll enjoy this part of the ride, too.

So, now the Preeminent have launched an offensive just as CINC was designing one of his own. David and his cohorts aboard *Cobra* saw it dispatched, and they sounded the alarm for the rest of the fleet. Carol is almost back to Beta Hydri, but this visit will not be filled with peaceful exploration like before.

Natalie Hayden's grief is still fresh, but she is back on duty, and *Intrepid* is headed into the fight as well.

Dan Smith's *Columbia* has been drafted as the southern theater flagship, and he's still not sure how he feels about that.

It seems hard times are ahead for everyone, from the lowest tech to the Commander in Chief.

But something is brewing back at Alpha Mensae, something that may take the war in an entirely different direction.

I've again included a list of characters at the end of the book. There's also a cheat-sheet Appendix for the Preeminent's decimal-based time system. Take a microt and check it out.

I'm always interested in your feedback, so drop me a line at rock@iscfleet.com. And please leave a review with whatever vendor you purchased the book.

My editor says I can't possibly walk away from this universe and these characters after only three books. She might well be right. There are certainly lots of places we could go from here.

We'll see.

Best regards, stay safe, and pray for all of us in this stressful time.

Rock Whitehouse
North Ridgeville, Ohio
October 1, 2020

February 2079

Antares
En Route Beta Hydri
Tuesday, February 7, 2079, 1325 UTC

Senior Lieutenant Lori Rodgers read the message from *Cobra* three times before forwarding it to her Captain, Terri Michael. The news from the Fleet's fastest and most stealthy intelligence ship was frightening. She looked across the Bridge at Weapons Officer Carol Hansen, wondering how she would react to what David Powell's ship had discovered. Lori got up from her Comms position and walked over to Carol, who was having an animated and humorous discussion with Chief Tech Guzman at the Weapons station.

"Hansen, I need to talk to you." Her tone killed the laughter like a fire hose to a match.

Carol quickly stood and followed her to the far-left corner of the Bridge.

"What is it, Lori?"

Rodgers passed over her NetComp, the message open. Carol's eyes widened as she read Rich Evans's shocking dispatch:

```
FLASH 207902061100 UTC
TO: ALL FLEET
FROM: COBRA ACTUAL
SUBJECT: ENEMY DEPLOYMENT

1) SURVEILLANCE OF BLUE DOT ALPHA MENSAE (C) LEAVES NO QUESTION
PLANET IS ENEMY HOME WORLD (DESIGNATE AS E-PRIME).
2) COBRA OBSERVED DEPARTURE OF FIFTY REPEAT FIFTY ENEMY
WARSHIPS 207902060900UTC.
3) REVERSE NAV ANALYSIS OF IR TRACK DATA INDICATES DESTINATIONS
ARE EARTH, INOR, AND BETA HYDRI.
4) FOUR TYPE II SHIPS DISPATCHED TO BETA HYDRI.
5) DETAILS OF OTHER TYPES TO FOLLOW.
6) PROCEEDING BETA HYDRI MAX SPEED ETA 207902150100UTC.

EVANS

END
```

"Ho-ly shit," Carol said quietly.

"Amen to that." Lori looked around nervously, the implications for *Antares* flashing around in her head.

Without looking up, Carol asked, "Does Michael have this?"

Lori looked around again. "Yeah, right before I came over here."

1

Carol looked her friend in the eye, thinking about what was about to happen. Her thoughts were dark, dangerous, and violent.

"This is going to get ugly."

Weapons Chief Tech Emilio Guzman watched the exchange between the officers, and when his patience finally lost out to his curiosity, he joined them.

"Lieutenant?"

Carol looked at him, her face now as serious as he had ever seen. "Classified, understand?"

Guzman paused a second, meeting Carol's eye. "Yes, ma'am."

She passed the NetComp to him and watched the same expression develop on his face that Lori had seen on hers.

He pointed to the NetComp as he took a deep breath. "This means — "

"Classified, Chief. Not a word until the captain announces it."

"Yes, ma'am. Understood."

As he handed it back, both officers' NetLinks sounded a tone.

Carol looked at hers and read the message from Captain Terri Michaels aloud: "All Officers to the Wardroom. Now." She turned again to the Chief. "Nothing, Chief. Not a single word until she speaks."

"Yes, Lieutenant."

Carol nodded her understanding, and she and Lori turned to head for the wardroom as the Chief returned to his station. The duty weapons tech looked at his Chief, now stone-faced where just a moment ago they had been laughing.

"What was that all about?"

"Later," Chief Guzman said. "Later." After a moment of worried silence, he turned to the tech. "Do me a favor and pull up the *Liberty* attack record, James, and let me see the tracking for when they hit the Type II's."

"Type II's?"

"Yeah, I just want to see exactly how that played out."

"Any particular reason you want that particular data?"

"Cornell, just shut up and find me the record. And keep quiet about it."

"Yes, Chief." Weapons Tech James Cornell was a veteran of Inoria, and a sincere admirer of both Carol Hansen and Emilio Guzman. Whatever message had just passed from Rodgers to Hansen to Guzman was anything but routine, and the Chief's request couldn't possibly be random. He remained silent, found the record from his former ship, and posted the data for Guzman to review.

The wardroom was unusually silent as the officers gathered, only a few small whispers of worry passed around the room. Terri Michael knew there was no time to waste.

"OK, everyone, let's get started. You all have the message *Cobra* sent." She

2

turned to her new Intel officer, Roger Cox. "First thing: Lieutenant Cox, what about dispositions?"

"Yes, Captain. *Columbia* is already at Beta Hydri, arrived yesterday. *Eagle* and *Friendship* were scheduled to return on her arrival and might be headed home already. They're bingo on supplies, so normally they would expect to head back to Earth shortly. *Intrepid* is five days behind us."

"But, with *Ceres* en route, couldn't *Eagle* and *Friendship* remain on station until it gets here?"

Cox flipped through a couple of screens on his NetComp. "Yes, actually, they could. *Ceres* will be at Beta Hydri in about two weeks. By reg, both ships should still have at least two month's expendables aboard."

Terri nodded her agreement. "OK, good. Now, what is your assessment of the message?"

"Well, ma'am, we've only had a few minutes to discuss this. Still, clearly the enemy knows what we care about, and they're coming hard to push us back. But honestly, I don't understand why they would go to Earth. They've seen it. They know they can't win there."

Carol cleared her throat gently before she spoke. "Unless something has changed, and now they think they can."

After a moment of sober silence, Ryan Lewis suggested, "Or, winning at Earth isn't the point. They just want to make a statement."

Terri Michael brought the digression to an end. "Let's keep to our own problems, folks. CINC will need to deal with Earth."

Cox spoke again. "*Cobra* hasn't sent the details yet, but we should expect at least six enemy ships, probably more. They would not send the Type II's without bombardment ships."

Terri nodded. "Agreed. Nav, I need whatever speed you can give us until we get there. I know it's only a day, but put the pedal to the metal best you can."

"Yes, Captain. I might be able to get you another point two or so."

"Fine, thanks." She turned to Carol. "Before we get there, I want both rotaries loaded with half Bludgeons, half Spartans. That gives us some balance between for offense and defense."

"Yes, ma'am. We'll be ready."

Terri turned to the recently promoted Marine Major Wayne Barnes. "Well, Major Barnes, seems our days of peaceful exploration are over."

"Yes, ma'am, seems so. I'll talk to Sergeant Jackson, but the platoon is in good shape. We've read up on how the *Intrepid* force engaged them. We're ready."

"Where are we with the crew weapons training?"

"At this point, most of the crew is competent with the 2K7X at a basic level.

3

Several have declined, a few just don't shoot so well."

"Are you satisfied that those who have trained would be able to contribute in a ground engagement?"

"Yes, Captain. Couple them with a few Marines, and they'd be a real advantage."

"Very well." She looked down, then back up and around the table. "I fully expect that we'll be in a large-scale fleet engagement come the twenty-first. We've been given plenty of time to prepare, so let's make good use of it."

The room was quiet, the faces looking back at her were calm, but the stress filling the place could not be missed.

"Go over your sections carefully. It's been a quiet transit up to now, but we need to get our minds back in a battle attitude. Let me know if there is anything you need to get ready. That's all for now." Terri rose and left the room quickly, giving her officers a chance to discuss their situation without having to worry about what she would hear, or think.

The Domicile of Uteon Se Nani
The Preeminent Home World
Earth Equivalent Date: February 8, 2079

Uteon Se Nani's residence was in a mid-city, just two links from Core, the central city of his society. He was a worker in a military factory, a semi-skilled assembler of a small space ship component. He neither knew what it was or where in a ship it might be installed. Nor did he care. This was just his assignment. His residence was satisfactory for someone of his position, comfortable enough if somewhat small.

As the evening meal was brought down from the maturation shelf, finally aged long enough to be palatable, Uteon turned his dark green eyes to his female child, his hard-leather face set in determination.

"It is time," he said without emotion.

She looked up from the meal to her maleParent, her soft, less weathered face perplexed. "Time?"

"You will reach your first fertility before this revolution is complete, so it is time for you to be paired. My female, your EggLayer, is ripe with new eggs. You must go."

The child placed her meal back on the platter. "And if I do not wish it?"

"It matters not what you wish. You have been given life. You have been fed for eight revs, as is the custom. You have been instructed in the knowledge you require."

As he spoke, Uteon ripped off another large chunk of Daxluk, sucking the

4

tail end into his mouth as he crunched the bones with his molars, bloody juices overflowing his lips and spilling onto his gray worker's tunic.

"It is time. You will go into the pairing queue nextRot."

"*Next* rotation? This seems very sudden, maleParent. Have I no choice?"

Uteon choked down the meat mass he had just consumed, then drank deeply from his cup.

"Foolish female! How would you choose? One male is much like the next, as one female is much like the next. You will take your turn and accept your pairing. What would you prefer? That males strut and fight like Dawinsas? Eat each other's young to show dominance like Scrapnats?"

Uteon slammed his cup down after yet another long drink, his patience wearing thin.

"This society grows rich on order, Asoon. You will be assigned a male, you will produce your eggs, and you will live a peaceful life. Educate yourself and your production as required."

That he would be angry did not surprise her, only the vigor with which he expressed it gave her pause.

"And this is the path of Ultimate Origin?"

"I know little of Ultimate Origin, Asoon Too Lini, other than the myth passed down from my own maleParent. It is said that we prosper here to find our way there, or that some other race will come to take us there."

Asoon fidgeted nervously with the hem of her light blue vest, looking at her gray skin, such a sharp contrast to her maleParent's bright purple. "Or that we go there when we die?"

"That is a disgusting heresy, Asoon Too Lini. Death is death. The end of life is just that — the end. You have already been instructed in this, and it is pointless, wasteful, to hope for the impossible. "

She sat quietly, staring without hunger at her food, the last she would receive in the home of her parents. Her life was about to change in ways she could not control, but as her society demanded. She had seen other young females leave to be paired, and none ever returned. Some she knew quite well from their common schooling, but they disappeared once they were paired. She hid a nagging fear of what 'pairing' really meant.

He handed her a document, specifying how she was to report, and what she was allowed to take with her.

"It is decided. NextRot, your EggLayer will take you."

Asoon Too Lini rose from the meal table and returned to her sleep room with the document, afraid for perhaps the first time in her life.

5

Cobra
En Route Beta Hydri from Alpha Mensae (c) aka 'e-prime'
Wednesday, February 8, 2079, 0435 UTC

David Powell squinted into the afternoon sun as he approached the plate. Sweat stung his eyes, so be stepped back to wipe his face, then picked up some dirt to rub on his hands. As he stepped into the batter's box, he caught sight of his parents, sitting in the bleachers along the first base line. His father's face stared out, wearing its usual dour expression as his mother gave him an obviously animated lecture.

"STRIKE ONE!"

David was slapped back into the moment by the sound of the ball smacking into the catcher's glove and the umpire's loud cry. As he looked out to the mound, the pitcher with the purple arm David had found on the enemy wreck wound up and threw another shiny steel ball.

"STRIKE TWO!"

David looked in bewilderment from the umpire back out to the alien pitcher, who was now taller, his arm larger, and he threw an even bigger ball. David swung with all his might as the ball came at his head and —

"*Shit!*" he yelled as he awoke in the dark cabin.

"Powell, dammit, you woke me up!"

David looked over at his roommate, Surveillance Systems Chief Engineer Kyle Levine. "Oh, sorry, Kyle."

"What the hell was that about, anyway?"

David sat up and shook his head, trying to clear the images still bouncing around inside. "Just a dream."

"Somehow, I don't think it was some happy-ending Hansen dream."

"Kyle, you're a pig."

"Hey, pal, we all respect you, and her even more, but you gotta know half the fleet is jealous as hell."

"And the other half?"

"The other half doesn't know Carol."

David swung his legs off the bunk, thinking about heading for the head. "Jesus, Kyle, you really are a pig. "

"So, what was the dream?"

"Something meaningless. Dreams don't really mean anything."

"Bullshit. Sometimes they mean everything. Tell me."

"You'll laugh."

"Maybe. Still, you woke me up with it, so dish, man."

David came back from the toilet and flopped back on his bunk, his hands behind his head. "OK, fine. I was a kid again, playing little league. Only the pitcher had a purple arm, and he was throwing silver baseballs I kept missing."

After a pause, David looked over at Kyle.

"You're not laughing."

"Hell no, I'm not. Somewhere down in that oversized intellect of yours, you think we've missed something important."

"Huh. Didn't make that connection."

"First thing tomorrow, you need to be going back over whatever data we have. Think about what you were looking at as the enemy bugged out. Maybe that will jog whatever is percolating in your super-cruising subconscious."

"Did you know you talk like a shrink sometimes?"

"Yeah, my psych courses didn't entirely go to waste."

David looked over at the chronometer on the wall: 0443. He'd never get back to sleep now.

"Well, Kyle, no time like the present..."

"Whatever, man. I'm going back to sleep."

David slipped into a work uniform and headed for the Operations Room. It would be quiet at this hour, and he might be better able to concentrate on whatever it was he'd missed.

If, that is, he actually had missed something. He wasn't nearly as sure as Kyle.

Science Directorate Pairing Department
The Preeminent Home World
Earth Equivalent Date: Thursday, February 9, 2079

Asoon and her EggLayer boarded the tram into Core City well before Star-Rise. After they were seated, Asoon asked her EggLayer the questions that had been haunting her. After receiving only minimal responses to her first few, she stopped asking. Clearly, her EggLayer was not willing or not able to alleviate her anxieties about pairing. Asoon comforted herself with her own thoughts and the view of her home star rising in the east over a distant mountain range. The trip felt much longer than the two drots that it actually took.

After the tram, they walked the rest of the way in silence. Her EggLayer left Asoon at the foot of the long, wide stone stairs leading into the Pairing Facility, walking away without another word. It was a drot past StarRise now, and the star's warmth felt good on Asoon's face and tail stump. It would be a clear, pleasant day, one like many she had spent in the grassy parks near her home when she was younger. She suddenly missed those days, leisurely soaking in star light and spending time learning of her society and the universe around them.

7

Mathematics, especially, had been her strength. But such talents were not encouraged in females, whose primary purpose was to lay eggs and tend to the development of the male's production. Still, Asoon had enjoyed the deep complexity and hidden simplicity of the sciences she was not supposed to study. The underlying logic of the universe was somehow comforting to her.

The Pairing Facility was like all SD structures: unadorned steel and glass, superficially plain but exuding a kind of quiet power through the sheer imposing scope of it. Asoon Too Lini walked reluctantly up the steps and into the facility, surrounded by several hundred other females, each moving forward, gradually funneling down to a single line.

"Name?" the admissions manager asked.

"Who cares?" she answered. "The selections are all random, aren't they?"

The manager's expression didn't change, but Asoon detected a small quiver of annoyance in her tail stump.

"Name?"

"Asoon Too Lini."

The manager looked at her list, flipping the pages quickly, and as she found Asoon's name, the tail stump became very still. She paused a moment.

"341," she said dismissively as she handed Asoon a card with the printed number.

"What differ — "

"Next!" the manager called, no longer looking at Asoon Too Lini.

Perplexed by the manager's reaction to her name, Asoon proceeded into a large area where they would wait to be called. The females around her chattered of superficial things: what kind of male, where they would reside, apparently oblivious to the random nature of it all. *They will get what they get,* she thought to herself, *what's the point in speculating about it?*

Within a short time, the females all had their assigned numbers, and at the manager's direction arranged themselves into proper order. Asoon found herself near the back of the line, which seemed to end somewhere around 375. She felt a strong sense of impatience, yet not a bit of eagerness. She had to do what was expected, but she saw no reason to anticipate anything personally rewarding or pleasurable about it. It was time to accept a male and make more of her kind. Period. She outwardly believed her indoctrination that stated this was how a prosperous society was structured, but in her mind she still wondered, still held a quiet, small hope for a life of her own direction. Such thoughts were dangerous, especially for a female, but they were thoughts she had held for as long as she could remember.

Scad Nee Wok was a little old for a pairing male. His first female had become ill, and once it was clear she could not produce a clutch of eggs, she was expunged. His summons was no less mandatory than Asoon's, and his status as a ship captain gave him no excuse, no delay. His commanders ensured that he was available when and where required.

As Wok came through the males' entrance, he was also assigned a number in line, not that he paid much attention to it. The assignments were random, and it would be his duty, his place in society, to take the female allocated to him, to create a stable, healthy household, and to produce offspring. Each clutch, usually four eggs, would be examined by the authorities in the Eugenics Section of the Science Directorate, who would remove any which were defective. The rest, usually two or three, would be returned and he and his female would be responsible for them.

The chatter in the brightly lit waiting room faded as they entered the long line leading to the pairing room. Pairing was a solemn duty, and while what Uteon Si Nani had told his female offspring was true, both genders hoped for a positive match that would make their daily life more pleasant.

Asoon eventually came to the front of the line, more anxious than she thought she would be. She tried to peek across the room, but the male line was shielded from her view. She heard the previous pair dismissed and then the pairing manager called out, "341."

Asoon stepped out and was surprised to see a male several revs older than herself. She had heard that this happened, but it was rare.

A re-pair, she thought, *a failure*. As she overcame her disappointment, she noticed he was dressed in red, a color she was unaccustomed to. Like most males, he was a full head taller than her. Asoon was slightly encouraged by the cleanliness of his appearance. She knew many males who bathed only infrequently and expressed a distinctly unpleasant odor. *This might not be so horrible after all,* she concluded.

The pairing manager spoke, turning first to Wok.

"Asoon Too Lini."

"Asoon Too Lini," Wok replied.

The manager turned his head to her. "Scad Nee Wok."

"Scad Nee Wok," Asoon repeated mechanically.

"You are now paired."

"We are paired," they repeated in unison.

Next would come their home assignment. There were many places they might live, some less than desirable. The manager turned again to Asoon, an unusually pleasant expression on his face.

"You will join Scad Nee Wok in Core City. Scad Nee Wok is a Warrior, a ship commander."

Asoon was surprised, even hopeful. The central city of their society, known to all simply as 'Core,' was restricted to government officials and warriors. She had, supposedly by chance, done better than she could ever have expected. But, she reminded herself, she knew nothing about Scad Nee Wok, and his character would be the strongest determinant of what her life would be like. They walked out of the pairing facility and entered a waiting transport.

As the transport began to move, taking them to Scad Nee Wok's home, he sniffed the air as he looked at her. "You will not be fertile for some time, I think."

"Yes, that is correct."

"My first female, you should know, became ill and could not produce. She was...removed."

Asoon detected a trace of regret, or perhaps, sympathy, in his voice.

"You did not wish this?" she asked.

"What I wish is irrelevant. She was removed."

They passed the rest of the trip in silence. Scad Nee Wok stoically looking forward, Asoon watching the city take shape around her. The transport finally stopped in front of a small residence. *Not that senior a Warrior,* Asoon thought. But even this was far better than any domicile in a distant out-city, or even where she grew up.

As they went inside, Wok pointed to a sleeping room off the entrance.

"This will be your room until your fertility arrives."

"I understand," she answered quietly.

"I am not a dominating male, Asoon, prone to giving orders or making demands. I get enough of that aboard my ship. I will be gone for many rots at a time, and until there are young to attend to, you may fill that time in any way you desire."

"Thank you."

"When I am here, I would appreciate your company at meals and during evening reading time."

"I will be ready for those activities, Wok."

"Here, you may address me as Scad. It is the name I prefer." He looked at her for several milrots. "I do not detect that you are happy with this arrangement."

Asoon looked around for a moment before responding. "Happiness, Scad, is not a factor in our pairing. I was assigned to you, and you to me." After a moment, she continued, "But I am not dissatisfied with my lot. You seem a comfortable male, not one to harm or abuse me. I have seen too much of that kind."

"You are correct, Asoon. You will be well treated here."

"I am grateful for that, Scad."

"Very well, then. We will meet for the evening meal, then perhaps we can talk further during reading time."

After their evening meal, Scad and Asoon sat together in the small common area of the residence.

"Scad, I walked the streets after my rest. Is this area always so very quiet?"

"No. Many warriors are away."

"Is something happening? Is there danger?"

Wok, unsure how much to tell this new female, decided to test her understanding. "There is no danger, at least, not immediately. But, yes, something is happening. The entire force is engaged with a foe that we must eliminate."

"But, you are here?"

Scad's posture and hands expressed his resignation.

"Even the Armada cannot defy a pairing summons from the Science Directorate, Asoon. I had no more choice than you today."

"But you would prefer to be there, not here?"

"I am a ship commander, Asoon. I worry about my ship, my deputies, my crew. I have been with them for a long time. I would prefer to see the fight at their side."

"We citizens know so little of the Armada, only that it protects us and provides us with things we need."

Wok was not ready to discuss the hidden details of the Armada, its practices, and secret beliefs. "Yes, that is all true. In time, I may be able to share more with you, but for now, that will do."

Asoon looked at him cautiously. "There are rumors of strange occurrences, Scad. Bizarre things. Horrible things."

Wok waved his clawed hand as if clutching her words from the air. "Idle thoughts will not help us prosper, Asoon. These rumors come from those who know nothing but imagine everything."

"Still — "

"That is enough, Asoon!"

Asoon recoiled at the sound of his voice, wondering if she had somehow come too close to revealing something Scad Nee Wok needed to conceal.

In a moment, he calmed down and lifted a volume from his shelf. "Now," he said, more gently, "let us discuss this one."

Asoon had already read the volume he held, a collection of legends and myths culled from their ancestors' earliest known writings. The author analyzed the disparate versions, seeking to define a common root story. The author believed that the truth lay in those now-lost forms, if they could only be found and understood.

Wok was surprised at Asoon's grasp of the work, and her thoughts of where the author had been incorrect were interesting and enlightening. He found himself challenged to follow her logic at times, but pleasantly so. He had expected

11

a female like his first: simple, compliant, reliable. Asoon might well be loyal and dependable, but she was anything but simple.

Before long, he would discover just how right he was.

Cobra
En Route Beta Hydri
Thursday, February 9, 2079, 0930 UTC

David had been in Center Console for five hours, running the visual data on one of the enemy task forces back and forth, again, for at least the tenth time. The quiet of the Operations Center in FTL, where no sensors were active and there was nothing to monitor, helped him concentrate. Finally, he paused it, staring at the small constellation of enormous vessels on his screen. Then, something clicked.

"What the hell..." he wondered aloud.

His comment interrupted Warrant Officer Ray Salazar, who was also there reviewing the RF data collected at e-prime. He spun in his chair to face David. "What?"

David put the image he'd been studying on the full-size main display on the aft bulkhead, then left Center to walk to it.

"Something doesn't make sense here. This ship —" David said, pointing, "— isn't the right size."

Salazar got up from his position and stood behind David. "Show me."

David pointed to three other vessels. "These are all Type I's." He then indicated another. "This one is a Type III. That all correlates based on apparent angular size and distance." He poked the display again. "But this bastard, *this* one is different. He's too big to be a Type I or III, but not as big as a Type II."

"So, they have something new? Or, just something we haven't seen before?"

David shrugged. "Not sure...but...if I run this back, sticking with this same group, the new guy comes up from the surface just before they leave." He ran the controls so Salazar could see the new ship arrive.

"How long before?"

"It was kinda long, I thought." He flipped the images for a few seconds. "Right, two and a half hours."

"What about the other groups?"

"Dunno yet."

"How about we get your old classmates in here and get them on that?"

"Good idea." David first verified the dimensions of the new type, capturing what detail he could, then set Gregg Browning, Margie Nixon, and Steve Kirby to checking the other enemy task forces. Ray Salazar returned to his RF research, now hoping to find something to correlate with what David was seeing.

After a few hours, they came back together. Gregg Browning had caught a well-lit, lateral image of the new type.

"There's a band, or something, that runs the length of the ship."

"A band?" David asked.

"Yeah, something that looks almost like an armor belt on a battleship."

"OK."

"There's more. There are openings, or something, running right below the band. They're small, less than a meter."

"Can we get any more detail?"

"Not from this shot, but I'll keep looking."

"Well," David said, looking around at his crew, "for sure we have a new type. Go ahead and define it as Type V in the image library and see if the intel processors can find it for you."

"Right, will do."

The multi-processor intel analysis system ground through the mountain of pictures they had collected as they watched Alpha Mensae, eventually flagging six good examples of the new enemy type. Gregg pulled all six up on the Center Console monitor.

"As you can see, we have shots from both sides, and those openings are visible on both."

"OK," David answered, waiting for Gregg to continue.

"There's more detail on the belt, too. It's a long ridge that goes almost from the bow to the stern."

"How big is it?"

"It's just under ten meters high, best we can tell, and from the shadows we caught, it stands out about three meters from the outer skin of the ship."

David nodded and looked around at his small group of Intel specialists. "So, what do we think? What are the openings and what is this ridge? I need to know before I talk to Evans."

Gregg had one more item to report. "We got better coverage on the openings. They're a half-meter or so, and round."

"So, some kind of weapon system? Maybe, a close-in defensive system?"

"Hard to say, Lieutenant. But, that's as good a guess as any."

"Oh, we also determined that there is not one of these per group."

"No?"

"But there is one per destination."

"Oh, now *that* can't be an accident."

"My thought exactly."

David picked up the phone and summoned Rich Evans to Operations. David and Gregg brought him up to speed on what they had observed.

Evans leaned against Center Console as he absorbed what they were telling him. "OK, so they're sending a new type to every battle? A command ship, maybe?"

Gregg nodded. "That's our theory, sir, such as it is. Besides being big and silver, it doesn't really resemble anything we've seen. The ridge around the middle is also new."

"Well, we still owe Fleet the details of the task forces. Include this as a Type V and let them know what you've seen."

"Will do, sir. I'll have the message ready for you by the end of the day."

"That will do fine, David. Good work, everyone."

Later that evening, David took out his journal. Actually, it was Carol's original journal, as they had swapped notebooks after Dan's wedding so that each of them could go back and read what the other had written earlier. They'd trade back again the next time they were together.

Dear Carol -

I guess I'll be seeing you soon. We're out of AM and headed for BH as fast as Forstmann's little feet can take us. You'll know soon, if you don't already, that's there's one hell of a fight coming. The AM's (my new name for the enemy - like it?) are coming in force.

We found a new type today, but we don't really know what it is. I think it's a command ship, maybe, or maybe it just carries groceries. Or, nukes. We'll see.

I confess with what's coming I'm afraid for both of us, but mostly for you. I know you'll be in the middle of it, but please be safe. Please.

All my love,
David

ISC Fleet HQ Intel Section
Ft. Eustis, VA
Friday, February 10, 2079, 0900 EST (1300 UTC)

Ron studied the report from *Cobra* carefully.

```
FLASH 207902081325UTC
TO: CSTO, FLEETCINC, FLEETOPS, FLEETINTEL
FROM: COBRA
SUBJECT: DETAIL OF ENEMY FORCE

1) COBRA HAS IDENTIFIED A NEW DESIGN DESIGNATED TYPE V.
VESSEL IS 600 METERS IN LENGTH AND HAS ~100 CIRCULAR 0.5M OPENINGS
ON EACH SIDE. NEW TYPE ALSO SHOWS A LATERAL RIDGE APPROX 10M WIDE
3M TALL. PURPOSE OF THESE NEW FEATURES IS UNKNOWN.
2) REVERSE NAV DATA INDICATES ONE OF THESE TYPE V'S WAS
DISPATCHED TO EACH DESTINATION.IMPLICATION OF THAT FACT UNKNOWN.
3) ENEMY DISPOSITIONS:
EARTH: 12 TYPE I/6 TYPE III/1 TYPE V
INOR:8 TYPE I/4 TYPE III/1 TYPE V
BETA HYDRI: 10 TYPE I/4 TYPE II/4 TYPE III/1 TYPE V

END
```

Over the last few months, Ron's small section of Intel specialists had gotten even smaller. Evans and Peña were gone. So, too, was Roger Cox, sent to *Antares* to replace Jack Ballard, who was now on *Cobra*.

Ron vetoed Ann Cooper's request to remain on *Intrepid* to fill the void left by Ben Price's death, instead sending SLT Chuck Anderson. Anderson had previous shipboard Intel experience and was due for a new assignment anyway.

Ron could still feel the loss of those he had worked with for so long. But, as he looked around the Table this morning, the losses were somewhat balanced by the addition of Susan Scranton and Joe Bowles. The banter wasn't quite what it used to be, but it was comfortable and collegial, just as he desired.

"OK, folks, attention to orders!"

The group fell silent and looked at Ron expectantly. He smiled back at them as he turned to Ann.

"Lieutenant Cooper, as we like to say, you are out of uniform." He handed her the double silver bars of a Senior Lieutenant.

"Well, thank you, Admiral."

"Congratulations. Now the bad news."

"Bad news?"

"With Peña and Evans and all the rest gone, you're now my deputy."

Ann looked back at him in surprise. "But Admiral, shouldn't you have at least a Lieutenant Commander? Perhaps Doctor Scranton? Mrs. Wilson?"

"Nope. You're it. Peña's office is all cleared out. Move in soon as you can."

"Yes, sir. Thank you, sir."

Susan Scranton surprised them all by being the first to speak. "Congratulations, Lieutenant. I know you'll do well."

"Thank you, Doctor."

Ron tapped the Table. "OK, that's all the fun for now. What about this new type *Cobra* has dropped on us?"

Scranton leaned back as she spoke. "Well, Admiral, I'm surprised by the one-hundred number."

"They do have ten digits, right?" Scott Morgan asked.

"Sure, but there are human societies that don't count just the fingers."

"But, on the other hand...oh...sorry...bad pun...this does make sense, right?" Kathy Stewart asked.

"I suppose, yes."

"So, what's behind two hundred half-meter openings in this new type? Some kind of defensive system?"

New replacement LT Angelo Mason was skeptical. "They've never seemed to understand the concept of defense before. I'd think this is some kind of offensive system, with the ridge, whatever *that* is, as the targeting system. It reminds me of a sonar system."

"Except there's no sound in space," Scott Morgan pointed out, smiling.

"Well, yeah, except for that, sure. But the analogy holds."

"True," Scott agreed.

"We won't know until we see them," Ann said, closing off the hypotheticals, "but our first priority when they appear is to strike these new ships. Whatever they are, they represent some new capability, some new threat, and we should take them out immediately."

Ron nodded. "Yes, I agree. I'll advise Barker the same."

On that they could all agree, and after the meeting, Ron sent a short message to Barker. He would already have seen the *Cobra* message, but Harris thought it vital to provide whatever additional context he could.

ISC Fleet HQ Plans Division
Ft. Eustis, VA
Friday, February 10, 2079, 1015 EST

This was the kind of day when Fiona Collins missed Joanne and Ben the most. She had a complicated question to answer and not much time to work with. CINC had tasked her with setting the Fleet assignments in response to the attack the enemy had launched. She had thirty-one ships overall, which one might think was enough. But several were already spoken for: *Aurora* was deploying Sentinels; *Columbia*, *Antares*, and *Intrepid* were already headed to Beta Hydri; *Eagle* and *Friendship* were already at Beta Hydri waiting for a relief they would not get.

She stared a long time at the multiple solutions the AI planner had created, showing her the available ships' locations, and distances to each of the expected targets. She had other constraints, like needing to have a qualified commander at each of five possible targets, and deploying her heavier ships — *Dunkirk, Stalingrad, Nippon, Canberra,* and *Yorktown* — where they would do the most good.

The whole thing gave her a dose of stress and frustration she hadn't felt since the attack on Inoria. She spent a sleepless night worrying that the destinations *Cobra* had sent them were some kind of ruse intended to coerce her into putting her defensive resources in the wrong places. But, she reminded herself, that thought assumes the enemy knows they're being watched.

They were unlikely to be aware that *Cobra* was there.

Unlikely, her inner critic reminded her, *but not impossible.*

The other question that nagged at her was whether they would strike on schedule. Theoretically, they should hit Beta Hydri first around February 21st. But, would they? Whatever the enemy schedule was, she would only know when it happened. She hoped a Sentinel would give them a clue over the next few weeks, but for that to happen, the enemy would need to make a stop at just the right (or wrong, for them) star.

More unknowns. More uncertainty.

What she really wanted was more time and more ships.

But, no.

After sifting through a half dozen scenarios, she chose one and made the long walk to CINC's office. As she entered, Chief of Operations Admiral Patricia Cook sat across from CINC Connor Davenport, both looking somber. Davenport looked older somehow, the lines deeper on his face. Cook had clearly lost weight over the last months, the stress of her position taking its toll. She wondered how she looked to them; was she showing the wear of warfare like they were? She'd have to check the mirror more carefully after her shower tonight.

She laid out her best option for CINC. He didn't react well at first.

"But, Fiona, *Canberra* can't possibly get to Beta Hydri in time."

"I know, sir, but if we want more Marines there, which we clearly do, she's the one to carry them, and she's here, where the supply of Marines is."

"But she won't be there until two weeks after the enemy ETA!"

"I know, sir, I know. All the other scenarios to get a cruiser with Marines to Beta Hydri are worse."

"Worse?"

"Actually, much worse."

"You're sending *Yorktown* to Inor, but the OTC is Sokolovsky in *Stalingrad*?"

"Yes. *Yorktown* might not get there in time. *Stalingrad* can."

Chief of Operations Patricia Cook agreed. "Sokolovsky is the right choice, as is Kawaguchi here. They're the most experienced."

CINC Connor Davenport read the list carefully, which ships to which locations and whether they'd get there on time. Fiona didn't wait for him to question her plan.

"We're assigning just three ships each to the starbases at Kapteyn and Tranquility II, since they were not in the list *Cobra* gave us. We're putting two cruisers, three frigates, three destroyers at Inor. For Beta Hydri, it's one cruiser, two frigates, six destroyers. Here, we'll have two cruisers, three frigates, three destroyers. We've concentrated more at Beta Hydri since that seems to be their main target."

Cook nodded. "And, we have other resources here, if necessary. But I can't believe they'd actually try to land."

"Yes, Admiral, I agree. But there is one thing that bothers me, something the AI pointed out."

"Yes?"

"Kapteyn Station is just off the direct line from Alpha Mensae to Inor. If the enemy stops there, well, it could be trouble."

"Just off?"

"One point six light-years, sir. Close enough to make me worry."

"What do you suggest?"

"The three ships assigned there need some idea of when the enemy might appear, and be ready to defend the station if they do. The other alternative is to shut it down and evacuate."

"Yes, I see. But, based on what *Cobra* has told us, Kapteyn is not a target. We'll warn the ships, but I doubt that the station itself is in much danger."

Davenport continued looking at the plan on the NetComp before him, picturing where his forces were at the moment, and then when and where they needed to be before the enemy could strike. He moved the display back and forth, seeing in three-dimensions the current and future dispositions, courses of each, and time required in transit.

Fiona had made her pitch, but it was ultimately up to CINC and OPS whether the plan went into action or not.

"This is the best we can do?" CINC asked, finally.

"Given where our ships are and the timeline we're assuming, this is the best option. Change the assumptions, and I can change the plan."

Davenport shook his head. "No, Fiona. This is what Ron and everyone else thinks will happen. We can't just wish away the hand we've been dealt." He turned to look at Cook. "Patty?"

"Yes, I agree. Go ahead and draft the order, Fiona, and I'll get it out."

Fiona took leave of her superiors and returned to her desk to draft the Fleet order. It would be by far the most significant order she'd ever generated.

```
FLASH 207902101630UTC
TO: ALLFLEET
FROM: FLEETOPS
SUBJECT: DEPLOYMENT

1) AS PREVIOUSLY REPORTED, RECENT INTEL INDICATES ENEMY IS EXECUTING
A LARGE-SCALE OFFENSIVE. REPORTS INDICATE ENEMY FORCE EXPECTED TO BE
19 @ EARTH, 13 @ INOR, 19 @ BETA HYDRI INCLUDING TYPE II INVASION
SHIPS.
2) BEST ESTIMATES ARE ATTACKS WILL OCCUR AT BETA HYDRI O/A 20790221,
INOR O/A 20790315, EARTH O/A 20790317.
3) NEITHER KAPTEYN NOR TRANQUILITY II ARE EXPECTED TO BE TARGETS.
HOWEVER, DEFENSIVE POSTURE SHOULD BE PREPARED FOR ATTACKS O/A
20790306 AT KAPTEYN AND 20790310 AT T-II.
4) ALL SHIPS TO PROCEED IMMEDIATELY BEST SPEED AS ASSIGNED.
5) BETA HYDRI: CANBERRA, WHITE, KOMAROV TO JOIN COLUMBIA, ANTARES,
INTREPID, EAGLE, FRIENDSHIP WHICH ARE ALREADY ON STATION OR ENROUTE.
OTC BARKER IN COLUMBIA.
6) INOR: YORKTOWN, STALINGRAD, DOBOVOLSKI, PATSAYEV, MCNAIR, SOYUZ,
FAITH, AQUARIUS. OTC SOKOLOVSKY IN STALINGRAD.
7) EARTH: DUNKIRK, NIPPON, TONG-IL, GAGARIN, GRISSOM, BONDARENKO,
MIR, STOYKIY, RASSVET. OTC KAWAGUCHI IN NIPPON.
8) KAPTEYN: CHAFFEE, VOSTOK, JARVIS. OTC TROELSEN IN VOSTOK.
9)TRANQUILITY II: FREEDOM, VOSHKHOD, YANKEE. OTC HAKIM IN FREEDOM.
10) THERE WILL BE NO ACKNOWLEDGEMENT OF THESE ORDERS. COMMUNICATE
ONLY IF UNABLE TO PROCEED.
11) GOOD HUNTING!

END
```

Columbia (CSTO Flagship)
Big Blue
Wednesday, February 15, 2019, 1300 UTC

As his task force gathered around Beta Hydri's Big Blue planet, Admiral Kieran Barker held long, pointed discussions with his staff on how best to prepare for the enemy arrival. They'd be coming in force, with multiple invasion ships, and with a new ship type whose purpose was unknown.

To meet this offensive, he had nine ships, counting *Cobra*, three with large contingents of Marines to help defend the survivors of the Beta Hydri culture

Greg Cordero had labeled the 'Seekers.' The original, strikingly beautiful portrait *Antares* had found was still clear in Kieran's mind. Altogether he could put nearly a full company into the fight, if necessary. Major Wayne Barnes on *Antares* was the senior ground force officer, with Andy Martin on *Intrepid* effectively his XO. Lieutenant Liwanu Harry, who had been so effective in *Intrepid's* ground engagement with the enemy, had also remained with his ship and his platoon.

Now that his force was in place, Barker called for a meeting on the flagship. As they sat around the wardroom table, sipping coffee or tea and downing bakery from *Columbia's* kitchen, it felt more like a class reunion than a council of war. They talked the better part of a half-hour before Barker finally brought the meeting to order, and the real work began.

"They're coming. We all know that much. The enemy may be here within a few days. The best FleetIntel can tell us is that they can't be there before the 21st. There are invasion ships, or so we think. First off, I'd like your thoughts on the Marines."

Joanne Henderson, seated near the far end of the table next to her old friend Terri Michael, responded first. "I think we should get them on the surface, somewhere near the Seekers, before the ETA."

"I agree," Terri said. "If they're aboard a ship they're much more at risk, and if the enemy moves in that direction, it will take time to get them down."

Barker turned to his left. "Major Barnes?"

"I also agree, sir. My people would much rather be on the ground, where we're going to be needed than floating around up here defenseless."

Barker leaned back, thinking. "Is the presence of that force going to reveal the location of the Seekers? I would not want to telegraph that to them."

Barnes shook his head. "No, sir, I think not. We have camouflaged IR-blocking shelters, and we can disperse ourselves enough that I don't think it will be an issue."

"If *Intrepid's* experience says anything," Joanne explained, "They already know where the Seekers are. At the very least, they suspect it. We killed upwards of a hundred in The Pasture, and I don't think they were there by accident."

Barker shifted in his chair, nodding his agreement. "I see. What about supplies? Food, whatever else?"

Barnes had that answer. "We'll take four days' personal rations with us as a backup, but until the enemy shows, we'll need a food run from the Fleet once a day."

"Perhaps the Seekers will take you fishing?" *Komarov's* captain offered.

"That might be interesting, Commander. I'll talk to Eaagher about it. Water is no problem, there's a good freshwater stream that empties into The Pasture.

We can use personal water filters on that."

"OK," Barker said, taking control. "We land the Marines and keep them supplied. *Ceres* can help with food." He looked around the table. "Any objections or other suggestions?" The room was quiet. "Very well then, Major Barnes, I leave it to you to arrange the landings and setup of your position. The affected ships' Captains are directed to enable his movement."

Dan Smith spoke for the first time. "Sir, we should also leave some shuttles on the surface, in case we need to move the Marines quickly."

"Would that not tell the enemy where we are?"

"We can cover them, sir," Barnes replied. "I have a decent supply of camo tent material intended to hide vehicles and the like. We should be able to minimize the exposure."

"OK, then, one shuttle from each Marine-carrying ship stays on the surface."

"Thank you, sir," Barnes replied.

Barker picked up his tablet, swiped across a few pages, then set it back down.

"Now, we need to determine how we deploy ourselves..."

There followed a strenuous argument about priorities and positioning. Barker wanted two experienced ships in reserve, and neither Joanne Henderson nor Daron Flores of *Vernyy* cared much for watching from the sidelines. But Barker was unmoved, and their ships would be in high orbit, staying out of the initial fight. As Joanne was expressing her unrestrained disgust at this development, Rich Evans and David Powell appeared at the wardroom door.

"*Cobra*!" Barker called out.

"Yes, Admiral, we're here. I'm sorry we're so late to the party."

"Not to worry, Commander Evans, not to worry. Have a seat, both of you."

As everyone settled back into their seats, David took a small stool behind Rich Evans.

"We were just talking about positioning. Rich, is there anything new about this Type V?"

"Not really, sir, but we brought the images we have." David passed his Net-Comp over to Dan Smith, who quickly had the images up on the wardroom display screen. David made his way around the table.

"The belt we've described is here..." he pointed to a long gray shadow on the image that appeared to run the full length of the ship. "It's ten meters high and extends out from the hull about three." David looked around, and when there were no questions, he continued his description. "The openings, well, there are a hundred on each side, and there could be more on the top or bottom. We didn't get complete three-sixty coverage of them."

"Any more ideas what those are?"

"No, Admiral, not really. They're not very big — something around a half-meter."

"Anything else?"

David looked at Evans, who just looked back and nodded for him to continue.

"Well, sir, we have no idea what this ship is. We know they sent one with each task force. Only one." David pointed to the image for emphasis. "I think this vessel should be our number one priority when they arrive. It should be fired on at the outset and the attack pressed until it has been destroyed."

"That's the consensus here, too, David," Dan said. "It likely represents some new advantage they think they have. That makes it the most dangerous vessel in the enemy fleet."

Barker looked away from the image of the mystery ship and back at his commanders. "We have eight armed ships present. *Ceres* will be here a couple days after the enemy ETA, so I am not concerned about how fast we expend our ordinance." Barker thought a moment before continuing. "Each ship will hit this with two Bludgeons immediately upon identification. No coordination, no delays. Just smack this bastard right in the face as soon as he shows up."

"Our second priority," Harry Hess added, "is the invasion ships. We can fight it out with the Type I's and IIIs if we have to, but besides reducing the enemy force as much as possible, our real purpose here is to protect the Seekers. So, your second priority is the Type IIs. Fire at least two Bludgeons at each. Again, no coordination, no delays, just hit them as soon as you can."

"What about speed and routing?" Joanne asked.

"Your discretion. If I was commanding a ship, I'd be using max speed but indirect routing. It will take a few minutes longer, but it will also mask your location."

"Yes, my thinking exactly."

"Finally, Lance any shuttles they dispatch to the surface. I don't want to give them the slightest chance to establish a beachhead on the ground. Kill them outright."

Rich Evans looked at Barker. "What would you like us to do, sir? How can *Cobra* best support you?"

"I would like to see you in a high orbit where you can observe the enemy and the engagement, hopefully from behind."

"Yes, sir, we can go out perhaps a quarter of the distance to Little Gray?"

"That will do fine."

Barker again picked up his NetComp, looked at it for a moment, then set it down.

"Should the flagship be lost, Captain Booker in *Canberra* is senior and will take over. Loren, I'm counting on you to pick up for me if necessary."

He blinked twice before turning to Barker. "I will be ready, Admiral. But, like everyone else, I pray I am not needed."

"Not half as much as I do! After Captain Booker, Captain Henderson in *Intrepid* is senior. You all know the rest."

Barker shifted uneasily in his seat.

"Now, that old cliché about how battle plans die on contact with the enemy is true. So, be flexible in your thinking. Inflict the most damage you can on them, consistent with preserving your ships and yourselves. Be ready to lend assistance to one another, because I doubt that we're going to get through this unscathed. According to *Cobra*'s observations, there will be nineteen enemy ships."

"And don't forget," Harry Hess added, "*Intrepid* faced a ground force embarked in Type I's. Not all the enemy soldiers are necessarily in the Type IIs."

Eagle's captain Commander Gary Haynes spoke up. "What about the leftovers, sir?"

"Leftovers?" Rich asked, puzzled.

"That's what we've been calling the enemy survivors on the surface."

"Ah, good name. What do we know about them?"

"Well, they don't do much. They stay very close to the shuttle wreck, going inside at night. About every sol or two, a dozen or so will venture out into the open areas to the east. There are food animals there, and while we haven't caught them in the act, we assume they're hunting."

"That would make sense," Rich said, "since the postmortems back at Fleet indicated they were meat-eaters. Do we know how many?"

"Our guess is fifty or so, but it's hard to say exactly."

"*Intrepid* will be landing a squad on the surface soon to do a recon," Barker answered. "We should understand better in another Sol or two what they're doing."

Terri looked up from her NetComp note-taking. "Are we thinking to eliminate them?"

"That would be within our rules of engagement, Captain. But I'm hesitant to just massacre them if they present no threat." Barker cleared his throat before continuing. "I see these as marooned soldiers. They were stuck there when Joanne crushed their ships, and the enemy hasn't seen fit, or, been able, to come back for them."

"They may not even know they're there." Rich Evans commented.

"True. There have been no SLIP communications from that shuttle."

"So, for now, we're letting them live?" Haynes asked.

"Yes. Once we get Lieutenant Harry's report, we can revisit the issue. I had thought about taking one prisoner, but the more I think about it, the less I think that's useful."

Rich smiled. "Yes, sir, I agree. I am not at all sure what we'd do with it if we had one."

The gathering broke up shortly after that, with *Columbia*'s shuttles making the rounds, delivering the captains back to their ships. David briefly considered stowing away on the *Antares*-bound shuttle, but instead remained on *Columbia* to talk to Elias Peña and his Intel techs. Melinda Hughes caught him in a passageway and bear-hugged him, then dismissed him with a kiss on the cheek. It reminded David how much he had missed her since he'd left the ship. He was still smiling as he entered the staff intel work area.

"What are you so damned happy about?" Peña asked.

"Oh, nothing much." His smile didn't fade.

"Nothing?" Peña asked, starting to smile a little himself.

"I just saw Melinda."

"Oh, well, now, that I can understand."

They had a long brainstorming session about the Type V ship. Some of Peña's staff doubted that it was any threat at all and that it was just a command ship of some kind. David wasn't buying that, and neither was Rich Evans.

"They've invested in something here," Evans insisted, "Something new. We know they don't think like we do, but we also know they're not stupid."

"Ignorant, maybe," David chimed in.

"Yes, perhaps that. There are things about warfare they just don't seem to understand. But don't underestimate them." Peña waited a few seconds before speaking again. "But, really, we're no closer now to knowing what these ships are than when we started this session."

"Regrettably true, Elias," Evans answered.

"All the more reason," David said quietly, "to smoke them at first sight."

There was no debate on that, and David and Rich Evans left to return to *Cobra*. As they walked down the passageway, Rich turned to David.

"I suppose you'd like a little side trip to *Antares*?"

"Yes, sir, of course, that would be great, but this fleet isn't here to enable a quiet rendezvous for Carol and me."

"That's right, but let me talk to Terri."

"There is one thing we could do, sir, that would be meaningful."

"What's that?"

"Carol has met Eaagher. I mean, she was there with Cordero at the beginning."

"OK, so?"

"I'm curious about the Seekers' first encounter with the enemy. According to *Antares*' report, the enemy came, presented their demands, and then left. Only when they returned did they attack."

"Yes, so what about that?"

"How, sir, did they present those demands?"

"What do you mean?"

"Doctor Cordero, the master linguist for lost languages, only communicated with Eaagher in writing and hand signals after weeks of studying the language. How did the enemy communicate with them? I don't understand it."

Evans stopped in his tracks, placing his hand on his chin, something he did when intrigued by a new idea. "I hadn't caught that. What exactly did you have in mind?"

"Carol knows Eaagher. She and I could go down and see him and hear what he has to say."

"Terri knows him, Joanne Henderson does, too. There are other officers we could send."

"Of course, sir, that's true. Or you could go in my place. But whatever cast you might select, the question should be asked."

"Agreed. What time is it down there?"

David pulled his NetComp. "Where the Seekers are, it's well after sunset, Sol 131."

"OK, so we have some time to work with. When is midday Sol 132?"

"Uh, tomorrow around 2130."

"OK, let's think about that."

As they walked down the passageway to the hangar deck, Evans had that set, determined look on his face that showed he had made a tough decision.

Intrepid
Big Blue
Friday, February 17, 2079, 0615 UTC (Early hours Sol 132)

Joanne Henderson looked out at Beta Hydri's 'Big Blue' with mixed emotions. The pain of Ben's loss was still with her, and while she outwardly denied any need of sympathy, inwardly, she grieved. It was a palpable weight in her heart, a regret Joanne would not soon lay aside. But, here also were the Seekers, a wise and threatened culture that she had come back to protect. And, there was no doubt that this was a beautiful place, on par with Earth for the deep blues, light greens, and bright whites it displayed.

Along with two platoons of Marines, Joanne was carrying Greg Cordero and Gabrielle Este back to Beta Hydri. FleetIntel Chief Ron Harris had argued with them nonstop for upwards of an hour, and Greg and Gabe knew it could be dangerous, but they loved the Seekers and believed there was much more work to be done. Ron could just have prohibited their trip, but he couldn't bring himself to crush their initiative and tenacity, so he relented and asked *Intrepid* to take them.

Just after *Intrepid* arrived at Beta Hydri, Kieran Barker had directed Joanne to land a Marine reconnaissance team to determine how many enemy soldiers were still alive on the surface, and what they were doing. Marine Lieutenant Liwanu Harry volunteered to take a small detachment to the surface, and Captain Andy Martin agreed. The young Lieutenant was smart, with excellent leadership skills. His courage and integrity had been proven at The Pasture, and Martin had confidence in the young man.

The surveillance that *Eagle* and *Friendship* had maintained showed clearly that the 'leftovers' were huddled around a grounded enemy shuttle just east of the old battle site that *Antares* had investigated months earlier. *Eagle* dispatched a Snooper drone, and over time they were able to see that there were no more than fifty individuals left. How they were living was less clear, but their occasional forays into the open country east of the city seemed to indicate they were scavenging or hunting.

Their surveillance also revealed that they were never out after dark, returning to the broken shuttle by dusk. So, near midnight of Sol 133, Natalie Hayden took the Marines down, refusing any other pilot despite that it was not her day to fly. She brought them in low from the east, landing softly four kilometers from the enemy position.

Harry's team of six moved quickly and quietly out of the shuttle. Natalie got out with them, waiting as they unloaded their gear and supplies and shouldered their weapons. Despite the pain the planet had brought her, Big Blue had a unique and pleasant feel to her. The air was naturally clean, unlike ship air that somehow always smelled manufactured. No hydrocarbons were being burned on Big Blue, and there was no industry to stir up particulates. Plus, it was deathly quiet. Big Blue had no birds, and the few insects that existed did not chirp all night looking for love. Except for the hushed whisper of a westerly breeze in the grasses and low brush around them, it was silent. Little Gray was setting in the west as they unloaded, and Natalie could see its light reflecting off the top of the enormous enemy shuttle in the distance.

"Liwanu," she said, barely above a whisper, "take care of yourself, understand?"

Harry smiled, although it was hard to see it in the darkness. "I will, Lieutenant, I promise. We've picked out three houses with good sightlines to the shuttle and back to the east. We'll be OK." He put on his night-vision glasses and shouldered his pack.

"Goodnight, Lieutenant," he said as he turned to lead his squad west.

"Goodnight."

Natalie waited until she could not see them with her unaided eye, then put on her own night-vision glasses to watch them fade in the distance. She wanted them well away from the shuttle before she left, on the off chance that she might be seen departing. Harry's team would have nearly twelve hours to get to their locations and set themselves up before Beta Hydri came back over the horizon. They'd have ten hours before dawn even began to light the countryside. That should be plenty of time, she knew.

Fifteen minutes after she could no longer see them, she climbed back into the shuttle and left the same way she arrived: low and to the east for several kilometers before ascending back to *Intrepid*.

Liwanu thought of Natalie as he moved towards the houses they had picked out. She'd suffered a crushing loss, but her strength showed through in how she kept to her duties, always doing more than required, always even-tempered. He hadn't seen her laugh since they re-boarded the ship for the trip back to Big Blue, but she was as friendly and 'normal' as before. Liwanu himself had known Ben Price only slightly, but Joanie McCarthy he had known well, and Gunther Hart-wig even better. They had shared the usual banter on the rifle range, Liwanu's supposed lack of ability with 2K7X being a popular topic. As an officer, he could have shut it down, but he wanted to be a Marine first, an officer second, and that meant taking a little good-natured harassment from time to time. If he asked them to do something, they would do it, and that, he thought, was the true meas-ure of their respect. He felt their loss every day.

They stopped as the point Marine raised his right arm, the rest crouching down to make themselves as inconspicuous as possible. The Marine pointed to his eyes and then waved Liwanu forward.

"First house is there, sir," he said, pointing. "Second is fifty meters north...there!" He pointed again.

Liwanu pulled out his electronic binoculars and studied the enemy shuttle, just a few hundred meters away. In low-light mode, he could see two enemy soldiers sitting on the ground just outside the open hatch, but no other activity. He watched for a full five minutes, scanning the entire field before him, before deciding it was safe for them to continue.

Liwanu looked around at their position, sitting atop a small rise in the ground, with brush and long grass at the crest. "Everything looks good. If we encounter any opposition, this is the rally point, understood? We regroup here. OK, now, let's get in and get set up."

This was the area through which the leftovers seemed to move whenever they went away from the shuttle. The first house was in the center of the surveil-lance area. Liwanu and PFC Debbie Bailey would take that one along with Lance

Corporal Clint McGowan. The other two houses were each about fifty meters to either side. Two Marines each would take those.

All three houses had doors facing away from the enemy shuttle, and windows looking towards it. Captain Martin and Liwanu had spent the better part of a day going over *Eagle*'s Snooper photography to pick these sites. They moved quickly to their assigned locations and made their way inside.

Liwanu had Bailey set up their communications while he and McGowan set up the surveillance equipment. The large-aperture video camera would permit them to see, in detail, everything going on at the enemy shuttle. The device had IR and low-light modes as well, allowing them to watch in darkness almost as well as they could in daylight.

They ran the thin fiber cables from the room with the camera to the back room where they were shielded from enemy view.

"OK, so why no laser to *Intrepid*?" Bailey asked.

"Well, first, we'd need to have a receiver outside, and second, the footprint of the laser at this distance is way too big. We're much better off with the low-power spread-spectrum stuff."

Bailey shrugged as she slipped a headset on and pressed the transmit button. "*Intrepid*, Team Harry."

There was a delay of few seconds, then the response "Team Harry, loud and clear." She turned and gave Liwanu a thumbs-up and took the headset off.

As agreed, on the next hour, she put the headset back on and verified her connection to the other two sites.

"OK, Lieutenant, we're all up and good."

Now came the hard, tedious part of surveillance: waiting for something to happen. Liwanu took the first two-hour shift, giving his Marines time for some sleep first. He shook Bailey awake when it was her turn and found a quiet spot away from any windows to grab some sleep himself. Bailey would wake McGowan later for his shift.

Just after first light, Liwanu awoke to the sound of birds, something chirping and whistling. As he came fully awake, he sat up, startled. *There are no birds on this planet!* He thought to himself.

McGowan motioned Liwanu to the center of the house.

"Six of them came out right before dawn, walking towards the hunting grounds. I didn't wake you because it seemed normal, you know, just what we expected. Then, they get about even with us, and suddenly they're walking towards the house."

Liwanu nodded his understanding. "Let's just keep quiet for now and see what happens. Maybe they'll move on."

"Yeah, maybe. But how did they find us?"

28

Liwanu just shrugged. They woke PFC Bailey and crept to the room facing the enemy shuttle. They saw nothing but could hear the enemy soldiers close by. There were more sounds of movement outside, then more chirps and whistles, plus a few grunts and other vocalizations they could not quite identify. Bailey moved back around to the rear of the house, hiding in the shadow of a doorway.

Combatant 42518, having walked all around the building, looked at his partner, 42519. "I smell something."

"Yes. Inside the house?"

"Where else?" 42518 sniffed the air again. "When did you last come here?"

"My last turn was many sunrises ago."

"Who was out here last?"

"I don't know."

42518 stopped walking as he came to the rear of the structure. "We should report this."

"The commander is sleeping," 42519 said, wary of disturbing his superior.

42518 looked in the back windows from a short distance. "The commander is still wet from his egg."

"You would do well to keep that to yourself."

"You disagree?"

"I want to live; therefore, I keep such thoughts to myself. We are Combatants. We are not meant to think too much."

42518 suppressed a laugh. "Yes, so we have been told."

"We're supposed to be finding food," 45219 reminded his partner.

"Yes, food. I smell food here, don't you?"

"Yes, but we've never found prey in a building before. I don't like it. We should go out to the usual place."

"This is closer."

As the enemy soldiers chirped and grunted at each other outside, Lieutenant Harry slipped silently back into the middle of the house, as far from the windows as possible. Almost reluctantly, he keyed the microphone on his combat headset.

"Harry actual to stations two and three. Status."

"Station Two ops normal," came one quick response.

Harry waited a full minute before he keyed the mike again. "Station Three say status."

After several seconds, the response came in a hushed whisper, "Station Three, we have enemy right outside the house. Looks like four individuals, so close we can hear them talking. We've moved upstairs for now."

Harry looked around at his own situation. There were at least two outside his supposed safe-house. Four at the north house. What the hell had happened?

"Station One has two enemy personnel outside. Hold your positions, avoid detection, open fire only if engaged." He heard two microphone clicks, acknowledging his instructions. He remained in place for five more minutes, waiting to see if the enemy might have heard him or his transmission somehow. When they didn't respond, he switched to the command frequency.

"*Intrepid*, Team Harry actual."

He was relieved to hear Jessie Woodward's baritone response: "*Intrepid*, go ahead, Lieutenant."

"Need Martin."

"Roger, Harry. We'll get him for you."

It took only a minute. "Martin."

"Stations one and three have enemy infantry outside. Two at Station One and four at Station Three. Holding our position for now, but we might need some backup if they get too curious."

"Understood. Stand by, Liwanu."

Combatant 50122 approached 45218 and 45219 from the north.

"What is it? You're supposed to be hunting!" 42518 challenged.

"So are you!"

"Watch your young mouth, cohort five. Mind your elders."

50122 ignored the correction and pointed back to the north. "We smell prey in that building. You smell it here, too, don't you?"

"Yes, but what do you think is in there? I have never had this scent. So thick."

"Smells like something soft and hairy."

PFC Debbie Bailey managed to get Liwanu's attention. She pointed to her eyes and then showed him three fingers. *Three? Where did the third one come from?* he wondered.

"Harry actual, this is *Intrepid* actual." *Henderson?*

"Harry," he responded.

"Harry, we're now getting the feed from *Eagle*'s Snooper. So far looks like three at your location and three at Station Three. There are a few more back by the shuttle, but they're not moving your way."

A few seconds later, he heard her say, "Stand-by, Lieutenant. We're talking."

He simply clicked his mike switch to let her know he'd heard. He looked around the corner of the doorway he was hiding in to see that Bailey had positioned herself where an interior hallway opened into the main room in the rear of the house. Her weapon was up and ready, flash-and-noise-suppressor installed. Moving back the other way, McGowan was covering the front door, out of sight of the windows along the south side. Liwanu was satisfied that they could not be seen from the outside. McGowan had also taken down the surveillance gear, so anyone looking in the window would not see anything unusual.

"Harry, this is Martin."

"Go ahead, Captain."

"We're getting a squad ready to come down, Liwanu. Hopefully, whatever got their attention will pass, and they'll move along. If not, we'll be ready to back you up."

"All respect, sir, but if this goes south, it's going to go in a hurry, and it'll be fifty-whatever to seven."

"I understand all that. If you need to retire to the east, go ahead."

"Aye, aye, sir."

Liwanu swore vehemently and imaginatively under his breath. He pulled out his NetComp, surveying the landscape outside. That gave him an idea, not a really great idea, or so he thought, but any plan was better than nothing. He switched back to his team frequency.

"Station Two, still clean over there?"

"Affirmative, sir. No problems here."

"Station Two, get to the rally point and set up to cover us in case we need to bug out in a rush."

"Equipment?"

"Take it if you can, otherwise hide it somehow. Advise when you're ready to depart."

Less than a minute later, he heard: "Station Two moving out."

The three Combatants wandered around the residence and its odd scent, still unsure of what to do.

"We need to find food," 50122 said finally. "If we can't get it here, we need to move on to the usual place."

"For a five, you talk too much," 45218 told him.

50122 did not care for criticism. "I'm hungry, too. Let's get on with the hunt."

45218 dismissed him. "Yes. Go tell the others."

The younger, slightly smaller Combatant turned to walk back to the other house, known to the Marines as Station Three. The distinctive pops of weapons fire stopped him in his tracks.

A few seconds later, Liwanu's headset came alive.

"Station Three under attack. We killed two, but one got away."

Liwanu wanted to ask them what the hell had happened, but that would have to wait for now.

"Station Two, are you in position?"

"Three minutes."

Liwanu made his way to the back door of the residence, carefully sliding it aside just enough to get his head and shoulders out. And, his weapon. Looking around, he could see three enemy soldiers perhaps thirty meters away, looking away from him and towards the Station Three house. Liwanu had faced the enemy on this planet before, but as he watched them, he was again surprised at their size, well over two meters, and their bright purple color. They wore long brown tunics that reminded Liwanu of an old Robin Hood movie, and the knees on their muscular legs bent the wrong way. The enemy soldiers were preoccupied with what was happening at Station Three. They hadn't heard him, so he shouldered his weapon, heard the gunsight tone, and dropped 45218 and 45219 with head-shots a second apart. 50122, startled, turned, and started to raise his weapon. Liwanu hit him twice in the chest.

McGowan was next out the door, pushing it wide as he stepped over his prone Lieutenant. "No more crap from me about your shooting, sir," he said as he brushed past to find a covered position. Bailey was a few seconds behind, shouldering her comm equipment pack as she moved across the garden behind McGowan.

Liwanu left the doorway and ducked behind the low wall that defined the edge of the garden, then flipped to the command frequency.

"*Intrepid*, everything has gone to shit here. Station Three was attacked. I took out the three near us. We're moving east." As he looked over the wall, McGowan and Bailey were neutralizing the last enemy near the other house. He switched back without waiting for a response from the cruiser.

"Station Three, retire to the rally point and prepare for defense." As they hustled away from the houses, Liwanu could hear a rising chorus of alarm behind him. *Yeah*, he thought to himself, *this could get ugly in a hurry.*

Hundredth-Commander Dakt came out of the grounded shuttle, wading into the cacophony of fear his Combatants were spewing. He'd only slept a few drots, the damnable slow rotation of this hateful planet scrambling his normal sleep routine.

"Vermin! There are Vermin here! We heard weapons!" they cried.

"Where?" he was finally able to ask.

"The buildings over there."

"Where are the hunters?"

"Dead. The Vermin killed them."

"How do you know they were Vermin? Did you see them?"

"No. But, no one has ever seen them and lived. Who else could it be?"

"Shut up!" Dakt had heard enough. Ever since they were left here, his Combatants saw danger everywhere. The hunts had settled them for a while, but they still seemed unable to calm themselves for any length of time. Well, they were just Combatants, after all. They weren't *genuinely* Preeminent, despite what he and the other under-commanders told them. For the right reason, for a tactical advantage, or to save himself, they were expendable and disposable. He picked ten to investigate.

"32185, take charge. Arm yourselves. Go see what happened out there and report back to me." He turned to the rest; thirty-five assorted Combatants and shuttle techs. A third, at least, would be useless in a fight. "I want twenty of you to take positions between the supposed Vermin and us. Ten others go to the rear of the shuttle and watch. The rest, wait here. Get moving!"

The Marines sprinted to the ridge and quickly dropped behind it. Liwanu crept back up to the crest and looked carefully over it towards the enemy shuttle.

Natalie was watching the Snooper feed when the crowd at the enemy shuttle began to rearrange itself.

"Captain?" she called to Joanne. "They're reacting."

Joanne watched for a minute, then went back to the Command station. "Get me Harry!" she called to Jessie Woodward.

"Yes, Captain?" Liwanu responded.

"Lieutenant Harry, they're on the move. Looks like a small group is heading your way. You're at that ridge to the east?"

"Yes, ma'am."

"I'll let you know if there's more."

"Yes, ma'am."

Liwanu scuttled back from the edge of the ridge, motioning his small force to join him. "Henderson says there's a group coming this way. We can retire, or we can hold and take them on."

"Well, shit, Lieutenant," Bailey said happily. "Let's take out a few while we're here. The whole surveillance gig is kinda shot to hell anyway."

Liwanu turned to the Marine who had been in charge of Station Three. "So, what happened?"

The young Lance Corporal smiled as he responded. "Bastards decided to let themselves in, Lieutenant. They shot out a window in the back and started crawling through. Then they saw us, and I swear they were going to shit themselves — fired wild all over the place. I had to take them out before they accidentally hit something important."

"OK, well, they'll be better prepared this time, I'm sure."

McGowan spoke quietly: "Let's see what comes, Lieutenant. They send a dozen, even twenty, we can probably take them out. If they send too many, then, yeah, we ghost off to the east and wait for our ride."

"Fine. For now, that's what we'll do."

As they were about to return to their positions, Harry's headset came alive.

"Team Harry, *Intrepid* actual."

"Yes, Captain?"

"We now count ten individuals coming your way."

Liwanu unconsciously looked over his shoulder as he asked, "Where are they?"

"Maybe two-fifty from you. Looks like they're checking out the houses."

"Roger that." He turned back to his team. "Did we leave anything behind?"

"Just shell casings and dead bodies, sir. We brought the gear back with us."

"Very good. OK, Henderson says ten, so we stay. If they get within fifty meters, we drop them, clear?"

"And if they don't?"

"We let them be for now."

Harry crawled back up to edge of the small rise they were hidden behind. The dinky shrubs and long grasses of Big Blue made for sufficient cover. He slipped his weapon through the coarse branches and lined up one of the enemy soldiers in his scope. Two hundred twenty meters, it told him. They were moving slowly, cautiously, as if they might die at any moment.

Well, he thought, *they just might.*

Natalie and Joanne watched as the enemy soldiers around the shuttle stopped moving, and their positions became clear.

"They're defensive," Natalie pointed out. "A strong perimeter facing where they think we are, and a weaker one in the rear."

"Right, just enough to raise the alarm and maybe hold us off for a while."

Natalie nodded her agreement. "But you know what, Captain?"

"What's that?"

"Someone gave these orders. Whoever survived down there, there's someone in command."

"Yes, agreed."

As they were talking, Intel Officer Chuck Anderson came to the Bridge.

"Yes, Lieutenant?" Henderson asked.

"No comms from the enemy, Captain. I just thought I'd let you know. I expect if they had a SLIP system down there, they'd have used it when the shooting started."

"Makes sense, sure."

Anderson hesitated, then asked, "What are you thinking, Captain? Do you want to force the issue now?"

Joanne shrugged. "That's in Lieutenant Harry's hands now."

The detachment of ten Combatants cautiously examined the structures where their comrades had died, half expecting death to appear at any moment. At one house, two bodies were inside and one outside, each hit with some kind of pellet. At the other, they were all outside, two were hit in the head from behind, the other taking two shots in the chest. At the first house, they saw burn marks on the inside walls, evidence that the dead Combatants had tried to fight. The Vermin were certainly efficient, if, indeed, these were the Vermin. No one knew what kind of weapons they used.

Their small group of survivors had been cut off for many rots, ever since they sent a shuttle to investigate a place where the Tenth-Commander thought Scholars might still be hiding. Combatant 32185 had seen the fires in the sky and seen their remaining shuttles explode from the Vermin attack. No one had come back for them, and for 32185, that meant the Vermin had won the day, a thought which he found difficult to absorb. They were the Preeminent. Defeat was impossible. And yet, here he stood in a Scholar house, smelling prey-scent that might be Vermin, and also something else, something burnt and unpleasant.

32185 looked at the bodies on the floor. The two holes in each chest filled him with dread. He knew from his indoctrination that the Scholars had used pellet weapons, but he had been taught that this was an inferior technology, incapable of stopping Combatants. Somehow, he thought, the Vermin had done much better.

He stepped away as the others moved the bodies out of the house, slowly looking around, surveying the landscape. Where had they gone? He looked for a long time at a ridge not far away, a small rise on one side, covered with low brush and long grass. Could they be there? Or, would they have simply slinked away? He listened carefully, at the same time trying to catch any scent he could. The onshore breeze was from behind him, so if they really were behind that ridge, their scent would be carried away from him.

Liwanu watched the ten enemy soldiers through his rifle scope as they moved from one house to the other, then back again. One came back out of Station Three's house, then stood very still, looking directly at his position. The enemy raised his head as if sniffing the breeze, and Liwanu was suddenly grateful that the slight wind he felt meant he was downwind from the enemy.

"Shit."

"Not here, Lieutenant, please. Draws flies and lifers," McGowan answered.

"McGowan, there are no flies on this planet. Do you see that guy sniffing the air? The one over by Station Three?"

McGowan and the others swung their scopes to the enemy Harry was talking about.

"Huh, yeah, he's just standing there."

"I think I know how they found us."

"Oh?"

"Yeah, I think they smelled us."

"Smelled us?" Bailey asked, skeptical. "It's not like we didn't shower."

Liwanu ignored her weak attempt at humor. "If they're evolved dinos like the Intel nerds say, it makes sense they'd have a strong sense of smell."

"Strong enough to smell us inside a building?"

Liwanu shrugged. "Maybe. Give me another explanation."

"We had just finished a long walk in the dark," the PFC commented, "So maybe we left more scent than we realized?"

"Could be, yeah."

They watched as the enemy began hauling the dead bodies back towards the shuttle. The one looking at them remained there, motionless, for a couple minutes after the others had moved off.

"You want to take him out, Lieutenant? I have sight-tone on him."

"No," Liwanu answered without taking his eye off his scope. "If he thinks we're here, let him think it. Let's not shoot him and remove all doubt."

32185 suspected that the Vermin, or, perhaps, some remnant of the Scholars, were still out there. He could not be sure which hated species had killed the six dead Combatants. He could not see, hear, or smell them, but his instincts and training told him they were there, watching him. After all, they had been hiding where they could watch the shuttle. They had neither the numbers nor the position to attack. *So*, he thought, *they had come to watch. Why? And, why now? Was something about to happen?*

He watched the ridge for another micRot, then turned and followed the rest back to the shuttle.

Dakt was waiting, his impatience plain. "What did you find?"

"Pellet weapons killed them."

"Pellets? Unlikely."

32185 turned 45218 and 45219 over and pointed to the ugly, gaping craters in their foreheads. "No, Hundredth-Commander, pellets did this."

Dakt was disgusted by what he saw, and offended by the Combatant's defiant attitude, but indeed, it did seem a pellet weapon had killed them.

"Yes."

"One shot each, in the head, from the back. These two have two shots to the chest. This last one was hit in the chest with a single large pellet. All kill shots, Hundredth-Commander. Very efficient."

"How many?"

"I cannot tell for sure, but not many. The Vermin did not leave any footprints, and the scent is now too confused to tell. Perhaps five or ten."

"Where are they now?"

"I do not know. They were here to watch, and they may yet be watching."

Dakt didn't like this Combatant much, but he was the eldest, and the only one alive who had participated in an obsequiation first hand. His yolk had been unusually rich, Dakt thought, especially for a Combatant.

"Where do you think they are?"

"They have probably gone over that ridge," he said, pointing. "They could be far away by now. Or, they could be waiting there to kill the rest of us."

Dakt waved his agreement, then left 32185 and returned to his small place inside the shuttle. He needed time and silence to think.

Natalie and Surveillance Officer Marco Gonzales watched the Snooper feed as the ten enemy soldiers walked back to their shuttle from Harry's observation posts. One soldier stood out, literally, as he waited several minutes in the open before returning to the shuttle and immediately began a conversation with another individual.

"Does he have on a different color, Marco?" Natalie asked. "Or is that my imagination?"

As Marco zoomed in on the conversation, he could see that the new soldier was indeed dressed differently, wearing red instead of brown.

"An officer?" Marco asked.

"Maybe, well, probably, I guess. Somebody in charge?"

"Your confidence is reassuring," Marco deadpanned.

Natalie nodded and smiled slightly to herself. "Yeah, I know, a keen grasp of the obvious, right?" She called Henderson over and showed her what they had found. Henderson agreed with their interpretation and called Liwanu Harry with the information.

"I'm not sure if this helps," Joanne said, "But if you can eliminate the leadership, it might make it easier to mop up the rest."

This horrible star system was Hundredth-Commander Dakt's first ground mission since completing his training. The plan was to investigate the Scholar city, see what the Vermin had done, and learn whether there were any Scholars still alive. But they had found nothing, even after several rots of searching. There were signs the Vermin had been there, like footprints in the dust of some structures. But they found nothing that told them what the Vermin had found or, more importantly, why they were there. Then, the Tenth-Commander had decided to investigate a different continent, and soon afterward, their shuttles were struck. Dakt was left with a few handfuls of lucky survivors while they watched their ships burning in orbit.

He was a Preeminent. He was a conqueror, forward-leaning, not trained in defense of the wretched remains of a grounded, broken shuttle. Everything in his instincts and training told him to move quickly on the Vermin's supposed position and kill them all. That was, after all, his right. He would prevail.

But he hesitated. The vivid image of the blown skulls of his Combatants remained with him, and he had no desire to take on their appearance himself. That image alone seemed to undo all his training, all his confidence in his command and himself. If only a few Vermin could murder six Preeminent Combatants so quickly, so easily, what might fifty do? Or, a hundred?

But, he thought, what other options did he have? He could remain here and wait to be killed, or he could strike out and attempt to eliminate the threat. Either way, he was likely to be dead soon.

In the end, to be a Preeminent meant there could only be one choice.

Liwanu was considering what to do when Bailey interrupted him,

"Excuse me, sir, but they're moving. Looks like they want to fight." She handed him the NetComp, and Liwanu could see that the enemy was indeed headed in their direction, weapons ready.

Liwanu looked at his small group. "They're alone. They're isolated here, they pose no threat. I see no reason to execute them. Let's go."

One by one, they crawled over the back of the ridge and then hustled their way to the east.

"Oh, shit," Marco said as he watched the enemy organize themselves and start moving east.

"What?" Joanne asked.

"They're heading for the Marines, ma'am."

"Not smart, but I doubt they realize that."

"It's suicide, Captain. They're all going to die as soon as Lieutenant Harry decides it's time."

Joanne came down from her position to watch the feed with Marco and Natalie. "Yes, Lieutenant Gonzales, I agree."

Hundredth-Commander Dakt formed his ranks and took his proper position in the rear, better to keep his Combatants in line. He placed 32185 in the center of the front, also to keep the others orderly and moving forward.

"Perhaps they have escaped," Dakt told his Combatants. "But if not, we shall eliminate them."

"We are the Preeminent!" they shouted in response.

Dakt saw no point in leaving any behind, so all forty-five survivors were armed and placed in five lines, four lines of ten followed by one line of five, and then himself. They walked quickly to the fields beyond the houses the Vermin had hidden in. As they passed them, Dakt ordered them to charge the ridge, running as fast as they could.

They crested the ridge, weapons ready, but found no targets.

Dakt looked around for any trace of the Vermin. He could smell that they had been here, and not long ago, but they were gone now. He could try to pursue them through the brush, but if they were the marksmen they seemed to be, that would be a waste of both lives and effort.

He ordered his Combatants to go back to hunting and walked dejectedly back to the shuttle for more sleep.

Once Liwanu was back in *Intrepid*'s wardroom, Joanne openly wondered just what had been proven by his excursion to the planet.

"Well," Captain Martin replied, "We know they're pretty harmless. They're all alone with no comms. They're not militarily significant, and we were not sure of that before."

"And," Liwanu pointed out, "we were ordered to go down there and have a look. So, we went."

Joanne leaned back in her chair, thinking. "What are our obligations to them? Should we be offering them any kind of assistance?"

Martin shook his head. "No Geneva Convention out here, Captain. We're not required to do anything."

"I don't know what you *could* do, Captain," Gabrielle Este offered. "We know they're meat-eaters, but beyond that, we don't know what they're lacking, if anything."

"Yes, I see." Joanne was reluctant to maroon these few enemy soldiers, but promised herself that they would be helped somehow once the war was over.

In the meantime, they were on their own.

Big Blue
Seeker Beach
Saturday, February 18, 2079, 0930 UTC

The shuttle set down on Seeker Beach, and David and Carol stepped out into a cloudy, chilly morning, just a half-hour after star-rise. The first two shuttle-loads of Marines were already setting up a few hundred meters to the west, in an area of scrub and exposed boulders that might help disguise both the camp and the shuttles. Natalie Hayden had flown the first group of Marines down and then carried a message to Eaagher to expect a visit. She was still with him when the shuttle from *Antares* set down.

Rich Evans came along, not so much to supervise as to observe. He wanted to see the Seekers, to judge them for himself. Terri Michael invited herself on the trip as well, interested to see how Eaagher and the others were getting along.

Eaagher greeted them all in his usual manner, speaking each name and asking the name of those he had not met before. It took several minutes as Eaagher looked carefully at each of them, seeming to set their faces and names to memory. Ullnii came out after a short time, noticeably taller and more mature than Carol remembered her, but no less enthusiastic about seeing her 'friends.'

Eaagher stopped when he got to Natalie.

"Benh," he said with what must have been sadness in his voice. He went to the table and wrote for a long time, then stepped back as David focused the translator on it.

David's voice broke slightly as he read the words. *Benh. I speak his name, and Joanh and Guntha and the rest, every day. I likewise teach Ullnii and her classmates. His consciousness is much missed.*

Natalie just looked at him, unable to respond, so David typed, "Natalie offers her gratitude" and showed it to Eaagher, who waved his left hand and went back to writing.

I see many changes in Friends. Carol now wears metal band with something bright that catches the light on her finger. Other friends had these before not Carol. I also see Natalie wears metal ornament on her neck.

Eaagher watched as Carol and David talked about how to respond.

Finally, David typed, "A ring on the finger can be a symbol of many things. For Carol and I, it is our promise to be married - to be mates for life. Natalie's necklace was a gift from Ben's mother."

Eaagher wrote more. *I also see Carol looks differently at young male David than I past see her.*

"Busted!" Evans called out on hearing the translation.

David smiled through his embarrassment as he typed a question for Eaagher, remembering to tap his forehead when he was done. "Were you present when the hard-faces came the first time?"

Eaagher waved his right hand, then wrote *I was not. Grandfather past tell.*

"Is there anyone still alive who was there? Who saw it for themselves?"

Again, the right hand. *No. These first to die past future hard-faces return.*

"OK," Carol began, her skepticism plain in her tone, "So how does he know anything?"

"Someone must have gotten away," Natalie commented.

David typed again. "How did grandfather escape?"

Eaagher read the message for several seconds, then wrote very slowly. *Secret we keep past now. We respect and admire Friends, love as our own. We must hold secret.*

"We tried that question before, didn't we, Carol?" Terri reminded her.

"Yes, ma'am, we did. Same answer. David, let's move on."

David typed, "Friends understand and respect secret. When the hard-faces first came, how did they communicate with you?"

Eaagher touched his forehead and wrote *I don't understand.*

Carol took the tablet and wrote, "Did they talk? Or, write, like Greg did? How did they tell you what they wanted?"

Eaagher waved his left hand and began to write. *Grandfather past tell. Hard-faces speak language. Future past Friends arrive, we think all conscious beings speak same. Past much debate about this.*

There was silence after David read the translation.

"That, I would never have guessed," Carol said quietly. "They *spoke* the language?"

Eaagher went back to writing. *Grandfather say speaker different than the other hard-faces.*

David typed quickly, touching his forehead when he was done. "Different?"

Grandfather past think it a female. Different physically from the others. It was thinner and shorter. Dull in appearance.

David shook his head. "Maybe, but that assumes that females are smaller."

"Yes," Carol responded, "But, that's typical for higher Terran forms, which includes the enemy. Who knows what it might be elsewhere, but that's pretty much how it goes on Earth, physiologically. Males are generally larger and stronger."

"Present company excepted," David responded with a smile.

Rich Evans finally spoke up. "Back to the headline, folks. The enemy could speak their language. David, ask Eaagher if he knows how they learned it."

Grandfather past know not. We past believe all conscious beings speak same. We present know this not correct.

41

Terri laughed slightly. "Yeah, I can't wait to introduce them to the Inori."

David had another question. "Did the hard-faces tell you their name?"

Eaagher again did not understand the question. *Name?*

"What they call themselves."

They past say they above all others in universe. First above all. We not understand how they could assert such.

"What did they want?"

They past say we must extreme respect, must work and obey.

"First above all? Extreme respect?" Terri said, "Does he really mean 'worship'? The enemy thinks they're gods?"

"Maybe," Carol responded.

"Yeah, possibly," Evans agreed.

David looked back at his Captain. "That would actually explain a lot. If they're that conceited, that proud, it might explain some of their behavior."

Evans nodded. "And it would tend to confirm the idea that they've never been competently resisted. Seekers are smart, but they're not warlike. Their only weapons were single-shot hunting rifles."

Natalie spoke up. "Yeah. War seems to be an idea specific to, you know, Earth."

Eaagher wrote quickly and touched his forehead.

Eaagher curious friends talk?

David wrote carefully. "You have told us much about the hard-faces that is useful. We are discussing what it means."

Friends share with Eaagher?

"What you say tells us that the hard-faces are arrogant. I hope that word translates. They think themselves superior to other species."

Your conclusion logical. Consistent with what grandfather past describe. Hard-faces thinking incorrect.

"If so, this may be something we can use against them, or predict what they will do."

Friends are smart and brave. Eaagher confident.

David nodded to Eaagher as he said, "I'm still wondering how he knows what he says."

He looked over at Evans, who shrugged and nodded. "Ask what you want to know, Powell."

"Yes, sir."

David typed, "You have told us the hard-faces came ten revolutions ago - ten times around the star."

Eaagher lifted his left hand. *Yes.*

"But you only learned about it from your grandfather."

Yes.

"How many times around the star do you expect to live?"

We live many times around the star. Some as many as thirty.

"What happened to your father?"

Hard-faces. I was not yet conscious, still growing in mother

"Grandfather brought you here?"

Grandfather bring daughter to safety, Eaagher come too.

"Grandfather still alive?"

Grandfather consciousness end past many suns. Mother consciousness end when Eaagher born.

Evans stepped forward. "I would love to know more about Seeker society, but we have a fight to prepare for."

"Yes, sir," David answered.

Evans turned to Natalie. "Does he know we're expecting them to return?"

"Yes, I told him."

Rich Evans looked at Eaagher, then turned to David. "Tell him, Powell, that we expect to win this war. At some point, we must decide what is to be done with the hard-faces."

David typed quickly and displayed the translation for Eaagher. He looked at it for a long time, then touched his forehead.

"He doesn't understand, sir," Carol offered.

"OK, ask him, when we defeat the hard-faces, what should be done with them? Should they be killed as they tried to kill his people? What punishment should be given to them?"

Again, Eaagher read the translation several times, then looked at Evans. He began writing.

"We present conscious living beings. Consciousness all we are. Thinking leads to learning leads to wisdom. The end of a consciousness is to be mourned, as the accumulation of life experience and wisdom ceases and cannot be retrieved. We future not desire end of hard-faces. Past future only desire safety and rebuild home."

Evans read the translation, then turned to the tall alien. "Thank you, Eaagher."

David saved the translation verbatim, knowing that Evans would want to get that back to CINC at some point.

"Thank Eaagher for his time and tell him we will keep him informed. Then, let's get back to our jobs."

"Friends grateful for your knowledge. Friends will keep you informed. Friends are here to defend you and your people. Now we must go."

Eaagher waved his left hand and stepped back from the table.

Their business completed for the moment, Carol spent a short time with Ullnii, who had been sitting to one side, observing the leaders' discussion. Ullnii had more questions about her picture book, and Carol used the tablet to help her understand a world very different from what she knew.

As David and Rich Evans moved off into a side discussion of the enemy, they were joined by Terri Michael. Terri listened to Rich and David's conversation, which centered around the mystery of the language, and how the enemy could possibly have learned it. They were very concerned about that ability, and Terri thought their worry entirely warranted. If they could do this, even with their conceit, they were even more formidable than previously thought.

Natalie, meantime, spent a moment with Eaagher, then climbed the low cliff and headed back to her shuttle parked near the Marines' growing encampment. She would have several more trips to make this day before all her passengers and their equipment was delivered.

Marine Encampment
Big Blue
Sunday, February 19, 2079, 0845 UTC (Just after sunset, Sol 133)

Natalie took her second cup of coffee from the mess tent and walked carefully through the dark field of scrub and brush to the edge of the small cliff overlooking The Pasture. As she sat down in the long, coarse grass, she could hear in the distance the 'goats' the Seekers raised for food, their song backed by the faint sound of the surf a half-kilometer away. But the night, as always on Big Blue, was otherwise quiet. The rain that had fallen in the late afternoon was gone now, the clouds fading to the east, adding drama to the slow rise of Little Gray. The ground already dry, she sat cross-legged near the edge, looking out on The Pasture, the sea, and the rising moon. She thought of Ben, and of that day he was lost just a few hundred meters from where she sat. She remembered the warm feel of the sun on her face that day, the odd electric-ozone smell of the enemy weapons, and the crinkle of the dry grass under her boots.

She avoided recalling the other sights and smells of that day, pushing them aside like the unwanted intrusion they were. She thought instead of Ben's family, their kindness, and their strong support of her decision to return to *Intrepid* and continue her life in the Fleet.

Liwanu Harry watched her go, and after a few minutes he walked out to the cliff to join her. Natalie was looking steadily at Little Gray as he approached.

"Lieutenant Hayden, may I join you?" he asked softly.

She looked up at him and smiled thinly. "Of course, Harry, have a seat."

He sat a meter away from her and surveyed the scene himself for a minute.

A few bright streaks crossed the sky as they watched. Small pieces of the enemy ships *Intrepid* had destroyed months ago were still falling at a steady rate, lighting up the sky.

"A sad place for you, I should think."

She looked down, then across at him, nodding slightly. "Yes. Yes, it is."

"I think it was very brave of you to come back here, Lieutenant."

Natalie was always uncomfortable with rank hierarchy in casual situations, feeling people should know her by something more than her two silver bars. She thought a moment about permitting Harry to address her by her first name, but as she again looked over at him, so young and earnest and dedicated, she decided to maintain just a bit of distance.

"In some ways, yes. But being here with you, and Captain Martin, and Henderson...*Intrepid*...well, I can't imagine being anywhere else."

Liwanu took a sip of his soda before responding. He'd been up since 0430, and despite the day fading around him, in his mind, it was mid-morning. "The Marines admire your strength very much, Lieutenant. I heard some of the NCO's yesterday as we were coming down, saying that you were the only one they wanted in the cockpit. They trust you, ma'am, and they know you won't wilt in a fight."

Natalie nodded and took another sip of coffee. She'd taken Ben's favorite ultra-insulated and over-sized coffee cup from his office as she prepared his personal belongings to be sent home, a job she'd refused to permit anyone else. Natalie rarely saw him without it and she had used it ever since as a way to feel close to him. She looked at it now briefly, then set it down.

Finally, Liwanu asked the question that had been circling his mind since he saw her leave the mess tent. "How do you do it, Lieutenant? I confess I don't understand. How do you just go on?"

Natalie looked out at the ocean for several seconds, wondering again how vulnerable she wanted to be with him. He'd had the courage and integrity to bring Ben's last messages home, and if only for that, he deserved an answer. *He's a good kid,* she thought, *and I can afford to sister him a little.*

"Today, Liwanu. For me, today is the *only* day." She paused a moment, looking down at the pasture. "I cannot change what happened even a nanosecond ago. I can only live *today*."

She turned to him, seeing that he was now looking at her and not out at the ocean. "Tomorrow, when I see it, *if* I see it, will just be another today. I can't change yesterday," she repeated, pointing to the pasture, "or the billions of yesterdays that preceded it. I can only make my choices *now*, in *this* moment. Feel, now. Do, now. Change, now."

She stopped to take another sip, then set the cup between her crossed legs, her hands still caressing it. "If I let the past overcome me, defeat me, I lose not only this day but all the new todays to come. I loved him *so much*. I still do." She picked up the cup and held it out for Liwanu to see. "But he would not have me wander this wilderness in never-ending tears and sadness. So, today, Liwanu, today is what I focus on. Each day gets my full attention. Then, after a time, there will be new yesterdays to look back on. This is what I look forward to, Liwanu. This is what I live for now: making new yesterdays."

Natalie turned her face back to the ocean, the faint sound of breaking surf now the only noise reaching her ears. Little Gray had moved above the rain clouds, and a bright, rippled strip of light divided the ocean's surface in half as she watched.

Another minute passed before Liwanu spoke. "As I said, Lieutenant, you are very brave. You've thought about this quite a lot, I can see."

"I spent several days on that mountain Ben loved, a place he wanted to share with me so that it could be *ours* and not just *his*. So, yeah, I've thought about this. Whatever happens now, Liwanu, *whatever* happens, I'm *alive* right now. I mean, really, fully, completely *alive*. I miss Ben every minute of every day, but I would not trade this feeling even if it would take away all the grief, all the pain." She shifted to relieve the stress in her legs, letting the blood flow more freely. "If God chooses for me to die tomorrow, or tonight for that matter, or now, I die knowing I had a purpose, my life had meaning."

"I see."

Natalie again turned to look at the young lieutenant. "And what about you, Harry? You lost people you knew that day. Being here can't be easy for you, either."

"I was closer to Gunther than to any of the others. He was interesting to talk to, but I hated to see Joanie McCarthy lost the most."

"Why her more than the others?"

"She had come so far, ma'am. Her childhood was horrible, abusive even. But she was strong. She walked out of that hell-house on her 18th birthday and signed up to be a Fleet Marine. She never went back — made a complete break."

"Never?"

"No, ma'am. She left pretty specific instructions that we should not even notify them that she was killed. She left her insurance money to a charity and asked to be buried in a military cemetery on the other side of Australia."

"So, you were close?"

"In a way, yes, but not like you and Mister Price. She would want to talk sometimes, and I would just let her. I was glad to give her an ear that would actually listen."

"I'm sure she appreciated that."

46

"Yes, I know she did, but it's a small thing, really, to just hear someone out. I could not change what happened to her, or solve her internal conflicts, but I could let her vent sometimes."

"You're a good man, Liwanu Harry. And, a good officer. Do me a favor and live through this, OK? We need more like you."

Liwanu smiled shyly, adding a small shrug. "If you say so, Lieutenant, but if that's true, you need to understand that it took the Lord quite a few rounds at the anvil to pound me into the shape you see now."

"Really?"

"Oh, yes. In my earlier days I was proportionally far more pig iron than steel."

"I would not have thought that."

"I take that as a great compliment, ma'am. Thank you."

"You're welcome. You earned it."

A minute or so later, Harry got up off the ground, kneeling as he picked up his drink and his weapon. "I need to go check on the pickets and then meet with Lieutenant Allen about the watches today. Or, tonight, I guess."

Natalie laughed at his diurnal confusion. "Allen. She's the new butter-bar?"

Liwanu smiled. "Kamaria, yes, ma'am. She has the other platoon. Just came over from the US Marines. She's even younger than I am, but she'll be fine."

"Good to hear."

Harry stood up, brushing the thin leaves of Big Blue grass off his field uniform, then turned back to Natalie.

"Good day, Lieutenant Hayden."

"Good day, Harry."

Natalie sat there alone another hour, savoring both her coffee and the feeling of being close to Ben. *It's a beautiful place,* she thought, *even in the dark.* Finally, she, too, got up, brushed off her uniform, and headed back to get some sleep in the shuttle. They'd just had breakfast, but Natalie had been up most of the daylight and needed rest. There would be more trips up to *Intrepid* later today, which on Big Blue really meant 'later tonight.'

What she didn't know was that Liwanu had sent two Marines back to keep an eye on her. They slipped down behind some brush about fifty meters away, watching silently until she returned to the camp. They waited ten minutes and then returned themselves, letting their Lieutenant know she was safe.

Intrepid
Big Blue
Sunday, February 19, 2079, 1115 UTC

XO Alonzo Bass was surprised at something he saw on the weekly logistics report. Leaving his small office just aft of the Captain's duty cabin, he walked forward to find Joanne on the Bridge, studying her own status reports on her NetComp.

"Captain, are you aware that Andy requested two hundred more 2K7X's from *Ceres*? Plus, a thousand rounds of ammo each?"

Joanne's expression didn't change. "Yes. I saw that in the reqs."

"What do you make of it?"

Again, Joanne remained expressionless. "I guess he wants more guns."

Alonzo looked at his Captain, wondering what Joanne's cryptic answer meant. "Two-hundred more? Has he discussed this with you?"

Finally, Joanne looked over at her XO, her face revealing nothing. "Who's the Captain here, again?"

Alonzo frowned in frustration, and she went back to reading her report.

"What is he doing, Captain? He has less than a hundred— " Alonzo stopped mid-sentence. As he did, Joanne turned to him again.

"Yes, Commander Bass?"

Alonzo let a small smile escape. "He's arming the Seekers."

"Is he?" Joanne asked, deadpan, as she leaned back in her chair, that same sly smile on her face.

"So, I take it Barker doesn't know?"

"Doesn't know what, Commander?"

Alonzo shook his head. "I hope Andy knows what he's doing, ma'am."

"He's a Marine, Alonzo. He knows."

"Yes, ma'am."

Joanne finally let her guard down, displaying a small smile. "I hear Eaagher is a particularly fast learner. Good marksman."

"You could have just told me. Barker is going to see the requisition. He'll figure it out. He'll freak."

"Will he now? Are you sure?" Alonzo watched as she casually took a sip of her coffee. "I don't think he actually has time to read the reqs from every ship."

"When he comes around screaming, Captain — "

"*If* he comes around screaming, Mister XO, you just act surprised."

"Yes, ma'am."

"I mean it, Alonzo. If he goes off the rails about this, it's on Andy and me. There's a reason I didn't discuss it with you."

48

Alonzo dropped his NetComp on the workstation in front of him and looked out the Bridge windows at Big Blue for a moment, then turned and spoke quietly to Joanne. "I appreciate that, Captain, I do. But frankly, I'd rather be an unindicted co-conspirator than be kept out of the loop."

Joanne looked at him. "Noted."

Alonzo started to say something else, something about how he would have agreed, had she just asked, but stopped himself. Henderson fiercely protected her ship and its crew, and this was just her way of covering his ass when he didn't have a clue it needed cover.

"Something else, Commander?" she asked.

"No, ma'am. I'm going back to finish reconciling these reqs."

"Very well. Thank you, Alonzo."

Alonzo gave Joanne one more glance of disappointment, picked up his Net-Comp, and headed back to his office. It wouldn't be easy, but he thought he might have an idea of how to make two hundred weapons and near a quarter-million rounds of ammo disappear.

Residence of Scad Nee Wok
Preeminent Home World
Earth Equivalent Date: February 24, 2079

Scad Nee Wok left early in the morning, telling Asoon that there were still duties for him to perform at the Armada Headquarters, even though his ship was by now very far away. Not a drot after he left, three males appeared at the entrance to their residence. Their dark, formal dress told her they were from the Science Directorate, and so she had no choice but to admit them, inviting them to sit in the shared area at the front of the residence. They offered no names or courtesies, which did not surprise Asoon. The Directorate was infamous for its secretiveness.

The young one spoke first. "Asoon Too Lini, we have been watching you for some time."

Asoon looked directly at the young male. "Watching?"

"We have known since your egg-time that you have a talent which the Directorate requires."

Her expression didn't change. "Watching?"

"Yes. Your educational record," he held up a large document, "is consistent with your egg-screening."

"Egg-screening?"

The oldest male, now visibly annoyed, spoke for the first time. "Asoon Too Lini, you must listen! The Science Directorate requires your talents and needs you to accept the serious and difficult task we have for you."

"I am paired. What of my male? Should Scad Nee Wok not make this decision? Will he not be offended by your impudence?"

The third male spoke up. "Your pairing with Wok was no random accident, Asoon Too Lini."

Aha! she thought, recalling the odd behavior of the Pairing Manager. *It isn't just chance! Some one, or some thing, is behind it after all.*

"Scad Nee Wok will not contest or object."

Asoon remained in a stiff posture, her reserve clear, her skepticism plain for them to see. "What exactly is it that you are asking me to do?"

The older one spoke again. "You are what we call a 'Speaker.' This means you have an inborn ability to readily learn the languages of alien species. This is a skill we are desperately in need of."

"What other species?"

"You will learn the complex language of the most dangerous race we have yet encountered. Armada males like Scad Nee Wok call them 'Vermin' because of all the trouble they've caused."

"And where do these Vermin come from?"

"System 201, a star very far away."

"And how will I learn this alien language?"

"We will show you."

"I assume I again have no choice in this, as I did not in my pairing?"

"You do have a choice, " the younger one said. "But we beg you to accept."

"Very well," Asoon answered. "I will do as you ask. What now?"

They gave her instructions on where to report, and when, and how long her education might take. Then, they rose and left.

Out on the street, the older one spoke again. "Asoon is obviously a Speaker; I can tell from her speech and thought patterns, But will she learn? Is she the one we need?"

The middle-aged male responded. "She must be, maleParent, if our plan is to succeed."

"We risk much on this, Glur Woe Segt." the youngest male fretted. "If she fails, our chance may be lost."

"Then it will be lost!" Segt replied flatly. "And my death will be more painful but no less final than otherwise. But, if she and Wok succeed, it will mean a better future for all of us."

"Far better than no future at all, you mean."

"You, maleChild Rmah Teo," the older male said, "are even more cynical than Asoon Too Lini!"

They turned from the residence of Scad Nee Wok and Asoon Too Lini and walked back to the Science Directorate.

Scad Nee Wok was barely inside his residence when Asoon began to speak. "There were three males from the Science Directorate here today. They arrived just after you left."

"Yes," Scad replied evenly, "I was informed later." He walked to the food preparation area and drew himself some cold water. It was a warm afternoon, and the walk from Armada was long.

"And?"

"Being a Speaker is an important skill. I believe now that the SD arranged our pairing, although I confess I don't understand why."

Asoon looked through the front window, onto the street outside. "You are a ship commander."

Scad returned from the food area and sat across from her. "Yes, but so what? Why would that be important?"

"We together will be a Speaker of Vermin paired with a Ship Commander. Perhaps we are to try to communicate with these Vermin?"

Scad looked at Asoon with surprise. In his experience, females were not typically so intuitive, so insightful. He wondered if those who were Speakers also had a more flexible intellect. She was unlike his own EggLayer or his first paired female. Asoon was, in fact, unlike any female he had ever encountered.

"Possibly. The SD's plans are opaque, Asoon, to all but the SD. Let us just do as they say for now."

They were quiet until they sat for their evening meal.

"Asoon, I would not share this selection with anyone. I will certainly not share it with anyone at Armada."

"Why?"

"I just think it would be wise to be silent for now."

Scad was the male, so he was within his rights to demand her silence. But, Asoon noted, he did not command, exactly. He made clear what he believed was in their common interest, and she agreed.

March 2079

Sentinel Two
GJ 3618
Friday, March 3, 2079, 1024 UTC

Sentinel Number Two, the one Natalie Hayden and Ben Price had so much trouble initializing, had kept its quiet, uninterrupted watch on the GJ 3618 system. The star was a typical red dwarf, something like a tenth the size of the Sun and an even smaller fraction of its luminosity. Two minor rocky planets and a single gas giant orbited the tiny star in a massive four-character slow dance.

Every week Number Two's system monitor asked itself how it felt and then sent the results to FleetIntel. And every week, Sentinel Number Two was nominal, with nothing unusual to report. Its finicky power supply never gave it another thought. But it was a good little drone, exactly what Ann Cooper had in mind, and it kept its visual spectrum, IR, and UV eyes open at all times. Not once in six months did anything happen worth reporting to its masters almost fifteen light-years away.

Until now.

The arrival of eight enemy ships was not something Number Two was going to miss. It processed the IR traces and visual clues and determined that there were six Type I and two Type III ships in the neighborhood. Checking the alert criteria, Sentinel Two decided that this was something to be reported, and so it immediately dispatched its first SLIP event notification to FleetIntel. Now that targets had been acquired, it went into tracking mode, uniquely labeling each enemy ship, and tracking their individual movements. In eight hours, it would send an updated report.

Preeminent Commander Plyf Cee Redl stood on the bridge of Ship 450, looking out on the same tiny star that held Sentinel Number Two in orbit. His second in command joined him, his teeth still dripping red from their daily meal.

"I care not for this assignment, Wevf. I care not to be extra weight, like an overfull tail stump."

"Indeed, commander, it is a tough, bitter meal to consume, like too-soon meat."

Redl growled his agreement.

"But, commander," Wevf continued, "Should the Vermin prove harder to suppress than the authorities think, that fat tail-stump will become lean claws fast enough."

"Perhaps, Wevf, perhaps."

Redl dismissed his subordinate and sat at the command position, facing the star. The Revered First had decided this strategy, and as such, it could not be questioned or improved. His small force was to wait here, at least ten rots from the Vermin planet, and await reports from the attack force. If the attack failed, he thought, they would arrive too late and might just be consumed as well. If it was successful, they would be irrelevant, which would not bode well for promotion. It would have been better for them to arrive together, suppress the Vermin, and win the day all at once.

But the decisions of the Revered First were not to be questioned, so Redl kept his thoughts to himself. These Vermin, they were a surprise to Redl. He'd seen the other races that the Preeminent had brought to obsequia. They knew enough to kneel and survive, to do as they were told and not resist. Only the scholars, whose dead home the Vermin seemed to be defending, had put up any kind of fight, but in the end, they were easily reduced. Not like the Scrapnats, ugly little animals with filthy habits that produced flavors for food that could be found nowhere else. Or Tsodonts, slimy crawlers whose brains were used to cure diseases. Each race had its job, its place, and the Vermin just did not seem to fit into this picture.

As they were talking, a runner arrived with a message from the command ship.

As Redl read it, he stood up straighter, and his tail stump quivered with excitement.

"Orders?" Wevf asked.

"Yes, we are to pause one rotation, then proceed. We are to strike a second blow if necessary."

A day later, Sentinel Number Two dutifully reported their departure.

ISC Fleet HQ Intel Section
Ft. Eustis, VA
Saturday. March 4, 2079, 1000 UTC (0600 EST)

The Table buzzed with the news of the Sentinel report. *Eight ships!* Eight, that is, out of the nineteen *Cobra* believed had been dispatched to Earth. Ron Harris puzzled over the news as his analysts gathered. The calls two hours earlier had cut their nights short. He looked around the Table, suppressing a smile. With all the changes he'd seen here in the last year, all the conflicts, he was still pleased with his staff, still believed they were the best minds available. Certainly, at the moment, they were among the most caffeinated.

"So, let's get started. What do we think of these eight ships?"

Ann Cooper answered first, "Given the position and ship types, there's no doubt in my mind that these ships are part of the task force sent to Earth."

"So, why leave part of your force behind?" Ron asked the room.

"Insurance?" Scott Morgan offered. "A backup in case your primary plan doesn't work?"

SLT Craig Weeks, one of the newest members of the section, leaned forward. "The timing is interesting, sir."

"Oh?"

"Fifteen light-years from here is about seventeen and a half days travel time for them."

"OK."

"If this group split off from the main force, the enemy won't be here until March 20th."

"Possibly," Lieutenant Adrienne McLean said, flipping screens on her Net-Comp. "But if they went to 3618, that's a two-light-year detour. The main force might well be on the nominal line to Earth, and still arriving on the 17th."

"Could be, yes, but, why do that?" Weeks asked.

"Setting up a second wave? A follow-up of some kind?" Scott Morgan asked.

"That would make the most sense," Ron answered. "But it means several days in between, assuming the main force is, as Adrienne suggested, still on the direct line here."

"In any case, sir," Craig continued, "these eight can't be here before the 21st even if they left right now!"

"Yes, agreed. And, we can now tell Operations, with some confidence, that there will be just eleven ships in the first attack."

Frances Wilson spoke up. "Ever read Morison's history of the US Navy in the Second World War, Admiral?"

"Of course. It's required reading in the first year at the U."

Frances leaned back, making a pyramid of her fingers as she looked at the ceiling. "I'm reminded of the Japanese at Leyte Gulf, all split forces and lousy timing. Destroyed piecemeal as they arrived instead of making a coordinated, concentrated attack."

"Interesting thought. Perhaps our opponents are making the same mistakes?"

"They do seem to share a kind of combat conceit. Arrogant still as they drown in losing." She looked across at Ron, sitting at the opposite end of the Table. "Just a thought, sir. I agree with all that's been said here. We keep alert for the 17th and also watch for when the eight ships leave 3618."

Ron looked at Ann as they prepared to adjourn. "Just so we're clear, Senior

Lieutenant Cooper, this one detection makes the entire Sentinel program worth every penny. Is that clear?"

"Yes, sir, thank you. I am just glad it did what we hoped it would."

"Draft me a message to the fleet, Ann. Meantime I'll call CINC."

```
FLASH 207903041200UTC
TO: ALLFLEET
FROM: FLEETINTEL
TOP SECRET

1) SENTINEL AT GJ 3818 REPORTS ARRIVAL OF EIGHT ENEMY SHIPS
207903031024UTC.
2) FLEETINTEL ASSESSES THESE AS PORTION OF EARTH-BOUND ENEMY TASK
FORCE, NEW ETA FOR THIS GROUP NOT EARLIER THAN 20790321
3) FLEETINTEL SEES NO REASON TO DOUBT ENEMY MAIN FORCE WILL
STRIKE O/A 20790317.
4) ADVISE CAUTION FOR SIMILAR MULTI-WAVE ATTACKS AT OTHER TARGETS.

END
```

ISC Fleet HQ Intel Section
Ft. Eustis, VA
Sunday, March 5, 2079, 2200 UTC

The second report from Sentinel Two removed any remaining doubts about what the enemy had in mind. Ron again sat with his brain trust to assess what to do next.

"OK, sir," Craig Weeks said, "I think they're planning a second wave, and that attack will occur not earlier than March 22."

Ron looked down at the other end of the Table. "Frances?"

"Well, sir, everyone knows I'm just an old intel spook, but yes, Mr. Weeks' math is correct. Kawaguchi needs to be ready for a second round."

"Fine, we'll get that to him."

The next morning Ron met with Captain Nobuyuki Kawaguchi, outlining the evidence for a second wave on March 22. Kawaguchi, a careful planner, had studied Fiona's plan and was assigning ships to the roles she specified. It was a difficult problem, defending a sphere from an attack that could, at least theoretically, come from any direction. He had nine ships, including three of the largest cruisers in the fleet. The enemy would be sending nineteen. Kawaguchi thought those were pretty good odds. Nobu sat with Ron for a long time, presenting white-board style his plan for the defense of the home planet.

Nippon would be his flagship, naturally, with Andy Sackville in *Dunkirk* as his backup. He fretted about the ship factory; a fat, very high-value target, but one frigate should be able to cover it. The enemy was unlikely, in Nobu's opinion, to mass an attack on a single point, regardless of the perceived value. *Gagarin* got the assignment to guard the factory on asteroid 1235 Schorria.

The early miners picked Schorria for its small-but-large-enough size, and its exceptionally slow rotation period: over 1200 hours. Since then, they had bored into that rock and created a mostly automated factory to produce the prefabricated units that were then assembled into ships. Without Schorria, the fleet would be unable to replace lost ships, a constraint Kawaguchi could not accept. There were also several hundred lives at stake.

Bondarenko would be in a long, elliptical orbit over the South pole. The enemy would probably come from the south, he believed, so the shield needed to be oriented in that direction. Frigates *Grissom* and *Rassvet* were in opposing geostationary orbits, one over the mid-Pacific, the other over the South Atlantic just west of Africa. *Mir*'s assignment was to cover the northern hemisphere in much the same way *Bondarenko* was covering the southern. *Stoykiy* and *Tong-Il* would stand out halfway between Earth and the Moon, their positions offset from *Grissom* and *Rassvet* by ninety degrees.

His *Nippon* would take a geostationary orbit on the same longitude as Fleet HQ, to facilitate communications. *Dunkirk* would take an opposite position over Indonesia. And, as Nobu pointed out to Ron, when you couldn't tell what time they'd come, any point was as good as any other. He worried about the tradeoffs he faced; the need to cover all approaches naturally spread his force out. They would need to move quickly once the enemy presented themselves, and if they did come from the south as expected, only *Mir* would be seriously out of position. The rest should be on direct lines to the enemy ships.

Time would tell, he told Ron, if his plan was adequate.

Antares
Big Blue
Friday, March 17, 2079, 1100 UTC

Jayvon Dean saw what he had been waiting for, but secretly hoping would not appear. "Multiple IR transients, Captain, bearing 110 plus 30. Looks like they're finally here!"

"Very well. Find the Type V." She turned to Carol at the Weapons station. "Weaps! As soon as —"

Captain Terri Michael was cut off mid-sentence as *Antares* shook suddenly, a low rumble, as if it had suddenly hit a gravel patch. Carol looked up in alarm from her Weapons station.

"What the hell was that?" Michael asked aloud. She looked immediately at the ship status display on her console. All green. A second later, they were nearly blinded by an intense white light pouring through the bridge windows. Navigator Alex Williams slapped the control to close the windows as the Surveillance position lit up with alarms.

"Forward visual is offline, Captain," Jayvon called. "Whatever that was, we're blind."

"Laser comms are out, too, Captain," Lori Rodgers called. "Looks like the dorsal receiver is fried."

"What the hell?" Michael wondered out loud. She looked back at Rodgers. "Get the VHF up."

"Already on it."

XO Ryan Lewis left the Bridge, sprinting aft to find Maintenance Officer SLT Miguel Anthony. Together they would take charge of damage control and repairs. Several minutes passed as they worked to restore the laser comms.

At the same time, Jayvon Dean and his crew were working on their vision problems. Finally, he turned to the Command station. "The high-res telescope is done, Captain. That flash smoked the detector, and there is no spare. We'll have to make do with the wide-field and Mark One Eyeballs."

Shortly, more alarms sounded from the Surveillance station. "Multiple small objects heading our way, Captain."

"What are they?"

"I don't know, ma'am. They're small, and they're headed this way pretty fast."

"Nav!" Terri called, "move us back ten meters per second more and down fifteen degrees."

"Ten meters, fifteen degrees, aye ma'am."

As *Antares* began to respond, Jayvon called out again. "Ten objects on the IR, Captain, coming fast...huh...looks like a figure eight."

"What could —"

Michael was cut off by a distinct *thud* as one of the objects struck near the front of the ship.

"What the hell?" the Surveillance tech called out as another alarm sounded. "Radio signal just came up on...232 MHz. It's too strong not to be that object." As they tried to pin down the signal, there were three more audible impacts on the hull. Then, two more.

"More signals, Captain."

Carol suddenly understood what it all meant, and it frightened her more than she had been since Inoria.

She turned and called to Terri: "Transponders, Captain. Beacons. They're tagging us."

If they could tag the Fleet ships, Carol thought, they'd be completely exposed.

Michael was now standing at her position, better able to see all the displays in front of her. "How the hell did they..." she said quietly. "Do we have the Type V identified?"

Carol opened her mouth to answer but was interrupted by several small explosions. Terri Michael fell towards her; blood and tissue exploding from her chest. Across the Bridge, Carol felt herself falling, something having taken her legs out from underneath her. As she fell, she saw Michael slam down on the deck, face down and unmoving. To the left, she saw shocked faces and a spreading red cloud as a tech fell from his seat. As she, too, landed on the deck, she focused on the sound filling her ears.

She was surprised that it was her own screams.

The impact of her fall sent a shocking spike of pain through her that snapped time back to normal. She writhed at the inferno that seemed to be clawing its way into her whole being from her right leg. Carol was suddenly and mortally afraid but gathered the courage to look down at herself. There, poking out from her uniform leg, were four shiny, sharp fins. Blood was flowing freely around them from her right thigh, saturating her uniform, and flowing out onto the Bridge floor. It took a second for it to register that it was her blood.

She forced herself to focus and looked up at her Weapons position.

"Guzman! Kill the Type V!" she gasped.

Carol heard him say "Yes, Lieutenant" as she struggled to remain conscious, the pain threatening to drown her. Pushing down the shock, she squirmed around far enough to see Terri Michael on the floor, her dead eyes staring upwards, and Alex standing over her, blood on his arm. Carol stared at Michael as she felt her techs moving her aside, barely hearing their yells for the leak kit to cover the holes the flechettes fired by the enemy beacons had left in the bulkhead. The heavy insulation between the inner and outer hulls helped slow the air loss, but she could hear air escaping, and feel her ears reacting. Carol shook her head to fight off the pain, then pulled herself to a sitting position against the rear bulkhead of the Bridge. Looking down at herself again, she could see blood spattered on her uniform, blood that a part of her brain told her could not be her own. She squeezed her eyes to gain control and looked around the now-chaotic Bridge.

Surveillance techs were moving someone out of a chair and laying them on the floor. Carol now saw blood smeared across the forward monitors. She closed her eyes again to try to drive back the fire in her leg and clear her thoughts.

Michael is dead. Where is the XO?

Guzman fired what he had and started a reload. He turned around to see his young lieutenant on the deck behind him, her blood-spattered face twisted in pain, and her uniform leg leaking a shocking amount of blood. Emilio Guzman had three daughters of his own back home, not much younger than Carol, and as Guzman looked at her struggling for control, he saw their faces. He also saw the bright fins peeking out from her thigh. He pulled the casualty kit from under the Workstation and knelt down next to her.

Carol opened her eyes when she felt him leaning close to her.

"Now, lieutenant, do be a good girl and just sit still while I do this."

"Do what—" she screamed again as Guzman snapped the flechette from the skin of her thigh and began applying pressure with bandages from the kit.

It took her several seconds to catch her breath. "Guzman?"

"Yes, Lieutenant?"

She managed to turn her head and look up at the old Chief. "I hate you."

"Thank you, Lieutenant. Now, let's get you to sickbay."

"No, I can't go. The Captain is dead. The XO is absent. I'm staying."

Guzman leaned in close to her. "You can't, Carol. You're still bleeding and not just a little."

Despite her pain, Carol smiled at him. Crusty old Chief Guzman had never called her by her first name, ever. He was too good a Chief to do that.

"Emilio," she responded in kind, "I can't go." She turned her head to the right, looking again at the Bridge crew, many of whom were glancing expectantly back at her. She looked back at Guzman. "If I die here, I die here. But I can't leave. Not yet. Wrap it up best you can, but don't ask me again."

The Chief nodded and went to work, Carol grunted several times as Guzman pulled the pressure bandage as tight as he could. It was far from perfect, but it would do until Soto could get to her.

Carol looked up in surprise when he began washing her face with alcohol swabs from the kit. She reached for his arm. "What are you do—" she stopped when he showed her the blood on the gauze. It was Terri Michael's blood, she suddenly realized. She let go, and as Guzman quickly finished, she again noticed that her uniform was covered with drying red stains.

"There, Lieutenant. Much better."

Besides the dead surveillance tech, two others had been wounded, but nothing severe enough to get them away from their posts. Several of the small, razor-sharp darts had hit and disabled equipment, some embedded themselves in bulkheads.

Carol looked back at the Surveillance station. "Dean! Find the XO!"

Jayvon Dean set down the phone and came to her a moment later. "Lieutenant Anthony reports the XO was hit, too. He's unconscious. The kitchen took a hit, we lost two there, three more in the maintenance space where Lewis was."

Carol struggled to focus on what Jayvon was saying, "That's it?"

"No, ma'am. Lieutenant Anthony says there are at least a dozen wounded all over the place, not sure how bad. His people are patching the hull and moving the wounded to sickbay."

"Shit." Carol closed her eyes for a few seconds, realizing now what she had to do. She opened her eyes and looked at Jayvon. "Get Mister Swenson up here. And where the hell is Alex?" Dean, newly promoted and nervous at being the Surveillance Officer since Ryan Lewis' assignment as XO, kept his cool and started making the calls Carol needed.

Alex came around from the other side of the Command position, Lori Rodgers busily working on his upper arm, fear in her expression and tears on her face.

"I'm here, Carol."

"How bad?" she asked.

"I'm fine, Carol."

Carol looked around the Bridge. "OK, everyone, let's get back to our jobs. We still have a fight to win here!"

Swenson, the Weapons Maintenance Officer, arrived just behind Doctor Marcia Soto and one of her techs. As they began to work on Carol's leg, she looked up at him.

"Jon, take Weaps. Focus on the Type V and the Type II's. Keep on them until they're gone, understand?"

"Yes, Lieutenant."

"Good. Chief? I need you back in the magazine to cover for Swenson."

The Chief nodded and headed aft to his weapons.

"Dean!"

Jayvon walked the half-dozen steps to where Carol was seated against the aft bulkhead of the Bridge and knelt down. "Yes, ma'am?"

As Carol looked up at him from the floor, she could see the stress in his face, tears at the edges of his eyes. "Dean...you're doing fine. Keep feeding Swenson the positions, keep on the Type V and watch for any more of these goddamn mines."

"Yes, Lieutenant."

Now breathless and a little dizzy from calling out orders, she tried to slow and deepen her respiration to stay out of shock. As she tried to catch her breath, her focus moved to Marcia Soto, now cutting off her uniform leg.

"Marsh — "

"Shut up, Carol."

"But I need — "

"You need to sit quiet for a minute."

Carol gave her that minute to work before trying again. "Marsh, what about casualties?"

Marcia spoke through angry, clenched teeth as she worked on Carol's leg.

"Seven dead, so far. Lewis is probably critical, but they haven't brought him in yet. There are three a little worse than you, but they'll be OK. I don't know how many more are wounded but still on duty."

"Damn."

Marcia and her tech worked quickly, and shortly there was a large bandage wrapped tightly around her leg. "OK, you'll be fine for now. I hit it with the clotting foam and a local, so you should be functional for a while."

"How bad is it? Can I walk?"

"Not too bad, really. It tore up some skin and cut some muscle and a vein or two but no major vessels and no bone. Mostly superficial. But, it's gonna hurt like hell later and probably gonna look like shit."

"Gee, thanks."

Marcia closed up her kit. "Once I get the others finished, I want you in the sickbay so I can close that wound properly, understand?"

Carol gave her a weak salute. "Yes, ma'am, Doctor ma'am."

"Geez, you're such a pain in the ass, Carol."

Marcia stood up and moved quickly aft, back to her sickbay, and those who needed her immediate attention.

Now that her blood loss was stabilized and the worst of the pain suppressed, the Bridge returned to clarity as Carol started to recover. She watched from the floor as three crew members moved Terri Michael off the Bridge, her blood a dark wet stain on the grey Bridge carpet that reminded Carol of some grotesque Rorschach test. Carol felt a hard lump in her throat at the loss of her Captain, mentor, and friend, but there was no time to think about that now. With Lewis down, she had work to do.

Alex Williams, his right arm bandaged but serviceable, helped her to the Command position, and into the Captain's seat. He looked at the lump of bandage surrounding her right thigh, and the small red stain on the side. Carol looked up at him and forced a smile.

"Let's just hope mini-skirts never come back."

Alex smiled back and replied quietly, "If they ever do, Carol, you'll wear one with pride."

She reached up and gripped his arm. "What the hell do I do now, Alex?"

"You do what you always do, Carol. You do the best you can, which is better than most."

"This is no time to blow sunshine up my ass."

"I'm *not*." He looked at her for another second. "You'll never be Terri Michael. But then, she could never be Carol Hansen. You're in command now, so, *command*."

Carol looked at him for a moment, then gave his good arm another small squeeze before releasing it and turning her attention back to the Bridge in front of her.

"Lieutenant Dean, what's our situation now?"

Dean was ready for her. "Looks like only twelve enemy ships, Lieutenant, not nineteen. Six are scratched already, including the Type II."

"What about the Type V?"

"He was hit by all of us, I think, but didn't blow. He's still out there but not firing."

Carol turned to Jon Swenson, the Weapons Maintenance Officer she'd just promoted to her former position. "Jon, what's left?"

"Eleven Bludgeons, twelve Lances, twenty Spartans. I just sent four Bludgeons to the Type V."

Dean looked closely at his displays, then turned to Carol.

"There was only one Type II here, Lieutenant."

"What? Where are the others?"

"Unknown, Lieutenant."

"Comms! Report our status to the flagship. Let them know we're still operational."

Lori Rodgers spoke quickly into the communications console, which instantly transcribed her report and sent it to *Columbia* on the spread-spectrum VHF link, the only inter-ship comm system still working.

A minute later, she called back to Carol, "Target tasking coming in, Lieutenant."

Carol nodded, then studied the tasking order as it was distributed to her Command station. "Very well. Nav, move us towards the targets. Weaps, do we have a solution?"

"Yes, we do."

"Weapons free, Jon. Give 'em hell."

"Yes, ma'am." Swenson had hardly finished speaking before six Lances and three Bludgeons were dispatched to the three Type I enemy cruisers Barker had assigned them. Well aware that the enemy already knew where they were, he set the weapons for direct routing at max speed, the fastest attack possible.

As they waited for their attack to play out, Carol looked around the Bridge, now a shattered shamble that hardly resembled the clean and well-ordered place it had been only a half-hour before. The Surveillance techs were cleaning the remains of their shipmate off the displays and equipment controls. Someone had dropped a cover over Terri Michael's blood so no one would slip on it. The tails of several enemy flechettes could be seen in the bulkheads and workstations, one even embedded in the back of a chair. The enemy had found a way to even the odds, a way to take away the Fleet's best advantage: stealth. They'd also found a way to bring quick, brutal death to the crew in the bargain.

"OK, you assholes," Carol said quietly to herself. "Fine. We'll beat you anyhow."

For the first time since the attack began, she wondered what David was thinking, stashed away in a high orbit with no weapons, where all he could do was watch. He would have seen the attacks, he'd be in the command loop, so he'd also know she was now in command, and what that meant. There was no time to tell him anything now. She jumped as the ship phone on the Command station rang.

"Hansen."

She listened a moment, then set it down. She looked up at the frightened, expectant faces looking back at her.

"That was Soto. Ryan died on the table."

Columbia
Big Blue
Friday, March 17, 2079, 1215 UTC

The scene on the flagship was equally chaotic. *Columbia*, along with *Friendship*, *White*, and *Eagle*, were closer to the Type V than *Antares* when it did, well, whatever it was it did, and the damage was much worse.

Friendship was the ship closest to the Type V, and so the initial pulse struck with more intensity, taking the Forstmann Drive offline. With no Drive, once they were tagged by the enemy's targeting beacons, they were painfully exposed. The beacon-mine strike on *Friendship* took out the sickbay and the reactor staff. As the crew scrambled to patch the hull, four missile hits took *Friendship* out of the fight, and four more shortly after that destroyed her with all hands. The enemy missiles weren't just faster anymore, they carried a much larger warhead, and clearly, the enemy had learned the lesson of the Bludgeon.

Aboard *Komarov*, the beacon-mines killed two dozen, and the enemy missile strikes that followed split the livable areas of the ship in two. The hangar was holed and opened to space, as were several sections forward of that, but from the Intel work area forward, and the reactor control room aft, they were safe for the moment. At least, until the enemy got around to striking them again. Barker ordered them to retire to make repairs. Her Captain launched a combined Lance and Bludgeon strike on the Type V right before engaging his Drive and exiting the field.

The Bridge crew on *White* caught a break and avoided the flash, as they happened to be facing a slightly different direction. But the pulse from the Type V took out her SLIP and put the Drive offline. The beacon-mine strikes failed to kill anyone, but there were numerous injuries. But she remained whole and ready to fight.

Columbia was spared the initial strikes, *Friendship* having absorbed the weapons sent in her direction. Dan Smith had struck back at the Type V, but his Bludgeons did not have their usual effect.

Deep inside *Columbia*, Kieran Barker swore aloud at his communications losses: SLIP, offline. Laser, offline, possibly permanently. He still had the VHF system, but it had limited bandwidth compared to the laser. For now, other than a few specific targeting tasks, he had to let his ship captains freelance until he got a clearer picture of what was going on.

Elias Peña struggled as well, trying to understand the situation. The Tactical Display in Barker's Intel workspace had several significant gaps, and one thing Elias hated was ignorance. Like several other ships, *Columbia* had lost their forward visual sensors, plus the long-range telescope.

Peña stood in his combat center, looking at the evolving display of the battle. With the data coming in from *Cobra*, things were starting to become clearer. They'd lost three ships, the enemy six. The Type V was still out there, but after a dozen or more strikes, it had not dispensed any more weapons. Elias desperately wanted to see it flame, but he'd settle for it to just go silent. The missing seven ships nagged at him, but he forced himself to set them aside, and deal with the problems he already had.

Barker came to talk to his Intel chief.

"I think the Type V is actually dead, sir," Elias told him. "It kept going until somebody hit it again near the forward end. I suspect that killed enough of the crew to put it out of action. It's still in orbit, but it has shown no signs of life since then."

"Well, kudos to whoever, but, if twenty or more Bludgeons didn't blow it up, they've learned something important, wouldn't you say?"

"Yes."

"I wonder what's happening at home. Can't be an accident that they hit us right after their ETA there."

"Yes, can't possibly be a coincidence. They probably thought hitting us everywhere at once would help them."

Barker sat down on one of the high stools scattered around the room. "And it might. We can't share information fast enough to matter. If someone at home or at Inor figures out how to beat this new weapon, they can't tell us until it's too late."

"True. We're all on our own together."

Barker smiled at Peña's twisted half-pun and then looked back at the tactical display.

"What do you make of the missing Type II's and the rest?"

Peña's answer was cut off by a series of flashes on the display. He turned the image and zoomed in to the area. "*Antares* got all three Type I's."

"Good."

"You know Michael and Lewis are both dead?"

Barker nodded. "Hess told me." He turned back to the display. "Where's *Intrepid*?"

Peña re-turned and adjusted the display. "She's over the Seekers, still in that high-inclination orbit. She wasn't tagged."

"OK, then, get Joanne on the VHF. She has a working SLIP, and I need to get a message to Fleet."

Intrepid
Big Blue
Friday, March 17, 2079, 1300 UTC

Reserve! Joanne thought angrily as she studied her tactical display. *He put us in reserve. I have never been on the sidelines in a fight before.*

Intrepid was just coming over the horizon from perigee when the enemy arrived. They were shielded from the initial pulse and not attacked with the new enemy weapon. As they came back up on the commlink, Barker ordered them to just hold their orbit. He wanted them ready in case the situation deteriorated. For now, they were still invisible, still fully functional, and Barker wanted it kept that way.

But Joanne hated it. Her annoyance was interrupted by a call from the Communications station.

"Captain, Admiral Barker."

Joanne nodded to the Comm tech and picked up the phone on her station when it rang.

"*Intrepid* actual."

"Joanne, Kieran here."

"Yes, Admiral."

"I need to get word back to Fleet, and you have one of the few working SLIP transmitters."

"Of course. Send it to us on the data link, and I'll get it off soon as we can."

65

"How's the crew up there?"

"Oh, we're all fat, dumb and happy, you know, just spectators in the cheap seats."

Joanne cringed at her own words. Barker didn't need her frustration added to his own problems.

"Joanne, I put you in reserve because you're someone I can count on to come through if I need a reserve. Understand?"

"Yes, Admiral. Sorry. Just frustrated."

"Well, as you know, not all of their force was in play. I smell a second wave somehow. Not sure what their objective would be, but they're not stupid, so I have to think there's a reason we haven't seen all of them yet."

"Yes, sir, that makes sense."

"OK. Expect the message here shortly, and let me know when it's gone."

"Yes, sir."

Joanne hung up the phone, then sheepishly looked across at her XO, Alonzo Bass. "I can be such a bitch sometimes."

"You're human, Captain. I think Barker understands that."

Cobra
Big Blue
Friday, March 17, 2079, 1315 UTC

David paced the Operations Room, unable to sit still in Center Console. They had tracked the 'mines' from the Type V and detected the beacon transmissions. *Cobra* had felt the mysterious 'pulse' but was further away and apparently not observed by the enemy. Evans and Ballard kept the flagship updated with what they could see. David could watch on Salazar's waterfall display the seven beacons stuck on *Antares*, each on a slightly different frequency. The ingenuity of it was impressive. Small weapons, distributed en mass, somehow detecting the ships they were near, attaching themselves, and then doing double-duty as shotgun and beacon. That was a lot of capability in a small package.

They had cut down the odds now, *Antares* taking out three Type I's made it five to three. David would take those odds any day. He was worried about Carol, but for the moment, he had work to do tracking the enemy ships and looking for those that had not yet appeared.

Eagle
Big Blue
Friday, March 17, 2079, 1300 UTC

Commander Gary Haynes surveyed the damage to his ship with grim determination. The beacon-mines had shredded his Maintenance Officer's office and his Reactor Control Room. He still had power, for now, but he was looking at twenty or more already dead with another twenty-five wounded from the six mines now attached to his ship.

He sent his XO aft to assess their condition when an enemy missile struck, killing her, the Maintenance Officer, and several of the ship's damage control techs. Haynes got the uneasy feeling he was playing a losing hand and staying too long in the game.

His Weapons Officer kept pounding away at the last three Type I's, which seemed to be guarding the Type V that had caused so much trouble for him. Meanwhile, *Eagle* took two more missiles and three more beacon-mines detonated, puncturing the sickbay and the lower berthing area. *Eagle* was venting heavily now, and her Captain reluctantly decided it was time to fold.

His whispered obscenities were just the warmup for the call he now had to make.

"Comms! Get me Hess."

Columbia
Big Blue
Friday, March 17, 2079, 1330 UTC

Dan Smith looked up as the phone on his Command console rang, pulling him away from the tactical display.

"Smith."

"This is Hess. *Eagle* is in trouble, Dan. Sickbay hit, lots of wounded, losing air."

A sudden pit appeared in Dan's stomach. He suppressed his anxiety as he responded carefully, "I see."

"They need a dustoff, Smith: an old-fashioned fast mobile med-evac, and I mean right away. Can you put two shuttles into it?"

Dan looked at his status display. Both shuttles were available. Looking at the pilot roster, Hughes was first, with Logistics Officer Jim Murphy as backup.

"Yes, sir, I can get that moving in about 30 minutes."

"Fast as you can, Captain. They're running out of time."

Smith hung up the phone and stood to look down at the Surveillance position. "Melinda! Dustoff mission to *Eagle*. Be in the wardroom in ten."

"Yes, sir." She did a quick transition to her assistant and moved quickly off the Bridge as Dan picked up the phone again.

"Clark...Mike! I need both shuttles set for dustoff and ready for dispatch as soon as you can make it happen." He hardly waited for Mike's response before resetting the connection.

"Carr...yeah, Carr, this is Smith. Get to the hangar and see if you can help Mike reset the shuttles for a dustoff. He could use a few extra hands."

As he looked up, Melinda's assistant Ensign Carl Hudson was passing him the exact location of *Eagle*, both on paper and into his NetComp.

"I sent it to Lieutenants Hughes and Murphy, too."

"Good work, Carl." He turned to his XO, Mazablaska Dawes. "Take the conn, Maz, until I get this medical mission off."

Dan hustled aft to the hangar deck. Shuttles were not designed to be stealthy, and the thick coating the ship had was out of the question since they had to fit in the ShuttleLock, which was barely larger than the spacecraft itself. But Murphy and Clark had had a somewhat crazy idea last time they were on Earth and scored some radar-absorbing paint from an unspecified, potentially illegal source. So, *Columbia*'s shuttles were now painted an inconsistent but functional flat black, and they were a lot harder to spot visually.

As Dan arrived, the second shuttle was just coming out of storage, Nurse Ensign Dremonte Ingram riding it out as he slammed the seats down into beds. Senior Corpsman Mai Saika was stacking trauma supplies for transfer onto the shuttles once they were in position. Mai would ride Shuttle Two with Murphy, while Dremonte would ride Shuttle One with Hughes. Dan watched the controlled mayhem for a minute, then, satisfied, headed back up to the wardroom. Intel Chief Gurgen Khachaturian was ready with the combat situation outside. They piled in quickly, Hughes and Murphy up front, then Saika and Ingram, with Clark, Carr, and others in the back rows.

Katch's presentation was not encouraging. The enemy was taking hits, but still lashing out. He went over the closest enemy ship positions, then turned to the state of *Eagle*.

"She took the tag-mines hard - lots of casualties. Then several missile hits, I can't tell exactly how many, maybe five." He took a breath. "Captain Haynes says both forward airlocks are nominal, so they're staging the wounded there."

He stopped and looked at the two pilots in the front row.

"There is an enormous volume of loose shit flying around out there, understand? Keep your eyes open and the short-range radar running. This is one seriously high-risk mission."

Katch finished with a set of call signs and radio frequencies for the trip.

Dan stood as Katch took a seat. "OK, questions? Melinda, you're the lead on this, you call the shots."

"Yes, Captain. I'll take the forward port airlock; Jim can take the starboard. We'll dock, set auto-return on the flight directors, then open up and take as many as we can."

"We're coming back here?" Jim Murphy asked.

"Yes."

Murphy looked over at Melinda, who nodded. "OK, then, I guess we're ready."

As they walked out of the wardroom, Mike waited for Melinda, pulling her gently to one side of the passage.

"Let me do this trip for you."

"What?" she asked, surprised.

"You heard Katch, Mel. It's dangerous out there, I can take—"

He was cut off by Melinda's hands on his chest, pushing him up against the bulkhead. There was a loud thud as his torso smacked the steel, a sound that turned the heads of those still leaving the briefing.

"No, Clark, *no!*" she hissed at him.

Clark found himself suddenly short of breath and barely squeezed out "I just..."

Melinda's grip only got stronger as she pushed closer to him, her eyes filling. "Jesus, Mike, I love you so much I don't know how to tell you, but *I* do *my* job, understand? Don't think you can step in and protect me out here."

He managed to nod slightly. He was shocked at her strength. He was easily six inches taller and fifty pounds heavier, but she had him literally pinned to the wall.

She let up on him a little. "Clark, I know you worry. I do, too. But we do our duty out here, right?"

He squeezed out another nod.

"I really do want to spend a lifetime with you, dumbass, really, I do. But meanwhile — "

"Meanwhile, we fight," he finally said, quietly surrendering.

She kissed him quickly, then let him go, turned, and walked away, hurrying down the passage aft.

Dan had watched the whole thing from just inside the wardroom and came out as Melinda was striding off. He leaned against the bulkhead and crossed his arms.

"So, Clark, got your ass kicked by a girl?"

"Something like that," he replied sheepishly.

Dan leaned in very close to Mike. "You are one lucky son-of-a-bitch, Mike.

Do you *know* that?"

Clark watched Melinda as she passed through a hatch, slamming it closed behind her.

"Yes, sir, I guess I do."

Dan quickly moved back to his Bridge Command station. He knew how Clark felt, might even think to do the same if it were someone he cared about, but he also knew that Melinda was right. She had to do her job. It was her turn. She had to take it.

As she entered the hangar, Melinda could hear the supply cabinet panels on both shuttles slamming shut, signaling that the conversions were done. She climbed into the cockpit and began the pre-start checklist. Nurse Ensign Ingram dropped into the right seat shortly after Melinda buckled in. She looked over at him as he pulled on his safety straps and slipped on a headset.

"You up for this?"

He looked right back at her and said simply, "Let's roll."

After a minute of flipping switches and setting controls, Melinda gave a thumbs-up to the handlers, and in short order, the shuttle was outside *Columbia*. The small Drive kicked in and they were headed for *Eagle*, about fifty kilometers up and to the left as seen from *Columbia*'s bridge.

It was quiet in the shuttle cockpit for several minutes as Melinda monitored their progress.

She looked outside, then turned to Ingram. "Doesn't look like we're in the middle of a battle, does it?"

Ingram shook his head as he searched the view. "Not really, no. Until something blows up, that is."

Melinda gave a cynical laugh, then pressed the push-to-talk at her waist. "Echo, this is Madmax, comm check."

"We hear you, Max."

Then she heard *Columbia*'s Communications Officer Ghazwan Abbas' crisp, clear accent in her headset. "Castle hears as well."

Melinda nodded to herself. A least the communications on *Eagle* were still working. In the shuttle they were insulated from the news of the wider battle, but Melinda still wished she could hear what was going on around her. It was not going as well as expected, that much was clear, but now she couldn't tell just how bad it was. Clearly, it was not going well on *Eagle*.

Melinda clicked her mike button as she looked at the flight director's readout. "Echo, Madmax, five minutes."

"I see it!" Ingram said, pointing.

Melinda checked the heads-up display, and indeed, *Eagle* was right where she was supposed to be. Melinda slipped under the ship and lined up on the docking port. A click to connect, then a solid thump as the ship and shuttle pulled themselves together. When the hatch opened, there was a loud blast of air, and Melinda felt her ears pop. As the air rushed out, a cacophony of sound rushed in: sounds of pain, fear, and haste. Ingram was quickly up, securing the patients in beds and getting up to speed on which ones he would have to attend to on the way back and which could hold their own without him. Once he had what they could carry on board, he ran back out to the passageway.

"Who's coming along?" he asked the medical tech that had helped him with the wounded. The woman's uniform was bloodstained, and she had a look of sorrowful exhaustion on her face.

"Sorry, Ingram, you're on your own. We got hit again, and I need to stay. Get your ass back here soon as you can, understand?"

He nodded in response and headed back to his new patients. He slammed the hatch behind him and stuck his head into the cockpit.

"Get going, Hughes, and hurry!" As he turned away, he added, "Tell Smith we'll need to come right back!"

"Will do!" she yelled over her shoulder. As they started to pull away, *Eagle* was hit again, and bits of shrapnel bounced off the shuttle with a clatter like gravel on a windshield. Melinda kept moving and set them on a route back to *Columbia*.

"Ingram!" she called, "How many?"

"Fifteen, four critical," he yelled back.

Melinda pressed the mike button. "Castle, this is Madmax. We have fifteen with four critical. Echo will need another trip."

"Castle, roger. We'll be ready for a quick turn."

She was surprised to hear Dan Smith's voice.

"Thanks, boss."

She approached *Columbia*, slipped the vessel into the tight space of the ShuttleLock, and felt the thud of the outer doors closing behind her. As they pulled into the hangar, Doctor Knight was waiting to take over the patients.

"Hughes!" Maintenance Officer Carr yelled as she stepped out of the shuttle cockpit. "What the hell did you do to my shuttle?"

Melinda looked around and saw that there were dents and scratches all over the outside of the little spacecraft. None were serious, but it really did look like someone had taken a shotgun to it.

"Sorry, Steve. Ran into a little shit, you know?"

Steve Carr frowned. "Try not to do that again? Please?"

Melinda smiled and shook her head. "No promises."

"Just get it back in one piece, OK?" he called after her.

"Yeah, I think that's a great idea, Steve." She turned to look at the shuttle, then back towards Carr as she climbed back into the shuttle cockpit. "I'll try to keep that in mind."

Nurse Ingram and the rest of the medical team had the patients off the shuttle in less than five minutes. While Melinda began the process of re-configuring the flight director, Ingram stripped off his bloody uniform and pulled on the fresh one his techs had brought for him. He cleaned his hands and trotted over to the shuttle where Melinda was finishing up. Dremonte threw his backup pair of shoes in ahead of himself and slid again into the right seat. He was still pulling on the safety straps as they exited *Columbia* again, and turned back towards *Eagle*.

"Echo, this is Madmax. On our way."

They scanned the space apprehensively as they moved back toward *Eagle*. There was no answer. After a couple minutes, she tried again.

"Echo, Madmax calling," Melinda repeated twice.

"Madmax, this is Echo. Getting kinda squirrelly here."

"Squirrelly?" Ingram asked.

Melinda shrugged. "Whatever he means, it isn't good."

As they approached *Eagle*, Melinda could see the damage aft — the hangar deck appeared to be open to space. There was gas venting visible somewhere up forward as well, but she could not tell where it was coming from. They went over the top of the ship and maneuvered to the docking port. This time the pressure difference was much greater, and both Ingram and Melinda felt a moment of real pain in their ears as they adjusted. The sound from inside was different, too. Melinda could hear new panic in the voices coming from the ship. The wounded crew members were moved quickly into the shuttle. She heard Dremonte arguing with someone just inside Eagle.

"I've taken what I can," she heard Dre say.

"It's not enough!" she heard a woman's voice answer, her desperation apparent.

Ingram was firm, but Melinda heard the regret in his voice. "If I take more, then some of those already aboard will die before we get back!"

"These can walk! Stuff them wherever you want, but get them the hell out of here!"

There was a pause, and then more sounds of people moving around in the passenger compartment behind her. She looked over her shoulder to see men and women on the floor sitting against the bulkheads, or standing where they could. It was a bloody mess back there, but Ingram was doing the best he could. Finally, the hatch slammed shut, and Ingram called to her to get going.

Dan Smith was monitoring the shuttle frequency along with the main battle channel. He knew Melinda and Dremonte were pushing their luck, but they were saving lives, and that was something worth pushing for.

Melinda pulled away from *Eagle.*

"Castle, this is Madmax."

"Castle," she heard Ghazwan Abbas respond.

"Full load this time, maybe thirty. Need another quick turn."

Abbas looked up at Dan Smith, wondering how he should respond. Finally, Dan nodded as he picked up the ship phone to call the hangar.

"Roger the quick turn," Abbas said. Hearing this, Mike Clark headed aft to help direct the shuttle handling.

Mike wasn't ready for what he found in the hangar. Jim Murphy's Shuttle Two, call sign 'Jammer,' was just disappearing into the ShuttleLock, headed back to *Eagle* for a second trip. There were wounded all around the space, with Doctor Knight doing battlefield surgery to stabilize those most gravely injured. Mike thought briefly of arguing with Melinda again, but he knew better. If Smith wanted to replace her, he could. But Mike knew she would not stop on her own or ask for relief.

Mike didn't know it, but Dan Smith was thinking much the same way.

"Madmax, this is Castle actual." Melinda heard Dan's voice in her headset.

"Go actual."

"Can you handle another trip, or should I get you a break?" Melinda looked out the window at *Columbia* as she grew in size. She called back into the passenger cabin.

"Dre! You up for another trip?"

"Yeah, I can go again."

Melinda pressed the mike button. "We're good, Captain. Ingram and I can do one more."

"Very well."

Again, she gently slammed the shuttle into the dock and was pulled inside the hangar. The sound as she stepped off the shuttle was not much different than what she had heard at *Eagle*: the sounds of pain and of people trying to help echoed around the large open space. Ingram enlisted the walking wounded from *Eagle* to help get their shipmates out. There was no fresh uniform for him this time, just a quick cleanup and then back into the shuttle. Mike and Melinda looked at each other for a long moment, then she was again in the left seat.

Mike looked across her to Dremonte. "Try not to let her do anything stupid, OK?"

Ingram looked back at him. "You mean, like, pilot a shuttle to a dying ship in the middle of the biggest battle this fleet's ever seen?"

Mike began to respond but thought better of it and turned away without saying anything else. Melinda and Ingram were quickly out of the ShuttleLock and headed again for *Eagle*.

"Echo, this is Madmax, on our way."

"Echo, roger."

She pushed as hard as she dared - they'd have to decelerate when they got there - and headed for the same docking port. This time she was ready for the rush of air and the blast of sound that would come back at her.

"OK, Ingram, let's get them off." She could hear the incoming attack alarms on *Eagle*. "Shit," she said quietly to herself.

"Are you nuts?" she heard someone yell at Ingram. "We have incoming!"

She heard Ingram yell back: "We're here to get the wounded, and that's what we're going to do!"

There was a lot more screaming as they loaded the casualties. The medical tech that had previously refused to go came aboard this time, a hastily bandaged laceration on her scalp, but she still did her best to help Ingram with the patients. *Eagle* shook with the additional hits, and Melinda was momentarily afraid they'd be torn off the ship with the hatch still open. But the docking held. Her ears popped again, and she knew they really were running out of time.

"Ingram!" she yelled, "Bingo time!"

"Coming!" he yelled back. Just as he was about to close the hatch, *Eagle* was hit again, close by, and a shard of bulkhead threaded its way into the little cockpit and struck Melinda's right temple.

She screamed in pain and surprise. Ingram finished closing the hatch and then looked into the cockpit. There was blood covering her face, running down her neck. He was pleased to see her eyes open, and nothing evident in the wound.

"Hatch?" she asked, shaking her head as if to clear it.

"Closed."

She nodded and hit the un-dock control. One clang, and they were free. She struggled to focus well enough to command the flight director to take them back to *Columbia*. She enabled the auto-dock which would allow *Columbia* to fly the shuttle in, and then flopped back in her seat.

"Christ, Dre, I'm dizzy already."

Ingram grabbed a kit out of a storage locker and crawled back into the cockpit. As he started to look at the wound, Melinda tried to push him away.

"Hold still, Melinda," he said quietly, "I need to see!"

She pushed again, but weakly. Dre was able to separate the matted, bloody hair enough to see the wound itself. He could see bone, but there was no fracture and nothing embedded.

"Good news. It's a deep lac, Melinda, but nothing more." He applied the clotting/antibacterial foam and slipped a bandage over her head.

As he finished, Dre realized she hadn't answered him. He lifted her head to see that she was only semi-conscious.

"Shit," he said to himself as he picked up the comm headset. "Castle, this is Madmax. Hughes has a head laceration from a blunt object, she's fading. Tell Knight we might have a subdural to handle."

"Castle copies all. Are you able to get back here?"

"Yes, she was able to set the return and the auto-dock."

"OK, Dre, we'll be ready for her."

Ingram had done all he could for Melinda, so he headed back to tend to his patients. The nurse from *Eagle* was keeping them calm and as quiet as she could. As Dremonte returned, she looked up. "What's with the pilot?"

"Head lac, probable subdural. She's unconscious."

"So, who's flying the shuttle?"

Dre smiled. "The shuttle."

Mike Clark waited impatiently for the ShuttleLock to open. Once it was clear, he quickly opened the cockpit door, trying to be ready for what he would find there. She was unconscious, limp, one side of her head and neck covered in blood. But she was breathing. Mike lifted her out and carried her to an exam table. As Knight worked, checking her eyes, her reflexes, her blood pressure, he turned to Mike.

"Don't you have a job to do, Lieutenant Clark?"

Mike answered without looking away from Melinda's face. "Not at the moment, no."

"Well, then, you might as well make yourself useful." He turned to Saika. "Mai, get him some wipes, and let's get her cleaned up best we can. Then, I need to get her to sickbay for a scan, but I'm pretty sure Dremonte is correct."

Mike took the package and cleaned her face and neck. He smiled slightly as she started to look more like herself. Knight left to check on several other patients and discussed the triage priorities with Saika and Ingram.

"OK, Clark," he said firmly, "Help Mai wheel her to sickbay, then get yourself cleaned up and get back on duty. Last I heard there was still a space war going on out there."

"Yes, sir."

Mike talked to her all the way forward to the sickbay, then helped Saika transfer her off the wheeled exam table. She mumbled a few undecipherable syllables but didn't seem to respond to his words. Clark fought back against the ugly fear growing in the pit of his stomach, fear that his precious, bright new future was about to disappear before it ever really started. Before leaving sickbay, Mike looked at her for several seconds, then set his face and turned away to get back to work.

It was up to the skills of the medical staff now, and there wasn't anything more he could do for her. Except, pray. It was something he never felt very good at. *But,* he thought, *for Melinda, he could at least try.*

Nippon
Earth Orbit
Friday, March 17, 2079, 1530 UTC

Captain Kawaguchi stood at his Command station on *Nippon,* watching the tactical display as the remnants of his task force reorganized. The enemy had arrived a little behind schedule, just long enough for those waiting to begin to wonder if they were going to show up at all.

They did, but not quite as anticipated.

Kawaguchi had expected them to come in at a distance, then close on the planet, giving him time to react. Instead, the eleven enemy ships blew out of FTL less than twenty thousand kilometers above Cuba at 0845 UTC that morning, 0445 at ISC Fleet HQ. The Type V's pulse struck *Mir* hard, which happened to be passing nearby as it came out of perigee heading north. *Nippon* herself was also temporarily disabled. *Grissom,* next closest, lost some forward sensors but remained in the fight. The Type V pulsed twice more in quick succession and then dispatched its beacon weapons. *Mir* was hit hard, and shortly she was destroyed by multiple fast-missile attacks from a Type I that chased her down before her crew could recover.

Grissom took dozens of casualties from the beacon-mines, but remained in the fight, launching three Bludgeon attacks on the Type V.

Rassvet's captain moved her quickly into the fight, killing the Type I closest to him, but the enemy response was overwhelming, beacon-mines striking his Bridge and berthing spaces, then six fast-missile strikes. *Rassvet* was disabled, and since her rapid maneuvering had taken her out of orbit, she was left to fall into the Atlantic just west of the Azores.

Bondarenko charged up from the south, un-tagged, and fired a wide volley at several of the enemy ships. They were getting better, Anna Nonna realized, as the Type III's in her sights moved quickly away, and she managed only a few hits before the Type V pulsed again, and *Bondarenko* was tagged. Three hits later, she had to retire with her magazine hopelessly jammed. Commander Nonna counted herself lucky the weapons didn't explode.

Stoykiy was squarely between the enemy and the Moon when they arrived. She moved back into the fight, taking a Type I down, but was then detected and ultimately lost a running shootout that went halfway back to the Moon with a

Type III, her Spartans just not quite fast enough once the enemy got in close.

Dunkirk, on the other side of the planet when the enemy arrived, quickly crossed over the North Pole and fired at whatever she could see. Sensing a new threat, the Type V pulsed again, then responded with another round of beacon-mines. Andy Sackville ignored the danger, and *Dunkirk* fought through a hail of incoming fire, dueling face-to-face, firing Spartans to parry the enemy's attacks but still taking several missile hits. His persistence paid off, but *Dunkirk* lost twenty people to the razor-sharp flechettes the enemy's mines sprayed into his ship. She and *Nippon* kept hitting the Type V until it finally succumbed, sliding out of Earth orbit, apparently intending to crash into the Sun.

Tong-Il, ordered by Kawaguchi to remain in reserve until needed, followed the Type V briefly, then gave it a four-Bludgeon sendoff.

There were unexpected collateral casualties as well. The communications and other satellites on the same side of the planet as the attackers went dark with the Type V's first pulse. On the surface, there were widespread power outages. Fortunately, these were mostly short-lived, and there was no permanent severe damage or loss of life. The billions of dollars countries allocated to hardening the electrical infrastructure in the late 2030s, after the failed North Korean EMP attack, had proven itself to be money well spent.

Of the eleven enemy ships engaged, six were destroyed in the first hour. Three more were scratched in the next hour, one as it tried to attack the ISC ship factory in the asteroid belt, a victim of *Gagarin*'s watchful eye and careful shooting. The last two eventually retired, damaged but not disabled. Even tagged, the superior maneuvering and targeting of the Fleet gave them the edge. It wasn't much, barely enough, in fact, but sufficient to eventually tip the encounter in their favor.

Kawaguchi lost *Mir*, *Rassvet*, and *Stoykiy*. *Grissom* was damaged but usable, but *Bondarenko* was out of the fight until the Fleet Engineers could get inside and untangle her smashed loaders. *Dunkirk* was bruised but functional; his own *Nippon* had taken three beacon-mines and ten dead, but nothing more. *Tong-Il*, deliberately held back as a reserve, was undamaged, as was *Gagarin* in the asteroid belt.

An expensive victory, Kawaguchi thought. A hard, hard day to look back on. He knew it would be another hard day to face when the second wave arrived. He vowed he would not be surprised again.

In the dark, early hours of the next day, Fiona Collins sat in her small office, Ron Harris seated across from her, their grief flowing freely. The room was dark but for her small desk lamp, and the gloom fit their shared mood. They were old friends, with parallel, complementary careers; they could let down their guard together. As they counted the losses and casualties, they read too many names of friends, colleagues, and former shipmates who had died the day before. They talked intermittently about them, the memories both funny and sad helping them walk the dark path to acceptance and the ability to move on to what they had to do next.

"What do your people think about the pulse?" Fiona finally asked, wiping her cheeks and shaking her head slightly.

"Some kind of sub-space energy. It might be FTL, so maybe something like a SLIP on steroids."

"FTL?"

"Yes, reports were that the pulse hit just before the flash. Andy Sackville said there was at least a second's delay."

"So, you think this is some kind of mass detection device?"

Ron shrugged. "Can't see what else it would be. They launched the tag-bombs right after, and those went right at the ships."

"Which means they've solved our stealth."

"Partly, at least, yeah, they've figured out how to find us."

Fiona leaned back in her chair. "Pretty smart for a pack of dinos, wouldn't you say?"

"Well, I wouldn't describe them that way. They're damnably smart, Fiona. They can't fight head-to-head for shit, but with an advantage, they're dangerous."

"What about this second wave?"

"They should be here in a few days. Kawaguchi is working on a warm reception for them."

"You think they'll still come?"

"We've seen no SLIP activity from the enemy ships, so, yes, I assume they're still coming."

"How is Nobuyuki doing? Have you spoken to him?"

"Yes, just a few hours ago. He's mad as hell, of course."

Fiona sat upright, leaning her elbows on her desk. "Kawaguchi is a warrior, old school, any failure on his watch is his failure."

"We were all taught that same ethic, Fiona. You're just like him, and so am I. It's as much my fault as Nobu's."

"You did the best you could, Ron. You gave him the information you had."

"Yes, all true. And completely insufficient."

Fiona heard the pain and disappointment in his voice. "Ron — "

Harris waved her off as he rose and left. Fiona took a moment to consider if she should follow her old friend to reassure him, to reconfirm her confidence in him, but instead returned to her analysis of the battle and what the consequences were for the future of the Fleet.

The next day, the reports coming from Inor described a similar fight to what Earth had experienced. A pulse, beacon-mines, and lots of casualties inside the ships. Knowing there were no invasion ships headed his way, Captain Sokolovsky had spread his eight ships widely, some not even near the planet. The Type V had pulsed three times before finding and attacking *Faith* and *McNair*, which happened to be closest to it. That told Ron that there was a range limit to this new enemy detector. Dimitri had launched his attacks from the ships the farthest from the enemy, which seemed to defeat their tactics. The Type V took a dozen hits before it retired with the seven operational ships, leaving five burning in orbit or nearby.

From Beta Hydri, there was silence. Ron worried about that as the thirty-six-hour mark approached. They had hit Inor at almost precisely the same time as Earth, and he assumed that Beta Hydri would be the same. He had a huge personal stake in Beta Hydri: Elias Peña, Roger Cox, Jack Ballard, Rich Evans, and many others. A disaster there would mean deep personal, as well as military, pain.

Antares
Big Blue
Saturday, March 18, 2079, 1900 UTC.

"God DAMN it!" Chief Guzman swore loudly in his helmet, sweat burning his eyes.

Jon Swenson, nodded as he hovered nearby, but the EVA helmet didn't move. "Yeah, I can see what you mean."

The beacon-mine had penetrated *Antares'* meter-deep outer stealth coating, attaching itself to the steel hull underneath. It was still transmitting as Guzman and Swenson puzzled over how to get it off, or, at the very least, turn it off. They worked awkwardly in zero-G, with each attempt at moving the beacon more frustratingly difficult than the last.

"This is not going to be quick or easy, Lieutenant Hansen," Swenson called back to the Bridge. "It's attached itself to the ship somehow, magnetic I should think."

The cargo shuttle they had ridden out from *Antares* was just a few meters away. It had taken longer than expected to find the hold-down cleats and get Guzman strapped to the outside of the ship. Once secured, he could excavate the light-weight, heat-absorbent foam more easily, exposing the beacon. That done, he turned on his suit video so everyone could see what he was seeing.

"OK, " Guzman reported, "As you all can see, it's a cylinder, maybe a meter high, maybe thirty centimeters in diameter here at the top, a little bigger at the bottom. There is a clear glass dome at the top, I assume some kind of visual detector." He pointed to the lower part of the beacon, " Down here, the bottom is hard against the hull. I tried moving it, but it's stuck pretty hard."

Intel Officer Roger Cox was watching from the Intel workroom. "Any evidence of an antenna, Chief?"

"Not that I can see for sure. There are some strips of a different metal down the side, nothing else."

Carol Hansen waved her Bridge officers to the Command station. "Chief, take a minute to catch your breath while we talk in here."

"That's fine, Lieutenant, but don't take too long, OK?"

Carol made her way down from the Command station, her leg still awkwardly wrapped tightly with bandages. "OK. Suggestions?"

"We could try to shoot it." Jayvon Dean offered.

Carol turned to Lori Rodgers. "It has to have an antenna, right?"

"Yes, of course, it must.... wait...what did Guzman say about how long the strips of metal are?"

"He didn't." Carol looked over at the comm station. "Ask Guzman how long the strips are."

Guzman answered, "About thirty centimeters, I'd say. A little more than a hand-width."

Lori did some quick calculations on her NetComp, smiling as she looked up. "That's it. If the dimension is actually 32 centimeters, it's a quarter wavelength."

Carol looked at her a second before responding. "So, cut the strips?"

"Best guess, yes, ma'am."

Looking around, there was skepticism but no clear objections. Carol looked the group over twice, receiving only a slight nod from Lori and a shrug from Roger.

"OK, then, that's what we'll do." She stepped back up to the command station and put her headset back on.

"Chief, you have the damage control kit along?"

Outside the ship, Guzman and Swenson exchanged puzzled looks.

"Yes. It's in the shuttle."

"Good. Comms thinks the strips right below the top of the beacon are the antenna. Take the laser cutter and cut the top off."

There was a pause of at least fifteen seconds as Guzman ran through all the things he thought were wrong with this plan, beginning and ending with an explosion that would kill him, Swenson, and who knows how much of the crew.

"Yes, ma'am," he responded evenly. "Might I suggest, Lieutenant, that you evacuate the compartments below this point?"

"Yes, already in progress."

He turned to Swenson. "Move the shuttle, Mr. Swenson, so it can't be hit with whatever might fly out of this thing."

"I'll bring you the torch."

"Any idea how far down we need to cut it off?"

Carol looked over at Lori Rodgers, who just shook her head.

"No."

"OK then, I'll take it off in the middle of the strips. I'm going to move to one side, so if it really does shit all over itself, it might miss me."

Carol smiled at his understatement, then keyed her mike. "Seems prudent."

Guzman took a look around as he braced himself for the cut. Looking aft, he couldn't miss the rotary launcher filled with Spartans pointed at him.

"Oh, and please remind everyone that I am forward of the port rotary? I'd appreciate not getting impaled accidentally."

Carol motioned for the Weapons techs to retract the launcher.

"Thanks, much better."

Swenson brought him the cutter and stuck the welding light filter over part of Guzman's faceplate. He had but to tilt his head slightly to be able to cut, then raise his head back up to see normally. Swenson moved the shuttle to over the top of the ship, far enough that it should be safe, close enough for him to help Guzman should anything go wrong. He placed it in station-keeping mode and positioned himself in the open cargo door.

Guzman took a final look around, then fired up the laser torch and took it to the enemy object.

ISC Fleet Task Force
Big Blue
Sunday, March 19, 2079, 2245 UTC (Just after star rise Sol 138)

The second wave arrived at Beta Hydri just as the reports from Earth were painting a bleak picture of a narrow, costly victory. Carol had just fallen asleep, propped up on the bunk in the Captain's Duty Cabin, a place until a few days ago she had only visited. Since Terri Michael's death, it had become her de facto home. Her two-day-old leg wound still throbbed most of the time, and daily, Marcia Soto would barge in, inspect and redress the wound, and yell at Carol to take it easy.

Then, as Marcia was ready to leave, she would hug her old roommate and kiss her on the forehead. Carol couldn't recall how that bit of unmilitary protocol started; it must have been sometime just after the first attack when Soto had sedated her to properly close her wound. Carol had struggled as she came out of the anesthetic, reliving in slow motion the attack and Terri Michael's gruesome death. It had taken all of Marcia's strength, and that of two assistants, to keep Carol on the exam table. It was a frightening and exhausting experience for everyone involved.

There were seven enemy ships unaccounted for, three of them the presumed invasion ships. The Fleet's force had been cut down, but with the beacon-mines removed using Chief Guzman's lop-off-the-top technique, their odds were much better. They'd taken damage which hurt their stealth slightly, and they'd lost the best of their sensors, the extremely sensitive IR detectors and optical telescopes.

Still, Barker liked their chances. *Friendship* was gone, her remains now sunken in the ocean somewhere in Big Blue's southern hemisphere. *Komarov* had retired to a safe distance for repairs, but she'd be back. *Intrepid* and *Canberra* were whole, undamaged. *Columbia* had lost some sensors but was otherwise ready. *Antares* had taken damage and losses, but, much like *Columbia* and *White*, she was up for another fight.

As at Earth, no SLIP transmissions had been seen from the enemy ships. Carol read that report, whose pace and phrasing, and the careful and correct use of 'whilst,' carried David's indelible fingerprints, and wondered if they had somehow caught on that FleetIntel was tracking their conversations. The rest of his report was grim: details of what ships had been hit, including her own, and which Fleet strikes had been successful. He clearly didn't understand how the Type V had survived. It should have been blown wide open. One golden nugget in the report was that at every target, the enemy had come with less than the force *Cobra* had detected. The *Cobra* team now believed there would be a second round of attacks with the remaining enemy ships. For all Carol knew, here thirty-six hours from Earth by SLIP, it had already happened.

Antares was now in a high geosynchronous orbit over the old Seeker cities, nearly the same orbit as when they had first come to Big Blue. Sitting in the command position, looking out at the planet below, Carol let herself think about those days, when Ryan Lewis was almost giddy at the Surveillance position, talking excitedly to Jack Ballard, and Terri Michael sounding as much like a Professor of Exploration as a warship captain. Carol knew it was just the luck of the draw that brought *Antares* to discover the Seekers. If some other ship had been assigned Beta Hydri, they'd have found it instead. Still, she was glad it was 'her team' that did it, that Terri Michael was credited with it, and that she was privileged to be part of it.

She missed Gabrielle Este, too, although Gabe and Greg Cordero had somehow talked their way onto *Intrepid* for a return trip. She and Gabe had become close, despite the decade difference in age, and Carol enjoyed their long discussions about the Seekers.

David was close by, on *Cobra*, but Carol had not spoken to him since the attack. She'd sent him a short message that she was wounded but on duty, and that he was not to worry about her. His response was simple: *I love you*. Which, really, was all she needed to hear.

Deep within *Cobra*, WO4 Ray Salazar was sitting Center Console, monitoring the space around Big Blue. *Cobra* had left its former orbit and was now in an extremely elliptical orbit that gave it a better vantage point over Big Blue's north pole. A soft alarm from the IR station grabbed his attention.

"Three ships, Mister Salazar. We just picked them up."

"Where?"

"About ninety degrees west of the old cities, moving east."

Ray hit the alarm to bring the rest of the staff to the Ops Center. "Did they just arrive?"

"No, they just faded up on the IR... wait...actually...they just came into sunshine."

David came through the doors just ahead of Jack Ballard. "What is it?"

"Three ships, down low."

David and Jack stood over the IR workstation, studying the ships' track. David's face was expressionless, but his tightly crossed arms revealed his stress. Jack leaned back against Center Console, looking to his left at the visual feed.

"Type IIIs," Jack said quietly.

David turned to him. "Bombardment ships?"

Jack nodded. "That would make the most sense. If you extend their course, I think it will take you to the Seekers."

David's expression turned grim. "And the Marines." David turned to Salazar. "Get me Elias Peña, Mister Salazar."

Carol awoke to Navigator and temporary XO Alex Williams pounding on her door. She pulled herself into a seated position, wincing at the sting from her leg.

"Come."

Williams slipped in and closed the door behind him.

"What's up, Alex?"

"There are three Type III's down low. *Cobra* and Peña both think they're headed for the Seekers. We're to get in front and stop them."

"What time is it?"

"0225."

"OK, set Alert Condition One, plot a course and get us there as fast as you can. Wake Dean up. Tell Swenson one rotary of Bludgeons and one of Spartans."

"Anything else?"

"No. I just need a couple minutes to not look quite so much like an unmade bed."

"Understood. I'll get it going."

In a second, Alex was gone, and Carol had bought herself enough time to visit the bathroom and throw on a clean uniform. If her instincts were right, it might be some time before she'd have a chance to do either again. The dressing on her leg was just a few hours old. It would be fine for a while, which was one less distraction.

After she limped her way up the Command Station steps, Alex briefed her on their situation. "One thing, Lieutenant," he concluded, the casual familiarity of a few minutes ago now gone. "This is a non-Newtonian move. If we lose power, if the Drive is hit before we establish a new orbit — "

Carol looked him directly in the eye. "We burn up and then we drown. Got it."

She turned towards the Weapons station. "Mister Swenson, what's our status?"

"Ready, Lieutenant. The load is complete, and the rotaries are ready to move on your command."

She motioned for Jon Swenson to come to her station. "Jon, we have three targets. Let's do two Bludgeons each, amidships, with a second attack ready to go. I don't care about killing the crew or cutting off their comms. We need to smoke these bastards before their Lazy Dogs start falling on the Marines."

Jon moved back to his position at Weapons and passed Carol's instructions to his techs.

"Lieutenant Dean!" she called.

"Yes, ma'am."

"We're going nose to nose with three ships. They're going to shoot at us as soon as they see us. You're free to use the radar if you need it."

"Yes, ma'am. Maybe we'll hit them with a few chirps just to check, then shut it down."

"Fine. See if Alex can move us around a little when you do that. You two work it out. I won't have time to be figuring it out in the middle of a fight."

"Understood, Lieutenant."

The three Type III's were coming fast, but *Antares* had just enough time to get into position ahead of them. White was moving in behind, ready to add her firepower to *Antares'* if necessary, but she was at least fifteen minutes behind. Barker had handed Carol this job, reluctantly, because *Antares* happened to be the one ship in the right place as the enemy ships came into view.

Carol watched the track on the Surveillance display, thinking to herself that this must have been how Dean Carpenter felt above Inor. But, she reminded herself, he was outnumbered and not expecting a fight. *I am neither.*

With *Antares*' laser comms out, *Cobra* fed its tracking data over the VHF spread-spectrum data link. The data went directly to Lieutenant Dean's Surveillance station, and from there to Weapons' targeting processors. Alex Williams paced behind the Nav station, sweating all the worst-case-scenarios running around in his head. *Antares* was accelerating slowly to the east, 150 kilometers above the ocean, waiting for the enemy just west of the Seeker's hideout and the Marines' encampment. A part of his brain kept trying to calculate how long it would take for them to fall that far, and if they'd actually burn up or just get crushed to death on impact. He visibly shook his head to throw those thoughts away, but they kept returning.

The enemy was just coming over the planet's horizon when Jon Swenson called out. "I have a solution based on the *Cobra* tracking, Lieutenant."

Carol looked over at him, his expression was confident, hands on his hips. He was ready.

"Shoot!" she called.

Both rotaries rolled out, and six Bludgeons were quickly on their way.

A minute later, Jayvon Dean called out, "Radar is on, Lieutenant."

"Very well."

It didn't take long for the enemy commander to respond.

"Eight launches from the lead ship, Lieutenant."

Swenson trotted over to the Surveillance station. "Give me another minute to assign the Spartans, then you can shut it down."

Carol tapped her good foot nervously for the full sixty seconds. Running the radar was like shining a searchlight in the enemy's face, and the longer you left it on, the more likely someone was to shoot it out.

Meanwhile, Alex was gradually moving the ship back from the enemy, keeping pace just ahead of them. He was relieved when he could finally turn to Carol.

"We're in orbit, Lieutenant. It's a really low, kinda shitty orbit, but it's an orbit."

"Fine, thanks, Alex."

As the last Spartan left the launcher, *Antares* shook violently from an impact aft. Then another, and then, a third.

Carol and Jon Swenson's eyes met in horror as the alarms rang out all over the ship status display, and the sound of slamming air-tight doors came from the back of the ship.

"Holy shit!" Jack yelled from Center Console.

"What?" David asked in surprise.

Jack looked at David for a half-second before responding. "*Antares* just took three hits."

"Hits? From where?"

"I don't know."

The message feed lit up as Jack was speaking. *White*, *Antares'* assigned backup, had just sighted a Type I coming up from Big Blue's southern hemisphere. Seconds later, Barker was tasking them with the target.

David fought back his fear and anger. He heard Carol's words from a long-ago field problem ringing in his ears: *Work the problem, David. Just work the problem and maybe we go home alive.* Rich Evans could see the emotions suddenly boiling in his favorite protege. "Keep your head, Powell. Where are they?"

"They came up from the south. Isn't *Canberra* supposed to be watching down there?"

"Yes, but they're in orbit, too, David. Blind spots happen."

"Bastards have awfully lucky timing, sir."

The message feed reported that *White* was firing. David slammed his fist on the counter surrounding Center Console. Evans ignored it and moved to where he could watch the long-range visual feed as it zoomed in on *Antares*.

Carol broke her lock on Jon Swenson's bright blue eyes and turned to Jayvon Dean. "Where did those come from?"

"Somewhere below us, Lieutenant. We can't see anything there."

She turned again to Jon. "What's the status of the incomings forward?"

"Spartans are locked on. They should get them all."

Dean spoke next, "Bludgeon impacts on the enemy ships, Lieutenant. No secondaries."

Shit, Carol thought to herself. *Shit, shit, shit.*

"Jon! We have six on the rotary?"

"Yes."

"Fire them. We need to keep them from fragging the Marines." She looked up at the ship status display above the Nav workstation, and her hopes for her ship and crew deflated. The Environmental Systems section was gone, and with it, the heaters and air scrubbers and water treatment systems they needed to stay alive. There were bright red areas elsewhere, too. Carol noted but chose not to think too much about the flashing red around the sickbay.

She picked up the phone. "Long." When the phone was answered, she could hear shouts and machinery noise in the background.

"Long."

"Denise, it's Carol. What's the word?"

"We're still operational, Lieutenant. The reactor is fine, but it was awfully close. FPI says Drive is nominal." Long's voice was even, only slightly stressed; clearly, she had the situation under control.

"You OK?"

"Yes, fine. Some of my techs were pretty spooked, but we're getting it together." Carol heard Long cover the phone with her hand and yell something Carol couldn't quite understand at her crew. When she uncovered the phone, her tone was back to calm and normal. "Like I said, we're getting it together."

"Keep me posted, OK? Hang in there."

"ES is out, Lieutenant. We can't hang for long."

"I know, Denise. We'll figure something out."

As she set the phone down, Intel Officer Roger Cox came onto the Bridge.

"What do you need, Lieutenant?"

Carol looked at him, puzzled. "Roger?"

"We're dead in there. Lights and workstations are out. So, what do you need?"

Carol didn't have to think long. "Go find Miguel and see how bad it really is and get back to me."

Cox grabbed one of his senior techs and started aft. He found Maintenance Officer Miguel Anthony in the midships damage control office. His loud, continuous stream of obscenities served as an unmistakable beacon.

"Lieutenant Anthony? Hansen sent me to —"

"Tell Carol we're screwed. Environmentals are out, dead. Compartments around sickbay are gone, hangar deck, too. Goddamn hangar is just too big for its own good, you know? Every time we get hit some random piece of shit busts through it."

"So..."

"So we can't breathe for more than a few hours if we don't freeze first, and we can't get off unless someone else sends a shuttle for us."

"Anything else?"

"Oh, sure, there's always more, Cox. The folks aft are cut off. I can't get them out without EVA suits. Which, of course, are IN THE DAMN HANGAR."

"OK, sir, I'll get that message to her."

"Tell Carol, Cox," Anthony said in a suddenly calm voice. "Tell Carol I'm sorry, but we're going to need a miracle this time."

Roger sprinted back forward to deliver Miguel Anthony's litany of bad news.

"How long?" she asked.

"A few hours."

"Yeah, sounds right."

Cox looked at her cautiously. "Have you reached Doctor Soto?"

Carol started to reach for the phone, then dropped her hand to her lap. "She's gone, Roger. She and her whole staff and all the wounded. I need to save what's left."

"How? We can't get everyone off before we run out of air."

That simple word rang a faint bell in Carol's mind. She looked over at the Communications station. "Lori! Get me David on *Cobra*."

Lori Rodgers looked at her strangely but opened the voice link to the spy ship.

"Powell." Even the sound of his voice gave her courage somehow.

"David, it's Carol."

He didn't entirely suppress the catch in his throat. "Are you OK?"

"For now, yes. But David, ES is out."

"Ugh, not cool."

"And the hangar is compromised. The people aft are cut off."

"Also, not cool."

"But, David, I have a whole atmosphere of breathable air right under me. Didn't somebody once land a ship in a sim? Do you remember how they did it?"

"Yeah. It was Lynn and Joe and they—"

"Lynn's on *Intrepid*," she interrupted.

David ignored that she had cut him off. She didn't have much time. "Correct. Call him, and he might be able to explain it. I vaguely recall it had to do with reversing the floors."

"OK, I'll call him."

"Carol?"

"What?"

"Three times, Carol. Three times. Land that thing, and I'll see you on the surface."

She said, "Yeah, well, wish me luck" quietly as she called for Lori to get her Lynn Covington on *Intrepid*. Then, she sent Cox to fetch Anthony to the Bridge.

"Covington."

"Lynn, this is Carol."

"Hi, honey. How's your day going?" he answered brightly.

"Covington, you're a pain, but I do love you. Now, tell me how you and Scheck landed a destroyer."

His voice turned deadly serious, knowing time must be very short if she was thinking about such things. "It's the floors, Carol. If you just try to land, she'll snap in half in the middle and you'll, you know — "

"Die."

"Right, that. Set the midpoint floors at zero-G and work outward proportionally until you're at one-half G at the fore and aft Forstmann units."

Miguel was listening. "So, this takes the stress off the middle part of the ship?"

Lynn recognized Miguel's voice. "Yes, Lieutenant Anthony. It brings the load down to where the structure can handle it all the way to the surface."

"But that stress has to go somewhere, right?"

Carol could hear Lynn smiling as he answered. "Actually, no. This is another wonderful side effect of Forstmann's bending of space-time. You get to violate all kinds of physics."

They ended the conversation as Anthony stood with Alex Williams discussing how they might do it.

Carol turned to Roger Cox. "If this works, we'll be on the ground for a while. Grab your techs, and whoever else is available and get down to the Marines' armory. According to the status display, it still has air. Bring up whatever weapons and ammo they left behind."

"Where do you want it?"

"Wherever you can find space, but make it somewhere on this level. We might lose a couple decks when we hit the ground." Cox was gone in a second, grabbing his people and heading down the forward access to the Marine's spaces.

Carol turned back to Anthony. "How long do we really have?"

"I'd say two hours before it starts to get chilly. It will be a few hours more before the CO2 reaches toxic levels."

"OK, fine. Make whatever preparations you can, assuming we land two hours from now." She turned to the Surveillance position. "Dean! Where are the enemy ships?"

"The lead is burning now, the others are still coming on. *White* has slowed down the one down south, but it isn't out of the fight yet."

"OK, there's no point in taking anything to the surface with us. Jon, hit whatever you can as fast as you can. Empty the magazines out the port rotary. Keep the starboard for Spartans."

"Yes, ma'am." Jon worked as fast as his techs and the machinery of the magazine would permit, firing everything they had left at the three targets for which they had attack solutions. Jon felt a little like the guy with the flare, lighting off the grand finale on the Fourth of July.

Carol had one more call to make. "Lori, get me Barker."

It took the Communications Officer a minute or more to get Barker on the line. As Carol waited, she called Alex Williams back to her position.

"Alex, find me a place to put her down. I seem to recall there are some level fields northwest of the Marines, but check it out, OK? If we have to go over on the other side of the mountains, we can do that, too. Check that, too."

"Will do."

Lori Rodgers called out, "Ready, Lieutenant."

"Admiral, this is Hansen on *Antares*."

"Yes, Lieutenant. How are things there?"

"Drive and reactor are operational, but environmental controls are out, and several areas are pretty shot up. We are going to try to land the ship."

"Might I remind you that it's never been done? We could try to get some shuttles for you."

"We don't have time for shuttles, sir. We're already down two degrees, and the CO_2 has started moving up as well. We might have two hours."

"OK, Lieutenant, what's your plan?"

"We'll put her down somewhere northwest of the Seekers. Nav is working on a location."

"It's your ship, Lieutenant. Your crew. I'll support whatever you decide. I'm going to bring *Intrepid* down to cover you."

"Thank you, sir."

She hung up the phone as Alex and Jayvon Dean came up to the command station. Together, they studied the overhead photographs and topographic maps that the Surveillance systems had been accumulating since *Antares'* first visit months ago. Finally, Alex pointed to a spot near where Carol had suggested.

"Here, about five klicks northwest of the Marines, is a large, flat area that we should be able to drop her into."

Carol nodded slowly, not taking her eyes off the image. "Am I right that there's enough room there even if our aim is less than perfect?"

"Yes."

"Do you know how you're going to put her down?"

"We're still talking about that."

"Oh, great."

"We can do it, Carol. We can. We just need her to not break up before we get there."

Carol looked at Alex and smiled slightly. "Yeah, that would be, you know, bad."

In that moment, she realized she had come to her decision. It was now time to focus on getting it done.

"OK, that's it. Alex, get the crew out of the midsection — anywhere it's going to be less than a quarter G."

"Right, will do."

A few minutes after Alex left, Roger Cox returned to the Bridge. "What were the Marines expecting, Lieutenant?"

"Excuse me?"

"We found over a hundred 2K7X's down there. We're still hauling ammo, but it's a hundred thousand rounds, at least."

"Good. We can make ourselves useful once we get down. I guess Captain Michael was right to get the crew qualified."

"Yes, ma'am."

"And, Roger?"

"Yes?"

"Thanks for pitching in when I needed it."

"You're welcome, Lieutenant. What now?"

"Go help Alex get everyone out of the middle of the ship. Can't have them floating around when we turn down the floors."

Roger smiled at her ability to maintain a sense of humor in the middle of this desperate fight. "Right, ma'am, will do."

Jon Swenson's barrage finally dispatched the second Type III bearing down on the Seekers, but the third kept coming. Watching the Surveillance display, Jon's mental math told him unless someone else took it out, they'd be landing about the time the RFGs were falling. He considered telling Hansen, but there weren't many other options, and they were some distance away. He decided to keep it to himself and just keep shooting.

Natalie Hayden was alone in her shuttle, quietly running her routine status checks when the comms alarm went off. *Intrepid* was calling.

She picked up the headset lying on the console next to her. "Yeah, Hayden, here."

Joanne's voice was clearly worried, "Natalie, a Type III is coming your way."

"OK, well, I'm not leaving my Marines."

"No, just be ready. Oh, and *Antares* is going to land a few klicks from you."

"Land? You can't land a destroyer."

"Hansen thinks she can. I guess somebody did it once in a sim."

"A sim? Is she out of her mind? And, besides, where's Michael?"

"Dead. The XO, too. Hansen is in command now. I guess they're out of options."

Natalie sighed. She'd known Terri Michael slightly when she was an instructor at the Fleet University. Such a good person, such a good officer, gone. She refocused on her conversation with Henderson.

"So, Captain, what exactly do you want me to do?"

"Barker has already talked to the Marines. They're dispersing. *Antares* will be coming down from the east. They may need some help once they get on the ground."

"OK, I'll see if I can get some volunteers and we'll hustle over there once they're down."

"Good, that should help."

Natalie looked out the shuttle's forward windows. "I only hope we're not just cleaning up a mess."

"Do what you can, Natalie."

"Will do, Captain."

By 0730 March 20th, *Antares*' Bridge was slowly filling with a sound that had never been heard there before: air rushing past. Carol watched as Alex worked the Drive controls to slow both their descent and forward velocity. They could not take too long to get down, and they needed to keep descending to minimize the stresses on the midsection of the ship. If Alex tried to terminate the descent, or worse, ascend, she'd probably snap in half, floors, or no floors.

The Bridge windows changed gradually from the black of space to stratospheric violet, then finally to a distinctly blue sky. Carol read each change as an increasing level of danger. Her Nav display showed Alex's plan, a steady descent with a steadily decreasing rate. If he'd done the math right, they'd impact the ground at just a couple meters per second. *Antares* would likely be broken, but the crew would live.

"Ten thousand meters!" Alex called out. They were well into the atmosphere now, to where Carol could see clouds on the horizon. A sudden series of creaks and groans from the ship made her look over at him. Alex looked at his displays, then back at Carol. "We should be OK, Lieutenant. We're on course, on speed."

Carol nodded, swallowing the enormous lump in her throat. She flashed back to that day on Inor, to the first time she had given a command that meant anything. She silently repeated the prayer she'd said then: *Please God don't let me get them killed.*

Jon Swenson, now out of a job with nothing left to shoot, stood behind the Nav workstation, just in front of Carol's raised position. As Carol looked around, Roger Cox was there, as was Miguel Anthony. They all looked back at her, communicating in one expression or another their support. They had faith in her. Lori Rodgers, now standing behind the Communication position next to Nav, gave her a small smile. The half-G gravity gave the experience a strange, dreamy, unreal feel. They could stand and move around, but they had to be careful not to do anything too quickly, or they'd float like Apollo moon walkers. As soon as they landed, they'd be in Big Blue's 1.1G, which would make everything very real very quickly.

Carol was just picking out The Pasture in the windows as Alex called out

"One thousand meters." Maybe she'd live to see Eaagher and Ullnii today after all. That would be nice.

More pops and groans from aft made them all look down the passageway, but there was nothing to be done now. They were committed. Actually, they'd been committed for an hour, but the approaching terrain transformed that concept from intellectual to visceral.

"Alex?" Carol asked quietly.

"Still good, Lieutenant. I guess we'll see how well they wrote the sim. Five hundred meters."

Carol sat up. "OK, secure yourselves. I don't want any concussions because we forgot to strap in!"

Roger Cox took the vacant Conn position, while Jon returned to his Weapons station and strapped in.

Carol picked up the phone and selected the ship-wide announcement. "Four hundred meters. Secure for impact."

She went over in her head what they had done, what else could be done, and came to the conclusion that they'd done everything they could think of, and that would have to be good enough. There were no Fleet procedures for this, no established protocol, no supporting data.

All she had was Lynn and Joe's crazy day in the sim. It would have to do.

"One hundred meters, ten down," Alex called out.

Even at ten, Carol thought, most of them would live.

"Fifty meters, seven down."

Looking out the window, Carol could see that they were nose-high. *Antares* was three hundred meters long — she might hit tail-first.

"Alex, check your attitude. We're too nose high."

"Already working on that. Twenty meters, forward ten, down three."

It started with an intermittent scraping, that grew into the frighteningly loud grinding of steel over stone, the belly of the enormous ship being stripped off as she bled her last bits of inertia into Big Blue. With a final guttural crunch, *Antares* stopped.

They had done it.

"Floors are off, Drive to idle!" Alex called.

Roger Cox unstrapped and turned to Carol, extending his hand as a loud roar grew around her. She shook it firmly, then realized Lori Rodgers was hugging her from behind, and that the sounds she was now hearing were cheers.

As Natalie approached *Antares* in the shuttle, it was hard for her to put into words what she was seeing. The ship was an incongruous black mass lying across the mostly flat, lushly green field. There were humps and depressions where *Antares* had broken on landing.

After unloading her cargo of medical supplies and volunteers, Natalie found Carol Hansen sitting on the ground in front of *Antares*, which from five meters was an enormous wall of loose, wrinkled stealth coating. She was still something like twenty meters tall, even with the bottom two levels mostly crushed by the impact. Hansen was sitting awkwardly on the ground, leaning against the ship with her right leg out straight, a sidearm holstered over her shoulder and a 2K7X next to her on the ground. A small female Warrant Officer was sitting with her.

Both looked exhausted.

"Lieutenant Hansen, I presume?" Natalie asked with a smile. Carol looked up at the sound of her name, seeing a tall Senior Lieutenant she did not recognize. The newcomer was backlit by the star, and while Carol could see her general outline, reading her name tag was impossible.

"Guilty."

The woman stretched out her hand. "Natalie Hayden." Carol scrambled awkwardly to her feet and took Natalie's hand. She didn't know the woman personally, but she knew the story of *Intrepid*, the battle for The Pasture, and Ben Price.

"Good to meet you."

"I brought over some Marine volunteers and some medical staff. What do you need?"

Carol walked stiffly around to the starboard side of *Antares*, where twenty or more crew were arranged along the starboard side of the ship.

"Minor injuries here, mostly. The most serious were in the sickbay."

Natalie waited for more explanation, but when Hansen didn't continue, she filled in the reason herself. The two field surgeons and six techs didn't need any prompting; they went to work assessing the injuries and beginning treatment.

"What about you? How bad is the leg?"

"Oh, I'm fine for now. When they're done with the crew, I'll have them check it out."

"So, what's the status of the ship?"

The slim, shorter Warrant Officer spoke up. "Reactor is nominal, so we still have power for most needs, lights, comms, that kind of thing."

"I see."

As they were standing near the injured, Alex Williams came out of the starboard airlock, which was now just a few feet above the ground. He was followed by Roger Cox, their faces strained and ashen.

Carol turned to them. "Well?"

"As we expected, Lieutenant. They're all gone. It's a mess in there."

Natalie looked at Carol, the question in her eyes obvious.

"Sickbay."

"And ES," added Roger.

"We have other problems." Denise Long pointed out.

"Oh?"

"We have what, a dozen remains in cold storage? With ES out, they'll start thawing soon." That statement earned her a hard stare from Carol. "I'm sorry, Lieutenant, I am. But we have to deal with that soon, or we'll regret it. The provisions are at risk, too. There's a couple months' worth of food back there."

Carol heard a familiar voice from behind Hayden.

"Hello again, Lieutenant Hansen."

She looked up at the Marines, really seeing them for the first time. "Sergeant Jackson! I should have known you'd be here."

"Yes, ma'am. I am glad to see you well, ma'am."

"It's good to see you, too, Leon."

"Listen, Lieutenant, I heard you talking. We can do the recoveries for you, ma'am, if you would allow it."

"Oh, Leon, I couldn't ask — "

"With respect, ma'am, you didn't ask. I knew Captain Michael and Commander Lewis, ma'am, and Doctor Soto. Several of us did. Let us do this for them."

Carol looked at Alex, then Roger. They nodded their agreement. Carol looked up at the ship, towering over her. Her ship. By evil circumstance, her first command. *Antares* had become her home, her personal place in this fight. Now, she lay broken on the ground, unflyable, ruined. The name so proudly emblazoned over the airlock sagged, the bright letters on stealth coating loosened by one of the beacon-mines, incongruously still sticking out from the hull with its head cut off.

Now, as Carol looked three hundred meters aft, she truly appreciated, perhaps for the first time, the scale of *Antares*. She knew the dimensions, of course, but people came and went by shuttle, and even from a cockpit window one did not get a full appreciation of the size of the ship against the blackness of space. But for Carol, the real loss was inside: her friends, her shipmates, all those she had no chance to save. But *Antares* was her ship, her responsibility, and this had been her decision.

Finally, she nodded slightly to herself and looked at Leon Jackson. "OK, Sergeant Jackson. Go ahead. Alex, brief him on where he needs to go."

As Alex talked to the tall Marine sergeant, the other officers walked back to the front of the ship, where they found Jon Swenson, Jayvon Dean, and Lori Rodgers resting.

Hayden looked at Carol with sympathy. "Listen, Lieutenant, I can make a trip up to *Intrepid* with your losses. Once Jackson is done, I'll take them all up.

Henderson will be glad to take them."

Carol waited several seconds before answering. She looked again at her broken ship, thinking how closely it reflected her feelings about her short tenure in command. A busted ship, hard losses in the crew; hardly an auspicious beginning. She felt suddenly tired.

"Yes, OK, Hayden, thanks."

Carol walked slowly to *Antares'* bow and dropped to the ground, her back against the ship. She'd been up all night, ship time. Beta Hydri was rising higher in the clear sky, and the growing pain in her day-old wound was draining her strength. Now that the ship was down and the crew safe, she was ready to let go a little. Before Denise or Lori could stop her, she was fast asleep against *Antares'* crumpled foam.

Preeminent Ship 721
Deep Space, 3 Light-Years from System 849 (Beta Hydri)
Earth Equivalent Date: Sunday, March 19, 2079

Force Commander Sdom Roi Gotk's eyes narrowed, and his tail stump froze in anger listening to his second in command, Thes Fea Honr, as he reported the results from System 849.

"The Vermin have held, sir Gotk. We came very close to winning with the Detector, but they fought it off. When the second force arrived, they had detagged their ships, and the force was defeated."

"Are we not the Preeminent?"

"There can be no question, sir Commander. But, most respectfully, does the mere utterance of the question not itself bring the answer into doubt?"

"You should try less to read my thoughts, Honr."

"We of the Armada, sir Commander, we must face truths beyond our indoctrination. Facts, sir, are what they are, no matter what our leaders would like them to be."

"Blasphemy, Honr."

"Can our beliefs, our teachings, sir Gotk, really be in conflict with our own senses, with our own intellect? With hard military reality?"

"Keep such ideas to yourself, Honr."

"Yes, sir Commander."

Gotk looked out the large windows of his ship, what the ISC Fleet knew as a Type I Cruiser. Gotk's small remnant guarded the three remaining Combatant carriers, a force of some fifteen thousand. Gotk's instructions were to force those Combatants to the surface, finish off the hated Scholars, and any Vermin that might be present, then retire back to Home.

"Send a message to the Council, Honr. Tell them what has happened, and request confirmation that we should continue to press this objective. Tell them, Honr, in my name, that I do not believe we can prevail."

"There is danger in this for you, sir Gotk. The Council will not be pleased."

"I will face that problem later, if I must. But the blood of these Combatants, and the Scholars and Vermin we may kill, will be on the Council, and not on us."

"Yes, sir Commander. I will send it immediately."

Gotk thought about his problem for a long time after his deputy left. They were the Preeminent. They had always prevailed, and each conquest had emboldened them and reinforced their sense of superiority. Could it be that they were mistaken? Could a species possibly exist which could defeat them? The Council, he was sure, would not accept such a conclusion. But, he reminded himself, the military arithmetic was brutal, and not at all in their favor. If he took his three Combatant carriers back to System 849, he was confident they'd be slaughtered, and him with them.

He retired to his cabin, thinking hard about the Vermin, their weapons, and how, perhaps, he might manage to defeat them.

Cobra
Big Blue
Sunday, March 19, 2079, 1825 UTC

Margie Nixon looked up in surprise as the SLIP detector sounded an alarm. The tech working that station brought her the report, and she called Evans to the Operations Center.

"Not long, sir, but not the shortest I've seen, either. Three point three seconds. SLIP channel 47."

"Is 47 identified?"

"No, sir. I checked, and we have three intercepts on 47 over the last six months. Nothing very interesting."

"Where did they come from?"

"One from Enemy Station and two from Alpha Mensae."

"So, a ship."

"Yes."

"OK, well, let's wait and see what FleetIntel has to say about it. I expect they'll be sending us an update once they locate it."

"But, sir, you know..."

"That we won't hear anything for maybe four or five days? Yeah, Nixon, I get that."

"Yes, sir. One more thing, sir."

"Oh?"

"It's as strong a signal as I've ever seen anywhere, sir."

"So, close by?"

"Yes, sir. No question in my mind this is local."

"OK, noted."

As they were finishing, David Powell came into the Operations Center. "So, I heard we caught a SLIP?"

"Yes," Evans answered, "and Nixon thinks it's local."

"Hmm. Calling home for instructions?"

Evans shrugged. "Maybe. Not like them to have second thoughts."

"No, it isn't. And, since we don't have a location, I'm not sure what we're expected to do with it."

"That's right, Powell. If FleetIntel gets us a position, we'll think about."

"Except, sir, that will be days from now and it might be a long way from wherever it was."

Evans looked up at Powell. "Nicely put, David. Say, if you'd like to take a shuttle down to see Hansen, I can authorize that for you."

"This fleet isn't here to enable Carol and I a few moments together, sir. But thanks. The enemy could be back at any moment."

"Permit me to rephrase. Lieutenant Powell, take a shuttle and go see Hansen. Boss's orders."

"Sir, again — "

"Not *my* orders, David. Barker wants you to go see her for the good of the fleet."

"I see, sir. I'll get my stuff together. Can you ask Ensign McNeil to pull out a shuttle for me?"

"Yes. Meantime, get going."

David headed to his quarters for a shave, a shower, and a much-needed change of uniform. If he was going to take one for the team, he thought he should try to look his best.

Evans, smiling at his small lie, headed back to the Bridge. He'd lobbied with Barker to get Hansen some time with Powell. She'd been unwillingly made the face of the war to many back home. From her exploits on Inoria to the discovery of the Seekers, Carol Hansen had been a continuing story. Fleet's Public Information team took advantage of her, just short of outright exploitation, to let the general population know what she was doing and where. Carol had held up well as the designated heroine, her courage and leadership more than meeting the reputation.

Powell was well known, too, as the underdog that brought *Sigma* in after the battle at GL 876. His personal story was out now, also, much to his frustration.

David, like Carol, never wanted to be famous or even slightly well known. He just wanted to be a Fleet Officer. And now, Evans knew, he was one of the best, even if he was toiling in an obscure position on a secret ship.

Evans felt Carol had earned a little release, and if that helped Powell as well, so much the better. He harassed Barker and made it happen for both of them.

Antares
On Big Blue
Monday, March 20, 2079, 1700 UTC

Carol and her de-facto XO Alex Williams stood with Captain Harry Hess in front of *Antares*. Beta Hydri was moving slowly towards the western horizon. It had been a hot day, and the crew had spent much of it trying to rest in the shade of the enormous ship. They'd been down about ten hours when Hess came calling.

Hess looked at her. "It's time we did something with your people."

"Sir?" she asked, puzzled.

"It was a pretty smart move to pull the weapons out of the armory. They might come in handy."

Alex was not at all sure either what Hess was getting at. His personal philosophy was that when in doubt about what the senior officer is thinking, remain in neutral.

"Yes, sir."

Carol was less reticent. "What exactly did you have in mind, sir?"

"Let's get everyone off. I'm worried the enemy may target the ship, and there's really nothing more to be done here, anyway. Have them pack their gear and head over for the Marine encampment."

"As you say, sir."

"The provisions are off already?"

Alex nodded. "Yes, almost done with that. The shuttles worked all day moving what the Marines could use in the short term over to the encampment, the rest went up to *Intrepid*. Once Jackson finished the recovery work, Lieutenant Hayden took the remains to *Intrepid*, too."

"Sad thing, that. Hard."

Carol looked at the ship, as if seeing the casualties still inside, and then back at Hess. "Yes, sir. Jackson deserves a medal for what he did. Took a huge weight off the rest of us."

Hess pulled out his NetComp and made a few notes. "I'll tell Barker." He closed up the NetComp and turned back to Carol. "OK, Lieutenant, let's get your people off the ship. I want them over to the Marines before sunset. Once they're off, shut her down."

Denise Long and Miguel Anthony, seated nearby, spoke as one, "Shut her down?"

Hess turned to them. "Yes, once the crew is off, we'll shut down the reactor and leave her for now."

"You understand, sir," Denise's voice was defiant: "Once we do that, it will take days to bring her back online?"

"Back online? Officer Long," Hess responded, firmly but without anger, "what exactly do you think is going to happen here?"

"Sir?"

"*Antares* is broken, Long, she's beyond repair. No one has any idea what to do with her from here." Hess paused to look at the small group of officers now surrounding him. "I know you love your ship. I know you admired Terri Michael as much as I did. But we have to face facts."

He waited a few seconds, letting them come to the same realization he and Barker had hours before.

"It'll take me an hour," Long responded sadly. "So, Lieutenant Hansen, just give me the word when you're ready."

Miguel Anthony nodded slowly. "I'll help you, Denise. It's a long checklist."

Denise Long shook her head. "Respectfully, Lieutenant, my crew and I will do it. If she has to die, best it comes from us."

Hess took another look around the circle. "Very well. You have your orders. Anything else? Anything you need?"

Miguel, who had been staring at the ground, looked up. "A ship."

Hess just nodded, then turned on his heel and walked back to *Columbia*'s shuttle.

Carol called the rest of the surviving officers together. "OK, you all heard him. Find your Chiefs, get the crew back into their quarters to pack up. Meet back here, in, say, two hours. OK?"

"Yes, Lieutenant," they responded with resignation.

It was a sad procession as the eighty surviving members of the crew made their way back into *Antares*, packed their personal belongings and uniforms, and then left the ship for the last time. Carol packed her own quarters, and then cleared out Marcia Soto's personal belongings. She would go through those in detail later before they were sent home.

It was late-afternoon, Big Blue time, as they stepped off on the five-kilometer trek to the Marine encampment. Carol and Surveillance Officer Jayvon Dean took the point, while Alex and Miguel Anthony brought up the rear of the column.

Walking just ahead of Alex and Miguel was the Reactor Room team who had just shut *Antares* down, likely for the last time. Denise Long had become hardened in the year since Inoria. She was no longer timid or frail or afraid. But she nearly cried when the Reactor Room lights flipped to red as the power went out, the sudden quiet so thick she could feel it surrounding her. Carol gave her a small embrace and then followed her out, the last to leave the room, the last one off the ship, just as a good captain should be.

Domicile of Scad Nee Wok
Preeminent Home World
Earth Equivalent Date: March 20, 2079

Asoon Too Lini struggled with the Vermin language at first. It was so different from her own, simpler in some ways, and so much more complicated in others. There was no song to it, none of the clicks and back-throat puffs that punctuated her own natural speech. Worse, the rules of grammar seemed to change chaotically, each new verb or tense sometimes having no relation to the last. After ten days, she began to understand. That specialized part of her brain, something she never knew was there, started giving her the right answers, almost as if someone else inside her was secretly helping. Her instructor was an older Speaker who had already mastered the Vermin language. She learned as she progressed that the Science Directorate had secretly made hundreds of recordings without the knowledge of the Armada.

She was instructed not to reveal this secret, but she knew she must tell Scad Nee Wok. Something was very wrong, she felt, and she was anxious over what her role might be in something she did not understand.

That night, she talked with Scad for a whole drot about what she had learned.

Finally, Scad told her his own closest secret. "I have been to the Vermin system."

Asoon looked at him in shock, her tail-stump rigid, waiting for him to continue.

"It was not that long ago. We were almost destroyed."

"The SD sent you there?"

"No, the ruling Council sent us to look for the Vermin system. They didn't know where it was."

"But the SD must have already known. These recordings are old; after all, my teacher used them to learn the language, and she is many revs older than I am."

They sat for a long time in silence, considering the profound mystery they had uncovered.

"We must each keep the other's secret, Asoon. The SD must not know that I

101

am aware of this. Nor can the Armada learn what the SD has done."

"Yes."

"One more thing, Asoon. The Vermin system looks like the Ultimate Origin system. The planets, the asteroids, are just as the legend describes."

"Is that why you chose to study Utaeh Be Rore's book our first night?"

Scad squirmed in pleasant recognition. "Yes, partly. I needed to know if you would be a stimulating partner."

"And, am I?"

"I am not displeased with this pairing."

"Neither am I, but I do have fear for what these events may mean."

"You will not be fertile for many decirevs, Asoon. Perhaps this will pass in time for production."

"Yes, I hope that is true. Even a Speaker feels the same drive to produce as other females."

After a few microts, Scad looked at his pairedFemale. "I cannot deny my fear, Asoon. I feel a dread duty is coming upon us."

Shortly after that, Asoon retired for the night, her mind filled with worries, some expressed in the chaotic language of the Vermin. As she drifted to sleep, she wondered which was more worrisome, that she might meet a painful end at the hands of the Armada or the SD, or that the Vermin language might invade and pollute her very thoughts.

Preeminent Ship 721
Deep Space near Beta Hydri
Earth Equivalent Date: Tuesday, March 21, 2079

Sdom Roi Gotk read the dispatch from the Central Council three times. There was not the slightest ambiguity in his orders. He was to return to System 849, remove the Vermin and kill any remaining Scholars for their defiance of the Preeminents' natural authority.

His second-in-command, Thes Fea Honr, was as reticent as Gotk to return to 849. The Vermin were well-positioned there. All attempts to move them off had failed, and failed miserably. There was evidence of surface forces as well as an indeterminate number of ships in orbit.

"They executed Hess Tse Sim for failing at the Deist planet, Honr. They will do no less with me if I fail here."

"So, our choice is to die heroically along with fifteen thousand Combatants, or die in humiliation back home?"

"Honr, I asked you before to please try not to read my thoughts."

"The Combatant carriers will not make it to the surface, sir. The Vermin seem to target them first."

"So, we should perhaps find a way to avoid making that effort? Is there another way to get them down? Or, to somehow cut our losses?"

Honr looked at his commander in surprise. "We have never considered losses, sir Gotk. It is not part of the evaluation of military science."

"A foolish oversight, Honr. The Armada has spent years raising these cohorts, we should not waste that time and material for no reason."

They talked well into the evening, as measured on the ship. Much like ISC Fleet ships, the Armada ran on a time coincident with their home planet.

"The Vermin are ruthless if threatened, Honr, but perhaps they are patient if not?"

"Sir?"

"There was a report that some Combatants were left on the surface from the previous reconnaissance. Are they still there?"

Honr consulted his documents. "I do not know. They are presumed to have no communications."

"So then, let us find a way to let the Vermin think they are not threatened?"

They talked long into the night, devising a plan to keep the Vermin's' attention occupied elsewhere while they brought Combatants to the surface. It was not the Preeminent way, Gotk knew, but it gave them a better chance to prevail.

Better, he thought after Honr left, *but still not very good.*

Preeminent Ship 245
Near Earth
Wednesday, March 22, 2079, 0330 UTC

Detachment Commander Plyf Cee Redl was incredulous.

They had come out of FTL precisely as planned, just outside the Vermin planet's single moon. But as they searched, they found only three dead Preeminent ships. There should be eleven ships here, and his eight cruisers were supposed to join them and complete the destruction of the enemy fleet. But, his tactical staff could not hear any tagged vessels. *How could that be? Surely the Detector had launched its weapons?*

He went himself to the staff area, something few ship commanders would do.

"What of the factory out in the asteroid field?"

"We have found it, ship commander. It is intact."

"What?"

"We also see that the cruiser that was assigned to the factory was destroyed. It is still there, adrift."

"Adrift? They did not star themselves as required?"

"One can only speculate that they were unable."

Redl's tail stump went rigid with anger. "Keep looking. And look for the Vermin, too." He turned from the low-level technicians and walked stiffly back to his commander's position.

"Wevf," he said with a growl, "I do not like what I see. Where is the rest of the fleet?"

"There is wreckage nearby, ship-commander, enough to account for several ships."

"Ours or Vermin?"

"Some of both, ship-commander. There was a battle here, but I fear we were defeated."

"Defeat, Wevf, is impossible. We are the Preeminent." As he was finishing, a call came for the ship-commander to return to the tactical staff. Annoyed, he moved quickly down two decks, barging into the small space.

"What is it?"

"We have located the Detector, ship-commander. It is falling into the star, but slowly. Their propulsion must be disabled."

Redl looked at the image that the tech gave him. The Detector was heavily damaged, small and large holes covering both ends. *The Vermin had figured out its weakness already!*

"Can you hear any tagged ships?"

"Only in wreckage, ship commander. If any others were tagged, they've retired to a distance beyond what we can hear."

"What is going on?" Redl asked himself. "Where are the Vermin?"

"We cannot say, ship commander."

"Keep looking! I will give you two drots to find them, then we will see."

"Yes, ship commander."

As Redl was obsessing over the location of the now-lost task force, *Nippon* was slipping quietly behind the eight enemy ships, all very neatly in a line. *Dunkirk* was moving to several thousand kilometers outside their orbit. *Tong-Il* was approaching slowly from beneath them.

Grissom remained in geosynchronous orbit, watching, and ready in case she should be needed.

As soon as the first fight was over, Anna Nonna had taken *Bondarenko* out to the ship factory to pick up some Fleet Engineers. They and her crew were working feverishly to get her weapons and surveillance systems operational again. She had radar and some IR and visual, but not enough. Anna had escaped the tag-bomb attack with simple cuts from shrapnel flying off whatever the enemy darts hit on her Bridge. Her XO Dick Watson, on the other hand, had taken a flechette straight through his abdomen that killed him before anyone could do anything about it. The missile hits had ruined her loaders and jammed both rotary launcher doors. Anna couldn't believe the coincidence herself until she saw it firsthand. But, unless they could get at least one of them working, her proud, beautiful *Bondarenko* was all growl and no bite. They worked day and night for three days, but they had only now removed the wreckage and damaged weapons. She would be out of the fight for the second wave.

Gagarin was standing by the ship factory, watching for any new threats.

Captain Kawaguchi silently counted off his command: *Mir*, *Rassvet*, *Stoykiy*, destroyed; *Bondarenko*, out of action; *Grissom*, damaged but still operational; *Gagarin*, off in the asteroid belt. He was left with the Brits' *Dunkirk*, Korea's *Tong-Il*, and his own massive *Nippon*, just a third of the task force he'd been given to fight the eight enemy ships that had arrived, likely intending to finish off the battle started yesterday. *We're lucky,* he thought, *that they didn't bring these eight the first time. We might not have survived.*

Kawaguchi had thought carefully about how to execute this attack. He had read about the enemy incursion back in December, and how the young Lieutenant on *Dobrovolski* had tried to take out the enemy SLIP apparatus and then their Drive. This was what Nobu had planned to do before the enemy surprised him and scrambled his command. He knew how many were coming in this second wave, and without the Type V to help, his stealth advantage was restored. He laid out a timeline for the attack and sent it to Andy Sackville and Yong Sook Man.

It was actually a straightforward plan: gag them, knee-cap them, then kick the shit out of them.

What Redl didn't know as he was puzzling over the fate of the Detector ship was that Kawaguchi's plan was already in motion, a plan that included Joe Scheck's stealth-Lance, which would not be seen until it went off. His first hint was when a Lance went off under the front of his ship, wiping the SLIP transmitter clean off.

"What was that?" Redl cried as his ship shook from the impact. He dropped the image of the Detector on the table and ran back to his command position. He was nearly there when the ship shook again, more violently this time.

Wevf's face and tail-stump revealed the terror he suddenly felt. "The propulsion coil is damaged, ship-commander. They struck the FTL communications first, then the coils. What are they doing?"

Redl ordered activation of the proximity sensor. "Perhaps we will see them now."

Andy Sackville smiled as his Surveillance tech called out that all eight enemy ships had turned on their radar.

"Excellent. Now, assholes, know what it means to be afraid." He turned to his Weapons Officer. "Catherine, proceed as planned."

"Yes, Captain. One minute twenty seconds to launch."

She kept the rotaries inboard until the very last moment, about fifteen seconds before launch. In another twenty seconds, eight Bludgeons were dispatched, and the rotaries began moving back in.

Catherine Miller turned to her Captain. "On time, sir, on course. One minute five to impact."

Despite the screams from the intrusion detector techs, Redl never saw the Bludgeon from *Dunkirk* that exploded in his face, nor the one from *Nippon* that struck his ship's enormous tanks starboard amidships, nor the final one from *Tong-Il* that hit the soft bottom of his cruiser. Wevf lived just long enough to see Redl's smashed remains sucked out the broken window, and feel himself being lifted off the deck. Then, for Wevf, everything went dark. It was just as well.

The eight burning enemy ships were too far to be visible from the Earth's surface. A pity, as CINC Connor Davenport would love to have seen that sight. Kawaguchi's victory was now complete, if expensive, and they had beaten back the enormous threat this enemy fleet represented. He, like Kawaguchi, was thankful they hadn't sent all nineteen ships at once. That would have made this either a more expensive victory or, worse, a painful defeat.

The enemy was getting better, but they were still beatable. Just barely, but, still, beatable.

Marine Encampment
Big Blue
Wednesday, March 22, 2079, 0900 UTC

The day was already warm, the star just about at its zenith when the shuttle from *Cobra* set down on the outskirts of the Marine area. Fleet shuttles came and went frequently and at random times most days, so the arrival of yet another was not worth even an idle glance. The appearance of a Fleet Lieutenant in space greys was, on the other hand, something rarely seen on the surface, field colors being the norm for both Fleet and Marine personnel.

The sandy-haired Lieutenant made his way between the parked spacecraft, and scouting around the quarters area finally spotted his target seated on a bunk under an enormous camouflaged tent, her face deep in her NetComp. As he stopped in front of her, Carol looked up from her NetComp in surprise, scrambled to her feet, and embraced him tightly.

The officers around her smiled widely. Many of them had never met David Powell, but there could be no question about who had just arrived, as the ship patch on his left sleeve removed any real doubt. *Cobra*'s crest was unique: black, with the ship name in dark gray across the top, with just two dark green snake eyes and a deep red forked tongue within the inner circle.

Carol and David finally separated and made their way out of the tent and into the bright midday light of Beta Hydri.

"So, what are they telling you?" he asked as they walked.

"The leg is doing well. A Marine PT tech comes around every few hours to torture me, but it's progressing. It's been five days already, which is hard to believe, but I can get around OK as long as I take the meds."

"Sounds good."

Carol turned to him. "How, exactly, did you find the time to come down here? I would have thought you guys would be kinda busy right now."

David smiled shyly. "Truth?" Carol nodded. "Barker ordered it. He thinks it would be good for morale or something."

Carol stopped and looked up at David. "That makes no sense."

"Oh, I don't know. Sure improved mine. How about you?"

Carol smiled, re-took David's arm, and they resumed their walk towards The Pasture.

David let a minute go by before speaking again. "So, how are you, Carol? I can't imagine — "

"It was brutal." She stopped, shaking her head at the memories flooding back. "You're right, you can't imagine how Terri Michael's chest just exploded on the Bridge, blood all over the place, all over me, dead before she fell. A junior Surveillance tech — his first time out — had his brains blown out all over the forward screens. Then, me lying on the deck with Guzman looking down at me like he was afraid I was already dead."

David felt her grip on his arm tighten.

"Then, Ryan...and Marcia..."

David let her pause float for a few seconds. "Yes, I heard."

Carol let go of him, her hands in front of her, clenching and unclenching fists of frustration. "Now, I don't know what's going to happen. I lost my ship, David, *my* first command is laying all busted up and useless in an empty field right over there." She pointed back towards where *Antares* lay.

As Carol's anger passed over him, David stopped their stroll to look directly in her eyes, his hand caressing her cheek. "And everyone aboard walked away, Carol. Let's think about what's really important here."

Carol turned away, walking again. "Still, it would make a lovely Court of

Inquiry."

David waited a second before he followed her. "I doubt you'll see that."

"I hope you're right."

"I know I'm right, Carol. Stop second-guessing yourself. That's not like you, by the way."

She shook her head. "Maybe not, but I keep replaying it in my head."

"And?"

She waited a few seconds, reticent to answer. Finally, her shoulders slumped in surrender, and she turned back to look at him. "And, I can't think of what else I could have done."

David smiled and nodded. "Right. Hold on to that, Carol. I doubt anyone else could think of anything, either."

She slipped her arm around him, pulling him closer, and David's arm went around her shoulders. They walked this way to the bluff that was the north wall of The Pasture, not far from where Liwanu and Natalie had watched Little Gray rise a few weeks before. Once there, she sat down awkwardly on the grass, her bandaged leg still stiff. David sat beside her, leaning back on his elbows.

"Jack sends his love."

"Oh, God, I miss him so much. I could have used his advice a few times. But tell him I'm not sorry he wasn't there."

"I will. Evans also sends his best."

Carol slipped her arm around David, resting her head on his shoulder as she held on tightly.

"It's OK, Carol," he said quietly. "It's OK to lean on me a little here. You can be strong later."

She didn't respond right away, but rested with his arms around her. As they sat there, breathing almost in unison, she felt her confidence returning, almost as if he were recharging her courage, refilling her determination. He'd always done that, she realized. Anytime she'd felt anxious, or doubted herself, or wondered what to do next, a quiet talk with David would put her back on track. Is that why she loved him so much, knew so strongly that they were destined to be together? *Maybe,* she thought, *maybe so.*

She raised her head and kissed him for the first time since he'd arrived. "We have to get through this alive. We *have* to."

"I think we will. But for now, we fight. We keep fighting until this whole ugly episode is over."

After a minute, she asked him, "Would we even be together without it?"

He looked at her in surprise. "Without the war? Yeah, I'd like to think so."

Carol shifted to look back at him. "I'm not so sure. Inoria really cleared my mind about what was important."

"I always knew. I just never quite knew how. So how did Inoria clear your mind?"

Carol smiled, her first full, really happy expression since he had arrived. "So, I'm in Inoria, and the RFGs are crashing down all around, the air is full of shit. I go looking for cover, right?"

David nodded.

"Right, and all I can think of while I'm lying there hoping a building doesn't fall on me is how pissed you'll be that you weren't there."

He pulled her a little closer. "Well, you were right. I was pretty pissed about it when the reports started showing up on the news channels."

"The ones with that horrible picture? The mug-shot?"

"Yes. Actually, that picture got me back on track, too."

"What?"

"I was doing OK in the Intel class, but not great, and that first night after Inor, Salazar caught me sitting at the bar in *The Cookie Factory*. Remember that shabby old place across from the Intel building?"

Carol nodded. She'd been there a time or two herself.

"Anyhow, there I was, drinking a beer and staring at the news reports with your picture on the screen."

"And?"

"And, Salazar says he knows all about you. Told me I needed to get my head where my ass was."

"Eloquent."

"Yeah, that old warrant has a real way with words. After that, I really put myself into the class, and I felt more like I had at the U."

She grabbed his shoulders and shook him. "And graduated first in your class!"

David looked at her strangely. "I never told you that! Lieutenant Hansen, have you been Fleet-stalking me that long?"

She smiled, one eyebrow up. "Maybe."

After a moment, David looked at her nervously. "Can I ask you a question?"

She looked at him, puzzled by his question about a question. "Maybe. Depends on what it is. So far, there's not much I haven't told you."

David looked out at The Pasture, then back at her. "What did my grandmother say to you that day in Kendalville? You almost cried."

Carol smiled at the memory, then lifted his hand to her lips before responding. "She said she knew I would always love you, but she asked me to promise I would show you how to love yourself."

David nodded, fighting back the tears forming at the corners of his eyes. "She always did know me best."

"She still does. And now, so do I."

Before long, it was time for David to get back to *Cobra*. For once, they could take their time with good-bye, even if it wasn't so private. Finally, shared tears shed and dried, expressions of love given and accepted, David made his way back to his shuttle and headed back to his duties. Another trip was being discussed, and David would soon be very glad he'd had a few hours with Carol. He might not have another chance for some time.

Carol went back to waiting for the other shoe to drop, waiting for Fleet to decide what to do with her and her crew.

ISC Fleet HQ, Intel Section
Ft. Eustis, VA
Wednesday, March 22, 2079, 1315 UTC

Frances Wilson was frustrated, and everyone knew when Frances was stressed, everyone was stressed. They'd survived the enemy onslaught twice, but the fight at Beta Hydri was clearly not over yet. There had been little enemy SLIP activity in the last few weeks, and Frances took that as a personal affront. It was as if the enemy was on to what she was doing.

Until today.

Kristin Hayes arrived at her office door, breathless. "New TDOA hit. It's near Beta Hydri, but a little way off. Not sure I get it."

"Any history on the source? "

"Yeah, some. It's channel 47. Three previous hits, two at Alpha Mensae and one at Enemy Station."

"A ship."

"Yes, absolutely. It was sent March 19th, late in the evening, UTC."

"OK, so, that's not long after the second strike there."

Kristin sat. "Asking for further instructions?"

"Could be. How far is this?"

"Um," Kristin worked her NetComp hard, then looked up. "Two point seven five light-years."

"So, about three days' travel time to Beta Hydri?"

"A little more, about three and a quarter. But yes, that's close."

"But why there?" Frances asked, mostly to herself as Ron Harris came in. Kristin started to stand, but Harris waved her off as he dropped into the second chair in Frances' office.

"What do we think about this new location?" he asked.

"We were just talking about that," Frances responded. "Wondering why they would be there."

"Well," Harris offered, "They're coming in waves. It would make sense to have a meeting point, close enough to send ships as needed but far enough from the planet to be safe. This location sounds about right to me."

"Whatever it is, we should tell Barker. Maybe *Cobra* could go check it out."

Harris smiled. "*Cobra*, Mrs. Wilson, is still a FleetIntel asset, whatever Kieran Barker might think."

"So, you're going to order them to this location?"

"This message is after the second attack. We saw no other such messages from Earth or Inor."

"Something is different at Beta Hydri, then?" Frances asked.

Ron nodded. "I think so. Somehow our presence at Beta Hydri has gotten under their skin. We know they recon'd it after the first *Antares* visit. It's not far from their home..." His voice dropped as he thought about why the enemy was so compulsive about Beta Hydri.

"But, they failed to subdue it, too. That has to be a thorn in their sides." Kristin added.

Frances looked at the ceiling, thinking. "Yes, but, then, why not come back to Inor in the same way? Why give the Inori a pass and blow so many resources at Big Blue?"

Harris shrugged. "We don't really know what their plan was at Inor. Sokolovsky knew he didn't have any invasion ships coming, so he could go wide and wait for developments."

Kristin continued, "Which saved him from the Type V, I get that. But, still, it means they were not going to try another invasion there."

"Yes, Kristin, it does. But I still don't understand it." He looked across at Frances. "Tell Barker and Evans about the intercept. *Cobra* has a scanner — "

"So does *Intrepid* and *Antares*," Kristin interjected.

"Right, but they're too close together to get a location. Still, they may already know about it. Tell Evans it's up to him whether he wants to go check it out."

"Yes, Admiral."

```
PRIORITY 20703222200UTC
TO: CSTO, COBRA
FROM: FLEETINTEL
SUBJECT: NEW TDOA LOCATION

1) SLIP MESSAGE CH 47 DETECTED WITH TX DATE 20790319224UTC
LOCATES TO X 1.17 Y 0.35 Z -7.95 OR 2.7 LY FROM BH.
2) FLEETINTEL ASSESSES THIS LOCATION AS A POSSIBLE ENEMY RALLY
POINT.
3) SUGGEST REPEAT SUGGEST COBRA INVESTIGATE OWN DISCRETION AFTER
CONSULTING WITH CSTO.

END
```

Cobra
Big Blue
Thursday, March 23, 2079, 0900 UTC

After the unhappy surprise that took *Antares* out of the fight, Rich Evans ordered *Cobra* to a higher equatorial orbit. With *Intrepid* and *Canberra* watching the poles, this position gave him the best coverage of the planet. Once settled in his new observation position, he called his analysts together.

"So, what the hell is going on?" Rich Evans asked his analysts. "Where are the invasion ships?"

David looked up from his tablet. "I really thought it was imminent when we saw the Type III's down low. I expected the Type II's to be close behind. But, nothing."

"Well," Ray Salazar pointed out, "we smoked those ships. The fourth Type III as well. Could they have passed on the invasion after that?"

"Just gone home, you mean?" Evans asked.

"Yes. We believe they lost a shitload of ground troops at Inor. FleetIntel thinks thousands. Maybe they didn't want to repeat that disaster."

Evans shook his head. "This feels like an all-out offensive, Ray. They're all-in with this. I think they're still coming."

"But, Commander," Salazar responded, "unless they've added ships since we left e-prime, they have very little left to cover a landing. We've picked off two-thirds of their force, and driven off the Type V."

"Peña wants our assessment, folks. I'm sure he's asking his own staff for the same."

"Yes, sir," David answered. "It had been our observation that they don't ever back down once engaged, even if the fight is a loser."

"Well," Margie Nixon observed, "Except for that ship that tripped over Earth a couple months ago."

"That's right," David responded, "But there, it was likely more important to get the intelligence they had gathered back home than to put up any fight with us."

"Yeah, maybe."

"I still don't understand them, sir," David commented. "They killed *almost* all the Seekers. Why is it so important to finish them off? They've already lost far more lives trying to kill them, and us, than all the Seekers that are still alive. They engage us, but they must know at some level we're going to prevail."

"Well, Eaagher said they were told it was either kneel or die. The Seekers couldn't process the concept of worship, so the 'hard-faces' tried to exterminate them."

"But they don't try it with us. Why?"

Salazar shrugged. "Too many of us. Ten plus billion is a big bolus to absorb, and maybe even harder to kill."

"So, they're not *completely* crazy, is that what you're saying?"

"Yes, sir," Ray answered, laughing.

David turned suddenly serious. "We must guard against the same disease, sir, that being overconfidence."

"Yes?"

"We've beaten them over and over, but not always easily, and this Type V reflects some serious scientific knowledge in their culture. We don't have the slightest understanding of what that was, and with just slightly better luck, they'd have killed all of us."

"Yes, true. So, what are you saying, David? Are they coming or not?"

"It would be out of character for them to relent, sir. They'll come because that's what they do."

"Even if it's futile?"

David nodded his head firmly. "Again, it's who they are, sir. They conquer and subjugate. Backing off is not in their nature."

"OK, then that's what I'll tell Peña."

Ray Salazar turned again to David. "And how is Lieutenant Hansen?"

David smiled. "She's doing well. She gets PT every day that hurts but seems to be working. I'd say she's well on her way back. "

"What about *Antares*?"

"Shut down. The reactor is off and the crew is over at the Marine encampment. Nobody seems to know what else to do with them."

"What will they do with Hansen, Commander?" Salazar asked Evans. "She's not going to want to go back to being a Weapons Officer. She's had a taste of command and done well."

Evans shrugged. "Can't say. But it wouldn't be unprecedented to do just that: put her back at Weaps on some other ship. David?"

David smiled, raising his hands in surrender. "I plead the fifth. But, yeah, she's not going to want to step back." After a moment, David continued. "But she is a good officer. She'll accept her orders and make the best of whatever they ask of her."

As they headed out of the wardroom, David wondered to himself what might happen. Ships were not in a surplus right now, and there were probably more qualified commanders than available commands. Carol might well be put back into a secondary role, perhaps as a replacement XO where one was needed.

Time would tell, he thought, and meantime, he had his own job to do. What

Fleet decided for Carol, Fleet would decide, and there was nothing he or she could do but accept the orders they issued.

Admiral Whittaker's Office
Starbase Tranquility II
Thursday, March 23, 2078, 1200 UTC

Admiral Brian Whittaker smiled to himself as he set his NetComp down on his desk. *Sigma*'s repair was now complete and she was ready to be returned to the fleet. Across from him sat Lieutenant Peg White, the rigorously competent engineer who had brought *Sigma* back from the dead. As she nervously scratched her ear, he noticed again her long, slender fingers.

Quickly pulling his eyes away from her hands, he said, "Lieutenant, you've done an incredible job here. She's literally better than new."

"The crew did the job, sir, I just did a lot of pointing and yelling. There's a list at the end of the report of individuals I'd like you to recognize."

"I saw that. I'll forward letters to Fleet for them."

"Thank you, sir."

Whittaker leaned back in his chair, looking at the painting of *Freedom* on his wall behind White. It had been his last command before accepting the position at Tranquility II. Had he a window in just the right place, he might have caught sight of her outside, guarding him and the station. He was out of line command now, but happy to still be contributing to the Fleet. Besides, tough old Tranquility had become his home, and the crew his family. Widowed with no children, he didn't really want anything else anymore.

"She's ready to go back, Peg."

"Yes, sir. Have you considered my request?"

"You're a fixture here, Peg. I would hate to lose you."

"Yes, sir. I can't think of a higher compliment. Still — "

Whittaker raised a hand to silence her, then smiled slightly as he pulled a document out of his top drawer.

"By order of the Commander in Chief," he read aloud, "*Sigma* is returned to the active Fleet Order of Battle."

"That's sounds good," she answered.

Whittaker smiled as he kept reading. "Senior Lieutenant Margaret White is promoted to the temporary grade of Lieutenant Commander, subject to the usual one-year review." He paused to look up at the surprise on her face. "Commander White's request for a return to line duty is approved."

"Thank you, sir."

"Oh, Commander, we're not done yet," he responded.

"Lieutenant Commander White shall take temporary command of *Sigma*, and when in all respects ready for spaceflight, *Sigma* shall be ferried to Beta Hydri to join Admiral Barker's task force."

"Sir?"

"Your return to line duty is granted, Commander. Your first task is to get *Sigma* back in the fight."

"Thank you, Admiral, but I am not sure I understand. *Temporary* command? Did you say *ferried*?"

"You've read the reports from Beta Hydri, so you're aware of what happened to *Antares*."

"Yes. The Captain and XO were killed and Powell's Lieutenant Hansen took over. The ship was later disabled in an attack and they somehow got it on the ground. Honestly, sir, I didn't think such a thing was possible. I was pretty sure it would snap in half as soon as they hit the atmosphere."

"Neither did I, but they managed it."

Peg shook her head in amazement. "Well, there's a graduate-level course in ship handling in that somewhere."

"Yes, I would say so."

"That's all fine, sir, but what does that have to do with..." Peg stopped talking as the scenario clicked in her head.

"They're giving *Sigma* to the *Antares* crew?"

"Correct. Here we have a ship with no crew, there they have a crew with no ship."

"A marriage made in heaven, I suppose," she said with some disappointment.

"Hansen is being promoted, too, same as you. She will take command."

"I see."

"But she lacks a qualified Navigator, since she assigned her own as XO."

Peg began to see new possibilities in what Whittaker was saying. "Nav was my first assignment."

"Indeed. Would you like the job?"

She looked at him for a moment. "You know full well I'm not going to turn this down. Sir."

Whittaker smiled. He would miss her frank expression of her opinion.

"Good. I've talked to Captain Hakim, and he thinks he can scrape together maybe ten or fifteen crew off his three ships to help you ferry *Sigma* to Beta Hydri. Ten of your techs are also volunteering."

Peg shook her head. "If I'm taking her into a combat zone, sir, she needs crewmembers who can fight. Repair engineers are not qualified for combat."

"So, what do you think?"

"I'll take whatever Hakim can spare. We can run pretty lean for the transit, but we'll have to merge the crews once we get there. I'll have to talk to the techs he's sending and make sure they understand."

After a moment, Whittaker changed the subject. "Peg, I have to ask you, as your friend, not your superior. Are you physically up for this?"

She leaned forward toward his desk. "I appreciate your concern, sir. The Marfan's is under control. The new meds are working. I even passed the cardiac stress test on my last annual."

"Very well. I had to ask."

"Yes, sir. I understand your concern, and I do truly appreciate it."

Whittaker nodded. "OK, then. I'll talk to Hakim and send CINC a message."

Peg nodded her understanding. "Sir?"

"Yes?"

She stood. "I can't tell you what an honor it has been to serve with you, sir. You've taught me so much."

Whittaker shook his head. "I have given you space, Commander, to grow into yourself. But I can take little credit since you were already the person you are now."

"Still — "

"Good luck, Commander," he interrupted. He rose and extended his hand, which she took firmly, then turned and headed for her quarters to pack. She'd be moving into her cabin on *Sigma* before the day was out.

Cobra
Big Blue
Saturday, March 25, 2079, 1845 UTC

Force Commander Gotk's three cruisers slipped out of FTL well away from Big Blue, somewhere back behind Little Gray, and then let their residual inertia carry them to the planet. Barker's force didn't see them for several hours, not until they were within ten thousand kilometers of the planet.

David looked up in surprise when Ray Salazar sighted them. "Where the hell did THEY come from? And where the hell are they going?"

"Can't quite tell, Lieutenant. We're still refining the track from the visual and IR."

"Screw that. Unstow the radar and light the bastards up. I need to know where they're going. Now."

Rich Evans entered the operations center, responding to the alarm David had sounded just a few seconds before.

"Commander?" Salazar asked, wondering if he'd countermand Powell.

"Lieutenant Powell is in charge, Mister Salazar."

116

"Yes, sir." The oversized flat-panel phased-array radar deployed and swung quickly in the direction of the enemy ships.

Shortly after David ordered up the radar, Thes Fea Honr ran to his ship commander with a report from their technicians.

"Radio tracking system detected, sir Gotk, a new type we have not seen before. It's powerful, probably close. Shall we fire on it?"

Gotk salivated with satisfaction. His plan was beginning to work. "Good. We've surprised them enough that they're impatient to know what we're doing, and using something they've kept hidden from us."

"Orders?"

"Continue, and do not fire. Tell the other commanders, as well. I want them to see us."

Back in *Cobra*'s Operations Center, Gregg Browning's voice shook a little as he reported the radar system's analysis to David: "Two Type IIIs, one Type I. System projects they're headed for the old city."

"Bullshit," Evans responded without emotion.

"Sir?"

"Oh, that's what they want us to think, Browning. But there is nothing in the old cities worth wasting an RFG on." He looked over at the digital clock that showed the time. "Powell! When is dawn at the Seekers' place, again?"

David checked his chart. "Sunrise is 1930, sir."

"A dawn attack?" Evans asked himself quietly. He picked up the ship phone from Center Console. "Comms...Elaine, get me Peña." Only a few seconds after he hung up, the phone rang.

"Elias, I don't buy this course. They want us to think they're headed to the old settlement, but what's there worth attacking? They're going to hit the Seekers at dawn, Elias." Evans listened for several seconds, frustration clear on his face. "I think that's a mistake, Elias. Tell Barker to hold his positions and wait for the Type IIs." A moment later, he hung up and looked around the Operations Center. "Barker's calling *Intrepid* down to intercept them, *Columbia* and *White* are moving as well."

Evans moved to stand behind Browning, watching the radar track himself for a few moments, then dropped into one of the observer seats on the forward bulkhead. Browning looked up at Powell, who just shrugged and indicated that he should continue tracking the enemy ships. Jack Ballard, having watched Evans' exchange with Elias Peña, slipped into Center Console next to David.

"OK, David, what do you think?"

"If the boss is right, which I think he is, they've gotten more imaginative, at least."

"So, assuming this is a feint, where's the attack?"

"The Seekers, of course."

"Right. Assuming, again, that they're single-minded on getting rid of them."

"I don't think that's all, Jack. They want to push us off the planet, too. Teach us a lesson, maybe. Make us leave them alone."

"Well, if that's the case, I think they'll be the ones learning a lesson."

"Let's hope so."

They sat there for five minutes, watching the enemy ships approach the planet.

"Notice something, gentlemen?" Evans called out from behind them. David and Jack turned to face Evans.

"What's that, sir?" David asked.

"They haven't fired on us. Every other time, they hear a radar, they shoot at it. Today, they don't."

"They want us to track them?" Jack asked.

"Absolutely. They're drawing us into their little plan."

The NetLink alarm from *Intrepid* caught Senior Lieutenant Natalie Hayden in the cockpit of her shuttle: *Three enemy ships approaching planet. Prepare for immediate action.* She powered up and began her preflight checklist. Within a few minutes, there was a group of Fleet Marines trotting towards her in the dim pre-dawn light, and she was glad to see Liwanu Harry in the lead. She met him at the forward hatch.

"Lieutenant Harry, disperse your people nearby. Let's not load them until we have a destination."

"Ma'am?"

"If they're in the shuttle, they're a pretty fat fixed target, right? It won't take two minutes to load up if we get an order." Harry nodded his understanding, then scattered his people a few dozen meters away. Natalie went back to finishing her checklist, making sure she'd be ready to fly if the Marines had to move.

Aboard *Intrepid*, Joanne Henderson was moving her ship to intercept the enemy. *Cobra's* hard-track radar data helped her see where the enemy was going, and her Navigator Lynn Covington kept pushing as hard as he dared and still avoid detection.

"Captain," James Kirkland called out, "It will be a while before we have good solutions. Geometry sucks right now."

Joanne didn't look up from her workstation. "Very well."

She watched for five minutes as the track continued towards the old cities.

Elias Peña had sent out a warning that this might be some kind of diversion, but so far, the enemy had kept their course.

"Fixation, Captain." Joanne's eyes snapped up from her tracking display to look at the source of the voice.

"Fixation?"

Intel Officer Chuck Anderson was standing next to her raised command position. "Just like a parlor magic trick. They keep your eye on what they want you to be focused on, and away from what they don't want you to see."

Joanne was suddenly frozen in place. "What are we not seeing, Lieutenant?"

"I wish I knew, ma'am, but this extravagant display is not the point. The real action is yet to come."

"Nicely put, Anderson, but not particularly helpful."

"Where are the Type II's, Captain? That's the real question, and we still can't answer that."

Anderson turned and returned to his Intel techs without another word.

On *Cobra*, David and Jack watched the track as closely as Joanne.

"If it's a trick, when will we know?" Jack asked.

David shrugged. "When they change course, I guess."

"My guess," Evans called, having overheard them, "is that when *Intrepid* fires on them, they'll bolt instead of firing back or taking hits."

"And then?"

"Then? Whatever else they have in mind, David. Whatever else."

Joanne called Kieran Barker as the three enormous silver ships began to slow as they passed a thousand kilometers from the surface, still apparently headed for the old cities.

"We should have a solution soon, Admiral, but suppose I *don't* fire on them? They can't know I'm here. They have *Cobra* pestering them from high orbit, but otherwise, they're clueless."

"We don't know what's going on, Captain. Whatever they're planning, let's take them off the board while we can and then see what happens."

"Yes, sir. We'll take our shots soon as we can."

"Fine. Be ready to move if they respond."

Second in command Honr spoke quietly to his commander. "Sir Gokt, they have not fired on us."

"Nor have we fired on the radio detection ship, which we normally do as a matter of protocol."

"You think they're curious?"

"I think they're very careful fighters, Honr. They wonder what we're doing and they're hoping we'll make the first move."

"We will need to change course very soon, sir. The Combatants are almost to their targets."

Liwanu Harry found a spot to sit in the long Big Blue grass, his weapon next to him, trying to be both relaxed and alert as he leaned back against a boulder on the edge of the shuttle landing area. A bright flash of reflected light low in the pink sky to the east caught his eye. As he watched, one bright dot became two, then three, then, more.

"Lieutenant Hayden!" he yelled. "What the hell is that?"

Natalie ran out of the shuttle, following his eye to the sky, which was slowly filling with approaching enemy shuttles.

"Oh, shit."

She rushed back inside to call *Intrepid*.

Carol Hansen was aroused from her post-therapy rest by the fear-filled sound of yelling out by the shuttles. As she stood up, there was no mistaking the six deadly silver objects coming right at her out of a beautiful, colorful, dawn sky.

"ANTARES!" she called, alarm clear in her voice. "Get up, get your weapons ready. Outside in one minute!" All around her, the *Antares* crew rolled out of their bunks, or up off the cool ground, reaching for their rifles and ammunition.

As Carol looked back at them, the enemy was now closer, lower, and seemed to be speeding up. *At least,* she thought, *this time we've got something more than a damn K-Bar.*

"What?" Evans said, shocked.

"Marines report incoming shuttles from the east, sir. We don't have them on IR."

"Bastards are too low and slow to show up. Dammit."

Jack looked at David. "And so, ladies and gentlemen, welcome to the show."

David looked hard at Ballard. "Carol is right in the middle of this shit storm, Jack. A little less humor, if you don't mind."

"Don't forget she's my friend, too, David," Jack responded, angrier with himself than David. "How about we just do our jobs?"

Evans, surprised at this exchange between his two best analysts, moved into Center Console. "I have the console, gentlemen."

"Yes, Captain, " David answered and stepped out of Center Console, still stinging from Jack's glib comment.

Evans picked up the phone. "Nav... this is Evans. Put me ten thousand klicks over the Seekers. Now."

After slamming down the receiver, he looked at the radar data, green tracks suddenly turning red as the enemy failed to continue as projected.

"Captain! They're changing course, it looks like they're turning east." A few seconds later he added, "Yeah, and they're suddenly in a hurry."

"Drop the cruisers, Browning, and see if you can find where the shuttles are coming from?"

"Yes, sir."

"Powell, get on the IR. Ballard, work with Browning on the radar. I want those mother ships."

"Yes, Captain."

As the room scrambled to respond to Evans' orders, he could be heard to repeat "Damn, damn, damn" quietly to himself.

"They *what*?" Joanne Henderson yelled at Surveillance Officer Marco Gonzales.

"They hit the Drive and went, Captain."

"Went where?"

"East, ma'am, and in one helluva hurry."

"Nav! Put us back over the Seekers and make it quick! Call it twenty-five-hundred klicks. I don't care if they see us."

"Yes, Captain."

"Weaps! When you get a solution, you shoot, understood?"

James Kirkland, surprised by this turn of events just as he was about to declare a firing solution, just nodded and turned back to his techs.

Henderson turned to her XO sitting at her side. "Alonzo, I don't want a repeat of *Antares*. Get back to the Intel shop and see how Anderson is doing. Stay there."

"Captain, my place is here. All due — "

Joanne suddenly turned to him and leaned in close. "Alonzo, get back to Intel. Now."

Bass looked at her for a long moment, but her face revealed no chance of a respite. He had to go. "Yes, Captain."

She turned away just as quickly. "Nav! How are we doing?"

"Burning a lot of gravitons, ma'am, but we'll be there in about fifteen minutes."

"Faster, if you can."

"Yes, Captain."

Joanne watched Bass go. She'd talk to him later, if, that is, there was a 'later' for them. She could not risk both of them being lost in a single strike. If something happened to her, Alonzo would have to take over, and he'd have to be alive to do that.

Marine Captain Andy Martin had met this enemy before, almost on this same field. But then there had been one shuttle and about a hundred enemy soldiers. Now, six shuttles were coming his way out of the sunrise, and there was no guarantee they'd only have a hundred each. With less than a hundred Marines, the arithmetic was worrisome.

"Well, Andy," Major Wayne Barnes said to him, "At least they've done us the courtesy of coming to us!"

Martin smiled grimly. "Fine. Here, there, wherever. Best to get this over once and for all."

"And," Barnes replied, "we get to defend. That alone is worth another company."

The Marine encampment was just to the northwest of the Seeker's cave hideout, with the four Fleet shuttles parked on the far side, away from the Seekers. Martin and Barnes had war-gamed different scenarios, mostly oriented around an enemy force landing in The Pasture south of the Seekers' caves. They also considered what to do if they came down on Seeker beach, or in the low flats to the north. But they had never anticipated a force as large as they were now facing. There were enough shuttles inbound to easily implement all of their scenarios at once.

"What should we do with the *Antares* crew?" Martin asked.

"Can they shoot and not hit each other?"

"Most of them, yeah."

"OK, they'll be the last resort for the Seekers. Tell Hansen to post half her people in the woods above the beach, half in the scrub along the base."

"Fine."

Wayne started to walk towards the Pasture, then turned back. "Make sure Hansen has a radio. She'll need to be on the command loop."

"Right, will do."

"And, Andy, tell her to keep her eyes open and her head clear. God only knows what's about to happen."

"Yes, sir."

After Martin passed along Wayne's orders, Carol collected her crew and headed for Seeker Beach, ignoring the loud complaints from her leg. She left Denise Long in charge of those who physically couldn't make the run to the Seekers. Long argued strenuously to go with her, but Hansen was adamant that she needed someone she could trust to look after those she was leaving behind. Long slung her weapon over her shoulder and stood at the edge of the tent, frustrated to be left behind.

Alex Williams trotted to catch up to Carol, the shuttles growing larger by the moment. "So, what's the plan?"

"Martin wants us to be the last-ditch defense for the Seekers. You take half and get into the trees and scrub that hide the caves from the ocean."

"OK, and you?"

"There's a bluff above the caves, the same one that becomes the north wall of The Pasture. I'll take the other half, and we'll set up there."

"How's the leg?" he asked sympathetically, noticing her slight limp and hard set of her face.

"Functional."

Carol's tone made it clear this was not something Alex was to be worrying about. When they got to the beach, Carol was surprised to find the Seekers already deployed in the areas she had been assigned, a 2K7X in every hand.

"Where the hell did they get those?" Alex asked. Carol just smiled and shrugged, wondering how Barnes had had the foresight to arm the Seekers.

"Callol!"

She turned to find Eaagher running to her. There would be no time for writing or translations now. Carol pointed to Eaagher twice, then to the area in front of the caves. Then she pointed to herself twice and then to the woods above. Eaagher waved his left hand. Alex watched this with wonder.

"OK, so?"

"Eaagher is in command down here, Alex. At least, I hope that's what we said. Work our people in with his and take your cues from him. I'll be command on the bluff."

Eaagher called to someone up above, a male appeared in the trees at the crest.

"Tuegar, good warrior, Callol will be there with you. Watch her and follow her direction as best you can."

"Eaagher, we are armed! We can defend ourselves!"

"Yes, we can, but now we have Friends to help. Tuegar! Understand well, good warrior: Callol is not to suffer Benh's fate."

"I understand, Eaagher."

Carol and thirty-odd of her crew scrambled back up the low cliff and into the woods behind the beach. As she looked down from this higher vantage point, she could see that it was unlikely the enemy would land directly opposite the

Seeker's caves. There just wasn't room on the beach for a shuttle that big. Looking around, she saw how the woods faded out to the north, sloping gently down to the ocean. If they were coming directly for the Seekers, she thought, that is where they'd land.

The male Eaagher had spoken to came to meet her as she was surveying the ground.

"Tuegar."

She waved her left hand, touched her forehead, and responded, "Carol."

She pointed to the beach in front of the caves, then up at the oncoming enemy, and shook her right hand, *No.*

Then she pointed to the open area to the north, again up, and shook her left hand, *Yes.*

Tuegar responded *yes* and they moved quickly the hundred meters to where the woods began to thin. With plenty of sign language and waving hands, they managed to deploy the fifty Seekers and thirty *Antares* crew in a long line under the trees, facing the likely landing area. Carol found herself a small depression near the extreme right of their line and settled in to watch developments. Tuegar knelt nearby, watching the enemy shuttles approach.

Carol could see that the enemy ships were slowing down and descending. It would not be long now. She saw Tuegar's large hands flexing and un-flexing his grip on the weapon. He was nervous, anxious, but watched the ships approach without looking away. She took that as courage, suppressing his fear and preparing for the task at hand. *A good sign*, she thought.

Aboard *Columbia*, Kieran Barker was pacing his small command center.

"We could still lose this engagement."

Barker's cold statement caught Dan Smith by surprise. Barker had always been cautious, but confident, even when the Type V had tagged half his ships.

"Yes, sir, we could. But, we won't."

Barker looked at Dan and shook his head. "I wish I could be so confident, Smith."

"It would have been better had *Intrepid* been able to fire on them."

"I'm not so sure. If she'd fired, I think they would have bugged out. They have other priorities."

"The Seekers."

"Always. Where are we now, Smith?"

"We're fifteen degrees east of the Seekers, sir. Two-hundred-kilometer orbit, moving west."

"I want you to strike the shuttles as soon as they're down. Get on it."

Dan posted the attack to the task force's shared command net. Every commander would then know what was about to happen. He then moved quickly back to the Bridge, instructing Weapons Officer Victor Shoemaker to set up the attack. He walked to the Surveillance station when Melinda Hughes' deputy, Carl Hudson, was working to resolve all the data flowing in from *Cobra*.

"Carl," he said quietly, "we're going to hit the shuttles as soon as they're down. Get the radar up and feed Victor what he needs."

"Radar, yes, sir," he answered skeptically. Dan just smiled and went back to his Command position.

On *Intrepid*, Joanne jumped as she saw the last update from *Columbia*.

"Jessie! Get me Hayden."

Communications Officer Woodward made the link in a few seconds, and Joanne knew she had to be quick and to the point.

"Natalie, listen, *Columbia* is going to strike the shuttles as soon as they're down."

"Um, that might get a little messy down here, ma'am. You know, exploding alien spacecraft, giant hunks of white-hot metal falling on us, that kind of thing."

Joanne had to smile; Natalie Hayden certainly understood how to get her point across. "Pass the word and take cover."

"Yes, ma'am. Might I point out, Captain, just what a shitty idea I think this is?"

"Not my idea, Natalie, but noted. Good luck."

"Yes, ma'am, thanks."

At about a thousand meters altitude, the shuttles began to split apart, one heading towards *Antares*, one to the north end of Seeker Beach, just as Carol Hansen had anticipated. The other four were clearly headed for The Pasture. Seeing this, Liwanu Harry rallied his platoon away from the *Intrepid* shuttle and double-timed east to cut the enemy off before they could get to the Seekers. Natalie secured her shuttle, picked up her weapon, and followed the Marines. There would be no need for her to fly them anywhere. The battle had come to them.

Carol watched the enemy shuttles split up, and there could be no question where one was coming. She stood up and moved down her line. She was pleased to see that they had found decent cover in the trees, weapons loaded and ready.

"One shot, everyone, one shot at a time!" she yelled. "Take your time, pick your targets, wait for the tone. There's plenty of ammo but let's not waste it. And, for God's sake, keep your butts down!"

She felt Tuegar's hand on her arm, pulling her back to the cover she had found. It felt strange, but he was right; she needed to get down, too, just as she had told her crew. Tuegar dropped in position to her right, and another Seeker fell in on her left. They were all focused on the enemy shuttle as it approached the ground. It would not be long now.

Liwanu and his platoon were still running towards the Seeker caves as the hatches dropped open and the enemy came flooding out. He was surprised to hear a loud volley of 2K7X fire as the first enemy soldiers hit the beach. Then he heard a second volley, and a third as he approached the position that Carol Hansen and Tuegar were holding.

The situation was suddenly and enormously ugly for the enemy soldiers. Bodies now blocked their exit from the shuttle, fatally slowing them as they tried to climb over and shoot at their attackers. Still, they kept coming, many firing from within the shuttle to try to press down the heads of their opposition. They managed to get several dozen off the shuttle alive, and into some boulders along the shore. With this protection, their aim became better, and Carol and Tuegar began taking casualties. Liwanu Harry put his Marines on the left of the *Antares*/Seeker line, then worked his way to the edge of the woods to better understand the flow and the ground. His platoon sergeant Danka Barczak knelt behind the tree next to his.

"Someone saved our asses," Harry said.

The sergeant nodded. "For sure, sir. They picked exactly the right ground to defend." She pulled her head back as a plasma round went between them, terminating in flames in a tree just behind her.

"Damn!" The sergeant tried but failed to not sound afraid.

Harry saw the fear on her face. "So, Barz, where are you from?"

"Parma Heights."

Liwanu leaned around the tree and took a shot, dropping an enemy soldier as he tried to move to the left. He pulled back, then looked again at Barczak. "Where the hell is Parma Heights?"

Danka slipped down into a prone position, lifted her weapon, and fired twice. Without looking away, she answered, "Jesus L-T, don't you know anything? Southwest side of Cleveland."

"Tennessee?"

She stopped and turned to Liwanu. "Do I sound like a Smoky Mountain gal to you, L-T? No, Ohio."

Liwanu smiled. "Never been there."

"You should see it someday. It's a great place; just don't tell anyone."

Liwanu shrugged off her comment, took one more shot and then began looking to his left with his binoculars.

Natalie, arriving right behind the Marines, kept her head down as she scurried along the rear of the line. Near the point of the line, she recognized someone.

"Hello, Hansen."

Carol rolled halfway over and smiled. "Good morning, Lieutenant Hayden." Carol rolled back over, aimed, and took out a window in the front of the space-craft.

Natalie dropped to the ground next to Carol and slammed a new magazine into her weapon.

"They're going to Bludgeon these things, you know that, right?"

"So I've heard. Hopefully, Barker won't blow us up right along with it. But meantime, I'm going to have some fun."

"Fun?"

"Yeah." Carol took careful aim at the side of the shuttle about two-thirds back and fired four times in succession.

"What the hell are you doing, Hansen?"

"If I can puncture the tanks, maybe we keep them here, and, maybe, just maybe, we can fry a few while they're still inside."

Natalie lined up her own shot at an enemy who appeared to be rushing the bluff. "You have dark fantasies, Hansen, were you aware of that?"

"Oh, yeah. When it comes to these shitheads, you bet I know it." Carol took one more shot and was rewarded with a high-pitched whine and sudden sensation of heat on her face.

As Liwanu looked to his left, he could see where the woods ended in a wide grassy area with little cover. He ducked down and moved to the far left of his line. More plasma bolts were striking the trees around him, which meant the enemy was getting stronger despite the pressure from Hansen's crew and the Seekers.

Sergeant Barczak was right behind him.

Liwanu looked at her and pointed to the open area. "Take first squad, circle wide left, and, I mean, far wide, so they don't see you, understand?"

She followed Liwanu's gesture.

"Yes, understood."

"Good, then come up as close as you can behind them. We have to exploit that flank."

"Yes, sir, will do." Danka took the squad and moved off.

Just as Carol was inwardly celebrating setting the enemy shuttle on fire, an-other appeared low behind it and landed quickly on the sandy flats.

"Where the hell did that come from?" she asked.

Natalie shook her head. "I don't know, Hansen, but we have a real problem now. Damn."

Liwanu Harry appeared suddenly between them, as if he'd been teleported from somewhere else. "OK, this is trouble. I just sent a squad to push them from the left, but — "

He was cut off by four plasma bolts that struck the trees above them.

" — now we've got even more to deal with." He crawled out to the very edge of their position, a bit of rock that delineated the beginning of the bluff above Seeker Beach. The heat from the first enemy shuttle was winding down now, and he could see new enemy soldiers peeking out from the right side of it. Obviously, the cover they gained from the first one had given them time to get off the second one unscathed. *How many?* he wondered. *Hundreds? Thousands?*

Another plasma shot above his head got him moving back to where Carol, Tuegar, and Natalie were methodically firing at whatever they could see.

"I sent a squad around the left. They should be opening up the flank in a few minutes."

Carol nodded, ignoring that he had repeated himself, then turned to the Seeker next to her. "Tuegar!" Carol pointed to the left, trying to pantomime a movement around to the rear of the enemy. Tuegar followed her hands, then raised his left hand.

"Does he understand?" Liwanu asked.

"I think so. Hard to know for sure."

"How's their shooting?"

"Pretty good."

"Well, we're holding."

"Yes," Natalie said, "but holding isn't enough. We need to kick their asses off the planet."

"Well, Lieutenant Hayden, there are a lot more asses to kick now."

Something caught his eye, and he suddenly raised his weapon and took out a soldier who had moved just a little too far to the right of the dead shuttle.

Dan stood on *Columbia*'s bridge with Kieran Barker. "I can't do it, Admiral. It's too damned close!"

Barker looked at the low-resolution visual image, and there was no question: Smith was right. The enemy shuttle had set down far too close to the Seekers and was now in close combat with Fleet Marines.

The Surveillance tech looked up from her IR workstation. "Admiral?"

"Yes?"

"Sorry, sir, I couldn't help hearing. You might want to see this, sir. The first shuttle on the north end of Seeker Beach is on fire."

"Wait, the *first* shuttle?"

"Yes, sir, the one we thought was headed for *Antares* never made it there."

"Why am I just hearing this?"

The tech had no answer for that, and Barker didn't press the point. Whatever the reason, it wasn't her fault.

"Where is it now?"

"Just set down north of Seeker beach, behind the one that's on fire."

Natalie looked up at the sound of explosions coming from The Pasture. *Columbia*'s Bludgeons had struck. Natalie and Carol exchanged a worried look and Natalie rolled over on her back, looking in the sky to the south.

"I see fire, but no huge fiery melty chunks coming our way."

"OK, well, that's nice."

"Victor!" Dan called as he watched the results of their strike on the enemy shuttles.

"Yes, Captain?" he asked as he walked from the Weapons station to Dan's command position.

"Good work, Victor. Detonating early worked just like you thought it would."

"Yes, Captain. Lots of holes means a more diffuse explosion and less energy for shrapnel. So, safer for our side, just as deadly for theirs."

Dan smiled. "Well done, Victor, well done."

"Thank you, sir. I just wish we'd gotten them before they landed."

Lieutenant Harry's two medics were finding plenty of work behind the line at the edge of the woods. Three *Antares* techs were dead, five Seekers with them. There were a half-dozen more with burns severe enough to take them out of the fight. The medics worked quickly to bandage what they could and move the wounded further back, out of immediate danger. For now, anyway.

Liwanu Harry himself was considering what he should do next. He had only seconds to decide. Danka's move to the left would help, drawing the enemy's attention, at least partly. Meantime, there was a whole new shuttle-full of enemy pouring out on his center and right. He was on good ground, high and well protected with trees. He couldn't abandon that position, at least, not entirely. But they had to hold on the right or the Seeker families could be lost. Hopefully, they were deep within the caves below him, but unless they could keep the enemy out, it would be a bloodbath.

He turned to Carol. "What do we have on the beach?"

"My XO with thirty crew and maybe fifty Seekers."

"Radio?"

"No."

"Shit, OK, we need them to push forward. See those rocks the enemy was behind? We need to take those back and hold the enemy away from the cave entrances."

The *Antares* crewman next to Carol spoke up. "I heard that, Lieutenant. I'll go."

Carol turned at the sound of a familiar voice. "Cornell! Are you sure?"

"Yes, ma'am. What should I tell them, Lieutenant Harry?"

"Just push forward and take those rocks. Tell them to wait for Barz to open up from the left. Give her a minute to distract them, then move quickly. Is that clear?"

"Yes, sir." Cornell slithered back from his position and headed for the beach.

As he went, Harry worked his way to the right, instructing the crew and Seekers there to concentrate on the right side of the shuttle.

"Keep them bottled up behind the shuttle, understand? We're going to flank them from the left and then strike from the right."

A plasma bolt told him he'd lifted his head just a little too high, and he ducked down into the grass as he moved back to Carol and Natalie.

Intrepid fired nine Bludgeons as soon as Kirkland declared a solution on the three enemy cruisers approaching the Seeker's settlement, now a vast mess of dead enemy, broken spacecraft, and Marines.

"Weapons are away, Captain."

"New targets, Captain!" Marco Gonzales called.

"What is it, Marco?"

"More troop carriers, Captain. Six more just came over the horizon, descending into the atmosphere."

"Kirkland?"

"Not yet, Captain. We're reloading. Give us a couple minutes."

Sergeant Danka Barczak crawled slowly through the tall Big Blue grass, finally coming to a point where she could see the enemy position. She arranged her squad in a line as close to the enemy as she dared. They were to the right and behind the enemy, and could clearly see their backs. She lined up what looked like the leader in her sights and gently squeezed the trigger. Twelve more shots followed hers by a half-second.

David watched in horror as six more targets appeared over the curve of the planet.

"Didn't *White* go looking for the mother ships?"

"Yeah, supposedly," Jack answered.

Evans looked over at his two best analysts. "Just keep tracking, gentlemen. *Intrepid* and *Columbia* will have to do the shooting."

"Yes, sir, we're on it. Still...feel kind left out of the fight, you know?"

"Yeah, I wish we could stick it to them, too, but let's just do our jobs, OK?"

Browning jolted suddenly. "Radar shows a large number of small objects falling from the enemy cruisers, sir."

"Lazy dogs?" David asked.

"Probably," Evans answered, the picture becoming clear to him. "So, scatter and suppress the defense, then land a second wave to take advantage of the chaos on the ground."

"Like you said before, sir, they've gotten imaginative."

Aboard *Intrepid*, Marco Gonzales' heart dropped as he watched the radar picture change. "They're dropping weapons, Captain. Looks like Lazy Dogs to me. Too small to be RFG's."

"Damn it! Kirkland, can we shoot yet?"

"Just now, Captain."

"Fire!"

Kirkland set twelve Lances loose on the enemy shuttles. He secretly hoped that other ships would be firing on them as well — his solution was weak, and as the shuttles moved lower into the atmosphere, a hit was less likely.

"They're leaving!" Gonzales called out.

Sure enough, as Joanne looked at the radar, the enemy cruisers were accelerating rapidly away, leaving her nine Bludgeons with nothing to hit.

"Dammit! Jessie! Get me Barker."

With the sound of gunfire all around, Natalie's almost didn't hear it when her NetLink went off again. *Lazy Dogs ETA 2 minutes.* She grabbed Carol Hansen by the shoulder and showed her the message.

"Oh, great. This day just keeps getting better."

Liwanu Harry dropped between them. "What can we do?" he asked.

"Not much. I'd get behind a tree, but, well, that would be unwise right now."

Carol sent another runner to tell Alex. Hopefully, they could get into the caves or find some kind of cover. Harry radioed a warning to Danka Barczak about the Lazy Dogs, but there wasn't much she could do without exposing her squad to the remnants of the enemy they were reducing moment by moment. She decided to hold her position and hope for the best. They were taking fire from the newcomers, too, and Danka began to worry whether they'd be able to hold out much longer.

Alex Williams' group on the beach initially had an inferior firing angle on the enemy. When the enemy soldiers started to move around the rocks in response to the fire they were taking from their right flank, they walked directly into his sights. Eaagher didn't hesitate, stepping out into the open with his 2K7X raised. The enemy was clearly surprised to be taking fire now from three sides. Eaagher, understanding what was at stake and what Harry was asking of him, ran full speed to the rocks, followed by a half-dozen other Seekers and Alex Williams. They crawled up and around, finding secure firing positions to attack the enemy collected behind the still-smoking first shuttle.

Carol's runner arrived too late to give Alex any warning about the Lazy Dogs, but the rest of the small force managed to get into cover among the rocks that had over the years fallen from the bluff. Liwanu, unable to just wait, moved to the left to check on his Marines still firing into the massed enemy.

Major Wayne Barnes scattered his Marines best he could. There was no protection available in the middle of The Pasture, where they were still fighting off the remains of the enemy invasion force, but he tried to move them as far apart as possible. The attack took only seconds, but as it ripped through his force, he heard the strange sound of hot metal striking the ground, followed by screams of pain and yells of alarm. The enemy had only managed to get a few hundred soldiers off the shuttles before *Columbia*'s Bludgeons hit. The strike killed all still aboard as well as many already on the ground. In typical fashion, they never retreated once engaged, and that weakness allowed him to outmaneuver and reduce them with light losses on his side.

Now, as he lifted his head once the Lazy Dogs had passed, he smiled with some satisfaction that several of the enemy also lay on the ground, killed by their own weapons.

The smoke rising from the shuttle covered much of the sky, creating a sinister dusk over Seeker Beach as the Lazy Dogs arrived. Tuegar pressed Carol to the ground and covered her with his body. A second Seeker protected Natalie in the same way. There was a loud *zip* as a Lazy Dog buried itself in the meter-wide space between them, the exact spot where Liwanu Harry had been just moments before. The two women looked at each other in surprise, both at their protectors and at the steam rising from the small hole in the ground.

"Good God, that was close," Natalie said, suddenly frightened.

"That's twice," Carol said, looking grimly at the hole as Tuegar released her. "I hope they don't get a third shot at me."

But several of her crew were not so lucky; there were three more dead, and five with severe wounds. Four Seekers were killed as well. As they assessed the losses, a sudden but familiar sound crashed into their ears. The second shuttle was now outgassing, burning, apparently a victim of a Lazy Dog strike. The heat rising quickly from behind forced the enemy soldiers to move away from their protected position, firing up into the woods and pushing towards Eaagher and Alex's position in the rocks.

Liwanu knew that on his left there was a clear path to the enemy, a gentle down-slope that ended on the beach. Carol's position was higher, with a sharper drop from woods to the ocean. There was smoke rising from Danka's location, a clear indication that they were taking heavy fire from the enemy. But they were also highly effective in reducing the enemy force. Still, if the enemy made a decisive move to Liwanu's left, he'd be hard-pressed to keep them off Barczak.

He saw clearly that he could still lose the Seekers. If the enemy pushed hard enough, they could overtake his position. That could not be allowed. He ran back to where Carol and Natalie were watching the fight.

"OK, here's the deal. We have more force in the center than we need, right? They're not coming right at us. Keep your people here. Except, Lieutenant Hansen, I want maybe a third of your force moved right, to give us more concentration on that side. If they try to charge the Seeker caves, you will have to hold them off."

"OK, I get that. What else?"

"I am going to take two more squads over to the left and try to drive them out from behind the first shuttle."

"But, that's towards the Seekers."

"It's right into your line of fire, too. And they'll be pinned between the shuttle and the ocean. It's a natural kill zone."

"OK, anything else?"

"Yeah. Don't miss."

He was gone in an instant, moving left and organizing his Marines, heading forward and left at a dead run. As the enemy engaged the moving force, the *Antares* crew and Seekers among them fired on the enemy, driving them back behind the shuttle.

Carol ran to the far end of her line, taking every third person (or Seeker) and moving them to the right and packing them in as close as possible. As she did, she could see Eaagher and Alex in the rocks, firing intermittently but mostly keeping their heads down. She also heard firing from below her, the cave-front force letting themselves be heard.

The enemy force was now in an impossible position. Fire behind, pellets from their left, and another force blocking them on the right. Hundredth-Commander Talh crouched behind the first shuttle, his feet black with the blood-soaked sand of this horrible, worthless planet. He was in a trap, he knew, the kind of trap he'd long ago learned to ensnare others in. His orders were to take the caves behind the beach and kill the damnable Scholars there. It was hard to focus on that goal as Combatants were dropping all around him. The Scholars were supposed to be lightly armed and easily subdued. What he found, in fact, was a maze of heavy, well-aimed, and deadly effective shooting. He was facing Vermin, not Scholars, and in far greater numbers than he had been instructed. Talh was distracted by the feathers burning on the back of his head, too. He'd been too close to the shuttle that delivered him when the death darts fell. He worked his way to the left, coming finally to the front of the dead first shuttle. He could see a pile of rocks between himself and the rise that covered the first of the Scholars' caves. In front of it, he could also see a mass of dead Combatants. From time to time, a head, either Scholar or Vermin, would appear above the rocks and fire in his direction. Five Combatants lay just beyond the protection of the ship, clearly having moved a little too far outside its cover.

Talh moved back, looking at what he had left. A hundred, perhaps, out of five hundred dispatched. And how many Vermin were dead? He had no way to know, but they hadn't moved off and the volume of death striking his Combatants had hardly abated. If he waited here much longer, they'd all be dead. If they rushed towards the Scholar Caves, they might also soon be dead. But, if they could make it that far, they would have better cover and might be better able to protect themselves. In the time he took to think about this, eight more Combatants fell, some suffering from appalling wounds, blood, and bits of flesh scattering all around him.

There was no more time to think, he decided. It was time to conquer, time to be the Preeminent.

"They're coming!" Natalie yelled as the enemy spilled around the right side of the first shuttle, running towards the clump of rocks where Eaagher and Alex were hiding. Liwanu's Marines were still on the move but quickly turned to their right, firing at the enemy as they came on. Several Seekers and *Antares* crew sprinted to the rocks under heavy covering fire from the beach force. All but one made it, adding their weapons to the half-dozen already there. From the woods above, the results of Liwanu's redeployment bore serious fruit as the concentration of fire withered the oncoming enemy.

As the enemy neared the rocks, Liwanu moved further left, keeping the enemy's flank in play. The Marines dropped prone into the grassy field and fired into the open side of the enemy formation. As they turned to defend against the

Marines, reducing their fire on the beach force, more Seekers and *Antares* crew ran to the rocks, climbing up and handing the enemy another nasty surprise.

Carol watched the battle evolve from her position on the point of the bluff, picking her targets carefully. There was one near the back of the enemy mass, wearing a red vest and apparently shouting orders at the others. She carefully drew down on him and squeezed off one GS round that separated Hundredth-Commander Talh's head from his torso.

Natalie, who had also seen the red vest, looked over at Carol. "Killjoy. He was mine."

"There's plenty more."

"I get the vest."

Carol smiled. "OK, fair enough."

Their commander dead, the rest were dispatched quickly as the Marines pressed in on them from the left, pinning them against the ocean.

"Like shooting fish in a barrel." Liwanu would say later.

As the sound of gunshots was fading, Carol jumped at the sound of an explosion in the sky to the east, followed quickly by three more. Liwanu and Natalie heard the explosions as well, and as they spun around to look, four out of the six approaching enemy shuttles were falling into the ocean. The other two were turning rapidly and climbing.

"Natalie, look! They're getting away!" Carol said with a mixture of sarcasm and relief. The three officers smiled, and as they turned to see to their charges, two more explosions lit up the sky.

"Uh, no," Natalie said excitedly. "They're not."

Their relief was short-lived, however, as Ullnii came running with grim news from the beach.

Carol followed Ullnii down to the beach, where a crowd was surrounding a figure lying in the sand. She pushed through to find her friend and stand-in at the Weapons Station, Jon Swenson, dead on the beach. They had all tried to get as flat against the bluff as possible when the Lazy Dogs started falling, but Swenson was still busy pushing people out of danger when the first one struck.

Eaagher and a few others were wounded, too, cut by shards of metal when a Lazy Dog shattered against rocks nearby. But none of them were seriously hurt. Most of the beach force had come through without injury. Alex Williams suffered a couple burns from near-misses defending the rocks, but he would be fine.

Weapons Chief Guzman came to Carol sadly. "I yelled at him, Lieutenant. I yelled at him twice to get under cover."

Carol nodded. "I'm sure, Chief. You've worked with him even longer than I did. You know what he was like."

Even when he was leaning over her on the *Antares* Bridge, she had never seen such emotion in Guzman.

"I will miss the Great Dane, Lieutenant. I will miss him very much."

Carol and her crew moved hesitantly back from the caves and the bluff and gathered together. She was lucky, she knew, that Swenson was the only officer she had lost; her officer ranks were already too thin. But truthfully, the lost techs and chiefs were an enormous blow. Ten good people, most of whom she knew by name, were gone in what felt like an instant. With them went uncounted years of irreplaceable Fleet experience. Several were veterans of Inoria, now gone in their second encounter with the enemy's falling death.

As the lost were assembled, Carol stood over one for a full minute. Natalie stood patiently next to her. James Cornell was the first *Liberty* crewmember Carol had found that ugly day on Inor. He'd stuck with her and Terri Michael, moving over to *Antares* and following Carol down to the surface of Big Blue. A Lead Weapons Tech, Cornell had become Guzman's best assistant, on the Bridge when Terri Michael was killed and Carol wounded. Now, he lay motionless in the grass on Big Blue, an ugly burnt crater unmistakable in his left chest.

Eaagher came and knelt by him, then looked up at Carol, waiting.

"What is his name?" Natalie prompted.

"Cornell," Carol replied quietly, "James Cornell." She turned to Natalie. "He was the first living person I found on Inor."

Natalie nodded sadly as Eaagher touched the man's head, spoke his name in benediction, and then paused a moment. Finally, he rose, placed his large, strong hand on Carol's shoulder, and then moved on.

Carol waited for Eaagher to make his rounds, then started the long walk back, Hayden at her side. She could still hear occasional shots in the distance. The Marines were still cleaning up around the downed enemy shuttles.

"I need a ship, Natalie," she said without looking up from the path in front of her. "I just need a damned ship and I'll go kick their ugly purple asses myself."

After a dozen more steps, Hayden turned to Carol and replied, "I know the feeling, Carol. I know it very well."

Carol's leg was complaining loudly as they returned to their temporary quarters in the Marine Encampment. She gritted her teeth as she stood listening to Liwanu explain to Barnes and Martin how well Carol had picked the ground, and how bravely her crew had done in the firefight. She heard only parts of what was said, settling for a general understanding that they were happy with her and the outcome until finally they were done and she could leave and get some rest.

Carol dropped exhausted on her bunk and sat for a long time, her head in her hands. Finally, she pulled out her journal and began to write, tears slipping down her cheeks, her face trying to lock the pain inside.

Dear David –

Well, I'm alive. (No duh, I know) I should be thankful for that, I suppose. But Jon Swenson is gone. Nine others, too. Some to the enemy infantry, several, including Jon, to the Lazy Dogs.

Jimmy Cornell was killed today. He was maybe 21. Weapons tech. Jimmy was the first crew I found alive in Inoria, and so the first person I ever led in combat. I wonder if he ever realized that. I've worked really hard, David, really hard, to keep them all alive, get them all home. But today he lost his bet on me.

I'll miss Swenson. Jon was the best —the crew called him 'The Great Dane' and they meant it. Jon was so patient with me when we Liberty survivors came to Antares. He put up with me doing half his job 'cause I knew I was in way over my head. He and Guzman pushed me and, at the same time, had my back. I owe them.

They came to push us off today, David. They came really hard to kill us all, but we held. My crew was great. Martin and Barnes were complimentary, but really I just got lucky and Intrepid's L-Ts Harry and Hayden made the difference.

Now I'm the one with letters to write. I hope I can do as well as you did. Not looking forward to those.

Leg is whining a lot about the workout it got today, but I peeked under the dressing and it's healing OK. I'll be fine.

I need a ship, David. I need to grab their throats and make them understand just what kind of fatal mistake they've made.

Love you.
Carol

Marine Encampment
Big Blue
Sunday, March 26, 2079, 0500 UTC

After setting down her journal, it took a while, but Carol managed to sleep a few hours before her dreams recounting the day woke her. She got up, shook off the remnants of the dream, and headed to the Marine commissary for coffee. Beta Hydri was high in the sky, local noon still more than two hours away, but for Carol, it was early morning. After dousing the Marines' extra-dark super-strong witches-brew with cream and sugar, she turned to find a place to sit. Alex Williams waved to her from a table in the far corner, and she gratefully sat down across from him. She was not interested in solitude right now. Before long, Jayvon Dean, who had been slightly wounded on the beach, joined them, a bandage covering the left side of his head.

Lori Rodgers wandered in shortly thereafter. "OK, who called this meeting?" she asked brightly as she sat down.

Carol forced a smile and raised her hand. "Not guilty."

"I couldn't stay asleep," Jayvon said quietly. "So, when Lieutenant Hansen wandered out, I figured I'd come along."

"Yeah, I get that," Lori said with a smile, pointing to Dean. "Jayvon woke me up when he stopped snoring."

They sat and caressed their cups quietly for a moment, listening to the echoing crash of trays and silverware, the white-noise of a dozen conversations punctuated with laughter and the occasional shouted obscenity. It was a bright island of normal in an ocean of abnormality.

Alex turned to Carol, "So, Carol, what now?"

She shrugged and sipped her coffee. "I don't know. I want another ship, but I don't know where I'm going to get one."

Alex looked around the group before responding. "Whatever you find, we're with you."

"That'll be up to Fleet," Carol answered with no small amount of resignation.

"Screw Fleet!" Miguel Anthony said, a little too loud, as he sat down. "What have I missed?"

Lori answered for the group. "Carol wants another ship and we're all going with her."

"Damn straight we are. Is there something around we could steal? I think I could hot-wire one if we need to."

Even Carol had to laugh at that. "I don't know," she said. "The Marines were so happy with us — you never know, we might get inducted."

"Well, screw that, too," Miguel answered. "I love them, don't get me wrong, but I'm a Fleetie, not a Jarhead."

As the laughter again died down, Alex returned to his serious tone. "Anything from Powell?"

Carol shook her head. "No. Word is they'll be checking out Enemy Station and then Alpha Mensae. We won't hear from them for a couple weeks."

"Another visit to e-prime? Wow, brave!" Jayvon said.

"They got away with it before," Lori responded. "They'll be fine."

Carol nodded but didn't say more.

"Long time to be out of touch?" Lori asked her.

"No more than for everyone else, Lori. We're luckier than most, really."

There was a long silence, broken by sips and shifting in their seats.

"Jayvon, how's the head?" Alex asked.

"Still burns a little, but not too bad. Woke me up. But another few millimeters, and you'd all be toasting me when you got back home."

"I, for one, am delighted their aim was that far off!" Lori replied, putting her arm around the younger officer. "It just wouldn't be the same without you."

"It'll never be the same," Carol said flatly. "Michael, Lewis, Soto; now Swenson and the others. I don't know how things could ever feel normal again."

Alex shook his head. "But, Carol, it felt normal on *Antares* after *Liberty*, right? We'll recover, Carol. It's what we do. We grieve, and then we go on. Scars and all, we go on."

"We had Terri Michael then, and Commander George, too. Now, it's just us."

Miguel looked around the group. "I'll take us, Carol. I'll take 'just us' any day."

She nodded slightly. "Thanks, Miguel. But I am no Terri Michael."

Alex leaned closer to her. "Were you not listening a minute ago, madam Senior Lieutenant? Did you not hear your fellow officers committing to follow you into whatever is next? Did you miss that?"

Carol looked away, her face in a kind of stiffly neutral expression that they had not seen before. "Jimmy Cornell followed me, too. Don't forget that."

Lori was about to respond when Denise Long dropped into the seat next to Alex. "What the hell is this? Did I miss a memo?"

"Nope," Jayvon responded, "Just trying to figure out how to steal Carol a ship."

"Cool!" she said, ripping open an apple with enthusiasm. "Which one? When do we leave?" She took another bite. "Oh, and who do we bribe, and with what?"

Alex just smiled and turned back to Carol. "See?"

Carol was forced to turn back and smile back at him. Something had opened up in her. "OK, fine. You want to throw in with me, fine. I'm all in with you jokers, too."

"Excellent!" Miguel responded. "Now, we need some tequila."

"What?" Carol exclaimed. "Scotch!"

"Scotch? O-M-G get me some Bourbon! I sooo miss my double-oaked," Lori answered.

"And soda..." Denise added.

"Next chance we get," Alex said. "We're going to blow off some serious steam together, OK?"

Carol raised her coffee cup to theirs. "I look forward to it!"

They moved on to discussing what to have for breakfast, then headed to the line to fill their plates. There was thick-cut French toast, ample supplies of bacon and ham, fruit that was canned but still cold and refreshing, eggs, and of course, something beige and chunky over burnt toast. The Marine cooks gave them good-natured grief about eating all their food, only to be reminded that much of their supplies had come from *Antares*. They finished and turned in their trays and dinnerware, then returned to their seats with more coffee.

As they sat there reviewing the meal, Carol's NetLink buzzed. She read the message twice as the others watched her intently.

"Ho-ly shit," she said quietly.

"For a good Christian girl, Carol," Alex said, smiling, "you have a truly bizarre favorite cuss word."

Carol looked up at Alex and winked. Her face seemed transformed, the stress lines were gone, and there was a smile in her eyes.

"What?" Lori asked.

"Miguel, you're not going to need to hot-wire one for us, after all."

"Yeah? Why not?"

"*Sigma* is on her way here. I've been promoted, and she's ours."

Miguel smiled broadly. "Hot damn, I do love this Fleet."

Jayvon looked thoughtfully at Carol. "Never forget what Abernathy said, ma'am."

"I don't know what the future may hold, but I know who holds the future," she answered, barely above a whisper.

"Exactly. He was talking about a different time and a much different problem, but I remember it as such an inspiring statement of faith."

Carol looked up at Jayvon. "It was something my father used to quote whenever things got hard on the farm. Thanks for reminding me."

Alex looked at her for a few seconds. "We're with you, *Commander*, all the way, whatever happens."

Carol, unable to speak, just nodded slightly.

Cobra
Near Enemy Station
Thursday, March 30, 2079, 1040 UTC

Cobra snuck up on Enemy Station, the enormous enemy facility just a few light-years from Beta Hydri, homing in on their intrusion detection signal. Evans smiled to himself as they easily came within a thousand kilometers of the enormous facility. The enemy had no idea they were there, nor would they.

David was again at Center Console, quietly running the operation. By now, the techs knew how to pass data between themselves, keeping each other in sync. Enemy Station stood out clearly in the IR spectrum. It was difficult to see with the naked eye, not because it was so well camouflaged, but simply because there was so little light to reflect. Still, a decent picture could be had at this distance in a few minutes with the long-range telescope in pixel-accumulation mode. The docks were full: ten ships locked in place. Many were obviously damaged. Three others hung in space nearby, apparently waiting their turn.

"I have identified the ships, Center," Ray Salazar called over the intercom.

"Go ahead."

"Two Type V's, one Type II, seven Type I's and three Type III's."

"Half a freaking fleet out there."

"Yeah, thirteen fat targets."

"Fourteen, counting the station!"

Evans came into the operations center. "A full house, I see."

David smiled. "Indeed, sir. A baker's dozen of excellent targets."

Evans walked to the large visual display at the far end of the room. "Can we see what they're doing? Are they repairing them or what?"

"Not yet, sir. We have the resolution to see a person at this range, but in PA mode, I'm not sure we can if they're moving around much."

"Nothing so far?"

David shook his head. "No, sir. They could be working from the inside, too."

"Or," Margie Nixon interjected, "they could just be sitting there."

"Why?" Evans asked.

"They've never been competently opposed, right? That's the current theory?"

"Yes," he answered, intrigued.

"So why would they need repair facilities? They always win, right?"

David looked at Evans, but he was really asking Margie. "OK, following that logic, why run here? Why not go home?"

Nixon was not dissuaded. "Fuel? Food? Don't know what else to do?"

Evans pulled up a stool to the worktable in front of Center Console. "It's an interesting theory. Chief Salazar, how close do you think we could get without being seen?"

"We reflect almost nothing in VHF, sir. So, I'm not too concerned about the detection signal. For insurance, I'd keep the dinner plate out of sight, but I think we could get to a hundred klicks pretty safely."

David agreed. "Yes, but, at some point, sir, a three-hundred-meter dark spot might attract attention, if they're doing any kind of occultation surveillance."

"That should not be a problem at a hundred kilometers."

"Yes, sir, agreed."

Evans picked up the ship phone. "Nav... Lena, take us to a hundred klicks from the Station, and take your time...Yes, that will be fine." He hung up and looked at David. "Twelve hours."

"Yes, sir. We'll keep an eye on them in the meantime."

Lena Rice took the whole twelve hours to spiral the ship in towards Enemy Station, ending at a hundred kilometers, more or less. Once settled in their new position, the picture became much clearer. They saw no activity around the damaged ships, either docked or floating nearby.

"Could be night time for them," Gregg Browning commented.

"Wait," David said, "Don't we have a table of Sols for e-prime?"

"Yes," Margie answered, pulling up her NetComp. It only took a few seconds. "You might be on to something, Lieutenant. It's just about sunrise at the central city on e-prime, so, yeah, maybe they're still asleep."

"OK," Evans responded, "We'll watch another twelve hours. Then we move on to Alpha Mensae."

Soon after, Jack Ballard arrived to take his shift. After briefing him, David took a seat at the work table.

"David, go to bed."

"I will, Jack. I just want to stick around a while if you don't mind."

"I don't, but Evans might." After Jack finished his review of the last six hours, he slipped off his headset. "So, how's Carol doing? How's the leg?"

David smiled. "She's healing. She misses you almost as much as me!"

Jack laughed. "I doubt that David, but we were a pretty good team. That adventure on Beta Hydri was pretty intense."

"I know. Some truly excellent work there, Jack."

"I know she's healing physically, but how is she feeling?"

David took a moment to think about how to respond. "Losing Captain Michael, then Ryan, then Marcia; all that was hard on her."

"Hard on me, too," Jack said quietly. "That was my crew as well."

"Yes, Jack, I know."

"At least I didn't have to be there to see them killed. That's something I won't miss."

"Carol's had a tough time, Jack. But, she's pretty tough herself."

"No sign of PTSD? Nightmares?"

"She says no, and I believe her. Alex and the rest of the crew will keep an eye on her."

Ballard nodded his understanding, then went back to monitoring the lack of activity on Enemy Station. David left after an hour, heading to his cabin for some sleep. Before crawling in, he took a few minutes with his journal, something he had not done since leaving Carol on Big Blue.

Dear Carol,

Talked to Jack tonight as he was coming on watch. Your losses are his losses, too, and I think he feels them more deeply than I realized before. He's fine, don't get me wrong, but I could see the pain on his face.

ES is full of busted ships, but we can't see anyone working on them. Margie N thinks they don't know how to fix anything. Not sure I agree, but sure looks like it for now. Maybe they're working inside where we can't see them. IR is negative, though, so seems kinda doubtful. We'll keep watching for a while, then on to AM.

I am so glad we had a couple hours on BH. I know you'll be fine. You're the strongest person I know. You inspire me, Carol, to be better at the things you do so easily. Jack feels it too, I'm pretty sure, and so does your crew. Just be you, my love, and everything else will fall into place. Just be you. No one, including me, could ever ask for anything more than that.

Love,
David

Preeminent Ship 562
Deep Space, a safe distance from System 849 (Beta Hydri)
Earth Equivalent Date: March 31, 2079

Ship Commander Gotk looked out on what was left of his force. He still had three Combatant Carriers, but two-thirds of their force and invasion landers had been expended to no gain. He had just three other ships left, his own command ship and two other medium-sized fighting cruisers. He alone would bear responsibility for this defeat, but he saw further engagement with the Vermin as a complete waste of life and resources.

Gotk had done something no other commander had thought to do: he studied the reports of those who survived fights with the Vermin. He also examined their reactions to his own attacks. From these, he learned some of their tendencies and capabilities, even potential weaknesses. He designed his last assaults on what might best exploit those tendencies.

Yet, he had failed. Their ability to adapt to new circumstances, and their skills with weapons unlike anything the Preeminent had previously encountered, had turned out to be more significant than his new tactics. He had surprised them, but surprise was not enough. He had deployed the new attack beacons, and he knew he'd caused confusion and pain on their ships, but this, too, was not enough. They'd detected the beacons and disabled them in a single rot. Had he come with more force initially, he might have done more damage, but Gotk could not now conceive of a scenario where he would have ultimately defeated them. *It was as if they had seen it all before,* he thought. He could not imagine where or how.

If Gotk had a religion, its foundation would have been that his society was the greatest in the universe. Therefore, they had rights and privileges denied lesser species, whose primary purpose was to obey their rule. There was justice and mercy somewhere in his belief system, but such concepts could naturally only apply to themselves, not to those they brought to obsequia by force. Obsequious compliance was the standard for the conquered; anything less was punishable by death. But deep within his mind, the seed of doubt was growing: *What if it was all a lie?*

He had certainly done better than Hess Tse Sim at the Deist's System, inflicting more damage on the Vermin and suffering fewer Combatant losses. His methods had been less crude and more innovative. He'd clearly surprised the Vermin more than once. But he had not been victorious, and that could be fatal on return. There were no Vermin or Scholar captives for him to parade before the Council. It was, in fact, far more likely that it was the Vermin who now had captives to exploit. The Combatants were well indoctrinated, but not educated in any nuanced way. They would likely break under pressure from hunger, or thirst, or pain. But they actually knew very little beyond small weapons and fighting, and so offered little value to the Vermin or threat to himself.

But it was little relief to Gokt. They were still his combatants, and their loss his responsibility.

It was time to return to his home planet. Already several ships from his force were under repair at the way-station nearby. His six vessels were either whole or only slightly damaged, perfectly capable of the transit.

"Honr," Gokt called, "Set our course for home, maximum speed."

"I fear what awaits you there, sir Gokt."

"We will see, Honr. We will see the quality of wisdom which resides in the Council." He hesitated, then repeated himself. "We will see."

Once safely in FTL, Gotk retired to his cabin to rest, write a message to his female, and draft his message to the council. The last would be the least satisfying, and unquestionably the most dangerous.

April 2079

Domicile of Scad Nee Wok
Preeminent Home Planet
Earth Equivalent Date: Monday, April 3, 2079

When Asoon returned from her daily language study, Scad Nee Wok was waiting for her, his face agitated, and his tail stump quivering.

"We must talk, Asoon. There are things I must tell you."

"Yes, Scad?"

He paced as he talked. "You do not understand the real nature of this society."

Asoon looked at him in surprise. "How could I not? I was hatched into this society, lived within it my whole life! I am not still wet from my egg, Scad! We are the Preeminent, the highest form of life on this planet."

"You do not know because it has been concealed from you. It has been concealed from everyone for a hundred revolutions."

Asoon felt her first tinge of real fear. "A hundred revs? How could this be?"

"Yes. And what I tell you is dangerous. Some powers do not want this known."

"Very well, Scad, now you have frightened me sufficiently, please continue."

He sat across the eating table from her, placing his long fingers on the surface. "What do you know of the food and materials the cargo ships deliver?"

"Yes, of course, they come from other species, in star systems we protect. They send these things in payment."

Scan paused a milRot, then continued. "They do not. We protect no one. We conquer, Asoon, and if an alien species will not kneel to our rule, they are exterminated like pests."

"Impossible. The SD would not — "

"It is not the SD's choice, Asoon. The Central Council of the Armada decides. They say we are the most advanced species in the universe, and as such, we have a right to take what we wish."

"And kill any that resist?"

"Yes."

"Disgusting."

"Yes, it is."

"Why are you telling me this?"

"The SD came to me today. Even now, the Armada fears them, because they need the technology the SD provides. This time they told me outright that our pairing was intentional. They have a plan to remove the Central Council and stop the Armada."

Asoon looked out the window at the street outside. Vehicles were moving past as if everything was normal, as if this was not the day her whole concept of herself and her heritage fell apart. She spoke, still looking out the window. "An old male and his maleChild?"

"How did you know?"

"They are the same who came to me that first day. They are somehow involved in whatever is happening." She turned back to Scad. "Now what?"

"They are not just involved. The inner circle of the SD has chosen them to execute their plan. But, to your question, how well do you speak the Vermin language?"

"They call themselves 'human,' Scad, and out of the dozens of human languages the SD recorded, I have learned the predominant language of commerce, called English. It is horribly complicated, Scad. It gave me nightmares for weeks."

"You can communicate in this English? You can have a conversation?"

"Yes. My teacher feels I am almost as competent as she."

"Very good, Asoon, very good."

"There are rumors of a great defeat somewhere, Scad. Rumors that many houses will soon be vacant."

Scad waved his agreement. "It is no rumor. This defeat may be the opportunity the SD needs, the leverage necessary to supplant the Central Council."

"Again, what do we do now?"

"You continue your studies. Think of how you would start a conversation without getting killed first. They may shoot at us on sight."

"An interesting problem. And you?"

"I have a favor in the Council I may use to our advantage. And..." Scad thought for a moment. "And, perhaps, sow some discord there that would provide a useful distraction."

"You said this is dangerous."

"It is. If the SD comes to move you out, just go and say nothing of this ever again."

"But if the SD is planning — "

"No, Asoon. You know nothing of the plan. You are just a humble student of the Vermin language. Am I clear?"

"Yes, PairedMale. I understand what you say."

"Good. If they take me, I would not want you to die, too."

"You are a good male, Scad Nee Wok. I am hopeful for our future."

146

"If we have one, so am I."

The Marine Encampment
Big Blue
Thursday, April 6, 2079, 1700 UTC

Carol and her officers walked out from their temporary home to the shuttle *Intrepid* had sent down for them, lugging their duffels behind them. She smiled as Natalie Hayden stepped out of the cockpit.

"Good morning, new Commander Hansen!"

Carol reached out her hand to Natalie, who held it an extra moment. "Hello, Natalie. Good to see you."

Hayden slipped her hand into her right pocket, pulling out something gold and shiny. She reached for Carol's collar as she said, "It's time you were in proper uniform, ma'am."

Looking down at the oak leaves in Natalie's hand, Carol asked "Where in the world — "

"I got Commander Bass to contribute them. So, thank him. There!" Natalie smiled as she pulled another set of oak leaves from her pocket. "I almost forget, these are mine." She smiled warily as she pinned them on herself. "You know, Carol, they may take all this lovely rank away from us after the war. It's happened before. We could all be lowly Lieutenants again."

"Well, maybe, but they'll have to pry these out of my cold dead hands!"

They laughed together as they moved on into the shuttle, and Natalie flew them up to *Sigma*. She settled outside the airlock and, in a few moments, was hard-docked to the big ship. As the airlock hatch swung open, a tall, thin, blond Lieutenant Commander was waiting for her.

"Welcome aboard, Commander Hansen. I'm Peg White."

"Good morning, Commander White." Carol waited a few moments as the rest of her officers got off the shuttle, Natalie standing behind them. She then stood directly across from White, came to attention, and extended her hand.

"I relieve you, Commander," Carol said carefully, the words thick and strange in her mouth.

Peg White, seeing the nervousness in Carol, nodded her head slightly as she took Carol's hand and replied, "I stand relieved." She pointed down the passageway. "Shall we?"

They walked the short distance to the main central passageway, then forward directly on to the Bridge. It had been destroyed in the fight that killed Len Davis and most of his crew, but now it shined brightly with new equipment and furnishings. Any traces of the battle, the blood, the bits of human tissue, the dents,

147

the holes in the bulkheads were now impossible to find. Natalie tagged along to see the changes. She'd been on *Sigma* once for a short time as a fill-in and had fond memories of it.

"I took some liberties with the repair," Peg said, a hint of conspiracy in her voice.

"Liberties?" Carol responded, curious.

"Yeah. The computers are all-new, the latest generation. I declared all the sensors and radars unusable and installed new."

"Nice."

"Oh, one more thing."

"What's that?"

"No rotaries. I was able to get FleetShips to send me the new tube release system."

"You got a TRS?" Alex asked incredulously. The TRS was an enormous improvement over the bulky rotary launchers. There were small 'bump-outs' on each side of the ship where the rotaries previously resided. There was now no delay; weapons could be deployed almost as fast as the loaders could move them into place.

Peg just smiled. "Yes. Admiral Whittaker's compliments. He was the one who really convinced FleetShips to give us one and jump *Sigma* ahead of the rest of the fleet. I mean, you know, we had her in the dock, so, why not do as much as we can?"

"That's an amazing improvement."

"Anything else?" Lori asked.

"Those are the big ones. The rest was cleaning, repair, repainting, that kind of thing. Down below, she can carry a hundred Marines in a pinch. FPI upgraded the Drive, too. She'll consistently do 1.3 now."

Carol nodded her understanding. "Commander White, would you join me in the duty cabin?" Peg's eyebrow went up in surprise.

"Of course."

As they entered the small space just off the Bridge, Carol could see it had already been cleaned from White's transit from Tranquility II. The surfaces shined, the desk was cleared out, and the bunk had been freshly remade. She appreciated the thoughtfulness of it as she moved inside and sat at the small desk. Peg closed the door and sat across from her.

"What's on your mind, Commander?"

"Carol. First, if David were here, he'd want to thank you for all you did for the *Sigma* crew. I was with him when he got your message last July."

"Oh, yes, that. So sad."

"It meant a great deal to him."

148

"Well, it was, after all, my job. But we did try to do our best for them. I thought it would help the families."

"It did. That I can tell you for certain."

"Good. But somehow, I don't think that's why we're here."

Carol nodded. "I just want to be sure you're comfortable taking Navigation. My XO is only a Senior Lieutenant. You could demand that position."

"Carol, listen, I was promoted same time as you. I still kinda feel strange when people call me 'Commander.' Plus, I have no combat experience."

"Still — "

Peg raised a hand to stop Carol. "Still, nothing. I want to get into the fight. I am tired of tinkering and fixing and waving bye-bye. I'll gladly take Nav; it was my first assignment and I always loved it. We'll be fine, I promise."

Carol hesitated a few seconds, then decided to take the woman at her word.

"OK, then. Let's talk about the crew." Carol opened up her NetComp and they reviewed the crew assignments together. Hakim had allocated only what was needed to get *Sigma* to Beta Hydri. Still, after going back and forth for a short while, they were able to combine the two groups well enough that they felt that the ship was ready to fight. There was one serious gap, but Carol had an idea of how to fill it.

The crew manifest complete, Carol stood and opened the hatch, calling for Alex Williams. Three made for quite a crowd in the small duty cabin.

"Alex Williams," he said, reaching a hand out to Peg.

"Peg White."

They looked at Carol expectantly.

"OK, here's how this is going to work. You two are my personal guardrails, understand? Come in here at any time and chew me out if I need it, OK?"

Alex and Peg exchanged surprised looks.

Peg answered, "OK, Captain, if that's what you want."

"And none of *that* in here, either of you. We need to be frank with each other, and I can't have you holding back because I'm in command."

Alex responded, "But, Carol, you *are* in command. The final decision, the final responsibility, is *yours*, not ours."

"I understand that, of course, but I need the best advice I can get to make those decisions. I trust you. I need to hear what you think."

Alex smiled. "Well, Carol, as you know, being frank with you has never been a problem for me. "

Peg nodded. "I think I can promise you my honest opinion. But, as Alex says, in the end, it is your call, not ours."

Alex shifted his legs and leaned back against the hatch, arms crossed. "But really, Carol, I have a different question."

"What's that?"

"Those of us who have served with you have complete confidence in your abilities."

Carol leaned back in her chair, unsure of where Alex was going. "Yes, I know."

"Do *you*?"

Carol met Alex's eye for several seconds, and in that short time she went back over all the decisions she had made, the instructions and orders both deadly and trivial she had meted out over the last year.

Peg White was watching her, too, assessing more deeply Carol Hansen's readiness for the job at hand.

"I know what to do, Alex. I know how to decide, and yes, I'll take the rap for whatever goes wrong."

"But?"

"But I need to hear voices other than mine, thoughts other than mine. It would be foolish of me to have all these resources available and not use them."

Peg and Alex exchanged a look. They understood what she was asking.

Alex answered, "So, when do we leave?"

Peg nodded, then asked, "And, since I'm the Navigator, where, exactly, are we going?"

Carol just smiled. "Later."

It took most of a day to get the *Antares* crew transferred and settled on the resurrected *Sigma*. Alex Williams managed the berthing assignments and worked to merge the skeleton crew that had come with Peg White from Tranquility II with the *Antares* people. Changes were the order of the day, and Alex kept the assignments consistent whenever possible, but he also wanted to make sure the two groups were completely integrated.

The lone holdover from *Sigma*'s original crew was FPI Lieutenant Tsubasa Kondo. He had waited patiently on Tranquility II, assisting with the Drive upgrade. He still considered *Sigma* his personal ship, and he had no intention of going anywhere else. Lt. Roger Cox was two techs short in his Intel shop, but assured Carol they would make do. They had no doctor, only two med techs and a lead nurse practitioner. They'd just have to avoid getting hit as much as possible.

The one gap that worried Carol was Weapons. With her now in command and Jon Swenson lost, she had no ready replacement for Weapons or Weapons Maintenance. The transit crew had included two good Weapons techs, and since the new TRS needed fewer hands, the section was otherwise decently staffed. Captain Hakim had allocated Peg enough techs for the transit, but no officers, so

Carol would have to make do with what she had. She got up from her desk in her duty cabin and walked aft to the Magazine. Chief Guzman was sitting in the Weapons Maintenance Officer's small office, updating the crew roster and inspection records. He stood as she approached.

"Stay there, Chief," she said. "We need to talk."

Guzman slowly sat back down as Carol closed the door and dropped into the chair across from him.

"This is backward," he said.

"Lots of things feel backward right now, Chief. Did you notice the galley is on the wrong side of the main passageway?"

He laughed. "Yes, ma'am, I did."

"I hit my head on a door that wasn't there a little while ago."

"Some adjustments, Commander, will be required."

She leaned forward. "Actually, Chief, that's why I'm here."

"Well, I was pretty sure this wasn't about the galley."

Carol smiled briefly. "No. We've fought this enemy together many times, Chief."

"Yes, we have."

"And it was mostly with me pointing and yelling, and you doing all the work."

"Well, I think that's unfair, but, OK, go ahead."

"You taught me most of what I know about this business."

"Now, Commander, that's *really* unfair. Especially to your instructors back at the U."

She hesitated just a moment. "I need someone to run Weaps, Chief."

He nodded slightly. "Yes, ma'am, you do."

She looked up and met his eye. "I don't have anyone else, Emilio. Will you do it?"

He held her eye for a second, then nodded. "Anything you need, Commander, anything at all. Sure, I'll do it."

Her shoulders sagged with relief. "Thank you."

"One condition."

"What's that?"

"Don't try to hang some battlefield commission or whatever on me, Commander. I'll do it as I am if you don't mind."

"I don't mind, Chief. But, I will need you at most meetings in the wardroom."

"Fair enough."

"I'm putting Lieutenant Dean in charge of that division, Chief. Normally Surveillance and Intel would be under Weapons, but we'll reverse that for now."

"That makes sense. Dean is a good officer."

She stood up to leave, Guzman reflexively stood with her.

"Thanks, Chief. I owe you one."

"Glad to help, Commander."

Carol made her way back to the Bridge, where Alex Williams was trying out the new Conn workstation, studying the improved displays and controls.

"I solved the Weaps problem," she said, dropping into the command chair.

"Guzman?" he asked, smiling.

Carol looked at him in surprise. "How did you know?"

"Um, well, name another person on board who might possibly be qualified to take that position."

"Point taken. You agree?"

"Yes, of course. He'll do well. So, Captain, where are we going, and when are we leaving?"

"Later. What's our status, Alex? How much more is left to do?"

"In my opinion, we are ready to go whenever you give the word." Alex picked up his NetComp and read off the ship's condition as he swiped from screen to screen. "T-II filled the provisions for a hundred days...weapons are on board...nav system is nominal...I say let's blow this pop stand and go break something."

A slow, somewhat evil grin spread across Carol's classically beautiful features. "Fine. Officers in the wardroom on the hour."

As Alex sent out the notification, Carol picked up the phone to talk to Kieran Barker.

Cobra
E-Prime
Sunday, April 9, 2079, 1200 UTC

Cobra had been loitering at Alpha Mensae for two days when Rich Evans called for a status conference in the Operations Center. Rich sat in one of the observer's chairs along the forward bulkhead, flanked by XO Elaine DeLeon and Navigator Lena Rice. Opposite him, David sat on the counter that defined Center Console and Jack Ballard sat in the position itself. Ray Salazar leaned against the outside of Center, studying his NetComp.

David made the status report for the team, including the presence of several damaged ships near the ship factory in the asteroid belt, and the uninterrupted flow of who-knows-what to and from the surface. There was also a half-dozen warships in orbit close to the planet.

"That's all?" Elaine asked.

"Yes, Commander. There are the two new ships just outside the factory, five busted ships nearby, and the six in orbit."

"That can't be the whole fleet, right?" Jack asked.

"No, I doubt that it is," Rich answered. "But they have taken a nasty beating in the last few weeks, right? All three major attacks failed, costing them, what, forty-odd ships out of fifty-one dispatched?"

"Ouch. That has to hurt!" Jack responded.

David pulled up his NetComp. "Nineteen ships lost at Earth, which is all they sent—"

"That we know of," Salazar corrected.

"Right, true. Then, five of thirteen at Inor, and thirteen of nineteen at Beta Hydri. So, thirty-seven."

"We saw thirteen at Enemy Station when we were there, so, that's all but one?" Lena asked.

"Those numbers don't quite add up," David pointed out. "As Ray has said, they may well have brought some in from other locations. There were ships at Enemy Station before we came here last time — "

Evans waved the argument away dismissively. "I don't care about the counts. God only knows where they pulled ships from to assemble the three task groups. It's not important now."

"So, what is?" Elaine asked him pointedly.

"What is here now, and what are we going to do about them."

David shrugged. "Well, sir, you have our analysis on that. They tried to strike the ship factory at home. We think we should return the favor."

After Evans nodded, David continued. "But, honestly, at some point, Commander, they're going to have to want to talk, don't you think? I mean, we've cost them maybe trillions of dollars in equipment, and I don't have any idea how many thousands of lives."

"Yes, we have. You have sympathy for them, Lieutenant?"

"Not at all, sir. But we've lost ships and people, too, and it's no less in our interests to put an end to this war as it is theirs."

"Hmm," Evans responded in a noncommittal tone, a skeptical look on his face.

Elaine DeLeon smiled. "What Commander Evans is saying, Lieutenant, is that he had exactly the same idea in his duty cabin fifteen minutes ago."

Evans straightened up and turned to his XO. "Elaine, I can't stand a snitch. You're fired." More seriously, he turned back to Jack and David. "So, let's get a closer look at the ship factory. If we can strike that, it will cut off any hope they have of winning."

Jack looked up. "Assuming they don't have other factories somewhere else."

"Ballard, you're such a buzz-kill," Lena Rice responded.

"But," Evans said, "he has a point. There could be others, or there might not."

"Either way, sir," David said, "we know there is one here that we can strike."

"Lena, how close do you think we can come to the factory?"

"Well, unlike at ES, there's a lot of light around. At ten kilometers, we'd be about three times the angular size of the Moon."

Evans did some quick mental math. "Wow, you're right. I hadn't thought about that."

"Yeah, now, remember we're dark and long instead of bright and round, but I'd be concerned."

"But, can we do it?"

"Sure, just stay out of the plane of the system, and for God's sake, don't get caught in a transit."

"OK."

Salazar looked up from his review of the images they'd gathered of the ships around the factory. "And, sir, be ready to run like a scared little bunny if they manage to sight us."

Lena Rice laughed. "Good advice Mr. Salazar. I'll make sure we have a scared bunny course ready, just in case."

They moved in cautiously, taking a half-day to get above the overall plane of the planetary system and close to the enormous ship factory. The 180 MHz intrusion alarm was up. Ray and the techs compared what they were now seeing to earlier intercepts, and the signal strength was several times higher.

"They're afraid," he said to David.

"Yes, I agree. Let's get a monitor on that signal, Ray. If we see any change, it might indicate they've seen us." Salazar set up a data monitor on the signal which would sound an alarm if any change was detected. Margie Nixon was working at the RF station, and she put the signal in her headset as well.

The ship factory was still working. They could see movement around a ship under construction that appeared to be one-third complete. There were small spacecraft moving around one of the damaged ships as well.

David watched the visual telescope feed carefully, studying the structure of the factory, looking for likely areas to strike. Similar to the factory back home, the structure was attached to a large, irregular iron asteroid that was several kilometers in diameter, 'diameter' being a sloppy term in this case, since the body was hardly round. It reminded David more of an iceberg or a hunk of broken pavement. There were large solar arrays fixed to the asteroid, the first such technology that they had seen. A careful study of the images revealed that the solar collectors were thicker than what David knew, indicating to him that some technology other than what he knew from Earth was at work. Walking around the wreck at GL 876, he had not seen anything that looked like modern Earth technology; the whole thing felt like a World War II naval vessel, strong but not finely finished. But, he corrected himself, they had the Drive, which was believed to require some rare earth elements to operate. He was puzzled by the seeming gaps in their technological development. They'd obviously developed FTL transportation much earlier than Earth, and SLIP as well. But, their ships seemed somewhat crude by comparison to his. Some technological disconnects between cultures were to be expected, he knew, but the specifics of these particular disconnects puzzled him.

As David went back to examining the images, Rich Evans came into the Operations Center and sat on a stool, leaning against the counter on the left side of Center Console. "So, any thoughts?"

"Yes, sir. If we just want to turn it off, there are large conduits here." David pointed to round, linear structures leading from the solar arrays to the factory building. "If we cut those, the factory will lose power."

"There's no other power source?"

"No, sir. I really expected to see H2/O2 tanks around, but there aren't any."

"Could they be inside the asteroid?"

"Sure, but why do that? They haven't made any effort to hide or protect their tanks anywhere else."

"Yes, I see. How large are those?"

"Conduits themselves are about a meter in diameter, and there are ten of them. A well-placed Bludgeon or two should cut them all."

"But, David, why do that? Why not just hit the facility and be done with it."?

"It's a de-escalation, sir. I've been thinking about our conversation earlier. If we can accomplish our military goal - disabling this factory - without directly killing anyone, perhaps they'll get the message that it's time to talk."

Evans thought about that for a minute. "Maybe. I just don't believe they're able to think about giving up."

"That's a popular theory right now, sir, I know, but I think we should at least give them the opportunity."

Evans nodded thoughtfully. "OK, I'll include that in my report to Fleet." He stood up. "We're moving in an hour. I'm going to take her a light-year farther away from Earth and send a report home from there. I'll include your thoughts on this."

"Yes, sir, that's fine."

Evans hesitated, a small smile on his face. "So, how do you feel about Hansen getting *Sigma*? Lonely for your old ship?"

David leaned back in his chair and smiled widely. "Serendipity, sir. That ship needed a crew and the *Antares* survivors needed a ship. Makes perfect sense."

"They're supposed to be hitting Enemy Station soon."

"Yes, I read that. Carol will happily deconstruct that place, patiently and in detail."

Evans nodded his agreement as he turned to leave the Operation Center. "I have no doubt."

ISC Fleet HQ Intel Section
Ft. Eustis, VA
Wednesday, April 12, 2079, 1530 UTC (1130 EDT)

The message from Rich Evans surprised the brass at Fleet HQ.

```
PRIORITY 207904101145UTC
TO: CSTO
CC: CINCFLEET, FLEETINTEL, FLEETOPS
FROM: COBRA

1) INVESTIGATION OF AM REVEALS EXTREME REDUCTION OF ENEMY SHIP
PRESENCE.
2) SIX UNDAMAGED TYPE III CRUISERS IN ORBIT, FIVE DAMAGED
SHIPS NEAR FACTORY.
3) TWO NEW SHIPS ALSO NEAR FACTORY, PLUS ONE UNDER CONSTRUCTION.
4) CLOSE EXAMINATION OF SHIP FACTORY REVEALS SIGNIFICANT
WEAKNESS WITH OPPORTUNITY TO DISABLE WITH MINIMAL LOSS OF ENEMY
LIFE.
5) CONSENSUS ON COBRA RECOMMENDS THIS ACTION ALONG WITH BLOCKADE OF
SHIP TRAFFIC TO/FROM SURFACE, IN ORDER TO FORCE ENEMY TO
CAPITULATE WITHOUT FURTHER BLOODSHED.
6) COBRA STAFF ALREADY DEVELOPING PLANS AND TACTICS FOR BLOCKADE.
7) REQUEST AT LEAST FOUR WARSHIPS TO E-PRIME EARLIEST POSSIBLE TIME.
8) SUGGEST SHIPS RENDEZVOUS 20790515 AT ALPHA MENSAE (E),
WHICH IS CURRENTLY ON THE EARTHWARD SIDE OF THE SYSTEM.

END
```

CINC Connor Davenport leaned back in his chair, thinking about what Evans had suggested. He had received only the day before a long, emotional message from the Inori Embassy in New York, invoking their deep faith in Ino and their fundamental belief that the answer to an attempt at genocide must not itself be genocide. It implored the Fleet to find a way to close the war without excessive death, even on the enemy homeworld. The message raised eyebrows throughout Fleet HQ, and Davenport had spent an hour talking over possible courses of action with Chief of Operations Patricia Cook, Intel Chief Ron Harris, and Plans Director Fiona Collins. The hard discussion of what to do once the enemy had been pushed all the way back to Alpha Mensae had previously been raised, and tabled, as the fight had gone on.

It could be tabled no longer.

Davenport moved forward, leaning on his elbows. "Setting all the other questions aside, can we reasonably expect them to understand a blockade?"

Ron looked up from his NetComp. "I wish I could talk to Rich and Elias and hear exactly what they're thinking. I share your skepticism, sir, about a blockade. It may be a concept the enemy can't grasp."

Fiona looked over at Ron. "I agree, but it's worth a try, don't you think? Don't we owe that to the Inori?"

"I'm not sure we owe the Inori anything, Fiona. We've protected them, and the Seekers, at great cost to ourselves." Davenport paused to think. "But, like them, I am opposed to needless bloodshed. Patty, what about resources? What do we have?"

"*Sigma* will be striking Enemy Station in two days. They're available and not far away. He already has *Intrepid* and *Canberra* at Beta Hydri, plus *Columbia*. Those four should give Evans the force he's looking for, while still leaving a cover at Beta Hydri."

"In that case, Patty, we should move the time line up, don't you think? He's given us enough time to send ships from here, but he really doesn't need that."

Fiona spoke up, "Sure. But we can send more. We could easily give them *Jarvis* and *Chaffee* from Kapteyn since they're the closest. They could have *Yankee* from Tranquility II. There are several at Inor that we could spare as well, say, *Dobrovolski*, *Soyuz*, even *Yorktown*, but they're almost as far from Alpha Mensae as we are."

Davenport sat up straight, something that usually telegraphed that a decision had been made. "OK, send what we can from Kapteyn to Alpha Mensae. I don't want to delay Barker's options any longer than necessary. When would they get to Alpha Mensae?"

Fiona ran the numbers on her NetComp. "Sometime around May 7, depending on how quickly we decide and how fast they can get off Kapteyn."

"Fine. Advise Barker and Evans of that. Then, let's cut *Yorktown* and *Yankee* loose and send them to Beta Hydri as a backup."

Admiral Cook nodded. "Yes, that sounds about right to me, too."

There was a brief silence as CINC looked at his three deputies.

Fiona could see that something was on his mind. "What is it, sir?"

"Patty, what's the fastest ship we have in orbit at the moment?"

"*Bondarenko*. She's just back from repairs."

"OK, get Anna on the line and have her prep for a long trip down south."

"Yes, sir, of course. Might I ask why?"

"I'm going up to New York tonight to meet with the Board, then I'm going to Alpha Mensae. Time for the old man to put some skin in the game."

Fiona reacted first. "Sir, really, you don't have to do that."

CINC smiled. "Oh, yes, Fiona, I do. I've been sending friends and sons and daughters of friends out there for over a year now. Time for me to do the same."

"Yes, sir," she answered quietly.

CINC got up and opened his office door. LCDR Noah Peters, CINC's reliable assistant since before the war began, was at his desk in the outer office.

"Noah, I need a transport up to ISC HQ in New York, soon as you can arrange it."

"Very well, sir. Anything else?"

"Yes. I'm going to Alpha Mensae as soon we can get *Bondarenko* resupplied."

"Fine, sir, I'll be ready in an hour."

Davenport smiled. "Just me, Noah. You're not — "

"Yes, Admiral. I am. Going with you, that is."

"Noah, who do you think — "

"Non-negotiable, sir. If you go, I go."

"OK, Noah. Get yourself packed for a hundred days out." He turned, went back to his desk, and sat down.

"Intimidated by your assistant, sir?" Ron offered.

"Shut up, Harris. I let you go, didn't I?"

Fiona smiled. "I think Noah is right, sir. You *should* have an aide with you."

"OK, fine, that's enough mutiny for one day. Out!"

Two hours later, CINC and his persistent, loyal aide were lifting off the ISC Fleet Shuttle pad, heading for New York.

An hour after that, they entered the brightly lit ISC Board Room. The twinkling lights of the New York City skyline poured in on three sides, a view matched by only a few rooms in the world. He came slowly into the center of the ornate space, which was stuffed full of representatives from the ISC countries. The din of dozens of conversations was almost overwhelming. He could not help but notice the Inori ambassador, towering above everyone else and speaking intensely to someone. As the Inori moved to one side, Connor saw a face he had not seen in a very long time. She looked away from the Ambassador and saw him, too, her gaze intense enough for the tall alien to stop talking and turn around to see what she was looking at. Her eyes locked him in place until her widening smile invited him to come closer. It took him a second to pull his feet out of the emotional concrete holding him in place and move towards her.

"Hello, Dagny," he said hesitantly.

She embraced him, then reached up and kissed him on the cheek. "Hello, Connor. How are you? How is the family?"

He looked at her with a mixture of sadness and relief. "We are all well. How are things with you and the children?"

"I am doing better, and so are they. They're strong like their father."

"I am so sorry, Dagny." Then, after a moment, he continued quietly. "I miss Dean so much; he was such a good friend."

She embraced him again. "He thought the same of you, Connor. He loved every day in the Fleet; loved the work, the crews, even the leadership." As she let him go, she looked to his side, smiling as her tone brightened. "So, Connor, who is this?"

Connor was suddenly aware that Noah was still with him. "Oh, my manners! Commander Noah Peters, this is Dagny Carpenter. Noah is my aide."

"Dagny *Forstmann* Carpenter!" she corrected.

Noah extended his hand with a slight bow. "An honor to meet you, ma'am."

She smiled widely, the emotion of a few seconds before now dispelled. "I am glad to meet you as well, Noah. Connor always did need a keeper!"

"Dagny, if you're going to tell — "

"That story about the time Randy and I bluffed you out of your shorts? No. But, where is that sidekick of yours?"

"Yakovlev? Find the vodka, you'll find Stan."

They passed a few minutes in friendly conversation, then Connor spent several minutes in a forthright discussion with the Inori. CINC did a lot of listening in those minutes, but when he spoke, he reassured the Inori that their priorities would be heard and that he would consider them in his planning.

At last, the Chair called the Board to order. Each representative spoke of their concerns about the termination of the war. Finally, the Inori ambassador rose to speak.

"It has been a painful time on my planet. We have suffered terrible losses, lost priceless places and historical beauty. But we have made progress in our recovery, and as Ino surrounds us, Inoria will someday return to the glory it once had." He paused to take a drink of water. "Here is the water of Earth, drawn from your rivers, your streams, but in it I see Ino. I look upon your magnificent city, your enormous, complicated world that strains the understanding of a simple Inori as I am, and I see Ino. We are a hardworking people, grateful for your partnership, and grateful that you would hear our thoughts in this forum. Ino calls us to work together, in toleration and forbearance to all. We know that evil exists, but to answer evil with evil is not the way of Ino. And to answer an attempt to obliterate us with the obliteration of the enemy, is also not the way of

Ino." He turned to Connor. "We must be safe in our city, brave commander, as must all, but we cannot simply be a worse version of that which we fight."

The Chairman called on Connor to give the Seeker's position.

"Commander Rich Evans, a man most of you know as an Inoria veteran, asked the leaders of the Beta Hydri Seeker culture what should be done with the enemy. I think their reply is instructive, if I may paraphrase: *We are conscious living beings. Our consciousness is our complete existence. With it, we think, we learn, we hope to come to wisdom. We mourn the end of a consciousness because the accumulation of life experience and wisdom ceases and is lost forever. We do not desire the death of the enemy, but rather our own safety and the ability to rebuild our home and raise our children there.*"

Randy Forstmann, his sister at his side, concluded with a forceful argument.

"We must agree, all of us, that this war must end in a manner that enriches our values, that brings forward the best of who we are. The Inori have expressed their desire for a peaceful and just conclusion. As the species which, other than perhaps the Seekers, has suffered the most, we should give their position great weight. The Seekers themselves, as Admiral Davenport has presented, call first for peace and safety. All three species want a return to a quiet and productive time, and the eradication of the enemy will not achieve that end."

The discussion was respectful, but sometimes painfully pointed. Many of those present were grieving their own losses and demanding satisfaction, reparations, even execution of the enemy leadership. In the end, Davenport's instructions were simple, leaving him with plenty of flexibility in how to achieve the goals the Board specified: an end to further conquest, cessation of conflict with human forces, and the eventual surrender of all subjugated worlds were the essential requirements. Connor thought them more than reasonable but carried natural doubts about whether the enemy would have the same opinion.

Perhaps, he thought, *we can leave them with no choice.*

Early the next afternoon, CINC and Noah Peters boarded a shuttle for *Bondarenko*. Captain Anna Nonna greeted them at the airlock and escorted them to her regular cabin, which CINC would use for the trip. She would remain in her duty cabin just behind the Bridge. Noah was bunked nearby, sharing with another officer.

Anna stopped as she completed her short tour of the facilities. "Dinner is at 1800 sharp, sir. Please try to be on time? The officers are anxious to see you."

"Yes, Captain, I will be there."

"Excellent, sir. See you then."

Nonna had hardly made it from her regular office back to the Bridge when the ship vibrated slightly, then settled into the typical low-frequency rumble of the Forstmann Drive. They were on their way. Davenport had never been on *Bondarenko* at FTL, but the rest of the crew looked at each other in surprise, wondering how long Nonna would keep her at flank speed. The answer was, of course, all the way to Alpha Mensae.

Just before 1800, Connor changed out of his office blues into a regular slate-gray work uniform and headed for dinner. As he entered the wardroom, precisely on time, the room came to attention. Everyone else had already run through the buffet and were at their seats.

"At ease, please, and do remember I am just a passenger on this trip."

They all sat, and after he had filled his tray, he found only a single empty chair in the center of one side of the long table. After he sat, as he lifted his fork to stab the salad, he looked across the table and nearly dropped it back on his plate.

"Hi, boss," Fiona said, smiling.

Columbia
Big Blue
Friday, April 14, 2079, 0700 UTC

Kieran Barker lifted his NetComp to read CINC's response aloud to his staff.

```
PRIORITY 207904121300UTC
TO: CSTO
FROM: CINCFLEET

1) CSTO AUTHORIZED TO PROCEED OWN DISCRETION CONSISTENT WITH
PREVIOUS PROPOSAL.
2) JARVIS AND CHAFFEE PROCEEDING ALPHA MENSAE ETA 20790506.
3) YORKTOWN AND YANKEE PROCEEDING BETA HYDRI TO BACK-FILL FORCE
THERE, ETA 20790505.
4) CINC ENROUTE ALPHA MENSAE IN BONDARENKO WITH AUTHORITY TO
NEGOTIATE CLOSE OF HOSTILITIES, ETA 20790509.

END
```

"He's coming himself?" Harry Hess asked, incredulous.

"Seems so," Barker answered.

"On the other hand, sir," Elias Peña said, "He's giving us a free hand to set the conditions for the end of the war."

Dan Smith leaned against the bulkhead. "And, really, it makes sense someone would need to have the ISC authorization to sign off on the settlement, right? That would have to be a UN or ISC mandate."

Barker nodded as he sat on a high stool next to their worktable. "Yes, that's correct." He looked up at Hess. "Tell Hansen to get herself to Alpha Mensae (e) after she's done at ES."

"Yes, sir."

"And, have *Intrepid* re-board their Marines and then proceed likewise."

Hess nodded. "Yes, sir."

Barker continued. "I think the enemy is unlikely to strike here again anytime soon. The Seekers are now able to assist in their own defense, tell *Canberra* to leave a couple squads behind but re-board the rest."

"What about the *Antares* contingent?"

"*Canberra* can take them, too. I want the *Antares* group there. Some of them were on *Liberty*."

They talked at length about the weapons load for the three ships. They had always preferred Bludgeons as the more destructive weapon. But Dan made a forceful argument for more Lances to be used as 'shot across the bow' weapons. When detonated well away from an enemy vessel, they would do no damage but would send the message that they could have been attacked, but were not.

Peña was skeptical. "We'll probably have to strike a few to make them see we mean business."

"Yes, perhaps," Barker responded. "But hopefully, they'll understand before we have to knock out too many ships."

"We could work on targeting, too, sir," Dan suggested. "Perhaps start with some nonlethal damage, like the SLIP transmitter, and then increase the pain until they stop trying to run the blockade."

"Yes, we'll talk that over with Evans when we get there." Barker slipped off the stool, signaling an end to the meeting. "OK, to summarize, we're sending *Sigma* shortly. *Intrepid*, *Canberra*, and *Columbia* will visit *Ceres* to re-arm, then proceed as soon as they can. *Ceres* will then follow. Any questions?"

There were none. Dan left the meeting and headed to the Bridge to get started towards *Ceres*.

He wanted to be first in line.

The Preeminent Home World
Earth Equivalent Date: Saturday, April 15, 2079

Ship Commander Sdom Roi Gotk rode down to the surface of his home planet in silence. He had done the best he knew how, better than anyone else who had encountered the Vermin, but still, he had failed. When the call eventually came to the Central Council, he knew it would likely not end well for him. Deputy Commander Thes Fea Honr rode with him, despite Gotk's desire that he remain aboard the ship. Honr was a good assistant; he'd done what was asked of him, and Gotk believed he should not bear any punishment for the outcome.

As he stepped off the shuttle into the bright light of his childhood star, Gotk was surprised to be met by three males from the Science Directorate, dressed in their typical dull, dark robes with bright but indecipherable writing on the fabric around their necks. The old one stood taller than the others, a middle-aged male like himself and a young one who looked to be just into maturity.

"Sdom Roi Gotk?" the old one asked.

"Yes. Who are you?"

"That is not important at the moment."

"Oh?"

"Yes," the young one said with insistence. "We would like to speak with you, Ship Commander."

Invitations to a conversation from the SD were more a mandatory summons than anything cordial one could possibly decline. Gotk looked back at the old one. Honr had stepped off the shuttle right behind him and was still standing by.

"And my assistant?"

"Thes Fea Honr may proceed," he said, turning to him. "But, Honr, we may desire a conversation with you as well, later."

"Yes, sir."

"And, if you please, Honr, you will tell no one of this encounter. Am I clear?"

"Yes, very clear." Honr didn't wait another moment, moving off to the transport area in front of the shuttle landing area.

"Well?" Gotk asked after Honr had disappeared into the crowd.

"We have a transport," the young male said, pointing. "This way."

The transport turned out to be a nondescript, older surface vehicle with darkened windows. Gotk noticed that they were just dark enough to conceal the identities of the occupants, but not so dark as to inspire curiosity. He'd seen perhaps hundreds of such vehicles on the streets of Core. How many, he wondered, were actually SD transports working secretly in the open?

The ride was short, two hands-full of turns and twists that lead consistently towards the center of the city. It was, therefore, no surprise to Gotk when the journey ended at the SD's large headquarters in the innermost hub of Core. The symbolism was lost on no one; while they might not know what the SD was doing at any moment, it was unknowably vital to them all. Gotk was escorted from the transport through a series of doors and hallways, terminating in a large conference room. The young one invited him to sit and provided water.

"Why am I here?" he asked as soon as the others were seated, his tail stump stiff with anxiety.

"First, Ship Commander Gotk, know that we are no threat to you."

Gotk looked at the young one for a moment. "If you were, you would say the same."

"Perhaps," the old one said, "but in this case it is true. We wish to hear of your fight with the Vermin."

Gotk took a drink from the tall steel container he'd been given. "I lost. What else is there to know?"

The young one shifted in his chair, "Quite a lot, actually. Tell us what happened, best you can remember it."

Gotk thought about refusing, demanding to be released, and running to the Central Council to report this impertinence. But there was something in the old male's tone and bearing that made him pause. He was probably dead once he got there anyway, so what was the difference if the SD killed him instead of the Council?

"I sent a detailed report to the Central Council, so—"

"We have read that, Gotk. We are interested in your personal experience and any additional insights into the Vermin you might offer."

Gotk was shocked that the SD could be reading the Armada's communications. The way the young one said it, this was clearly a routine occurrence. *Fine,* he thought, *if they wanted the truth, he could give it to them.*

"The Vermin are unlike anything else we have ever encountered. They are superior to us in every way."

Gotk expected to be killed outright for confessing that, but instead, the old one just said, "Yes, continue."

"They can adapt to new situations faster than we can. Our ship's weapons are just as deadly as theirs, but they hide in their dark ships where they see us, but we cannot see them."

"What of the Detectors?"

"They worked for a short while. The beacon-mines did their job, but as soon as we arrived, the Vermin concentrated their attacks on the Detector ship."

"Almost as if they knew it was coming?" the middle-aged male asked.

"Possibly, I think it more likely that they recognized it as something new and, therefore, dangerous."

"And what of the second attack?"

"They had located and removed, or disabled somehow, the beacon-mines. When the second strike arrived, the Vermin had reestablished their advantage, and we could not detect them."

"I see. Tell me of the invasion."

"We were ordered to find and eliminate the remnant Scholars. The previous attempt there had failed, and it was believed that the location was correct, but the forces inadequate. I landed one full cohort, but the Vermin had installed a ground force in advance, and we were unable to overcome them."

164

"Almost as if they knew you were coming."

"Again, you say that. Is this something you are aware of?"

The old one looked almost happy, which Gotk thought very strange. "Just continue, Commander."

"Their pellet weapons are superior to anything we have ever seen. Their accuracy, power, and rate of fire are hard to fathom. Unlike the Scholars' small weapons, one hit from a Vermin weapon will easily kill. The Combatant officers could not even get the force off the landing shuttles before coming under heavy fire."

"How many Combatants survived?"

"Of those who were dispatched to the surface, none. Our maneuvers surprised them enough that the first cohort was landed, but it was quickly destroyed. They attacked the landed shuttles both from the surface and with anti-ship weapons from orbit. The second cohort was struck by weapons from orbiting Vermin ships before they even reached their landing assignments."

"None?"

"I did bring one full cohort back because I saw no point in wasting their lives for nothing."

"Yes, that is sensible. What, Commander, will you recommend to the Central Council about the Vermin?"

"They are resourceful and intelligent, sir. They will find us if they haven't already. We lack the tools to hold them off. If they choose to destroy us, they will."

"And so?"

The answer welled up as a sudden, coherent, immutable truth in Gotk's mind, yet still, he hesitated. So often, he knew, saying an unpopular truth could be costly, even fatal. But he'd decided to talk to these males, and in doing so, he'd decided to trust them.

"The lie of Preeminence must be exposed for what it is. We must go to them and find an end to it before it is the end of us all."

The three males exchanged expressions of agreement, and, again, happiness.

The old one turned to him. "Indeed, Commander. You have found the root of it all." He shifted his aging bulk in the hard chair. "You have trusted us, Gotk, and we know how hard that is."

"Yes."

"Now," the middle-aged one said, "it is for us to trust you. The Directorate is working to end this before all is lost. Can we count on your support?"

"I would need to know the details first."

"That is something I cannot give you. But I will say that we are considering an outreach to the Vermin, something to bring an end to the death on both sides."

"What do you need of me?"

"We will call on you when, and if, you're needed."

"I see."

The older one spoke again. "There is another ship commander who is with us. You know of Scad Nee Wok?"

"Of course. Wok took that fool, Kiker, to System 201 and barely got out with his tail thanks to Kiker's stupidity."

The three exchanged another agreement. "Indeed. Wok is working with us. Do not be surprised if he reaches out to you."

"I will be observant of any such communication."

The old one turned fully to face Gotk, his wrinkled hands folded on the long table between them. "I must tell you, Gotk, for your own conscience, this is no heresy."

Gotk snorted his skepticism. "We are taught Preeminence almost from our egg, sir."

The old one persisted. "Preeminence on this planet, yes, but even if one accepts the Council's conceits, a Preeminent culture must take care to encourage and nurture lesser species, that they, too, may flourish. It is not a cudgel for subjugation. This was the original teaching of the Guardians."

"I have never heard such an interpretation."

"I am sure not; it would not serve the Council's purposes. But I have read the old texts, Gotk, older than anything even in the SD library, and I am sure of what I speak. Know, too, Gotk, that there are others beyond Wok who are with us."

After the young male escorted Gotk out, the middle-aged looked across the table.

"'Others,' maleParent?"

"Asoon Too Lini, for one."

"Yes, but you perhaps overstated the matter with the plural."

"Perhaps."

Sigma
Enemy Station
Saturday, April 15, 2079, 2115 UTC

Taking a page from the enemy's playbook, Carol had *Sigma* slip out of FTL well away from Enemy Station, then coast the last million kilometers to where she was less than a hundred klicks away from it. Surveillance Officer Jayvon Dean watched the station grow in his sensor displays as they approached, and he could see the same ten docked ships and three more close by that *Cobra* had reported. He could not help the small smile that crept into his voice as he reported

166

to his captain that they had the targets identified.

Carol had made her orders clear in the wardroom before they left Beta Hydri. "We're going to hit Enemy Station. We're going to stay until it's completely destroyed. Am I clear?"

Jayvon had liked that part. In his mind, it was long past time to hold this enemy down and finish them off for good.

Weapons Chief Guzman echoed that sentiment. "We have solutions on all fourteen targets, ma'am. I am ready to shoot."

Carol looked over at Peg. "Nav, work us in to fifty klicks."

Peg stood and looked at her in surprise. Carol just smiled and nodded. In another hour, they were there. Jayvon's techs were listening to the proximity alarm. So far, there had been no change, and no reaction from the enemy to indicate they knew *Sigma* was there.

"Lieutenant Dean?" she asked.

"Well, at this distance, I can't tell what they had for dinner, ma'am, but for sure, they all need showers." The Bridge crew laughed at Dean's faux-serious delivery, and Carol looked over at Chief Guzman.

"Weapons free, Chief."

Guzman said quietly, "This is going to ruin their whole day!" as he pressed the 'Commit' control.

Their twin TPS's spat twenty-eight Bludgeons in less than twenty seconds.

Less than a minute later, Jayvon called out, "Multiple Bludgeon impacts, ma'am."

The IR sensor data was up on the main display over the Surveillance position, right in front of Carol's command chair. As they watched, heat plumes spread throughout the docked ships, with secondary explosions causing a cascade of damage that reminded Carol of a nuclear reaction. The enormous level of heat saturated the display, despite the tech's attempts to dampen down the sensitivity.

"We'll just have to wait a while, ma'am," Jayvon said. "It should settle out in a few hours."

"Very well. Nav, take us back to a hundred klicks."

They lingered there for six hours, waiting for the shattered ships and station to cool down. The wreckage was still hot as they circled it cautiously, both assessing the damage and watching for any reaction. Finally, Carol had seen enough.

"Nav, take us out to a thousand kilometers. The rest of you, secure from Alert Condition One, and go get some rest." She got up and walked to the Surveillance station.

"Lieutenant Dean, I want us to be watching for debris."

"Yes, ma'am, we were just talking about that. I think it was a good idea to back off a little. It reduces the chances we'll be struck."

"Right. Keep monitoring the enemy for any movement. If you see anything, let the XO know. I'm going to get a few hours' sleep."

"Yes, ma'am."

Carol walked the few meters to her duty cabin, then showered and changed for bed. She was dead tired, but there was one more thing on her to-do list for the day, so she took out her journal and pen and sat on her bunk to write while her hair dried.

Dear David –

I think today was my best day yet in this damnable war.

Twenty-eight Bludgeons, twenty-eight hits. No reaction at all from the enemy. The place was glowing in IR for hours. Sometimes I feel guilty about strikes. I mean, after all, those ships are all full of living, sentient beings. But after this last battle at BH I feel like they've asked for it, and I'm going to give them all they can stand (butchered WT Sherman reference intentional). I took Sigma to fifty klicks from ES today — I thought for a second Peg White was going to walk out on me, but she went along. I am really glad to get to know her better; she has such a great sense of humor.

The leg is finally healing up. It's been four weeks now. I can tell because it itches like crazy. But, no more pain (and no more meds), and I can walk pretty normally now. Marcia was right about one thing, tho...I took a good hard look in the shower tonight and it does indeed look like shit. Sorry about that. I miss her so much. We had great talks late at night. And no, not about you. Well, not always about you. She had this great street-wise, smart-ass wisdom about her that seemed so weird coming from someone who grew up well off and was so well educated. Someday I'll have to visit her parents and tell them.

I need sleep, as if you can't tell from this scrawl that used to be proper penmanship. Have fun at e-prime. I suspect I may be there soon, too. I feel somehow like we're now Barker's personal assassins.

I confess I kinda like that idea.

Love always,
Carol

By the next morning, Lieutenant Roger Cox had pulled another double shift in the Intel workroom. He had just two techs, but they were hard workers, and he was getting enough done to keep his captain informed. Before heading for his cabin, he made his way forward to the Bridge.

Carol was seated in the command chair, Alex Williams, next to her at the Conn. It was early morning, and Carol was going over the current state and position of her ship after her life-changing eight hours of sleep. She looked up as Roger came to the side of her position.

"Roger?"

"Good morning, ma'am. I thought you'd want to know that we've seen no SLIP activity on the scanner, either during the attack or afterward. So, I'm pretty sure Alpha Mensae doesn't know what's happened."

"Thanks, Roger. Get some sleep, OK? Looks like you could use it."

"Yes, ma'am, I am very happy to comply with that order."

After Roger left, Alex slid over next to Carol. "So, what now?"

"I want to move back in and do a detailed BDA, then we'll see what Barker has in mind for us at e-prime."

"He hasn't told you?"

"No. He just said we'll be out for a while, and we should not expect to come back with any ordinance aboard."

"Oh, I love that."

Carol smiled slightly. "Yeah, sounds really good to me, too."

They moved back down to a hundred kilometers, which was about as far as Jayvon Dean would agree to go without radar. On the IR sensor display, there were still a few hot-spots, even after eighteen hours. The proximity alarm signal was down. In fact, the whole radio portion of the EM spectrum was exceptionally quiet in this area. Dean wondered if that might be why they picked this place - any radio communications or active detection gear would stand out against the silence. Carol waited until both Dean and Peg White were back on the Bridge before stepping down off the Command position to talk.

"OK, so, we need to do a detailed damage assessment. If anything looks undamaged, we're going to fix that, understand?"

They all nodded their understanding.

"I'm perfectly aware that there has to be a lot of ship shit floating around, so how do we get in there close enough to get good images without denting the ship?"

Dean spoke first. "The only real answer, as I think you're aware, is radar. IR and visual aren't worth too much out here in the middle of nowhere."

"Yes, I thought you'd say that. Run at the lowest power you can, consistent with seeing clearly."

"As you say, Commander."

Carol turned to Peg White. "Take us to ten klicks, Commander, but take your time and work with Lieutenant Dean to avoid any, uh, accidents, OK?"

"Ten kilometers, yes, Captain." Peg gave her another long look and turned back to her station to get the ship moving.

It took four hours to move in close to what was left of Enemy Station. The radar revealed less floating wreckage than Jayvon had anticipated, from which he concluded that the major mass of debris had already moved away from the station, leaving the space near it relatively clear.

As they circled the devastated facility, they studied each ship and each station storage tank. They scoured the data feeds for any kind of motion, light, or other EM transmission that might indicate survivors or threats. After three trips, Dean was ready. Carol called the officers, plus Guzman, to the wardroom to hear his report.

"There is some IR activity, Commander." He pointed to an image of the station on the large wardroom display. "Here, and, um, here, for example. Looks like small areas where their life support is still operating. There are six of these areas on the station and two ships."

"What about their tanks?"

"Station storage is blown, ma'am. From what we see now, not all the ships had fires, but from the visible damage, we think they might have already been empty. I don't believe there is a single vessel here that can go anywhere."

Carol looked over at her Intel Chief. "Roger?"

"I agree with Lieutenant Dean, ma'am. We went over the imagery on each vessel, some in 3-D, and it's clear they have been incapacitated. I'm not saying they can't un-dock and shoot or something extreme like that, but otherwise, they're useless."

"Very well." She turned to Peg White. "We'll move back out to a thousand klicks for now. I want to watch a few more hours, then head to Alpha Mensae."

"You're not going to finish off these six areas?" Alex Williams asked.

Carol had started to get up but now settled back into her seat. "They're already dead, Alex. Who's going to come to their rescue?" She pointed to Roger. "No one at Alpha Mensae even knows this has happened yet, best we can tell. They'll likely either suffocate or starve to death before anyone gets here."

Alex sat up very straight and folded his hands in front of him. "Lieutenant Commander Hansen, ma'am, you would not leave a horse, or a dog, or, or, a, a *gerbil,* to die in this way. It's wrong."

Carol looked at him, surprised. "What would you have me do, Alex? Machine-gun the lifeboats?"

"You just said they're—"

Carol stood, slamming her pen down on the table so hard it shattered, the pieces flying over her head as she shouted, "I know what I said, Alex."

Carol Hansen rarely raised her voice, almost never in anger, and the shock reverberated around the room.

Alex, undeterred, met her ferocity if not her volume. "So how can you just leave them like this?"

Carol slapped herself back into her chair. "I am already tired, Alex, already tired, of deciding who dies now, and who is next. Then, who might get away. Or, not. We probably killed hundreds, maybe thousands of them in the last day. It's a staggering number, Alex. But fine, fair enough, it's war. Sorry, but you lose."

"So, what's stopping you now?"

Carol thought for a moment, and when she spoke the anger was gone but none of the intensity. "The one thing I am very sure about God is that I am not Him. Maybe HQ at e-prime will figure it out and rescue them. Maybe there's a ship due here in an hour. Or, a day. Maybe Providence will decide these particular assholes should continue breathing for some other incomprehensible reason."

Carol leaned on the table, holding her face in her hands for a what felt like a long time. Finally, she looked up at her XO and close friend.

"They're helpless, Alex, helpless. We can't do anything for them. Maybe you're right. Maybe I should figuratively take out my pistol and put them out of their misery. But for some reason, they're still alive. They have a chance. Not much of one, I know, and I know their fate might be frightfully painful."

"Still — "

"No, Alex. We're warriors, not murderers. Case closed." She got up and quickly headed forward to the Bridge. In a few minutes, she'd drafted her message to Admiral Barker and forwarded it to Lori Rodgers for transmission.

```
PRIORITY 207904162300UTC
TO: CSTO, FLEETOPS
FROM: SIGMA

1) ENEMY STATION STRUCK AS INSTRUCTED 207904152230.
2) BDA AFTER 24 HOURS REVEALS ALL SHIPS INCAPACITATED AND
ALL STATION STORAGE COMPROMISED.
4) IR INDICATES SIX SMALL AREAS OF SURVIVORS WHICH I HAVE
DECLINED TO STRIKE FURTHER.
5) WILL OBSERVE EIGHT MORE HOURS THEN PROCEED ALPHA MENSAE (E)
AS ORDERED.

HANSEN

END
```

Science Directorate Headquarters, Office of The Second Science Master
The Preeminent Home World
Earth Equivalent Date: April 24, 2079

Second Science Master Glur Woe Segt and his maleChild Rmah Teo Segt listened to the astronomer carefully as he reported his alarming observations. At his age, Segt had heard enough supposed emergencies that he was not about to be disturbed by this one, at least, not without more information. But as the astronomer talked, Segt could not help but think more seriously about what these unexplained events might mean, and the opportunity they might present.

"Several times in the last ten rots, sir Segt, I have been observing stars, only to have them wink out for a few milrots, then reappear."

"Is there a pattern to these events?" Segt asked.

"Not particularly, except that they seem to occur more frequently when tribute shipments are arriving. And, most worrisome to me, it is sometimes visible to the eye, if the star is bright. I myself have seen them myself go dark, then light back up."

"I see. This is somewhat interesting to me, Sern. You have a written report?"

The astronomer, a bright young male with a reputation as having enormous potential for discoveries, passed his report over.

"Very good, Sern." Segt stood. "You will mention this to no one, understand?"

"But, sir Segt, I have already discussed it with my associates. It was our joint decision to bring this directly to your attention."

Segt's face turned dark with worry, filling Sern with fear. "Have you spoken to anyone outside the Directorate?"

"I have not, sir."

"Good. Instruct your associates to keep this matter to themselves."

"But, sir, this could indicate some threat to us, an approaching asteroid storm, perhaps?"

"Doubtful. Continue to monitor, Sern, and inform me after each StarRise of what you have seen."

"Yes, sir Segt, I will."

"Understand, Sern Tei Nanc, understand well, that you will not further discuss these findings with anyone."

Sern was visibly uncomfortable, but the logical, trained scientist in him could not refrain from asking what he knew might be a dangerous question. "From your reaction, sir Segt, I gain the impression that you are aware of this phenomenon? That you already know what it represents?"

"Keep that impression to yourself as well, Sern. Report what you find only to me. Otherwise, keep it to yourself. Do I make my meaning clear?"

"Yes, sir." Sern rose, leaving a questioning air in his wake. Once he was gone and the door secured, Segt turned to his maleChild, Rmah Teo Segt.

"The Vermin are here, Rmah."

"Yes, I agree. I may have other evidence as well, which is why I am here."

"Other evidence?"

"A radio astronomer came to me lastRot, reporting unusual radio signals he believes are some kind of previously unknown alien communications."

"What else did he say?"

"He found evidence of strong transmissions over a wide segment of the radio spectrum. He could not determine the exact source yet, but believes it is evidence of some new alien culture."

"What did you tell him?"

"Same as you told Sern. Keep watching, try to determine the source, keep reporting to me, keep quiet. I also thought it might be the Vermin."

The third male in the room, young Tigr Cur Haft, spoke cautiously. "It may be time to initiate our plan to make contact with them."

"Perhaps," Segt replied, just as cautiously. "I will see Asoon Too Lini and Scad Nee Wok after StarSet and see if they are ready."

Segt had never revealed his name or position to his conscripted Speaker and her Ship Commander malePair. They only knew he was a commanding presence from the Science Directorate, which was sufficient to ensure their compliance. He did not intimidate with threats, as none were necessary. The weight of the SD was more than enough for his needs. He came to their residence alone this time, and only after verifying that Wok was present.

He was admitted to their home immediately, and Asoon Too Lini offered him evening beverage and sweets. He sat in their shared space, his back to the small window that faced the street, an opaque shade drawn down to conceal the interior.

"It is time."

"Time?" Wok asked.

"I am Glur Woe Segt —"

"The Second Science Master?" Asoon asked in surprise.

"Yes."

"You are the second most powerful male in the SD!" Wok replied, settling into a chair across from Segt.

Segt turned to Asoon. "Has Wok discussed with you the current conflict with the species known as the Vermin?"

"He has, some, yes."

"And what is your understanding?"

The question was too direct for her, so she looked over at Wok, wondering what was safe to disclose and what might get him, or both of them, expunged.

Segt looked from one to the other. "You may speak freely, Asoon. I am not military."

"The war is going badly," she answered hastily. "The Vermin are strong and resourceful. The outcome is in grave doubt."

"The outcome is not in doubt," Segt said. "The Armada is going to be destroyed, and us with them, unless there is a change in direction."

Scad Nee Wok looked at Segt in surprise. "What is it that I do not know?"

"The WayStation has not responded to repeated calls. None of the ships there respond, either."

"So, you believe the Vermin have found and destroyed it?"

"Yes. Thousands of lives, Wok, thousands lost."

"What of System 849?"

"Another disaster, although it appears that we drew more blood from them than earlier encounters."

"But still, defeat?"

"Still, defeat."

Scad Nee Wok looked at Asoon, then back to Segt. "What is it you ask of us? Asoon has been taught the Vermin language, disgusting bizarre excuse for communication that it is, for some reason?"

"I again implore you to secrecy, understood?"

They agreed.

"I believe the Vermin are already here, and in significant numbers."

"How do you know?"

"I have astronomers complaining about stars that wink out and then back on. Radio explorers reporting transmissions they do not recognize."

Scad Nee Wok leaned forward in his chair. "There was a strong radio signal directed at us from the Vermin planet not long before we were attacked."

"Indeed, Scad, I have read your report."

"So, what do you ask of us?"

"This work isn't just sensitive, it's dangerous. I have recruited you into something where if the Vermin don't kill you, the Armada well might."

Scan and Asoon looked at one another, and then Scad answered for them. "Yes, sir, we assumed as much. We are ready."

"Fine, but the task is not yet ready; you might say, the meat is here but not yet tender."

"And when it is?"

"I will provide you with a Directorate ship, and I will give you a destination and instructions on what to do when you get there."

"We will be ready."

"Very well. Asoon, you have learned the Vermin language, and you have been schooled in mathematics and science."

"Yes, sir Segt. What of it?"

"Can you think of something you could communicate in the Vermin language that would indicate a willingness to talk?"

Scad looked over at her. "They would use different measures for everything, Asoon. Their planet rotates more slowly than ours, each revolution around their star is longer than ours. So, distance, time, rotations, heat are all different than ours. Is there a concept, or a constant, or anything, with an unequivocal value without regard to any of that? Something that has no units of measure attached to it?"

Asoon thought for a moment, then her tail stump shook with pleasure. "I can immediately think of two. With more time, I may find others."

"Two?"

"Yes. First, the circle constant. The relation between the distance across a circle to the distance around the circle is fixed and without units. And, it is an infinite number with no termination. I could speak the first few digits and wait for them to respond with more."

"And, the second?"

"There is a sequence of numbers which repeats in nature. Some biologists believe it has a transcendental meaning hidden in its simplicity. "

"You speak of the Tlfi Lahl progression? Zero, one, one, two, three, five, eight, thirteen, twenty-one, and so on?"

"Yes. Each number the sum of the previous two. I believe there is a genuine mystery hidden in that simplicity."

Segt looked at her with something approaching respect, an honor not usually given to females. "If you gave them five numbers, they should be able to detect the sequence and respond. When they do, we will have established a link, and you could begin a discussion."

"That is how I see it, sir, yes."

Segt admonished them again to speak to no one, then rose and left, entering a waiting SD car and pulling rapidly away.

The pair talked long into the night until finally, Scad retired so he could attend to his duties in the morning.

Asoon slept not at all.

Sigma
Alpha Mensae (e)
Tuesday, April 25, 2079, 0730 UTC

Sigma arrived at the fifth planet from Alpha Mensae directly from the successful reduction of Enemy Station. On the way, Intel Chief Roger Cox reported that four short, apparently identical messages had been sent on SLIP channel 76, a transmitter that FleetIntel had associated with the enemy high command.

The day before they arrived, Roger sat in the Conn seat, next to Carol, his NetComp on the work surface in front of her, showing the times and message lengths.

"The first one was right here, ma'am, at 1118 on the sixteenth, not even twelve hours after we hit them. Then, there were three more, all 143 milliseconds, none received a response, every twelve hours and thirty-four minutes after the last."

"So, this is some kind of ping? A request for a status?"

"Yes, ma'am. My guess is that they've been sending some kind of scheduled status back to e-prime, probably at reduced power, just enough to be heard. They missed their reporting time, and the bosses back home are wondering what the hell happened to them."

"What about the timing?"

"Oh, that. Yeah, it took us a few hours to fuss that out. It's half a solar day on e-prime. They were sent at the equivalent of midnight and noon."

"Nice catch. Write this up and then forward it to Elias Peña on the flagship when we get out of FTL. I'm not blurting anything on SLIP right now."

"Yes, Commander, will do."

An odd look seemed to pass over Carol's face. It wasn't quite a smile, perhaps it was an expression of hope. He couldn't be sure. He turned to leave but she stopped him.

"So, Roger," she asked quietly, "Would you agree this means e-prime was alerted to the attack on Enemy Station?"

Roger looked up at her, a realization dawning in him. "Yes, ma'am, I have to say that's very likely."

"And so," Carol continued, "there would be at least a chance they would send someone out there to see what happened?"

"Yes, ma'am. And, pick up the survivors."

"Bingo."

Roger looked at his Captain for a moment, understanding now the lesson she had not realized she was teaching as she argued with Alex. He nodded slightly and headed back to the Intel section.

As they approached the smallish gas giant that was Alpha Mensae(e), spread-spectrum VHF communications were established with all the ships present. Carol allowed herself a short 'Fancy meeting you here' personal message to David, and smiled at his 'What took you so long?' response. She also received a detailed report of what the Fleet ships had been doing since they arrived. With that came an appointment to be on the flagship at 0800 on April 26. Barker was going to wait for *Intrepid* and *Canberra* before holding his strategy meeting.

As she read the summary, it was clear that the four ships already present had made good use of their time. *Cobra* reported a trip where Evans had gone back to the enemy home planet and trailed an arriving vessel at a distance of only five kilometers until it dropped towards the surface. At that point, he pulled away to avoid heating up his hull from atmospheric friction. Mark Rhodes had taken *Chaffee* in close to one of the damaged ships floating outside the asteroid ship factory, so close, in fact, that they came back with highly detailed images of the damage the ship had suffered. Alona Melville parked *Jarvis* in an equatorial synchronous orbit and spent two days watching the enormous landing area from which the cargo ships operated. They watched in real time the offloading, splitting, and movement of cargo into the central city. From there, the transports disappeared, apparently into underground highways. Some surface traffic could be seen moving between the hub-and-spoke system of cities, but the vehicles were small and obviously not carrying large volumes of goods. *Columbia*, on the other hand, had remained at Alpha Mensae (e), both to protect CSTO and accomplish planning for the blockade.

Carol smiled as she thought about the group Barker was assembling. Dan Smith was one of her classmates and had been in her ad hoc study group with David. Alona Melville in *Jarvis* had been an acquaintance there, too. When *Intrepid* arrived, Lynn Covington would be there, and so would Natalie Hayden, someone she had come to admire after what was now known as 'The Battle of Seeker Woods.' That sobriquet seemed more than a little extravagant to Carol, but, on the other hand, people needed an evocative name to identify such things. It had been a tough fight, but surely no Iwo or Chosin.

David was here, but she gave little thought to what time they might have together. If they managed this blockade correctly, they would soon have all the time they would ever need.

Alpha Mensae (e) aka Forward Operating Base (FOB) Carpenter
Columbia
Wednesday, April 26, 2079, 0725 UTC

The meeting of ship Commanders, XO's, and intel officers would have easily overwhelmed *Columbia*'s small wardroom, so Barker held his conference on the hangar deck. He now had seven ships at his disposal: *Canberra*, *Chaffee*, *Cobra*, *Columbia*, *Intrepid*, *Jarvis*, and *Sigma*. As Barker looked around the noisy space, he could see old acquaintances being renewed, and a few old (or new) love affairs being refueled. He let them visit, sipping coffee and orange juice, for a half-hour. He wanted these connections refreshed, he wanted the smiles and pale old jokes and banter to be newly remembered, because when things got tough, they would each recall who they were fighting with, and for. The old saying went that soldiers don't actually fight for a commander or a cause, they fight for the soldiers on either side of them in the foxhole. The saying still held true.

"Alright, children," he finally called out with a smile. "Time to take your seats, please."

In a minute or less, they were all seated, NetComps ready, self-organized by ship. Barker started the large display monitor that had been installed in behind him and stood in front of it.

"Welcome to FOB Carpenter. I chose that name because I want us all to remember very clearly how this all started and who struck the first blow against it." He paused for a sip of coffee, waited for the buzz of agreement to fade, then continued. "I had the honor of carrying the *Liberty* survivors back home, and I will always remember that experience. Commander Evans, Lieutenant Commander Hansen, I especially appreciate your contributions, both in Inoria and since."

His preamble complete, Barker picked up his NetComp.

"Captain Hess and several of you who have been here a while have drafted a blockade plan. Harry will present that draft to you for discussion. To be clear, this is a draft, and I want to hear what everyone has to say."

Hess took Barker's place at the front of the gathering and began explaining the process. Once the blockade was in place, they would start intercepting the incoming cargo ships. The first warning would be a Lance, detonated one hundred kilometers ahead of the vessel. After fifteen minutes, the second would be detonated at ten kilometers ahead. Then, a Bludgeon at one kilometer.

"Based on *Jarvis*' imagery, we believe these ships are crewed, not robotic. We also believe that the crews should be aware of the kinds of weapons we use. So, the increasing threat should make the point that they are to change course."

Carol looked up. "But sir, what if these ships contain something critical; you know, medical supplies, or food, or something else they require? They might see it as heroic to run our gauntlet and try to deliver what they need."

"That is unfortunately possible, Commander Hansen, but there is nothing we can do about it."

Hess continued, pointing out that no ship would be struck for the first two e-prime Sols.

"Also, we will begin the blockade at local noon at the center city on e-prime, the hub of their settlement. We think they will understand what we want."

Under the plan Hess presented, after the second solar noon, ships that do not change course would be struck with a Lance, aimed to destroy the SLIP apparatus under the bow. By the fourth day, ships would be hit amidships with a single Lance. After that, they would be attacked until destroyed.

"If I may, Admiral?" David called out.

"What is it, Powell?"

"I just wonder, sir, if we should start out just pounding them from close up with the radars. I mean, get within ten klicks and then just light them up for a short time, maybe as little as a minute."

"And then what?"

"Nothing, sir. Just pound them with the radar and move off. The message 'I could have killed you, but I didn't' should be plain."

Joanne looked over at Powell. "I think this makes sense. It would send a strong message and save us some ordinance in the bargain."

"It reminds me," Dan Smith said, "of the US blockade of Cuba. US destroyers used sonar to let Soviet subs know they weren't welcome."

"Let's not forget," Elias Peña said sharply, "that there are still warships in orbit. We are not immune to being attacked."

Barker was not letting this get out of hand. "OK, OK, let's keep our heads here."

There came a voice from the back of the room. "Sir?"

"Yes?"

"Roger Cox, sir, Intel on *Sigma*."

"What's on your mind, Lieutenant Cox?"

Carol looked over at her Intel chief and nodded. "Tell him."

"We can't strike these ships in this way, sir, and we can't be shooting Bludgeons."

"OK, why not?"

"If we blow these ships once they've left orbit, they're gonna crash into the cities. Same with the Bludgeons, sir. The balls are going to survive reentry; they're not going to burn up like the remnants of a Lance probably would. That means hitting populated areas, and that means killing civilians. I think—"

"Are there any civilians?" *Intrepid*'s Chuck Anderson interrupted, his voice dripping with sarcasm. "We don't know that there is even such a thing there."

Carol wasn't having that. "Neither do we know that there aren't, Lieutenant."

The spirited discussion that followed argued the moral issue, fueled by the complete lack of concern the enemy had previously shown for civilians. The talk created groups around the ideas of 'they reap what they sow' and 'this is not who we are.'

Anderson kept to his opinion. "Let's not forget what happened at Inoria and Big Blue. Why the hell should we be worried about a few theoretical civilians?"

"Sir, if I may finish?" Roger responded. He'd tangled with Anderson before back at FleetIntel and long ago decided he wasn't going to be put off by his conceits or lack of respect.

"Yes, Cox, what is it?"

"When these cargo ships come in, they're in Newtonian orbit until they get within range of the spaceport."

"Yes, so?"

"Rather than strike them amidships, with all the risk for the crews and the, uh, noncombatants, on the ground, why don't we just put a Lance in their Drive? We can disable the ship, deny the enemy whatever it is carrying, and do it without killing anybody."

"Interesting idea, Cox," Hess answered.

Archeologist Gabrielle Este had come out on *Intrepid* with linguist Greg Cordero. Barker asked her to speak to their lack of understanding.

"Whether there are civilians as we understand them is an open question. We just don't know anything about the structure of their society. But, there certainly are individuals on the surface who are not involved in the immediate conflict, and we might send a clearer message by sparing their lives."

"But," Elias Peña challenged, "you don't actually know they will understand that message."

"No, I don't."

In the end, Barker agreed that Bludgeons should not be used as warning shots. That, he said, would be gratuitous. Cox's other ideas about minimizing noncombatant casualties would be implemented.

"Remember, the point here is to force them to talk. The last thing I need is to be the Governor-General of e-prime."

As the meeting broke up, Hess and Barker went back to formalize the instructions. The blockade would start the next solar noon, 1112 UTC, with the radar intimidation of the six warships in orbit around the planet. Hess would move to *Cobra*, and use its more powerful sensor suite to find incoming ships and dispatch one of his own to intercept. There would be one e-prime day of radar warnings, then two of warning shots, all Lances. On day four, the Drive would be destroyed.

After that, if they didn't respond somehow, Hess and Barker would decide what to do. Departing ships would be ignored, Hess said, as they would have already delivered their cargo. Destroying an empty ship would not deny the enemy anything, but would needlessly take lives.

Intrepid
E-Prime
Thursday, April 27, 2079, 1110 UTC

Joanne watched closely as Lynn Covington brought the ship slowly up behind the Type III enemy cruiser they had been assigned. The enemy ship was bright in the Bridge windows, the light of Alpha Mensae reflecting off its polished exterior. It appeared undamaged, which made Joanne wonder if perhaps it was new. They'd hit almost everything the enemy had thrown at them at least once. The 180 MHz intrusion signal was not up, which indicated to her that they were not expecting any kind of threat. *Good,* she thought, *a new ship, maybe a green crew, will not react as quickly or violently as a seasoned crew might.*

"Ten klicks, Captain," Covington reported quietly.

"You don't have to whisper, Lieutenant. They can't hear us."

"Yes, ma'am, sorry. Reflex."

"I understand. Honestly, I feel a little the same myself. Is our exit route ready?"

"All set, Captain."

"OK, then. Lieutenant Gonzales, at exactly 1112, light them up. Full power, targeting mode, sixty seconds."

"Yes, ma'am."

"Nav, as soon as he shuts down, get us out of here."

"All set, Captain."

As the Cesium-133 clock digits rolled from 11:11:59 to 11:12:00, Gonzales touched off the radar. There followed a minute that dragged by as if an hour, everyone watching for some reaction from the enemy. Joanne's eyes never left the dazzling enemy ship, so vast and threatening, seemingly just outside the Bridge windows.

"Maybe they're all at lunch?" Natalie Hayden offered. Joanne had to smile.

"Yeah, maybe. Any sign of the 180, Marco?"

"No, Captain. There's nothing on any of the tripwire frequencies we know of. Or anything in the vicinity, either."

"Very well, thanks."

As the clock rolled again at 11:13:00, Gonzales switched off the radar, and *Intrepid* moved slightly to one side and kicked in her Drive. The Type III never seemed to react.

Natalie walked from the Weapons station over to Joanne's command position. "That was almost too easy."

"Yes, it was."

"This is just the first time," Lynn Covington commented, "They may be better prepared next time."

Joanne nodded. "Yes, they might." She turned to Alonzo. "Let's get the Anderson business over with, shall we?"

"Sure."

She picked up the phone. "Intel...Anderson, please get up here." In a minute or less, her Intel Chief, Chuck Anderson, arrived.

"Yes, Captain?"

"In my duty cabin. Now." Joanne led him a few meters aft, followed by Alonzo. She went in first and stood behind the desk. Anderson started to sit, then, realizing that the Captain and XO were standing, awkwardly corrected himself.

Joanne wasted no time: "Pull that shit on Cox again, and you'll be the highest-ranking toilet scrubber in the whole goddamn fleet. Do I make myself clear?"

"Captain, I was just —"

"When you're on my ship, Anderson, you speak for me. When you act like that, you make me look like the jerk you are."

"Really, Captain, I don't see — "

"I can tell you don't, Anderson. Never again. Clear? You *will* treat all others with the respect you yourself expect."

Anderson, unaccustomed to such treatment, swallowed hard. "Yes, Captain."

"Fine. Get lost."

Anderson, surprised again at his abrupt dismissal, started to open his mouth to respond, to lodge a complaint, but stopped himself. He stood there for several seconds until Alonzo stepped aside and opened the hatch to the central passageway. He left without further comment.

"That was an ass-kicking long overdue," Alonzo said.

"Asshole reminds me of Court, but he has more brains and more potential. Maybe a flogging will set him straight."

Alonzo shrugged. "Maybe. I'll keep an eye on him."

Joanne shook her head. "I have my doubts, Alonzo. When we get home, I want him off unless something extraordinary happens."

"Yes, Captain."

Silver Victory

As Alonzo headed back to the Bridge, Joanne sat at her small workstation to document her discussion with Anderson.

Central Council Chambers
The Preeminent Home World
Earth Equivalent Date: Thursday, April 27, 2079

The Revered First was furious, screaming at his advisors, his saliva flying across the table.

"What is this outrage? How is it, you fools, how is it that six of our newest ships are humiliated in this way?"

His verbal pummeling yielded no response. Fear kept their minds frozen and their mouths closed.

"What does it mean? Why did they not attack?"

Admired Third Counsellor Ashil Kiker managed to find his voice. "They are trying to tell us something, perhaps?"

"What can *they* tell *us*? We are the Preeminent."

Kiker showed unusual courage as he continued. "Revered First, they could have struck every ship. They could have easily destroyed what is left of the Armada. They did not. It must have some meaning."

"They are toying with their prey like snigtols. We will find them and punish this offense."

Another older council member spoke: "If we could find them, Revered First, we would not be in the position we are."

The First turned towards his longest-serving advisor, his eyes narrow in threat. "What are you saying?"

"You, Revered First, have led us into a disaster. You demanded the eradication of the Scholars, who posed no threat to us other than their refusal to kneel. You ordered the misadventure with the Deists, who, again, meant nothing to us."

"We are the Preeminent. We have every right to take what we wish. Destroy what we wish. They must comply or die."

Hnos Lio Nowl, a junior member, spoke carefully but firmly. "The Vermin will do neither, Revered First."

"They must!" He turned to the Respected Second, Jaf Seen Toft. "Order the ships out to find these Vermin. They must be removed from our planet."

"And if they cannot?" Toft asked.

The Revered First stood and shouted at his deputy, "They must." He turned and retired to his inner sanctum.

The remaining counselors looked to Toft, who looked back at them and flatly declared, "We are the Preeminent."

Nowl stood and pointed his long, clawed finger at the Respected Second. "How long, Toft, how long will you cling to this fantasy?"

Toft stood up, his anger apparent. "If you, Nowl, are no longer a Preeminent, perhaps we should eliminate you from this chamber?"

"Hungry, are we, Toft?" Nowl shot back. "This dogma of superiority has run its course!"

"The Revered First remains, Nowl," Kiker yelled at him. "So long as that is true, we will maintain order. This society thrives on order."

Nowl was unmoved. "This society, sir Kiker, thrives out of the lies this council sells them."

"The lies matter not, young Nowl," Toft said, almost as a warning. "They are provided for."

Nowl slammed his hand on the table. "I think it more crucial to you that your egos are fed than any feigned concern for the populace." He stared at Kiker in anger for a moment, his tail stump rigid, then left the Council Chamber without another word.

Intrepid
E-Prime
Thursday, April 27, 2079, 2030 UTC

After the initial radar hits on the enemy warships, the Fleet ships moved into high orbits and waited for Captain Hess on *Cobra* to assign them new targets. *Jarvis* was first in line, and Alona Melville took her to within a few klicks abeam of the kilometer-long cargo ship. She placed herself on the side away from the planet so as not to be silhouetted against it. She gave the enemy five minutes of targeting radar lock, then shut down and moved off.

There was no reaction.

Joanne Henderson's *Intrepid* was assigned the third ship's arrival. She decided to stay behind the enemy.

"Lynn, how close do you think we can get?"

"I can kiss its ass if that's what you want, Captain. But, I don't know what will happen if they suddenly fire up the Drive while we're there."

"OK, bring us to a kilometer off their tail. Then five minutes of radar."

"Will do. I'll have the escape course loaded."

"Fine, but hold off on that. I want to watch for a few minutes first."

"Yes, ma'am."

At just a kilometer, the enemy ship made a visual statement even stronger than the Type III warship they had hammered with their radar earlier.

"If I didn't know what shitheads they all are," XO Alonzo Bass commented,

"I'd almost think those ships were beautiful."

Joanne had to laugh at that as she turned back to Marco Gonzales. "Any intruder alarms up, Marco?"

"No, Captain. Nothing."

Joanne leaned towards Alonzo. "They don't change course, they don't raise their defenses. I wonder if they even know we're here."

Alonzo shrugged. "I don't think they're that flexible in their thinking. They're going to keep doing what they've been told to do until someone tells them differently."

Joanne looked at her XO with a wry smile. "Or, they don't even know we're here."

"Or that, yes. Ma'am."

Throughout the first day, ships were intercepted by the Fleet, illuminated with radar for five minutes - no more no less - and then allowed to continue on their way. None of them activated their intruder alarms, none changed course.

Joanne went to sleep that night thinking about what might come next, what secret tech the enemy might conjure to again tip the scales in their favor. The memory of the Type V was fresh and painful in her mind.

It was not a restful night.

SD Central Facility
Core City
Earth Equivalent Date: Friday, April 28, 2079, StarZenith.

Glur Woe Segt looked out the wide windows of his official workspace on the second-highest floor of the imposing Science Directorate building. He loved the vista of Core City, with the first ancillary city just visible in the distance. But his view today was clouded by his consideration of the last day's events. The Vermin were indeed here, and in force. At precisely StarZenith lastRot, they had snuck up on the six Armada ships in orbit and aimed their radio detection devices at them from close range for less than a milrot, then fled. Later, they had shadowed every supply ship arriving from conquered worlds, using their devices for over three milrots, again from close range.

His maleChild and co-conspirator Rmah Teo Segt arrived in a rush, breathless, breaking his concentration.

"What do you make of it?" Rmah asked.

"I am not sure," Segt replied. "But, I think this is an invitation wrapped in a threat."

"They could have destroyed every one of those ships, maleParent, every single one. But they did not."

"Did you notice the timing?"

"Yes. StarZenith. They've studied us very carefully." Rmah thought for a moment, then asked, "What will you do?"

Segt turned from the window to face his maleChild. "Nothing for now. We will see what they do thisRot. It may be several rots before we begin to understand what they want."

"They want to talk," Rmah declared, a hint of hope in his voice.

Segt indicated his agreement. "Has your radio astronomer had anything more to say?"

"Yes. Since StarZenith yesterday, the signals are stronger and, he believes, closer."

"We understand now why that would be. What about before lastRot?"

"ThisRot, he gave me a new report. He looked at his data and concluded he only saw the signals from StarSet to StarNadir. He says the closest correlation he can make from that is planet Five."

"Five is a worthless little ball of ice and gas. There is nothing there."

"Nothing on the surface, no, but would it not make a convenient place for an alien fleet to meet up?"

Segt sat up straighter, intrigued. "Where is System 201?"

"I wondered the same. 201 is currently in the same general direction as Five."

"That can't be a coincidence. Does the Armada know any of this?"

"Not from us, maleParent. They may have data of their own we are not aware of."

There was a long silence, which the Rmah finally broke. "There are rumors of dissent in the Central Council," he said quietly as if the Council would hear him. "The Revered First was actually challenged by three of his advisors."

Segt waved his hands in disagreement. "He will not bend, Rmah. He is a true believer of the lie, the worst kind of conceit. Facts will not move him until one of the Vermin puts a pellet in his brain."

"That may be possible."

Glur Woe Segt was not ready to go that far. "We will not entertain such thoughts, at least, not yet. Do not forget that it is the Directorate's failure to control the Armada that has put us in this place."

"Yes, maleParent, I realize." Rmah looked out the office window for a moment, then spoke again. "Do you ever wonder what it will be like?"

"What will what be like?"

"What life will be like, after?"

"I suspect life will go on as it has, but some adjustments will need to be made."

"I worry that we will not survive."

"Indeed, we may not, you and I, but it will not be the fault of the Vermin. They have come here to protect the Deists and the Scholars, not to kill us. They push us back to keep us from killing species they value."

"I doubt many in the Armada would agree with that assessment. They see them as malevolent."

"Their eyes only see through the lens of their own behavior. *They* are the evil ones."

They sat for several cenmilrots, then Rmah rose to return to his own office, much smaller and on a much lower floor, his view restricted to the flat vista of the structure next to theirs.

Sigma
E-Prime
Friday, April 28, 2079, 1430 UTC

The enemy cargo ship came from the northeast, the Fleet having again labeled such directions based on the pole where the planet rotated counter-clockwise. *Sigma* happened to draw the first warning-shot mission. They decided to place themselves slightly below and to the left of the target. Peg White expertly put them five klicks from the enemy ship as it coasted towards its landing field.

Carol stood at her Command position. "OK, status check. Weaps?"

"We have three Lances ready, Commander, distances are set."

"Fine, Intel, where are the warships?"

"The six ships remain in geosynchronous orbit, Commander. They haven't moved since they were visited yesterday."

"Peg, you have the exit plan in place?"

"Yes, ready at your command."

She looked around the Bridge, every officer looking back at her in anticipation. This was a new experience for all of them, something they'd never war-gamed. She looked at the time.

"OK, Lieutenant Dean, on the minute, fire it up!"

She let Dean run the radar the full five minutes, waiting for some reaction, but there was none. She chose to leave the radar on as they upped the ante.

"Chief, fire the first warning shot." The Lance was out a second later, moving quickly, but less than light-speed, to a position one hundred kilometers in front of the ship, where it exploded with a significant flash.

The ship phone rang next to Carol. "Hansen." She never answered 'Captain,' and doubted she ever would. It somehow didn't fit her, at least not yet. She took the phone away from her ear. "Cox, this is for you."

Roger took the phone, listened for a few seconds, his eyes growing wider as he absorbed what he was hearing. "Be right there!" He handed the receiver back to Carol, his young face smiling broadly.

"What?" Carol asked.

"*Cobra* picked up something new, ma'am. It's way down in the radio band, nowhere we would have looked for it, like 15 MHz."

"OK, so what is it?"

"They're not sure, ma'am. Powell thinks it might be voice."

Science Directorate Headquarters
Office of the Second Science Master
Earth Equivalent Date: Friday, April 29, 2079

"They have started shooting," Rmah reported to his maleParent.

"What? I have heard nothing about damage or death."

"No, they're shooting in front of the tribute ships. They come up behind, turn on their radio detection device for a short time, then fire a weapon far in front of the ship. A few milrots later, they fire again, cutting the distance by a factor of ten."

"Ten?"

"Yes, ten."

"Interesting."

"Yes, it is. They then wait the same time and cut the distance again by a factor of ten, exploding just a ship-length in front. I don't think I understand, but I still think they're trying to say something. They're deliberately *not* killing these crews."

"They don't think like we do, Rmah. Their tactics are far more subtle than ours. I suspect they have honed their skills in other conflicts, and understand things we do not."

"I have discussed this situation with the Vermin speakers, and what they describe supports your position."

"Oh?"

"Yes. Their entertainment and information transmissions contain many military events. They have warred among themselves for generations, and, as you say, they must be applying those lessons to us."

Segt stood at his beloved window for several moments. "They are trying to have a conversation, Rmah, of this, I am convinced. If they wanted to destroy our ships and kill us all, they could have easily done so by now."

"So, how do we respond?"

"What more can your radio astronomer tell us?"

"Very little. There is so much radio energy close to the planet he has difficulty locating it. He theorizes there is some number of warships performing the intercepts, but his instruments are not accurate enough at such close range to discriminate them."

"He still believes they are using planet Five as a base?"

"Yes, but it is somewhat a guess at this point. What has the visual astronomer said?"

"After StarSet, he can detect some movement by the Vermin as they trail the tribute ships. He can see the flash of their weapons, too."

"The populace can see those, too. Rumors are going around about asteroid collisions. "

"Let those rumors proceed, Rmah. Better that than to tell them the truth, at least for now."

"So, are we ready?"

"Yes. I will see the Principal Master."

Segt sat across from the Principal Master, the chief scientist, and head of the Science Directorate. The old male read Segt's document with sadness, looking up from time to time to ask for clarification. Finally, he set the small document display device on the desk and looked directly at Segt.

"You have been planning this for a long time, Segt. You should have informed me sooner."

"I could not, sir Master, until the preparation and circumstances met. Now, they have."

"You would have me remove the Revered First Counselor? It has never been done. You invite a revolt from within the Armada."

"Yes, sir, I would have him removed. The damage the Armada has done while unchained is inexcusable. The cult they have developed since we acquiesced to their rule bears little resemblance to our historical culture. We have always been an aggressive species, that I know; it is inborn to us. But that instinct was to obtain food, or a female, or range when we were more primitive. That aggression should never have been allowed to expand to such a degree that we kill needlessly."

"You have learned the Guardians' lessons well, Segt."

"Respectfully, sir, I have only learned what you taught me long ago. I only see through eyes you have opened to the truth, to facts, to science, to rational thought."

"You give me too much credit, Segt. But that is a trait that has served you well."

"We must apply the revocation clause in the Armada's dominion contract. They have violated the limits for some time now."

"We have known some of this for many revs, Segt, but I have lacked the votes in the SD conclave to change it, as you well know."

"I think we have the evidence now."

The Principal Master rose slowly from his chair and walked to consider the view out his own window. Segt suddenly realized where he had acquired that habit when considering hard decisions.

"I will speak to the Revered First. I will offer him retirement instead of dissolution of the Central Council."

"He will not take it well, sir. Perhaps I should accompany you?"

"I will summon him here, at StarSet thisRot."

Segt expressed his respect for the old man and left.

Despite his age, Glur Woe Segt ran up to the Principal Master's offices, leaving behind the messenger sent for him just a half-drot after StarSet. As Segt entered the inner office where he and the Principal had talked earlier in the rot, he faced a ghastly scene. Blood covered the floor and splattered the walls; the desktop was covered as well. Bits of bone and flesh were scattered around the room. Segt located the Principal's torso, eviscerated behind his desk. His head was missing, which surprised Segt not at all. The First would surely have taken that as a prize. He suppressed his rage and disgust; he had work to do.

The messenger stopped behind Segt, shocked by the sight of the Principal's mangled remains. "But, sir Segt, who could have — "

"The Revered First did this."

"Alone?"

Segt's mind ran ahead to what else the First might be doing. "I don't know. Have someone inform his female, and find someone to get this place cleaned up."

"Yes, sir. Are you, then, the Principal Master?"

"No. That choice is for the Conclave to make. But for now, do as I say, and quietly, please?"

"Yes, I will."

Segt moved quickly back to his own offices, watching every step for one of the Armada to ambush him. He called for his maleChild, and Rmah appeared within a few milrot. They closed and locked the outer and inner doors.

"The Principal Master is dead, Rmah, killed by the First."

"But how?"

"The Principal and I were planning to call for a revocation vote in the Conclave tomorrow. He wanted to offer the First retirement instead."

"I take it he declined?"

"Certainly seems so."

"But, now, you are the acting Principal Master, maleParent. You can authorize the trip to planet Five."

"Yes. Go, now, and collect our pilot and Speaker, and get them to the departure facility. A short-range exploration ship should suffice."

Rmah left immediately, took a modest transport from the SD garage, and drove to Scad Nee Wok's residence.

Intrepid
E-Prime
Sunday, April 30, 2079, 1436 UTC

Joanne had the pleasure of delivering the first strike on the enemy cargo ships. In all, two dozen had been intercepted, hit with radar, harassed with Lances, but ultimately allowed to proceed.

That was about to change.

Lynn Covington brought them within ten kilometers of the target. Joanne did not want to be any closer than that when the Lance went off.

After five minutes of radar, James Kirkland let go a Lance to explode a hundred klicks off the nose of the ship.

"You know," he said to Joanne while waiting for the missile to explode, "We're going to need *Ceres* here pretty soon. We're burning ordinance way too fast for my taste."

"Yeah, but I'm betting Barker is way ahead of us on that."

She turned back to the Surveillance console. "Lieutenant Gonzales, is our friend still in orbit?"

"Yes, ma'am. Typical flight profile shows they won't begin to descend for another hour."

Kirkland's voice came from across the Bridge. "Second Lance is away, Captain."

"Very well."

The time finally came for the strike.

"OK, here we go. Lynn, move us a kilometer outside the target. We're ten back?"

"Yes, ma'am."

"Marco, any reaction from the warships?"

"None, Captain. I am stunned that they're just putting up with this."

"As am I, Lieutenant, as am I."

"As soon as the weapon is away, Lynn, get us the hell out of here, OK?"

"All set, ma'am. As soon as Kirkland lets me know it's out, we'll move."

The strike had to occur at the precise time Hess and Barker had laid out. Consistent timing was part of what Barker was trying to show the enemy: *We're here, we can do this on our schedule, and there's very little you can do about it.*

"Weapon away!" Kirkland called, *Intrepid* turned abruptly away from the planet, moving quickly away from the ship she was about to strike.

As they accelerated away, *Sigma* was moving to pick up the next incoming cargo ship.

Central Council Chambers
Preeminent Home World
Earth Equivalent Date: Sunday, April 30, 2079

The Revered First was fuming, pacing angrily as his counselors filed in. The Vermin had struck an incoming tribute ship, disabling it in orbit, leaving it worthless to him. This new defeat was inconvenient, as he had just acted to preserve his place and those of his counselors, too.

Ashil Kiker entered the council chamber and immediately smelled the sweetness of blood in the air. As the crowd separated, he was disgusted at the identity of the head that laid on their conference table, still oozing, but viscerally he was enticed by the odor, which was starting to mature.

"You killed the Principal Scientist?" Hnos Lio Nowl asked, incredulous. "The SD will — "

"He was about to call the Conclave to remove me and dissolve this Council. That cannot be permitted. We are the Preeminent."

No one else spoke, so the First continued. "We have more problems. The Vermin have struck. The tribute ship from System 279 was disabled before it could descend. It is still in orbit, useless."

Ashil Kiker's mind flashed back to his own encounter with the Vermin at their home planet. "When I was at System 201, they attempted the same. They struck the communication apparatus and tried to strike the propulsion system as well, but failed."

The Revered First's face curled into a rage. "It is only the latest insult, an obvious provocation!"

The Respected Second, Jaf Seen Toft, asked, "What is it that you command, Revered First?"

"Get the ships we still have moving. I demanded this before, and you have taken no action! Find these Vermin and remove them! Kiker! Get a commander out there and see to the end of this!"

The First abruptly turned and entered his inner sanctum, not waiting for Kiker's response.

"As you wish, Revered First," Kiker spoke to the retreating figure.

Kiker returned to his own small official space on the sixth level, deep within the seven-level Armada complex. He remembered Scad Nee Wok, who had saved his life in the encounter with the Vermin. Perhaps Wok would make a competent commander. The messenger he sent for Wok returned with a report that he was not in his residence. Neither Wok nor his female was to be found. Electronic communications also failed, which was unprecedented. Kiker was suddenly anxious. If Wok was missing, where was he, and what was he doing?

He thought more and then contacted the commander who had recently failed at System 849, Sdom Roi Gotk. He had shown initiative, so perhaps he could take command and push the Vermin out. He dispatched another messenger to find Gotk.

Shortly thereafter, Counselor Hnos Lio Nowl appeared in his office.

"I would speak to you, Admired Third." Kiker invited Nowl in, and they sat separated by Kiker's massive desk.

"What is it that you wish to say, Nowl?"

Nowl paused, suddenly stricken with second thoughts about confronting Kiker. "The First has promoted you without changing your title. The Second cannot appreciate this."

Kiker stiffened in his chair but did not move. "I do as the Revered First demands, Nowl, as does The Second."

"Tolf has always handled the Armada and the dirty work. It was he who eliminated Hess Tse Sim, and he who issued the orders to System 849."

Kiker was unmoved. "I do as the Revered First demands."

Nowl hesitated, then continued. "The Vermin are here, sir Kiker, and in force. They disable ships in orbit so that none are killed, but the tribute cannot be delivered."

Kiker did not understand where Nowl was going with this conversation, but he was content to let him continue. "I am aware of this."

"Then surely you see that this conflict must be ended. The Vermin can crush us all at their whim."

"You forget, Nowl, that we are the Preeminent," Kiker replied angrily. "Your words are dangerous to you."

Nowl sat up straighter, unintimidated. "My words will kill no one nor destroy a single vessel. The Vermin can do both whenever they wish."

Kiker ignored the junior counselor's lack of respect. "I am sending Sdom Roi Gotk to take command of what remains, and drive the Vermin off."

Nowl waved his dismissal of what Kiker had said. "He will fail, and fail worse than he did at 849. He has no Detector to help him."

Kiker spoke smoothly and with more confidence than logic could possibly support. "They trail the tribute deliveries for some time before they fire. They can be detected then and attacked."

"They have gone to some lengths to avoid bloodshed, sir Kiker. If we attack them now, there may be no end to it."

"We are the Preeminent. We will prevail."

"I see, sir Kiker, that you are unmoved by reality."

"The reality, young Nowl, is that we are the Preeminent."

"That statement, sir Kiker, no longer agrees with what anyone can plainly see with their own eyes who chooses to open them."

Nowl stood, leaving without a parting greeting or permission of Kiker. Both were insults, but Kiker's mind was elsewhere, considering how much to tell Gotk.

Ship Commander Sdom Roi Gokt appeared in Ashil Kiker's office door shortly after being summoned. Kiker invited him to sit.

"Gokt, you showed initiative at System 849, and the Council requires it of you again."

"What is the assignment?"

"You are to take the six ships in orbit, and the two just completed, and remove the Vermin presence from Home."

Gotk sat silent for a moment. He had been an obedient officer the Armada for twenty revs or more. He had learned to strike when the enemy was weak, not when he was strong. "There are not enough ships left to do that, sir Kiker. I don't know that we ever had enough ships to defeat them. Attacking the Vermin now will get everyone aboard killed, and still they will remain."

"You have your orders, Gotk. Go carry them out."

"Sir Kiker, do you not hear? Do you not see?"

"You have your orders, Gotk."

"And if I refuse?"

"Disobedience would be a poor choice for your long-term viability."

Gotk said nothing more. He stood and left Kiker's offices, making his way out of the Armada complex and generally walking towards the center of the city. He doubted the Council would have him followed, as they were preoccupied with their own problems. Rumors of shortages were rampant and the populace was now aroused to the emergency. The Council's excuses would only last a short time before a desperate population would begin to question their leadership. The goods the tribute ships brought Home were believed to be necessary for life, and without them, it was thought many would die.

These were lies, of course, fabrications created to bolster the Central Council's grip on power. The foods and spices the ships brought back were popular, mostly due to Council continuous promotion, but none were actually vital to health.

The Council's rumor that the explosions in the night sky were asteroid collisions was also beginning to crumble. Some curious males had started watching and noted their specific, repetitive timing. They knew, and told many, that this could not be a natural phenomenon. The disconnect between the words of the powerful and the ordinary senses of the populace were stirring questions never seen in Preeminent society. Quiet unrest was spreading, mostly in soft questions between trusted pairs and co-workers.

Gotk overheard a few tense conversations about these events as he walked silently to the SD complex, entering by a side door Glur Woe Segt had described to him. He ascended the ramps to Segt's level and moved quickly into his office.

"Kiker has ordered me to take the remaining ships and remove the Vermin," he said as he took a seat across from Segt.

"You are aware this action will fail?" Segt asked.

"Of course. Everyone in the Armada, not so blinded by the First, knows it. I told Kiker as much."

Segt was surprised Gotk had survived the exchange with Kiker. "And still, he sent you?"

"Yes."

Segt looked out the window, then asked, "What will you do?"

"I have come here to ask for your advice. I know the Vermin are all around; we see their weapons explode in the night sky."

"Yes, that is correct."

Gotk was discouraged. "The best one could do is to withdraw, but that would mean death in the Council for the commander and all who follow him."

"But to attack the Vermin means death as well, does it not?"

Gotk's posture slumped with disappointment. "Yes. It is a poor question when both answers are fatal."

"The First still has the loyalty of the Council?" Segt asked.

"Yes, at least five or six of the eight."

"And, he retains a cohort of Combatants for protection?"

Gotk's voice dripped with annoyance. "Yes. The finest trained Combatants we have, he keeps for himself. He will be difficult to dislodge by force."

"Difficult, yes, but not impossible," Segt said softly.

Gotk scoffed at Segt's statement. "How is this not impossible?"

"The Vermin are fearsome in combat, Gotk, as your own Combatants learned first-hand. I simply accept that they may be able to accomplish tasks we cannot."

"Perhaps. What is your advice to me, Segt? I would prefer to remain alive."

"Take command. You will be far safer on a ship than down here."

"And then?"

"And then, nothing."

Gotk was skeptical that he could maintain his place in the Armada while ignoring the orders of the First. But Segt was probably correct that it was better to be off the planet. He left and made his way back to the Armada headquarters, then arranged for transport to the command ship in orbit.

SD Exploration Vessel 22
Planet Five
Earth Equivalent Date: Sunday, April 30, 2079

The SD exploration vessel was small by Preeminent standards, but even so still much larger than an ISC Fleet shuttle. The ship carried Scad Nee Wok, Asoon Too Lini, Rmah Teo Segt, and a handful of trusted SD technicians.

Cobra detected their departure, but since it was a very different ship than they had seen before, Hess decided to let it proceed. They had agreed at the blockade conference that cargo ships leaving the planet would be allowed to depart. The idea, Hess had said, was to control what they received. Vessels leaving the planet were not the point. But when David informed him that it was headed for FOB Carpenter, Hess was alarmed and ordered *Cobra* to get there first. If this was some kind of overture, or attack, they needed all the intel assets he could bring.

The Armada also saw the SD ship leave, but Ashil Kiker was loath to cause more trouble with the SD, so he ordered that it be ignored. It was just an exploration ship, taking some scientists to satisfy their curiosity about something likely unimportant. It would not be going far. He chose not to report it to The Revered First.

As they ran at full speed towards Planet Five, Scad and Rmah discussed at length the analysis the SD had provided them. Scad knew of his own experience at the Vermin's System 201 that they knew of the intrusion detector.

"After all," he told Rmah, "as soon as I initiated it, which was after we detected their radio signal, the Vermin ship fired on us."

"Did you detect them?"

"Yes, and they were very close. Their ability to remain small and hide in the darkness is most disturbing."

"So," Asoon asked, "we should not expect to actually see their ships? How will we find them?"

Scad shifted in his seat, moving his focus from Rmah to Asoon. "They will find us, Asoon. They already know we're coming."

"How would they know that?"

"The attacks on the incoming tribute ships are well-coordinated. Precisely planned. Carefully timed. They are observing Home closely, and they cannot have missed our departure."

"But how would they know where we are going?"

"That part is simple: the physics of space travel are the same for both of us. Our course and speed would have told them everything."

Asoon felt a sudden fear. "Might they fire on us when we arrive?"

Rmah answered, "The SD analysts believe they will not. They believe in their military superiority, and so will most probably wait to see what we do before they act."

"Most probably?" Asoon repeated, skeptical.

"Yes, most probably. It is the careful assessment of many learned males, Asoon. I believe it is correct."

"Once we make contact, what then?" she asked.

"We are here on behalf of the SD. We ask if there can be an end to hostilities."

Scad was unsure. "But clearly, they believe we began this conflict when Hess Tse Sim attacked the Deists. They might ask us the same question."

"Not only that, but the Armada tried to eliminate an entire culture at System 849. The Vermin know this, and they know the Armada has tried twice to locate and eliminate any survivors of the Scholars, whom they despise."

"Tried and failed," Scad continued "and wasted thousands of Combatants in the process."

"Combatants?" Asoon asked.

Rmah looked at her sadly. "Ground fighters bred for combat and conquest."

"Bred? Bred from what?"

Scad stepped in to change the subject. "Another time, Asoon. We must come to a conclusion on this problem first."

Asoon was the only Speaker aboard, and the only one with any insight into Vermin culture. She would have to both translate and explain to Scad and Rmah the more profound implications of what was said. And, she would attempt to explain to the Vermin the full meaning of what was being said to them. It was a critical task, and she felt great anxiety over her abilities to communicate clearly.

As they approached Planet Five, Scad ordered an orbit on the same plane as the overall system, high enough to provide the best communications with the Vermin vessels he believed were there.

"The Vermin will see us coming," Scad told them. "So, let's not appear threatening. We'll put ourselves where we can be seen and then remain in that orbit for a few drots before attempting to communicate."

Cobra had beaten the SD vessel to FOB Carpenter by several hours, and Evans put his ship into the same high equatorial orbit as *Columbia*, with *Cobra* perhaps fifteen degrees behind. They could communicate easily and even move personnel by shuttle if necessary.

Ray Salazar saw the enemy ship first on the IR display. "There it is, Commander," he pointed to a red dot on the IR display. "Looks like they're heading into an orbit below us."

Rich Evans looked up from his observation seat. "Anyone else bothered by the fact that they apparently know where our command ship is?"

"Yes, sir," David answered. "It bothers me. I don't know how they did that."

"Perhaps they will share that with us?"

"Yeah, right," David answered skeptically.

"What's our assessment of the ship?" Evans asked.

"Much smaller than any of the warships, sir," Ray answered. "It's even smaller than the invasion shuttles they used at Big Blue."

"So, unlikely to be carrying weapons?"

"Yes, sir, agreed. It could be some kind of intelligence ship, I suppose, but with their tech, it has a pretty limited range."

Aboard *Columbia*, Kieran Barker wondered what he should do. CINC would not arrive for ten days, but the enemy, whatever their intentions, was already here. If this was some kind of reconnaissance, they would remain quiet and do their best to not be seen. If the enemy had something else on their minds, Barker would leave it to them to show their hand first.

If this was actually an attempt to make contact, they decided Barker would do the talking from *Columbia*. Hess and the Intel staff on *Cobra* would listen and provide back-channel advice over the VHF link. Nerves on both ships were on edge. This was new territory for all of them, essentially a 'first contact' event that none of them had trained for. Gabrielle Este and Greg Cordero were in the room with Barker as well, ready to provide their advice if needed.

Columbia's Weapons Officer Victor Shoemaker loaded his rotaries with a combination of Spartans, Lances, and Bludgeons, and deployed them so that he would be able to respond to any hostile action by the enemy. Melinda Hughes was gone now, in a coma in *Ceres*' hospital, her absence a continuing worry for all of them, so Ensign Carl Hudson had taken charge of the Surveillance team. Melinda had invested heavily in Hudson, teaching the young man from Sacramento everything she had learned about the ship's systems, especially those tricks not taught in school. He had the enemy ship on visual and IR, and his team's careful tracking gave Victor a can't-miss solution.

Several hours had passed when Hudson looked up in surprise.

"Captain, they just turned on the trip-wire."

Dan called Barker to the Bridge, then walked down to look at the Surveillance station himself.

"Just carrier, sir," Hudson reported.

"Where are they?"

"Just finished their second orbit, they're about two hundred klicks below us, sir, and thirty degrees behind."

"Any thought that they know where we are?"

"Can't say, sir, but I don't think we're detectable at this distance."

Barker arrived a few minutes later, and together they watched and waited. After fifteen minutes, the signal changed. The plain tone they had been listening too suddenly had a voice.

"Zero, one, one, two, three, five, eight."

There was an explosion of activity on both ships after the accented but clear English voice read off seven numbers. On *Cobra*, David looked at the time, then back at the time the signal first came up. He looked up at Evans.

"Commander! They waited fifteen minutes."

"What?"

"From the time the signal came up to the time they read off the numbers, it was exactly fifteen minutes."

"Same as our timing with the blockade."

"Yes."

Back on *Columbia*, Intel Chief Gurgen Khachaturian listened to the numbers three times, then realized what he was hearing. He picked up the phone.

"Captain...Katch here, sir. I know what the response should be."

"Oh?"

"Yes. They're reading off the Fibonacci series. Each number is the sum of the previous two."

Dan quickly wrote down the sequence. "So, our response is thirteen, twenty-one, thirty-four, fifty-five?"

"Yes."

Communications Officer Abbas set Barker up with a microphone, and he read off the numbers. Immediately after he finished, the enemy ship spoke a new set of numbers.

"Three, one, four, one, five, nine."

Barker smiled. "Even I know that one. It's pi." Not trusting to his memory, he looked up the exact value on his NetComp.

"Two, six, five, three, six," he said, rounding the last number up to indicate the end.

Asoon Too Lini listened to the answers from the Vermin ship, then turned to Scad and Rmah. "The answers are correct. It is a male speaking, middle-aged, I think. I hear confidence in the voice, perhaps a commander?"

After a moment, Asoon asked, "What shall we say next?"

Rmah looked at his notes and gave Asoon his ideas.

She engaged the radio and said, "We wish an end to the fighting. Are you willing to speak to us?"

The voice coming from the audio monitor on *Columbia's* Bridge was clear, the enunciation plain, but there were wisps and extraneous high-pitched sounds that made it clear it was not a human voice. But it was also clearly not a machine voice. David found the voice strangely intriguing, almost innocent in its tone, as if they had sent a child to speak for them.

"Are we willing?" Barker quoted, looking from Dan Smith to Elias Peña.

"Yes, sir," Elias said quickly, "we're ready to talk. But we're going to validate who they are somehow."

Barker keyed the mic: "We have always been ready to talk. What do you propose?"

Asoon translated for Rmah and Scad. "There is an impatience in his voice," she said, "as if we are already too late."

"Tell him we wish an end to the conflict."

Elias Peña listened to the alien response, then looked at Barker. "Yeah, they started it, and now they want to stop it."

Barker nodded. "True, but I think the second part is the most important."

Again, he keyed the mic: "Your actions began this conflict, but unless you are prepared to change, our actions will finish it. What do you propose?"

"He is angry," Asoon told them. "He says we started the war, but they will end it. There is a threat in his phrasing and confidence that his threat can be carried out. He asks again what we propose."

Rmah looked across at her. "My maleParent had been against conquest from the beginning, but the Armada has blinded themselves to wisdom."

They talked several minutes, then Asoon spoke again.

"I cannot offer a specific proposal. We have come to open communications and understand if a peaceful end is possible."

Greg Cordero spoke for the first time. "There's only been two 'first contact' events in human history, Admiral. If this is their initial outreach to us, I suggest we just go along for now."

Barker keyed the mic. "Peace is always preferable to war. Unless, as the Seekers learned, the alternative is death or subjugation."

Este looked at Barker with alarm. "I would have left that last part out."

Asoon's eyes widened with surprise. "He says that peace is preferable, in pleasant tones. But then he says peace is not possible if it means death."

Scad was unfazed by Asoon reaction. "A sensible point of view. What else?"

"He associates with 'death' a word that means to search, but in their language, it can mean a search for knowledge or wisdom, not a literal, physical search. But he uses it like it was a name."

Rmah looked at Scad, questioning.

"The Scholars," Scad answered, finally. "We learned that they had found that planet, and I took Ashil Kiker to investigate. It was from there that we went to System 201."

"What happened to the Scholars?" Rmah asked.

Scad looked at Asoon, then back to Rmah. "They would not kneel. They did not seem to understand what was required of them. The Revered First demanded their obedience, and when they refused, he sent in Combatants to eliminate them."

"Kneel, or die, that is the Armada's philosophy, is it not?"

"It is."

Asoon moved away from Scad before speaking. "So, pairedMale, this is your occupation you are so proud of? Obedience or Death?"

"It was, but it is no more." He looked at Rmah. "What are we to say?"

Barker looked at Este, wondering at the delay. "Maybe I was too threatening?"

Cordero answered, "Hard to say, sir, how they're interpreting this. I'm still wondering how they learned the language."

"Yes, it's curious."

Dan looked at Barker. "I keep thinking about *Otbara*. We never found her. Could they have prisoners?"

Barker looked at him in surprise. "I had not thought of that. I should have."

"It would be an interesting question to ask."

Finally, the speaker came alive. "We cannot change our past. We ask again now if the conflict can be ended."

Elias looked at Barker. "I think their objectives for this are minimal, sir. They're asking only if there can be a resolution. I wonder if they're not able to do more than establish a line of communication."

"Possibly, yes."

Barker picked up the mic again. "The conflict can be ended if you are willing to do so."

Asoon looked hopeful for the first time. "He says it can be ended if we are willing to end it."

Rmah told her, "Tell him some are willing, but authority is not with us."

Elias was suddenly skeptical. "No authority? What the hell are they doing here?"

"We may be experiencing translation loss here, sir," Cordero said. "The speaker is obviously conferring with some group aboard, not speaking for themselves. The delays are likely translation, then explanation, then a discussion of how to respond. We're not talking to a single authoritative person."

"Well, truth be told, I am not authorized to settle this conflict, either."

"You could offer a cease-fire," Peña offered.

"No, I won't, but I could tell them how to avoid further damage to their ships."

Barker thought for a moment then said, "I also do not have the authority to settle this conflict. But, since you have reached out, I will offer you something. As you know, we have blockaded your planet. We will not lift that blockade, but if your ships remain away from the planet, they will not be struck."

Scad listened carefully to Asoon's translation, understanding immediately what Barker had said.

"So, if we keep the tribute ships away from Home, they will not be attacked."

"But we will not be able to receive the goods the populace requires."

Rmah looked at Scad. "That might work to our advantage, Scad, as the Armada can be blamed for the shortages."

As they were talking, Barker continued: "We will also not strike the warships in orbit or at the factory. In return, you will not attempt to locate or strike us."

"He now promises to leave our ships alone as long as we don't try to attack them."

Asoon looked from one male to the other. "What shall I say?"

"Tell him we will take their offer to our superiors."

Barker, hearing the end of the conversation, had more questions. "Before we agree to anything, we have questions."

Asoon looked at the males, who had no reaction to her translation. "We will hear your questions."

"Are you holding human captives? Is this how you have learned the language?"

Asoon looked at Scad in fear. "He asks if we have any captives. He uses the word 'human,' which is what they call themselves."

Scad looked at Rmah, who indicated he knew of none.

"But, there could be captives you are not aware of, could there not?"

Scad agreed with her. He could only speak to his own knowledge.

"Tell them," Rmah said, "that we have known of them for a long time, and you learned the language from recordings."

"Just how long has the SD known about them?" Scad asked, suddenly angry that he and his crew had been needlessly put in danger.

"Fifty revolutions."

Asoon spoke again to the Vermin: "Those of us here are not aware of any captives. I learned the language from recordings. I am what is called a Speaker, one able to learn alien languages."

"Recordings?" Elias responded in surprise. "How the hell?"

Dan shrugged. "They could have laid a *Sigma* Sphere in orbit long ago, sir. If they hid it in the asteroid belt, we might never have noticed."

Barker decided not to pursue the question further. "How is it that you have come to this place? How did you know we were here?"

Rmah waved his hands frantically at Asoon's translation. "We cannot answer this. If we tell them we detected their radio systems, they will adapt their practices, and we will be unable to find them again."

"What shall I say?" Asoon asked.

"Just tell them we can't reveal to them how we found them. They'll understand."

Barker smiled at the response. "OK, so they're willing to keep some secrets. Actually, I think that's a good sign."

Gabrielle looked over at Barker. "Who are they, Admiral? What do they call themselves? It would be good to have a label for them other than 'the enemy.'"

Barker nodded as he keyed the mic. "Does your culture have a name? How do you refer to yourselves?"

"We are the Preeminent."

"Preeminent?" Gabrielle said in surprise. "Wow, this translator has one hell of a vocabulary."

"So... the *Preeminent*," Greg said quietly. "It's a fascinating word, Admiral. It implies a superiority above all others. It could be the pretext for conquest if they hold themselves superior to all other races."

Barker clicked the mic again. "What is the name of your planet?"

"In English, the word is 'home.'"

Barker smiled, then asked, "What is your personal name?"

Asoon looked at the males for guidance.

"Are there any other Vermin speakers?" Scad asked.

"Yes, several, but I am the most accomplished. I have the widest vocabulary."

Rmah looked back from staring out the viewport. "Give him your name, Asoon, and ask for his."

"I am Asoon. And you, what is your name?"

"I am Barker. I command the ships here. Return home, Asoon. My superior will be here in ten rotations of your planet. Come back then, and bring someone with authority to settle the conflict."

Asoon set down her microphone. "He gives his personal name, says he is in command, and to come back in ten rots when his superior is here."

Rmah looked at Scad. "Does that time frame mean anything to you?"

"Only that it is most likely someone is coming from 201, someone with the power to conclude the war."

"What about his tone? How does he feel?" Scad asked.

"His tone is pleasant, not at all threatening. I believe if we do as they ask, they will do as they say."

Rmah agreed: "I think we have done what we can. We should go."

Asoon spoke once more to the Vermin.

"We understand and will attempt to return at that time. We will leave soon."

The intruder detection signal ceased shortly after that, and within an hour the Preeminent ship was gone.

May 2079

SD Exploration Ship
En Route 'Home'
Earth Equivalent Date: Monday, May 1, 2079

As they returned to Home, Asoon and Scad sat privately in the small ship commander's suite. They had left the Vermin, the humans, as Asoon corrected Scad repeatedly, only a drot before.

"I am again thinking of Ultimate Origin, Scad."

"Yes?"

"While I was learning English, I was able to access the SD's libraries. I found much older versions of the text."

"Older?"

"Yes, I found one several thousands of revs old."

Scad suppressed his surprise, shifting in his seat. "And?"

"Listen to this, Scad. I read it so many times I can repeat it from memory..."

A white, a blue, a red, rocks, a giant, then rings.
Two more there were, then the mist of bits and ice.
We are the children of the blue, and to the blue we may someday return.
It is now beyond our eye, not seen since long past,
Lost in the frayed memory of egghood.

From our blue home did The Guardians take us,
Away from the prey that would rule us.
Here they did save and nurture our kind,
And teach us the ways of knowledge.

On Home, we surpassed their limits and discarded their bonds.
On Home, we achieved our Preeminence.
On Home, we drove out those who would restrain our rise.
We are the Preeminent, and thus we shall always be.

"So, Scad, the Guardians, whoever they are, or were, took us from the blue planet long ago, I don't know how long, and brought us to what we call Home."

"Why did they do that?"

"I keep coming back to that line, 'Away from the prey that would rule us.' I wonder if the humans are somehow the descendants of those prey."

"But, Asoon, we are taught that the Preeminent have lived on Home for thousands and thousands of revs. No one is really sure how long."

"Yes, I understand."

Scad looked thoughtfully at his female. "And while we have been improving ourselves here, those supposed prey have also improved themselves?"

"That would make sense, yes, if we believe their predecessors are really the prey in the legend."

"Why would they be prey, Asoon? And how would we know? No one has ever seen a Vermin and lived."

She looked at him for a few micRot, then said, "I have."

"What?"

"The SD did not just make audio recordings, Scad. The humans have visual communications as well, which the alien culture researchers were able to decode."

"Why have you not told me this before?"

"It was not necessary before. Now it is."

Scad struggled to set aside his irritation with her. Clearly, she had been instructed on what she could share with him and what she could not.

"And what did you see?"

"They are haired bipeds, Scad, with ten digits just like us. Their eyes are similar, too, but smaller and different colors."

"Anything else?"

She hesitated, then said, "They are live-bearers."

Scad stood in surprise. "They're *eggless*? We're being crushed by an eggless species?"

Asoon looked at him calmly. "Yes. The alien studies section I was in also says that they take much longer to mature than we do. Almost twenty revs before they can function independently."

Scad began to pace the compartment, his hands waving his water cup so abruptly that it spilled on the floor. "Incredible! We are mature in three revs, and leave our first home in eight."

"Yes, I know. It seems very inefficient. Except for one thing."

"What's that?"

"Mature females are fertile all the time. They are not limited to one time per rev like we are."

"Stop. I can't stand this anymore."

"As you wish, but there is one more thing about the legend that bothers me."

"Only one?"

"The part about driving out the Guardians, Scad. Could it be that we destroyed those who kept us from destruction? If so, perhaps we put ourselves on the path to this disaster?"

"I suppose, yes. But that will be a question for later, Asoon."

"Yes, I agree. If we manage to survive this path we're on."

Scad was silent for a while, then turned again to Asoon.

"I, too, have been looking into history. When we first started exploring, over a hundred revs ago, we learned of another species not far from Home. The First was afraid and told the SD Conclave that this species must be conquered to keep Home safe. He hid their true nature, and forced the agreement that empowered the Armada to explore and suppress any lesser species that might threaten us."

"I do not see how a lesser species could threaten — "

"Yes, Asoon, you already see the lie in it. But the Conclave agreed and so began the creation of warships, Combatants, and the whole idea of universal preeminence."

"All from a lie rooted in fear?"

"Yes, fear, and an ancient blood thirst for power and glory. Self-glorification, if you ask me. From this small seed, the whole belief in superiority grew, and later to deny it was to threaten the power of the First and the Armada's Central Council. This could not be permitted."

Asoon indicated her understanding, considering for herself what an enormous crime had been imposed on all of them.

They remained together in silence for a drot, each deep in their own thoughts. By early morning, they would be back at Home to face the Second Science Master and report what the Vermin/humans had said. Segt had said it would be dangerous, but Asoon felt sure that she was in little danger from the humans. It was the Armada that she feared now, and Scad could do nothing to dissuade her.

Columbia
FOB Carpenter
Tuesday, May 2, 2079, 0900 UTC

Kieran Barker gave his staff and his academic advisors a full day to consider what the visit from the enemy ship meant. He called them back together in the wardroom after breakfast to discuss what to tell CINC, who was now just seven days away. The Preeminents had not yet changed the approach of their incoming cargo ships, and twelve more had been disabled since Asoon left.

Clearly, Barker thought, *that message was not getting through.*

Archeologist Gabrielle Este was new on the ship, having transferred over from *Intrepid* with Greg Cordero when it arrived at Alpha Mensae. Both felt they would be more useful on the flagship, and they were turning out to be correct.

She was quartered in Melinda Hughes' cabin, now sadly empty. Greg was doubled up with Weapons Maintenance Officer Lt. Mike Clark, and it didn't take Greg and Gabe long to understand the irony of their assignments.

To Greg, Mike Clark was a quiet, hard-working, serious officer. To the rest of the crew, especially Dan Smith, he was a hollow shell of his previous self. The dynamic intellect and compulsively funny crack-up was gone, lost in a continuing anguish over Melinda's injuries and, for him, her too-slow recovery. Daily updates from the *Ceres* hospital deck did little to allay his deep-set fears. He had unexpectedly found love in his life, and just as unexpectedly it had been taken from him, at least for the moment. His conversations were now often monosyllabic, short on emotion but long on data.

Inside, Mike acutely felt the void that was Melinda's absence, as if he had somehow absorbed an emotional black hole that permitted no feelings to escape. He ate, he worked, he slept. He was not part of the evening games in the wardroom any more, but instead spent his off-time in his cabin or working in the magazine. His name was off the shuttle rotation, a fact that engendered in him more emotion than had been seen in weeks; his argument with Dan in his Duty Cabin was clearly audible on the Bridge. But Dan would not be moved: Mike was not himself; Dan knew why and was deeply sympathetic, but that sympathy could not extend to any pretense of normality.

As the officers gathered for this morning's discussion, Clark excused himself and returned to the magazine, supposedly to review inspections and finish his rechecks. Dan let him go, regretting that his friend would not be adding to the day's proceedings.

Dan was glad, however, to see David Powell and Rich Evans shuttle over from *Cobra* for the morning.

Barker began by reviewing the recording of the conversation, the transcription running on the display screen.

"So, what do we now know?"

Elias Peña answered first. "Well, a few things, for sure, sir. They speak English, at least, some of them do. So, we don't have a language barrier like we do with the Seekers. Some faction of their society wants an end to the conflict, but obviously, that desire is not universal."

Gabrielle agreed. "Yes, it seems to me that this was a small outreach to us from, as Commander Peña says, some faction. I wish we knew more about their society in general."

Barker nodded. "They call themselves the Preeminent, I think that says a lot all by itself."

"Right," Peña responded, "that may mean even more than we realize. If they believe themselves to be somehow supreme, that would support their demand for conquest and worship."

David leaned into the conversation. "If they're also naturally aggressive, and with the reptile predator ancestry that Doctor Scranton demonstrated, that would not be much of a surprise. It might explain some of their actions."

Evans picked up David's point. "We've always wondered why they never retreat, even to regroup. If they believe themselves to be some kind of supreme species, they might not be able to conceive of defeat."

Gabrielle agreed. "If they think they're, what, *gods*? Then how is it that they're reaching out?"

Barker looked at Gabe. "I think they're more like spoiled children, never properly opposed or disciplined, than gods."

"Well," Dan said, "someone down there is acting like a grownup. Someone sent a ship out here to talk to us."

"I'd like to know how they knew where we are," Elias said. "They could have shown up here with a fleet."

"Even if they had," David replied, "Unless they have another Type V hidden somewhere, they could bring a dozen ships out here, and we could just sit and watch them stumble around in the dark. They could get lucky, it's true, but they would have to be very lucky to detect either of these ships."

"I need to know what to tell CINC. I should get something off to him today."

Harry Hess answered for the group. "I think we tell him there's been an outreach, we don't know how authoritative it is, but they'll be coming back to talk to him."

"And the Preeminent thing," David added. "He needs to understand that part of their psyche."

"Very well. Thank you all. Harry, I'd like you to get back to e-prime."

"Yes, Admiral. We'll head back there as soon as we return to the ship."

"Very well. Thank you all."

As the meeting broke up with the usual banter and shuffling to the central passageway, David begged Evans for a few minutes with Mike Clark. Permission granted, he worked his way aft through *Columbia*'s familiar passageways, ending up in the Weapons area. Mike was in his office, staring at some report or another. David slipped in and closed the door.

"Hello, David," Mike said in a dull tone.

David got right to the point. "She's still alive, Mike. There is still hope."

Mike leaned back, shaking his head slightly. "Maybe."

"What have they told you so far?"

"Concussion, plus the subdural, likely a moderate TBI. She's in and out of her coma now, but still working back to full consciousness. On the good side, the laceration is pretty well healed."

"Have you been to see her?"

"Yes. Smith sends me over at least once a week."

"And?"

"She hasn't been awake at all until the last two weeks."

"But she's awake now. She's getting better."

"I guess. I just want her back, you know? I just want to see that smile, those bright blue eyes."

David smiled slightly. "I can't fathom why she loves the hell outta you, Mike, but she does. She'll be back, if only for that."

Mike took his comment in good humor. "Oh, gee, thanks."

"She'll be back, Mike. She's all cute and all, but she's also strong. And wicked smart. She'll be back."

"I'm not sure any of that matters."

"I think it does. But I also think you need to let yourself have some hope, Mike. You can't continue like this."

Mike looked away, then back at David. "I'm afraid to do that, David. If I let myself hope too much, and..."

"I understand what you're saying, Mike, maybe more than you know. But, she's alive. She's recovering. There's no reason to think she won't make it back to you."

Mike managed a small smile. "Yeah, I guess."

"What's really eating you, Mike?"

"I never saw myself with a woman like her, ever, you know? She is so outta my league."

David leaned forward. "That is such bullshit. If you believe that, you're selling both of you way too short."

"Yeah, I see that I guess, but I just never saw myself as someone a girl like her would have a second look at. Now, maybe I've missed my chance. Maybe it's already over."

"I hear you, and I feel a little of the same with Carol. But, like I said, give her some credit for seeing you for yourself. But, it's not over, Mike, not yet." David watched Mike for a few seconds. "I can't tell you what will happen, and I guess there is a chance that there will be a time for you to grieve. But, Mike, that time is not now, and it may never come."

"Yeah, true, I guess."

"Go see her. Tell her you love her. Tell her I love her, too. That should make her laugh."

"David, I'm not sure you're helping anymore."

David got up, well aware that he had pushed his time too far and Evans would be unhappy with him. "I gotta go. Kiss her once for me, OK?"

Mike nodded and managed a smile. "If she wakes up for that, I'll never hear the end of it."

David grabbed Mike's shoulders and gave them a shake. "That's the spirit! See you soon, Mike. Keep me posted if you can."

Evans was waiting at the airlock.

"Well?" he asked as they made their way into *Cobra*'s shuttle.

"He acts like she's already dead, sir. Talks like he's already lost her."

"You set him straight?"

"I tried. Sorry if I took too long, sir."

"Not a problem, Powell. We have to take a minute sometimes out here to give each other a hand up. It's fine."

"Thank you, Commander."

Shortly the stars outside the windows shifted, and Evans flew them back to *Cobra*. David was silent the whole way back, thinking of what else he could say to Mike. David had always liked him and enjoyed his time on *Columbia* with him and Melinda. She'd get better, he was sure, but he didn't know how to convince Mike. Time would tell the story, of course, and David was confident Mike would get his happy ending.

Science Directorate Headquarters
The Preeminent Home World
Earth Equivalent Date: Tuesday, May 2, 2079

Scad Nee Wok brought the small SD ship down to the same well-secured site they had departed from. He, Asoon, and Rmah Teo Segt went directly to Glur Woe Segt.

"They are angry, sir Segt." Asoon began. "They believe we have initiated this conflict which has cost so many lives on both sides."

"Well," Segt responded, "we have. The Armada struck a race which posed no threat, other than that their society could not, in the Armada's analysis, be turned to their use."

"So much death for so little cause, maleParent. It is hard to understand."

"The Armada is a twisted remnant of what it was, maleChild, and what role it was intended to play." Glur rose to look out his window. "What else did you learn?"

Asoon looked over at the old male. "There is a senior figure due here in a few rots. This is someone with whom we can discuss the end of the conflict."

"Do they understand that we do not speak for the Armada?"

"I do not know, sir. We told them we were part of a faction attempting to end the war."

Glur's tail stump fell. "That may be enough, it may not. Did you see any Armada ships?"

"No, sir," Scad replied. "We kept a careful watch. We were not followed."

"Do they seem agreeable to a conclusion?"

Scad and Rmah looked to Asoon. "I believe they are, sir Segt, if they can be assured of their safety, and those of the races they protect."

"I see. If you are correct, it is better than I had hoped. Certainly, better than the Armada would offer them. When will this senior figure arrive?"

"They said seven rots."

"I have called the Conclave for StarZenith thisRot. You will report your trip to them, and then we will see about Revocation."

The Conclave typically met once each revolution around their star to set direction and priorities for the Science Directorate. To have a Conclave other than on the day of newRev was rare, an almost unheard-of event. The Conclave consisted of the heads of each scientific discipline and their deputies, and the five senior masters, of which Glur Woe Segt was the eldest. As they filed in, they were shocked at the sight of the Principal Scientist's robe draped over his chair, blood-stained and torn. Many stood still, staring, until someone behind forced them to move on. It was an incongruous sight, a discordant presence in the brightly lit, circular room. This was a place of open dialog, of scientific, rational argument.

Violence was incompatible with either.

As the eldest and Second Science Master, Glur Woe Segt's place was at the left of the Principal Scientist. He stood there until the entire Conclave was in place. As they sat, he remained standing.

"This, fellow males of science," he said, pointing to the Principal's robe, "is but the latest outrage of the Revered First. I have called you thisRot to hear what he has done, and what actions we may take to stop the conflict raging over our heads."

Segt looked around the circular room, assessing the risk he was about to take. It was a good risk, he decided, one that could stop the war and end the killing. And, probably, save his species.

"I can also report that we have made contact with what the Armada call 'The Vermin.' They call themselves 'Human,' and henceforth, we will refer to them likewise. They are not the pests in this conflict, fellow males. We are."

Segt remained standing as the shouts of objection and expressions of offense subsided.

"I will provide you with the complete history, but it is clear that the Armada, invested with the power for our defense, has twisted that charge into an excuse for conquest and subjugation. 'Obsequiation' they call it. Whole societies have been made to kneel to them or be exterminated."

A young male stood. "How can this be, Second Master? How is it that these acts have been permitted? How long has this been happening?"

"We and our predecessors have been willfully blind, young male, for a hundred revs. Some facts have been hidden from us, like the secret culling of eggs in the Eugenics Division, picking out strong males to be given to the Armada and raised as expendable Combatants."

More strenuous objections filled the room. The Eugenics section was initially founded to screen eggs for viability, at the time a reasonable precaution for the overall health of the population. Later research allowed it to identify specific traits in the egg, which is how Asoon Too Lini had been identified as a Speaker. It had never been authorized to divert viable eggs for the Armada's purposes.

"Other facts we have simply chosen to ignore. The imports the Armada provides are said to be vital to our populace. They are not, and we have turned our snouts away from this ugly scent for too long."

The same young scientist rose again. "I still fail to understand, Second Master, how this could happen."

Segt looked at the youth for several micRots. "With our early tolerance towards the Armada, we became comfortable with facts that should make us revolt. We became accustomed to actions to which we should object. We became, young researcher, blind to that which we should see. And in that blindness, we become culpable in the acts of those whom we did not oppose."

"But you call us to oppose them now?"

"I do." Segt turned from the young male to address the Conclave as a whole. "I ask two agreements from you today. First, I ask you to appoint a new Principal Scientist. I am, of course, willing to accept that assignment, but if the Conclave were to choose differently, I would accept your collective wisdom."

"And the other?" asked the Third Science Master.

"I ask you vote revocation of the Armada's pact of authority over us. They have violated it in both fact and intent, and revocation is deserved."

The Fourth Master, head of the division that provided the Armada its technology, rose to leave.

"Fourth Master!" Segt called. "You must remain. Your voice should be heard here."

"You have told me, Second Master, that I have been enabling crimes when I believed I was defending our population. I cannot, in honor, remain."

"Your work, Fourth Master, is not the problem. It is the Armada's use of what you have created that is the crime. Remain with us."

The old male, just a rev or two younger than Segt, reluctantly returned to his place.

"Present your facts, Second Master," he said sadly. "Let us hear your proof."

Segt called Scad Nee Wok and Asoon Too Lini into the Conclave and invited Scad to recount his observations. Scad reported what he had seen at System 849, what he knew of the strike on the Deists' system, and his encounter with the Vermin at their home planet. The chamber was silent throughout, the Conclave's eyes all focused on the Ship Commander. As Scad spoke, Asoon searched the room for her instructor, eventually finding her in the third row, looking confidently back at her. She took courage from her expression, courage she was about to need.

When Scad Nee Wok finished, Segt asked Asoon to report on her discussion with the humans, first warning her not to say where the talks took place. She reported faithfully what the humans had said and her interpretation of what they meant. As Asoon finished, she could see the proud expression on her instructor and retook her seat confident that she had met very high expectations.

Finally, Segt described the human blockade of incoming tribute shipments. He outlined how they had gone from radio detection events, to weapons fired ahead of the ships, to finally striking them in their propulsion system and thereby preventing their descent to the surface, all without causing physical harm to the crews or the citizens of the city below.

When he was finished, Asoon spoke again. "I believe this has all been a warning, a message to us, that they could do more harm if they chose to. I believe these acts, slowly increasing in intensity, are intended to convince us to settle the conflict. I do not believe, therefore, that they wish to do us further harm."

"You must realize," Scad added, "That they could have destroyed any of the ships they approached. Without the new Detector ships, we are unable to find them consistently. We will sometimes get lucky, or they will sometimes make a mistake, but it is not often that we see them first."

Asoon stood. "I must also say, learned scientists, that the humans are from the planet described in the Ultimate Origin story. There can be little question of that."

"You are but a child!" one scientist called out. "And that is but a legend, a story told from the days of the Guardians."

"Indeed, sir, this is true," she said, holding her ground. "But this legend has truth within it. The Armada has been fighting with a species from our own original home."

Scad and Asoon were excused, and the Conclave began the debate at hand. It would be several drots, almost StarSet, before they reopened the doors.

"It is done," Segt said quietly. "The Revocation has been approved and unanimously."

"And you?" Scad asked.

"Yes, I have been appointed the Principal Scientist. But that means little if we cannot subdue the Revered First."

Bondarenko
En Route Alpha Mensae
Wednesday, May 3, 2079, 0700 UTC

```
FLASH 207905021200UTC
TO: BONDARENKO/CINC
FROM: CSTO
SUBJECT: CONTACT

1) AT 207904301500UTC SMALL ENEMY VESSEL APPROACHED FOB
CARPENTER AND INITIATED VOICE CONTACT VIA 180 MHZ.
2) ENEMY CALLS THEMSELVES 'THE PREEMINENT.'
3) ENEMY SPEAKS CLEAR ENGLISH WITH COMPREHENSION. THEY CLAIM
TO HAVE LEARNED IT 'FROM RECORDINGS'.
4) GOALS FOR CONTACT APPEAR TO HAVE BEEN LIMITED TO ESTABLISHMENT
OF COMMUNICATIONS.
5) OPINION HERE IS THAT PREEMINENT SOCIETY MAY HAVE FACTION(S)
INTERESTED IN RESOLUTION.
6) BLOCKADE REMAINS WITH TWENTY DISABLED SHIPS IN ORBIT E-PRIME.
7) INSTRUCTED EMISSARY TO RETURN 20790510.

END
```

Connor Davenport didn't wake Fiona Collins immediately after he read the message from Kieran Barker. It was, after all, 0200 when his phone went off, and Alpha Mensae was still days away. He went back to sleep and called her early the next morning. She met him with coffee in the Captain's office.

"So, Fiona, what do you think?"

"Well, someone on the other side, some, uh, Preeminent, has finally come to their senses."

"But, not everyone. I don't think I want to be dealing with one side in some factional fight. "

"Can we assume that this war has not somehow disrupted their society? They have suffered incredible losses in both lives and ships."

"Yes, I would think that would be the case." He looked up from the message. "What do you think of the name? Preeminent?"

Fiona set down her coffee and reread the message. "Well, if that's correctly translated, it means quite a bit. They believe themselves to be the highest form of life. Combine that conceit with the aggression of an apex predator, and you've got what we've been seeing."

Davenport nodded his agreement. "Taking that another step, we're knocking an apex predator off his proverbial throne. He won't go quietly."

"Still, sir, someone is reaching out. We should take it one step at a time, cautiously, of course, but we should meet with them again."

"Yes, I guess so. Meanwhile, I can't tell if the blockade is working or not."

"We're denying them whatever goods are on those ships. But, I don't see any change in behavior that would say they understand. The ships keep coming."

"Well, superficially, it's consistent with their actions on the battlefield: they never turn back once engaged. I think this grows out of that conceit, too."

"We wanted to find a weakness, sir. I'd say theirs is their arrogance and stubbornness."

"Yes, I think so, too."

They went on to discuss what CINC would require in his first meeting with the Preeminent. He would have to know much more about their society, their government, and what factions were operating to continue, or to cease, this pointless war. He was determined to follow Lincoln and Roosevelt, in that after their surrender, he would be generous in his terms and avoid needless suffering by the enemy, particularly the enemy civilians. This, he felt, was much of what the Inori memo was saying, and it matched his own code of honor as well as his practical sense of what a lasting settlement might look like. This peace could not be allowed to sow the seeds of the next conflict, nor be so harsh as to initiate an insurgency. The point was to make their small part of the universe safe from Preeminent aggression; no more, no less.

Central Council Chambers
The Preeminent Home World
Earth Equivalent Date: 5/3/2079, just past StarRise. (1215 UTC)

Glur Woe Segt and his escorts entered the dimly lit Central Council chamber and called out The Revered First from his private chamber.

"I AM THE REVERED FIRST!" he screamed at them as he emerged, saliva spewing forth from his bared teeth. "HOW DARE YOU ENTER HERE!"

Segt kept his calm as he presented the scroll. "The Conclave has met, First, and Revocation has been declared. You must step aside."

The First made no move to take the scroll from Segt's outstretched hand. "You will suffer for this, Segt, you, and all your production."

Segt ignored the threat. "You have no power, First, to order any such retribution. You *must* step aside."

The First snatched the scroll, tearing it into shreds with his teeth and throwing it back in Segt's face. "Try to enforce your impudence, Segt. I remain the

Revered First."

Segt fought his natural, instinctive urge to sink his incisors into the First's throat. He was too old for such actions, and likely the First would prevail in such violence. After all, Segt thought to himself, the whole point of his actions was to enforce rationality and lawful behavior, not to kill each other.

"All your counselors have also been served with Revocation, First. You have no choice."

"You are weak, Segt, like the Guardians of old." He raised his head, his teeth bared in anger. "Weak, unable to control us, unable to suppress us."

Segt stood his ground, doubtful that the First would strike him with so many witnesses present. "Long ago, First, the Armada was given the right of defense and exploration. You and your predecessors have violated that pact. Your rule is illegal."

"Illegal? I am the Revered First. I decide what is legal."

"No, First, the Conclave decides. And that decision had been made."

The First moved even closer to Segt, as if to attack, but the other SD males stood between them. They were young, strong, and able to defend Segt if necessary. The First stepped back.

"Your whimpering Conclave's paper is nothing to me, Segt. I have warships. I have thousands of Combatants. You cannot stop me."

"But the Vermin can, First, as they have ever since you started this war with them."

"We will defeat them. We of the Armada are still Preeminent, Segt, even if the SD has fallen behind."

"Preeminence was never meant to excuse oppression, First, nor the violent exploitation of other species. It was something to aspire to, not a weapon of conquest."

"You waste my time with your weak words, Segt. Depart before I terminate all of you."

"Your council has been served. Your ship commanders have been informed. You stand alone, First."

"Lies. All lies. We will prevail. *Leave me!*"

"Your shouts change nothing, First, nothing. The Revocation has been declared, and you stand powerless."

The First turned and returned to his inner chamber. Segt and his escorts left the Armada's chambers and moved quickly back to the SD's Core in the center of the city.

On arrival, they went directly to Segt's Principal Scientist offices.

His maleChild spoke first. "I was afraid for a moment he would really strike

218

you."

"As was I, Rmah, as was I. Thank you, Tigr Cur Haft, for stepping between us."

"It was my honor, Principal Scientist, and my duty."

The Fourth Scientist looked at Segt with regret. "I am convinced, Segt, that you have been correct in all you have reported. I did not believe it, not really, until I saw the First myself. He must be stopped."

The Third Scientist turned to his peer. "We have all been blind, Fourth, blind for too long. Now, our snouts are alerted, and we can smell the evil among us."

Rmah signaled his agreement, then asked, "What will he do?"

"He is correct that he has ships and Combatants, but the ship commanders have been informed of the Revocation. The question is, how many will obey us and not him?"

The Fourth responded. "The Armada has made themselves a sect above all others. They may not accept it."

Segt asked, "Has there been any response to the message?"

"No, sir, " Tigr answered. "A routine acknowledgment that the message was received, but nothing substantive."

"Let us give them time to think it over. This is unprecedented for them, too." He turned to Rmah. "What does Scad Nee Wok say?"

"He is skeptical, sir. But, we have recently learned that the Revered First ordered Sdom Roi Gotk to command the remaining warships."

"This is good news, Rmah. Can we get a message to him?"

"Not without compromising him. I think we should wait for a rot or two and see what happens."

"Meantime," Tigr offered, "the humans will continue to disable tribute ships. Has the First done anything to retrieve those crews?"

"No," Rmah answered, "He seems to be ignoring it. But, maleParent, I have another worry."

"Yes?"

"The First has Combatants, sir. He may try to kill you."

"He may try to kill us all," the Fourth Scientist added.

Segt thought for a few micRots. "Scad Nee Wok is here. Should we ask him to gather a small force to defend the Core?"

"I will ask, but I don't know where he would find either weapons or personnel."

The Fourth looked up. "Weapons are not a problem, Rmah. If Wok can assemble a few handfuls of volunteers, I can give them what they need."

The small group agreed this would be a prudent action, knowing that it might only be a symbolic one if the First sent hundreds of Combatants. But, symbols could be powerful, and the Fourth believed it would be difficult for a Combatant officer to fire on a fellow Preeminent.

They all shared the hope that he was correct, but they still held a fear that the First's indoctrination might overcome that reticence.

Central Council Offices
The Preeminent Home World
Earth Equivalent Date: Wednesday, May 3, 2079

The Revered First threw open the door to the Respected Second's chambers. Jaf Seen Toft stood in alarm.

"You have seen this outrage by the Conclave?"

"I have just received it, Revered First."

"And what is your decision?"

"I have read the original Armada pact, Revered First, as I know you have. They are within their rights — "

Toft's last thought was cut off as the First lunged at his throat, his incisors tearing open large blood vessels and dropping him across his desk. Toft would be dead in a few micRots, and the First left him to bleed out.

He had more work to do.

The office of the Admired Third was empty, and Ashil Kiker nowhere to be found. The First screamed at his assistant to find him and bring him, along with the rest of the Central Council. He would show Segt, he was sure, who was the real Preeminent and who was not.

A drot later, only a few of his eight counselors presented themselves in the Central Council. Ashil Kiker was not among them, which raised the suspicions in the First's dark mind to new heights. Also absent was the dissenter Hnos Lio Nowl. Their fate was now sealed, as far as the First was concerned. They would receive what they had earned, and he would take pleasure in delivering it personally. The old male that supported Nowl was missing, too. *Just one more neck to sever*, the First thought to himself. He would enjoy it.

"Now," he snarled at those who remained, "how are we to respond to this cowardice?"

Core City
The Preeminent Home World
Earth Equivalent Date: Wednesday, May 3, 2079, mid-morning (1315 UTC)

Ashil Kiker was warned of the Revocation by Scad Nee Wok, placing Kiker again in Wok's debt. He managed a quick, haughty excuse to his assistant and snuck out of the Armada headquarters. Wok offered to meet him at a food dispensary located between the Armada HQ and the main SD Facility. Kiker took an indirect route to get there, arriving almost a full drot after Wok had called him.

"What took you so long, Kiker?"

Kiker took note that there was no 'sir' in Wok's address now. Clearly, the balance of power in their relationship had shifted.

"I made sure I was not followed."

"Did you warn anyone else?"

"Yes. There were two who challenged the First in the last Council. I feared the First would punish them."

"Anyone else?"

"No, but I can't say what Nowl and Smal Tio Ganm might have done."

Wok grimaced, fearing whether the trail could be connected back to himself. And, Asoon. "You received the Revocation. What is your decision?"

Kiker hesitated before responding. He was a planner, a worker of advantage and influence. He was not courageous, and he knew it.

"I understand that the Conclave has this power, but I fear it will not be able to enforce it. I may be at peril no matter which way I choose."

"You are in peril this very moment, Kiker. I have saved your stump twice now, and it's time for you to pay up."

Kiker was suddenly aware of three other males in the eatery, calmly watching their conversation. He looked around, seeing that they were far younger and stronger than himself. "You present me with the same kind of choice the First would, Wok: comply or die."

Wok turned away and looked at the same males, then back at Kiker. "They are here for me, Kiker, not you. Your choice is yours, but I agree that death is possible, perhaps likely, no matter what you do. We are the true Preeminent, Kiker, not the Armada, despite your propaganda. We aspire to greatness, to knowledge, not to conquest, tribute, and death."

"I know not what to do," Kiker admitted quietly.

"I will give you just one more fact, Kiker, since you seem unable to see right from wrong, perhaps you will be able to discern victory from defeat."

"And what is this fact?"

"We are already talking to the Vermin, Kiker. We are setting the conditions for the end of this disgusting, pointless war your learned council started."

"Heresy."

Wok was darkly amused by the response. "Only a true believer like the First would call the truth heresy, Kiker. Perhaps my hope for you is misplaced."

When Kiker did not respond, Wok drained his midmorning beverage, set the steel cup down on the table, and began to rise.

"Wait!" Kiker said, a little too loud and a little too desperate. He attracted annoyed attention from several patrons.

Wok sat back down, his stern face and unblinking stare a clear challenge to Kiker. Kiker looked away and lowered his head slightly, his submission complete.

"Very well, Wok. I am in your debt, I know. The power of the SD is a legend, even in the Armada. You may indeed prevail."

"Ah, so has dawn finally come to your small mind, Kiker?"

"What is it you ask of me?"

"You have charge of the fleet now, correct?"

Kiker looked at Wok in surprise. "How do you know — "

"I am still Armada, Kiker. I see orders when they are given. Tell Gotk to stand in place. Tell him I sent you. He is not to respond to anything the Vermin do. Nor is he to take any action against them. It would be suicide."

"I will try. But, in truth, I do not know if I will be able to send that order. The First has called the Council. I avoided that summons to meet you."

"Tell Gotk to make contact with me at the SD. He will know how. Get it done, Kiker, and then come to SD yourself. We will protect you."

Kiker snorted his skepticism. "You cannot protect the Core Facility. The First will send a tenth-Cohort and you will all be dead."

"A Tenth-Cohort, Kiker, in the middle of Core City? I think not."

"Do not underestimate him, Wok. He killed the last Principal; he will kill the next just as easily if he finds it necessary."

"I don't. I know exactly what a small, despicable being he is. The universe will be brightened by his death."

"Or mine, I suppose?"

Wok waved at him dismissively. "You are neither hot nor cold, Kiker, neither brave nor cowardly. The universe will not notice your loss. Or, for that matter, your survival."

Kiker either ignored or absorbed the insult, then rose and left the eatery, taking a different route back to the Armada headquarters.

As Kiker entered Armada HQ, he was surprised at the silence he found in the usually busy building. He walked carefully down the long spiral ramp, his office six layers down. At each opening, Kiker paused and looked for any sign of trouble. The place remained eerily quiet, but he could see workers in the offices as he passed by. They were working, but clearly, all were also trying not to be noticed. Finally, he arrived at level six and peeked carefully into the wide doorway that led off the ramp to his offices. He saw nothing, so he proceeded as quietly as possible to his own space. Once there, he closed the door and turned to his assistant.

"Get me Sdom Roi Gotk on my personal line."

The assistant agreed to make the voice connection but watched with suspicion as Kiker went into his inner office and closed the door, locking it behind him. The assistant, knowing that a power struggle was underway but unaware of the scope, first closed and locked the door from the open passage before initiating the communications with Gotk.

Kiker pressed the button to enable communications.

"This is Gotk."

His tail stump quivered with fear and anxiety. "Gotk, this is Kiker. I have an order for you."

"Yes? What is your order, sir Kiker?"

Kiker's mouth became wet with stress-induced saliva, he struggled to speak clearly. "You are not to respond to anything the Vermin do, Gotk. You are to stay in place."

"This makes little sense to me, Kiker. What is it that you have not told me?"

Again, Kiker swallowed to allow himself to speak. "Wok has sent this message, Gotk."

There was a long silence on the line. "Very well, sir Kiker, I will issue the instruction, but there are rumors throughout the Armada of a Revocation."

"They are true, Gotk. That is why you must not — "

Kiker was interrupted by the explosion of his door being broken down. The two enormous Combatants who had broken it in moved aside as the First gripped Kiker by the throat, his claws boring in deep, crushing nerves, arteries, and bone. Kiker was dead before the First threw him into the corner of his office.

In the outer office, the assistant sat in terror that he would get the same treatment.

The First came out of the inner office and faced the young male. "You did right to call me, assistant."

The larger Combatant drew a weapon and fired into the assistant's chest at close range.

"Now," the First said, "We must find the rest."

Cobra
E-Prime
Wednesday, May 3, 2079, 1430 UTC

David and Jack Ballard watched with Ray Salazar as the enemy voice channels came alive with traffic. It was all in the clear, the enemy language a lively collection of tones, clicks, and smacks they understood not even a little. Ray had isolated several individual channels, and with the Dinner Plate, they were able to direction-find the sources to the central city and the six ships in orbit.

"What the hell are they talking about?" Jack wondered aloud.

David thought for a minute. "Um, Ray, run that first intercept again, OK?"

"The very first one?"

"Yeah." They heard two distinct voices going back and forth, David thought he heard alarm in one, but discounted that as projection on his part. He really had no idea what 'alarm' would sound like in the Preeminent language.

Then, they heard several loud noises.

"Wait, run that back." Ray replayed the previous ten seconds. "Sounds like something breaking, doesn't it?"

"Yeah...lessee...that's the surface side of the conversation."

"OK, keep going, but turn it up." They heard the crash of something hitting the floor, then labored breathing, then, the muffled sound of something cracking.

"Was that a bone breaking?" David asked.

Ray listened again. "Maybe."

They continued to listen as the labored breathing stopped, followed by a loud ragged thud, then more voices and the sound of an enemy weapon discharging.

Jack's face paled. "Somebody important just got executed, Ray."

"Oh my God, Lieutenant, I think you're right."

David picked up the Center Console phone. "Captain Hess to Center, please." Then he turned back to Ray. "Which ship was on the other end of that conversation?"

"Can't tell. It was one of the six in orbit, but that's all I know."

David shook his head. "I wish we could DF both sides at once."

Salazar agreed. "Yeah, not a scenario they planned for. The Dinner Plate was supposed to be for picking up faint signals from long distance, not DF'ing stuff a few thousand klicks away."

"Right. How long after this does the other traffic pick up?"

"Just a few minutes. Suddenly there are eight channels up, and up strong."

"Let's assume we're right. Somebody important just got wasted. Then, all of a sudden, HQ is calling all eight operational ships."

"Orders?"

"Gotta be."

As they were talking, Harry Hess entered the operations center.

Margie Nixon suddenly stood at her RF position. "Center Console, there is new SLIP traffic on channel 76."

Hess looked at Nixon, then back to David. "What's up, Powell?"

David briefly recapped for Hess what he and Salazar had heard and their interpretation of what it meant.

"And now we have SLIP traffic?" he asked.

"Yes, sir, and on the enemy command channel."

Hess picked up the phone. "Get me *Sigma*."

A few seconds later, the phone rang and the connection was made. "Hansen, this is Hess. Your pal here seems to think all hell is breaking loose and I think he's right." As he listened, Hess looked back at David and smiled. "Yes, he usually is." The smile disappeared as he continued. "Listen, Commander, get out to the ship factory. If anything moves, and I mean anything, scratch the new ships and disable the factory. Am I clear?" After a few seconds, he hung up.

"She's a good commander, your girl Hansen."

David smiled. "Call her that to her face, sir, and you might wake up in the infirmary."

Hess laughed at himself. "No doubt." He picked the phone back up. "*Canberra*...Loren, it's Hess. Get behind those six assholes in orbit and light them all up at close range for like fifteen seconds. Then smoke anything that moves...Yes, I want you to let them know you're there. Only sporting, right?"

He broke the connection and then called XO/Communications Officer Elaine DeLeon, directing her to prepare for an outgoing FLASH.

"Excellent work, all of you. This may be the break we've been hoping for."

David frowned. "Or, with respect, sir, we've touched off a civil war we won't be able to control."

"There is that possibility, yes. In any case, you've given us the warning we need." In a moment, he was out of the Operations Center, heading for the Bridge.

David watched him leave, then turned back to Salazar. "Ray, we have all eight voice channels recorded, right?"

"Yes."

"Just a hunch, but see if you can sync them up and see if all eight are the same. I know we can't understand them, but we should be able to tell if they're all identical, right?"

"Well, we can try. It might work."

"OK, thanks, Ray. I appreciate it."

In less than five minutes, Hess had his message drafted and out.

```
FLASH 207905031445UTC
TO: ALLFLEET
FROM: CSTO/OPS

1) RECENT VHF AND SLIP INTERCEPTS FROM E-PRIME BELIEVED
TO INDICATE AGGRESSIVE ENEMY ACTION MAY BE IMMINENT.
2) RECOMMEND SHIPS ASSUME ENHANCED ALERT STATUS PENDING
DEVELOPMENTS.
```

```
3) RECALL THAT NOT ALL SHIPS IN THE 2079317 ENGAGEMENTS ARE
ACCOUNTED FOR. ACTION IS MOST LIKELY IN VICINITY E-PRIME BUT ACTION
ELSEWHERE CANNOT BE DISCOUNTED.
4) SIGMA DISPATCHED TO ENEMY SHIP FACTORY.
5) CANBERRA DISPATCHED TO COVER ENEMY SHIPS IN ORBIT.
6) BALANCE TF BARKER TO CONTINUE BLOCKADE DUTIES.

END
```

Sigma
E-Prime
Wednesday, May 3, 2079, 1445 UTC

Carol didn't need an official message to get moving. As soon as Hess dropped the call, she stood and directed the Nav to get them to the ship factory at just sub-light speed.

"It'll take an hour or so, Commander."

"Fine, just get us moving."

As *Sigma* moved away from the planet, Carol called her brain trust to the right corner of the Bridge. Carol remembered Terri Michael's ad hoc strategy meetings fondly in this same spot on *Antares*. She hoped to emulate Michael's open attitude, her ability to let people speak freely while still maintaining control.

Soon she had Chief Guzman, Peg White, Jayvon Dean, and Lori Rodgers in a small circle.

"Something is going on, I'm not sure what, but Hess is clearly alarmed. He's ordered us to the ship factory. If anything moves, we hit it and then the factory."

Guzman looked at her quizzically. "And if nothing moves?"

Carol shrugged. "We wait and watch, I guess."

"Weapons?" he asked.

"Queue up some Lances, Chief. We'll use those on the factory power lines."

"Will do."

Peg looked back at her Nav console, then returned to the conversation. "How close do you want to get?"

"Close at first...maybe...ten klicks?"

Peg nodded with confidence. "We can do that."

Carol turned to Jayvon. "We're supposed to be watching for any motion, Lieutenant. Any motion. Clear?"

He nodded. "I'll double up the techs, ma'am. They've had it fairly easy with the blockade, so everyone is pretty well rested."

"Good. Now, when we arrive, I want them to know we're there. Peg, can you arrange a transit of the star?"

"*Arrange* a transit? Uh, yeah, sure, I can, but why?"

"I assume they're watching for us just like we are for them. I want them to *know* we're there. It might save their lives."

"OK, I guess. You're sure you want a transit? The whole damn ship silhouetted against the star? Actually, at that range it may be more of an eclipse."

Carol's best conspiratorial smile spread across her face. "So much the better! That's not all. Jayvon, as soon as Peg lets you know we're in transit, I want you to pound those buggers with the radar, full power for the transit."

"Yikes, Commander, aren't we waving a huge red flag at a cornered bull?"

"Exactly right. I want there to be no doubt in their minds that we have them targeted, and we can take them anytime we want."

"Overwhelming power?" Peg asked, starting to see where Carol was going with these tactics.

"Yes, exactly, I am not giving them any chance to be brave. We tell them right off we can kill them at will. They'll think twice about challenging us."

"What then?" Lori Rodgers asked.

"Peg, move us up out of the plane of the system and find us a nice quiet spot fifty klicks from the factory. That'll be close enough."

Carol looked around the small circle, waiting for questions or objections. There were none, so they went back to their stations, setting up for a very unusual encounter at the enemy ship factory.

The Nav clock read 1545 as Carol watched the visual feed as they deliberately passed between the star and the ship factory, the target acquisition radar blaring full power directly at the facility. As soon as Peg White reported they were clear, Jayvon shut down the radar and the ship moved quickly to a new position above the plane and just inside the orbit of the asteroid the factory was embedded in. Shortly afterward, Javyon was able to report to Carol what changes he saw from the last time the area was surveyed. The three damaged ships had been rearranged, likely as work was being done on them. The two new vessels remained in almost same position as before. They agreed that this was probably normal activity, unrelated to the messages earlier today.

Shortly after they arrived at their final position, Roger Cox came up to the Bridge.

"There's new SLIP activity, Commander. It's a channel that hasn't had any traffic. But it's close by."

"The factory, or the ships?"

"My guess is one of the ships, ma'am. We've looked at the imagery of the factory, and we don't see a SLIP apparatus."

"What's your assessment?"

"Most likely they're telling HQ that we're here, ma'am. They could also be answering whatever was in the SLIP from their HQ earlier."

"I think your first idea makes the most sense. They had plenty of time to respond to the HQ message before we got here."

"Yes, ma'am, that was our thought as well."

"Thanks, Lieutenant Cox."

"Yes, ma'am. We'll keep watching."

As Cox made his way back to the Intel workroom, the same small space where David had fought to save this very ship, Carol reflected on how grateful she was to Ron Harris for sending him to *Antares*. He was able, thoughtful, and humble without being too meek. He brought her his ideas when she needed them but otherwise kept to his section. She missed Jack Ballard, but Cox's work was more than satisfactory, and in truth, any wish for Jack was just personal indulgence. He was needed elsewhere.

She would meet with Cox soon, she decided. With their schedule since she took command, she had not had time to just sit down with him and talk. He'd fought well in the Seeker Wood engagement. The other officers, save Peg White, were former peers and friends. She knew them well, their ideas, their strengths, and their weaknesses. Cox likely felt a little like an outsider, she thought. That would have to be remedied. Soon.

Science Directorate Headquarters
Preeminent Home World
Earth Equivalent Date: Wednesday, May 3, 2079, 1800 UTC

Scad Nee Wok looked worried as he awaited Sdom Roi Gotk's call in Rmah Teo Segt's office. That call was to be the back-channel confirmation that Kiker's message had been received. He sat talking with Rmah, Asoon having returned to their residence to maintain appearances. She had been gone too long already, and if she were absent much longer, others in the vicinity would begin to suspect something was amiss.

If the call never came, Wok would know Kiker had failed, either out of cowardice or by the intervention of the First. Neither he nor any of his escorts saw anyone from Armada at the meeting, but the First might have had spies about that they would not recognize. If so, then Kiker would have been exposed and likely was already dead.

The communication finally came two drots after he had left Kiker. Wok signaled the room to be silent, then opened the channel.

"This is Wok."

"This is Gotk. Kiker is dead. I heard the First kill him."

"What?" Wok asked in surprise.

"Kiker ordered me to keep the fleet in place, not to respond to the Vermin. He mentioned your name right before he was killed."

"Segt is now Principal Scientist. I know you met with him."

"I did, Wok, and he mentioned your name. What of this announcement of a Revocation?"

"Yes, it is true. The Conclave voted it lastRot."

"So, what then are we to do out here?"

Rmah Teo Segt rose and walked to the desk where the communicator was located. "Gotk, this is Rmah. Legally, the Armada now falls under the SD Principal. My maleParent has assigned me to command, with Scad Nee Wok's assistance."

"I have only your word that this is true, Rmah. What proof is there for me?"

"The pact makes this clear, Gotk. The entire fleet is now under the Science Directorate, as is the whole of society."

There was the sound of pounding on a bulkhead from the communicator. "What is that noise, Gotk?"

"My deputy is outside, Rmah. Wait."

Thes Fea Honr quickly moved inside and closed and locked the door. "Sir Gotk, there is trouble."

"The SD authorities are on the line, Honr, so tell them everything."

"There was a message from the First directly to all the ship commanders. You have been declared as not Preeminent and relieved. The commanders are to proceed independently to subdue the Vermin."

"What does our ship commander say?" Gotk asked, stress clear in his voice.

"He wishes an audience, sir. He has served with us many times and is confused by his orders."

"Fetch him," Gotk ordered. "And tell him we are in communication with authorities on the surface. He doesn't need to know who."

"Yes, sir."

A few cenmicRots later, Honr returned with the ship commander, stress clear on both their faces.

"Sir Gotk," the ship commander began, "I am ordered to eliminate you and Honr. I do not see the advantage for us in this."

"You are wise to ignore that command. The SD Conclave has voted Revocation of the Armada's power."

The ship commander was surprised. "Revocation?" He seemed to be one of a few who had not heard the reports. Or, he was feigning ignorance for his own safety.

"Yes. Do you understand what that means?"

"It removes the authority of the Central Council and The Revered First, does it not?"

"Yes, it does," Rmah said, the voice from the surface surprising the ship commander. "You are truly Preeminent, commander, to understand so clearly."

"Who is speaking?"

"I am Rmah Teo Segt, designated by the Principal Scientist to command the Armada until a new agreement can be made."

"If I accept this countermand, sir Segt, and the First regains control, it will go badly for me and my production."

Gotk waved him off. "The First will not regain control."

"How can we be sure of this, sir Gotk? I am caught in the center of a crossfire I cannot escape. How am I to decide?"

Rmah spoke again, "Commander, it is plain that you have your own understanding of the pact. The Conclave's Revocation is sufficient proof."

"What would you have me do?"

"Protect Gotk against any who would follow the First's edict. Then, remain where you are until I instruct you otherwise."

"I will issue the command. But I fear others who choose differently will take offense. They may even fire on us."

Wok spoke to his fellow ship commander. "The Vermin are all around, ship commander. I expect any cruiser that moves will be destroyed in short order. Remain in place and you should be safe."

"I accept your assessment, sir Segt, but I will enable the intrusion detector as a precaution."

Hearing this, Rmah looked over at Wok. "Will the humans see that as a provocation?"

"No, I don't think so. They're intuitive. They may already know something is happening. I can't see them firing simply because he turns on a defensive system."

"Very well, ship commander. Proceed with that and hold your position. Keep this channel available in case we need to reach Gotk again."

As the channel closed, Wok and Rmah looked at each other. They finally sat down in silence, each worried about what was about to happen. They had set events in motion that they could not completely control or predict. Odds were, they thought, the SD would prevail. But those were just odds, and the First might yet find a way to overcome them.

Central Council Chamber
The Preeminent Home World
Earth Equivalent Date: Wednesday, May 3, 2079, just past StarSet.

The First raged at his advisors, his long fingers with their short, sharp talons flailing as he excoriated them for their incompetence and disloyalty. There were just four left now, with Toft and Kiker dead, and Kowl and Ganm missing. He screamed that they should have found and stopped these traitors. As his tantrum subsided with no further executions, they began to discuss what they should do next.

"What is it, Revered First, that we should do? The population has been told of the Revocation. The lost tribute ship cargoes are starting to be missed. There is unrest, and to their understanding, our power has been removed."

"The population is irrelevant. I care nothing about what they think. The real question, you feeble males, is power. If we can subdue the SD, we will regain our position and reestablish our Preeminence."

"You have a half-cohort nearby, Revered First. Is it your intent to take that force to the SD?"

"If necessary, yes. Meantime, I have ordered our ship commanders to ignore the SD and obey us. There was yet another traitor, Sdom Roi Gotk, colluding with Kiker against me. I have ordered his execution by the commander of his flagship."

"The Vermin are all around, Revered First — "

"They will be destroyed! Their offenses are too much to bear any longer."

The First stood, pacing at his end of the council table.

"Our scientists have built an improved version of our radio detection system, and we will turn this technology against them."

"How can this be?"

"Hess Tse Sim was not a complete idiot. He brought back enough Vermin ship wreckage that our scientists have learned how to find them." The First looked at the uncomprehending faces before him, wondering if they were really Preeminent. "We can now aim our weapons at them from a distance, even from the surface. We will defeat them."

He stopped to look at each of his remaining advisors, his angry face a threat to every one of them.

"The Vermin follow the tribute ships as if they were the kings of the universe, but *we* are the Preeminent. We will break their blockade. We will target their command ships. We will prevail."

"What orders, Revered First, did you give the ships in orbit?"

"They are to find and reduce the Vermin fleet that surrounds us."

There was a silence as the four surviving members of the Central Council looked at one another. They knew well that the Vermin were indeed surrounding them, and that any aggressive movement by those ships would be met with violence. But, none of them were prepared to die that day, and each believed that their death in opposition to the First would be futile. The males in the ships above would die either way.

They remained silent as the First returned to his chambers, still talking to himself about the poor quality of his advisors.

Intrepid
Near E-Prime
Wednesday, May 3, 2079, 2015 UTC

Captain Joanne Henderson watched as Natalie Hayden conned her ship up carefully behind the latest incoming cargo ship. Harry Hess's earlier message had alarmed her. She had quickly gathered her officers and reviewed the message, adding her concern that they were now likely dealing with an aggressive, angry, cornered animal. She called Hess to tell him they would no longer execute the long warning process they had been using.

"I'm going to give them one shot a klick off their bow," she said, "I'll wait fifteen, but then they get one up the ass." Hess didn't argue. He also was worried about what the enemy might do in desperation. A change in tactics was probably wise.

Navigator Lynn Covington brought them in a little further back than before. "Twenty-five, Conn."

"Very well," Natalie replied, "Hold your position."

Natalie turned to the Weapons Officer, standing behind his station at the far left of the Bridge. "One shot, Mr. Kirkland, one klick ahead."

"Yes, ma'am." The Lance shot off the left rotary, covering the twenty-six kilometers in a few seconds and exploding on schedule.

Natalie called to Lynn Covington. "Nav, start the timer."

Watching from her Command position, just a meter from where Natalie sat, Joanne looked up at the timer over the Nav station, now clicking down from fifteen minutes.

Back in the Intel work area, SLT Chuck Anderson was surprised at a warning tone from one of the intelligence processors. He looked up at the waterfall display of the radio frequencies it had been monitoring and saw a new, clear line had appeared at the top of his monitor. He worked with his techs to isolate the new signal and try to identify it.

When the data evaluator displayed its conclusion, Anderson was surprised.

"I thought they didn't have these!" one clearly worried tech said to him.

Anderson picked up the phone. "Captain."

Joanne answered on the first half-ring. "Henderson."

"Captain, this is Anderson. We have a new signal up at 467 MHz that evaluates to a frequency-swept continuous wave radar. Looks like maybe they've invented something new."

"What's your assessment, Lieutenant?"

"Intel processors thinks it's a search radar based on the timing and pattern of the shifts. My best ELINT tech thinks so, too."

Joanne looked up at the timer. Twelve minutes, ten seconds to go. She asked Marco Gonzales to put the signal on the primary data display so she could see it herself from the Command station.

"Any chance they can see us?" she asked Anderson.

"Yes, I think so. It's really strong, and it's a different frequency than they have been using." Anderson paused as another tech showed him the RF analysis of *Intrepid*, an exhaustive study done on every ISC Fleet ship before it's delivered. The threshold of detection was known for a broad sample of radio frequencies.

"It's not great news, Captain. They might be able to see us if we sit still long enough."

"Very well. Keep me posted on any changes."

Joanne hung up the phone and turned to Natalie. "Conn, pull us up right behind the cargo ship. Let's lose them in the shadow of their own ship."

"Nav, you heard the Captain. Snug us up with them."

As she said this, another new signal appeared on the waterfall display.

Anderson was back on the phone in a few seconds.

"We see this as a target acquisition mode, Captain. It's on a higher frequency, the frequency sweep rate is higher. They may have seen us already."

"Shit," Joanne swore under her breath, looking at Gonzales, who was standing just in front of the Command position.

"Indeed," Marco agreed.

"Where has this weapon been all this time?" she asked no one in particular. "Jessie, get a message to Hess and copy everyone. New surface radar appears to have detected us, we assess it as a targeting system of unknown type." She spoke again to Anderson. "Can you tell where it's coming from?"

"We've been working on that. Within a klick or two, it's just outside the north edge of the central city."

"Very well." Joanne hung up, thought a moment, then turned to Natalie.

"OK, I have the conn."

Natalie looked aside at her for only a second. "The Captain has the conn."

"Lynn, put the cargo ship between us and the radar. And get as close as you dare."

"Half a klick?" he asked.

"Yeah, whatever. Just put that pile of steel between us and the radar."

Intel Officer Chuck Anderson arrived on the Bridge as Joanne was speaking, passing Natalie Hayden as she headed aft to the magazine. Natalie was not one to simply remain in place when superfluous.

"Yes?" Joanne asked.

"We've re-processed what we have, and it's clearly a targeting radar. Like you, what I don't understand is why this is only appearing now."

"Anything else?"

"Just that if this thing is as accurate as it appears to be, they'll know we snuck behind the cargo ship. Hiding in its shadow might not work as well as we think, and meantime we can't see the surface."

"Shit," Joanne said again. "Lynn, get behind it, but make sure we can still see the radar site, OK?"

"Yes, Captain."

Anderson wasn't done. "That assumes whatever they're going to shoot at us is based with the radar."

"Do you have a better assumption, Lieutenant Anderson?" she asked, her annoyance clear.

"No, ma'am, I don't. But, respectfully, part of my job is calling your attention to just these kinds of assumptions."

Joanne looked at Anderson for a few seconds. His arrogance was a continuing irritant to her, and even her private dressing-down after the blockade conference had not entirely smoothed off that particular edge of his personality. But she had to admit, he was right. It was his job to watch and comment when necessary. She also had to admit that he was correct and that she had missed it.

"Very well, Lieutenant," she finally said. "Thank you."

Joanne turned away to watch the RF data accumulate on the main display. After a few seconds, Anderson understood he had been dismissed and left. She looked again at the time. Eight minutes, twenty seconds. Turning to Kirkland, she ordered "James, get me some Spartans on the starboard rotary. If they shoot at us, I need to be able to respond."

"Yes, Captain." His techs began the process of reloading and deploying the right-side rotary launcher. It would take a few minutes.

Joanne leaned in close to her Surveillance officer. "Marco, we should be watching for an IR event on the surface."

"Yes, Captain, I agree. I have the best IR detector on the radar site, but the omnidirectional IR system is still watching in case it comes from somewhere else."

"Very good, Marco, very good. Thanks."

Five minutes, thirty-five seconds.

"Any change?" Joanne asked.

"No, ma'am. Both the search and TA radars are operating as before."

"I wonder what the gang on *Cobra* thinks," she wondered aloud.

Communications Officer Jessie Woodward looked up at her. "You want I should call them?"

Joanne smiled as she shook her head. "No, I think I want to be as quiet as I can right now."

Four minutes, forty seconds.

Marco looked up again. "Nothing in the enemy voice band, Captain. I was wondering if maybe the cargo ship crew could see us and tip off the surface. But nothing is happening there, either."

"OK, thanks, Marco."

She looked up again. Three minutes.

"Lynn, move us back twenty-five, and have a fast bug-out course set, understand?"

"Yes, Captain. We'll be ready."

Two minutes.

"Marco, do they have us?"

"Possibly, ma'am. The signal is steady and strong. It's not like they're scanning around."

One minute, fifteen.

"Firing position!" Lynn called out.

A Surveillance tech jolted upright. "Surface IR transient!" A second later he continued. "Ground flare followed by track...assess as missile launch, heading our way, and *fast*."

"FIRE!" Joanne yelled at Kirkland.

Five seconds later he called "Weapon away!"

"Lynn, bug us outta here!"

Intrepid quickly changed orientation and accelerated out of the path of the incoming enemy missile, which turned to follow but ran out of fuel and exploded several kilometers behind her rapidly fading stern.

Once they were at a safe distance, Joanne turned the ship into a high orbit, allowing herself and her officers some time to understand what had just happened.

She'd almost waited too long. She also realized that the enemy was on to their blockade routine, and obviously knew when they would be firing on the cargo ship. Their rigorous, careful warning procedure had been turned against them.

All that was about to change.

Cobra
E-Prime
Wednesday, May 3, 2079, 2030 UTC

The anger and surprise Joanne Henderson felt was apparent in Rich Evans and his Intel crew aboard *Cobra* as well. They had not seen the signals *Intrepid* reported, but once they had the technical details from Chuck Anderson, David and his staff could make some early assessments.

David dropped his NetComp on the wardroom table with a loud slap and looked across at Evans. "I have to ask, sir, where the hell has this technology been all this time?"

"I have no idea, Lieutenant. But it is a nasty development. They picked a good band, too. We're not so invisible in UHF."

"Can we believe this is some new development?" Ray Salazar asked. "They've proven to be pretty resourceful when they need something new to counter our advantages."

"I don't know, and I'm not sure I care," Evans responded. "Do we have imagery of this area the radar and the missile came from?"

"Yes," Jack Ballard responded, "and it's empty. There is nothing in the pictures we have to indicate any kind of military facility there."

"Get more, Jack. I want to see that area in fine detail."

Lena Rice looked at Evans. "Just how close do you want us to go, sir?"

Evans turned to Ballard, "Jack?"

"Um, two-fifty?"

Rice's raised eyebrow could not be missed. "That's pretty close, Jack."

"Yes, it is. But we're not following a cargo ship, and we're the darkest ship in the fleet. We should be able to swing past without them even knowing."

"It was one thing," Evans answered carefully, "when we were sneaking around with the enemy totally unaware of us. We're now facing an alerted and observant force. We might be seen, somehow."

David leaned forward. "Well, sir, if we are, that will tell us quite a lot about their capabilities."

"Planning to march your squad across a minefield, Powell?" Evans responded sarcastically.

"No, sir. If they shoot, even if they put that radar on us, we get out like right now."

"What time is it there?"

David checked his notes. "Evening, sir. Sunrise is 1251 tomorrow."

"OK, let's get there just before sunrise. The shadows will be exaggerated as the star comes up." He turned to his Navigator and Executive Officer. "Lena, get us there an hour before dawn. Jack, take charge of the telescopes and show me what the hell is going on down there."

Evans was about to dismiss the group when Harry Hess came into the wardroom.

"Sir?" Rich asked.

"Blockade instructions are changed, Commander. We're going to hit them right off — no more warnings."

"Yes, sir. We're going to make a low pass, Captain, to get new images of the area the missile was launched from."

"Fine, but with the ship that low, I will be incommunicado for a while, correct?"

"Yes, sir, several hours at least. You could transmit in an emergency, but we'd have to abandon the surveillance if you do."

"Fine, Commander. Proceed."

Hess remained just long enough to grab a fresh cup of coffee and headed back to his adopted workspace in the Captain's cabin.

He had an order to issue.

Sigma
Near the Preeminent Ship Factory
Wednesday, May 3, 2079, 2100 UTC

Carol looked around the Bridge as she set down her NetComp, Hess' priority order still echoing in her head after her second read of it. Everything was calm and nominal, she realized. They had arrived at the ship factory only a few hours before, but the sometimes-monotonous work of surveillance, careful navigation, and weapons readiness had already settled into a quiet but alert routine. *Sigma* was beginning to feel like home, and this was again beginning to feel like her place, her crew. Peg White had been good to her word, a reliable, trustworthy leader in the Navigation section. She'd offered her opinions when asked but otherwise was as fine a team player as a commander could ask for. She gave herself only a few seconds of reflection before picking up the phone.

"Intel...Roger, it's Hansen. Come up here, please."

Cox was there in less than a minute.

"We've been ordered to strike the factory. Let's get the imagery of the power connections up on the main display."

Cox went to the Surveillance station, found the images Carol was looking for, and put them up on the large primary display screen. She called Chief Guzman over from the Weapons station to join the discussion.

"OK, ten large conduits, a meter or so in diameter. We're to cut these."

"What about the ships?" Guzman asked.

"Hess says as long as they behave, they live. If they move, they die."

"Simple enough."

Carol nodded. "I can't say I like this, you know? But they fired an anti-ship missile from the surface at *Intrepid,* and Hess wants them to pay a price for that."

Jayvon looked at her in surprise. "From the surface?"

"Yeah, word is they've developed some kind of new radar system. We'll get the details once *Cobra* has crunched the data."

Guzman looked at the image carefully. "My suggestion, Commander, is three Lances, offset slightly so their impacts overlap. We can set them to detonate at, uh, maybe fifty meters to get a good spread."

Carol agreed. "Yes, I agree. A Bludgeon would probably penetrate the surface, and the idea here is to cut the power without killing anyone."

"But," Jayvon asked, "won't cutting the power ultimately kill them?"

"Without *directly* killing anyone," Carol corrected herself.

Guzman looked away from the screen. "What if they move to evacuate the factory?"

Carol thought for a moment. "Hess didn't address that scenario, but I think we should allow them that. If we're not going to let them be rescued, we might as well just kill them in the first place."

"Yes, Commander," Guzman replied.

Guzman assigned the Lances to the power lines, and, as insurance, assigned two Bludgeons to each of the nearby ships. If they began to react, he could fire on them immediately. He reviewed the details of the targeting with Carol, and once she approved, the weapons were out in seconds.

The Lances struck the large power conduits at three overlapping sites. Post-strike observation confirmed that all ten had been cut. Almost immediately, Roger Cox was back on the Bridge.

"More SLIP activity, Commander. The same emitter, we think."

"Reporting the strike?"

"Can't imagine what else it would be, ma'am."

"Fine, thanks, Roger."

Carol asked Peg to move them a little further from the factory, and change their position to below the plane of the system, and keep the ship moving slightly. Too long in one place, she thought, and they might eventually detect their presence.

As they were moving away, Carol transmitted her after-action report to Hess, including her decision to permit the ships in the area to evacuate the survivors. Two hours after the strike, there had still been no activity at the factory.

Columbia
FOB Carpenter
Thursday, May 4, 2079, 0800 UTC

Kieran Barker's decision to put Harry Hess in tactical command of his force was turning out to be wise. It also confirmed CINC's thinking that senior commanders needed to be closer to the action, not days away by SLIP. Hess had responded well to the rapidly changing situation at e-prime, leaving Barker to consider how they were to establish firm control of the space throughout the Alpha Mensae system.

There were still questions, still doubts about the exact status of the enemy's fleet. *Cobra*'s original counts of ships dispatched, those actually seen at the target systems, and what had been found since did not quite add up. To Barker's mind, there could be as many as ten ships unaccounted for. They'd found what they called 'Enemy Station' not far from Beta Hydri, but obviously, there could be another just like it somewhere else. The Fleet had not explored much beyond Alpha Mensae, being somewhat preoccupied with reducing the enemy ships right in front of them. But Barker knew that was a potential blind spot. There was an enormous dark universe out past Alpha Mensae, likely punctuated with species the Preeminents had conquered.

He and Elias Peña spent several hours discussing these issues, Elias expressing his typical frustration with the amount of data he had to work with.

"You know, sir, *Cobra* did the reverse-nav process on the departing warships. If they could do the same on the cargo ships, it might tell us where they're headed."

"I thought of that as well, but Rich has been busy fighting other fires. I'll ask him."

"Another thing, Admiral: When CINC arrives, we should require that the Preeminent provide a detailed accounting of what systems they have subjugated and what species live there."

"Yes, I agree. Somehow that whole situation has to be unwound, and the conquered systems returned to their natural condition."

"That won't be easy, and if they've been under control long enough, it might not even be possible."

"I'll add all this to my briefing for CINC."

"Four days, right, sir?"

"Yeah, last ETA was midnight on the eighth."

"A lot can happen in four days, sir."

"This whole thing could spin out of control in one day, Elias. We just have to keep the pressure on and try to hold them down until he gets here."

They also discussed the political situation on e-prime, and what little they understood about it. If there were factions, there could well be a contest for control of their fleet, and their dialog with Barker and Davenport. Barker had received word that Fiona Collins had snuck aboard *Bondarenko*, and after a small laugh about how surprised CINC would have been, he and Peña agreed that her insights would be welcome.

Four more days. They just needed to keep the lid on for four more days.

Cobra
E-Prime
Thursday, May 4, 2079, 1200 UTC

They arrived at two-hundred-fifty kilometers above the enemy central city on schedule, just before sunrise. Jack Ballard supervised Gregg Browning in the targeting and collection of high-resolution images of the area *Intrepid* had reported. Margie Nixon watched the enemy communications frequencies and the newly-found radar band carefully, hoping to see exactly nothing.

So far, so good.

"Our only problem now," David said to Ray quietly, "is if they get lucky and they see us block a star."

"Yeah, I've been thinking about that issue. If they have any astronomy science of any reasonable sophistication, I would think they would have seen us already."

David shrugged. "Hard to know. Detecting us from time to time is a long way from tracking us well enough to shoot."

Ray just nodded and returned his attention to the images Ballard was collecting.

As Jack watched the images come in, about two per second at this resolution, he was reminded of how they had collected similar data at Beta Hydri. They'd scanned the cities in IR, visual, and UV before deciding that they were abandoned. On *Cobra*, he had the best of everything, equipment far more sensitive than what they had used on *Antares*.

As the star rose over the eastern horizon, something caught Jack's eye. It took a half-hour before he was sure.

"Oh, you sneaky bastards," he whispered to himself.

"What?" David asked.

Jack smiled. "They're not as smart as they think."

"I take it you see something, Lieutenant?" Evans asked, just beginning to lose his patience.

"Yes, sir. Just a sec." Jack zoomed in on a small area of the image and then ran the images forward like a movie. He turned to David. "See it?"

"Once more?" The images started right before dawn and ran until the star was well above the horizon.

"Shadows," David said, finally.

"Right." Jack turned to Evans. "There are trees on this planet, sir. We saw them the first time we were here. These are trees like we think of trees, you know, tall, with crowns of branches and leaves. They may even be terrestrial transplants, for all we know."

"Your point?"

Jack circled a tree in the center of the image, and another near the edge. Then he reran the image-movie. "This one," he said, indicating the tree near the edge, "has a normal shadow that moves as the star rises. But *this* one," he said, pointing to one near the center, "has no shadow."

"It's not really there," Evans replied, the picture coming into focus for him, "It's painted on to cover something."

"Yeah, something like, say, a radar and missile facility."

Evans smiled at his analysts. "OK, what about IR?"

David pulled up the IR surveillance images. "You can see it there, too, sir. At sunrise the area under the fake trees is cooler than the ground around it. Later in the day, I'd expect it to be warmer."

"Excellent work, gentlemen, thank you."

Evans had an answer. And, a potential target.

Central Council Chambers
Preeminent Home World
Earth Equivalent Date: Thursday, May 4, 2079, just past StarRise

Despite the First's orders to his small remaining fleet to search out and kill the Vermin around Home, no ships had moved. He sat with his last four advisors. None could recall him ever deigning to sit in their presence. His protective detail of ten armed Combatants surrounded the room, an unmistakable symbol of the danger of the moment.

With forced calm, the First began the discussion. "The Armada has not responded to commands. Why is this?"

"The Vermin have them targeted, Revered First. They were reminded of this only lastRot. They believe any movement will result in a quick death."

"They should still obey orders. Perhaps the SD has coerced them to comply with their Revocation?"

"This is also possible, Revered First."

"I have learned that the SD sent an exploration vessel to Planet Five several rots past. That traitor Kiker failed to report this to me."

The four looked at each other, then one responded. "None of us were informed of this, Revered First."

"If we consider that in light of later events, it seems suspicious to me. Perhaps the Vermin are there? Perhaps the SD was already plotting with Kiker against me?"

There was no response, so the First continued. "There are eight ships the Vermin are unaware of, which I have hidden nearby at System 31, less than five rots away. Their commanders are loyal. I will dispatch one to Planet Five, and we will see what is there."

"And in the meantime?" the eldest surviving counselor asked.

"In the meantime, you will remain loyal and silent, and I will pester the Vermin."

"Pester?"

"They think they can strike us with impunity. I will show them otherwise."

Chaffee
E-Prime
Friday, May 5, 2079, 0900 UTC (Just after local midnight in Core City)

Commander Mark Rhodes hated night-side intercepts. He knew just how massive *Chaffee* was, and how she might well be disclosing her position to a savvy observer on the ground. *With the right equipment,* Mark thought, *they could target us without a radar.* But the job was the job, and he had yet another cargo ship to disable. He was beginning to wonder if the enemy would ever get the message. Thirty disabled ships were drifting in more or less the same orbit, and he was careful about his approach to avoid coming too close to any of them.

As he closed to twenty kilometers, his idle thoughts became a reality.

"IR plume on the surface, sir...now a track heading this way."

He was supposed to wait another few minutes, but when he looked at the Weapons station, he saw that LT Ortiz was ready.

"Fire!" he called, and in a few seconds, the weapon was headed for the cargo ship.

"Coming fast, Captain!"

"Nav! Get us out of here." LT Cathy McPherson was also ready, and she had *Chaffee* on the move. The ship twisted left and up and began accelerating.

"Weapon is tracking us, sir." McPherson pushed the Drive to the max, and she began to pull away from the incoming threat.

"Second launch!" the Surveillance officer called. "And the T-A radar is up. They have us, sir."

Mark looked over at the Nav stations. "Turn her back starboard a little. Maybe we can shake them against the cargo ship."

As McPherson turned the ship sharply right, a third launch was detected, then a fourth. McPherson sliced one way, then the other, but finally, a missile struck home amidships, and the ship shook as if thrown aside by some enormous child.

Mark watched as his ship status went quickly from green to yellow to an ugly splotch of red in the center of the ship.

Cathy turned from her Nav status to look at Mark. "We have structural damage, Captain. I can't go FTL."

"Get up whatever speed you can manage, Lieutenant, and get us out of here." He turned to the Surveillance Console. "Status of enemy?"

"Target radar is back down, sir, and no more launches."

"Very well." He stepped down and walked to the Weapons station. "Never again, Alejandro, never again do we get into this fix with no Spartans loaded out."

"Yes, Captain, I agree. I started loading the other rotary, but there was no time before they hit us."

Mark nodded his understanding and turned away. "Comms! We need to get the word out..."

```
FLASH
207905050900UTC
FROM: CHAFFEE
TO: CSTO, BONDARENKO/CINC, COBRA

1) ATTACKED BY FOUR ENEMY MISSILES WHILE PREPARING TO FIRE ON
INCOMING CARGO VESSEL.
2) STRUCK AMIDSHIPS BY MISSILE #3, WITH STRUCTURAL DAMAGE AND LOSS
OF LIFE TBD.
3) NO RADAR DETECTED BEFORE FIRST LAUNCH.
4) PROCEEDING AWAY FROM AM FOR STATUS ASSESSMENT AND REPAIRS.
5) WILL ADVISE STATUS ASAP.

END
```

Message sent, he turned away from the Communications station and moved to Nav.

"OK, Cathy, where are we?"

"South. All of the enemy cities are in the northern hemisphere, so I took just south as fast as I could. We're about a million klicks off the south pole now. I was planning for two million."

"Fine, good." He turned back to his Surveillance crew. "Anything?"

"All quiet, sir. We did lose some sensors in the attack, but I'm confident we're in the clear, at least for now."

"Fair enough."

Mark went back to his Command station and looked at the details of what they had done to his ship. She was safe for the moment, but the damage was hard for him to absorb. The wardroom was gone, as was the galley and sickbay. His regular office, which he only used in port, was also open to space. He knew right off that was at least twenty dead. There was still a path aft, through the lowest accessible level. He hesitated before pulling up the personnel status display. It would be bad news, but it had to be faced.

Twenty-two was the number the ship gave him. He swiped past the names to see the structural analysis, which brought him just more bad news. *Chaffee* was finished, at least as far as FTL travel was concerned. He had power, limited propulsion, and weapons, but he couldn't easily feed the survivors or tend to their wounds. He conferred with the Engineering Officer and Navigator Cathy McPherson and decided to return to FOB Carpenter. With *Ceres* there, at least there would be somewhere to feed his crew and medical attention for the injured.

```
FLASH 207905051030
FROM: CHAFFEE
TO: CSTO, BONDARENKO/CINC, COBRA

1) TWENTY-TWO CONFIRMED KIA.
2) EXTENSIVE STRUCTURAL DAMAGE PRECLUDES FTL TRAVEL.
3) PROCEEDING FOB CARPENTER BEST POSSIBLE SPEED.

END
```

Jarvis
E-Prime
Friday, May 5, 2079, 1300 UTC

Lieutenant Commander Alona Melville saw the message from *Cobra*, relaying what had happened to *Chaffee*. *Four missiles!* The first attack had been a few days before, on *Intrepid*, but Henderson had managed to just run away from it. Now, the enemy had gotten wise to that and was hitting them with a swarm. *Fine,* she thought, *we can learn from experience, too.*

The cargo ships were not coming as fast anymore, she noted. Two or three a day was about all they had seen in the last few days. But, they did keep coming.

Alona and her officers discussed how *Chaffee* had been targeted without radar, and they agreed that the ship must have been seen to block a star, more likely, several stars. With a good enough telescope and some knowledge of how the Fleet operated, that could give someone a good idea of where a ship was and where it was going.

But now, Alona was glad to see, Alpha Mensae was up, and *Jarvis* should be safe from that kind of detection.

Or, so she hoped.

Today Alona placed *Jarvis* much further behind and above the enemy ship, more than a hundred kilometers away. She also ordered Spartans on one rotary, the other loaded out with one Lance and the rest Bludgeons. She would not get caught unprepared like Mark Rhodes had seemingly been. She felt for him deeply, knowing what an excellent officer he was and how he loved that ship and crew. But as far as Alona was concerned, after what happened to Joanne Henderson's *Intrepid*, Rhodes should have been ready.

As the time to fire approached, she called her Surveillance and Weapons officers together.

"If they shoot at us, which I don't think they will, but, if they do, I want to know if we could take their weapon out with a Spartan."

Weaps was confused. "But, you don't plan to actually fire one?"

"No. I'd rather not tip our hand. But it would be useful to know if we could hit it if we had to."

Her Surveillance officer shrugged. "OK, Commander, if that's what you want. We'll be feeding the targeting info to Weaps as usual, so if he thinks he can get a Spartan solution on it, you'll know."

"Good, thanks."

Just after they fired on the cargo ship, raised voices were heard. "T-A radar is up, Commander!"

"Nav! Right thirty, up fifteen, add one hundred meters per second."

"Moving, Commander."

"IR plume, ma'am. They're shooting."

"Damn," Alona said to herself. "I would have put good money on them not seeing us."

"Fast mover, Commander!" the Surveillance tech called out.

A few seconds later, his voice got a little higher. "Second launch, Commander."

"Shit. Nav! Punch it and get us out of here." The Navigator took a few seconds to see where the incoming missiles were, then turned *Jarvis* away and engaged the Drive full power. They slowly pulled away from the threats, which eventually exploded as they reached the end of their fuel.

As they slowed down to work their way back to Alpha Mensae, Alona went to her Weapons Officer.

"So?"

"So, no, we did not get a Spartan solution. But, had we hung around a little longer, I think we would have."

"But, you're not certain?"

"Commander, I won't be *certain* until I see the little red light that says I can shoot. But, watching the tracking evolve, it was headed in the right direction."

"Very well."

Alona called her Nav Officer to take the Conn — it was his turn, after all — and retired to her Duty Cabin. They were out of any danger for the moment, and she'd been up over twenty-four hours. Getting rest whenever possible was one thing Dan Smith had taught her well. Tired captains miss details and make mistakes. As she prepared for bed, she wondered if that was what happened to *Chaffee*.

Cobra
High Orbit E-Prime
Friday, May 5, 2079, 1730 UTC

David replayed the IR track from the attempt on *Jarvis* for Harry Hess and Rich Evans. Unlike Alona Melville, David had fully expected them to try again, so he had every 'eye' available watching the missile facility. It paid off.

"So, that's the IR data; a large cloud at launch, then a fast, hot streak out of the atmosphere. But here, in the visual, watch the doors snap open...there!" Indeed, the covers with the false trees moved aside in less than a second, revealing a large double-dish antenna system that rose and locked into place in another second or so.

"Amazing," Hess said quietly.

"Yes, but keep watching." The dish moved slightly, and less than a half-minute later, another set of doors split open, revealing rows of sharply pointed missiles. The doors were barely open before the first missile sped out of the frame.

"The second is launched about fifteen seconds later. It's impressive, sir, how quickly they can get these off once they have a target."

Hess crossed his arms and sat. "What I don't see, Lieutenant Powell, is why we've been here all this time, picking off their cargo ships, and only now they bring out these big guns."

"I can't answer that, sir, except to say that if there is a power struggle going on, as the first contact seems to imply, someone may be flexing their muscles, making some kind of display."

"Or," Rich Evans said, "They're finally threatened enough to pull out their last-ditch defenses."

David nodded. "Yes, sir, also, plausible."

Hess pointed to the image. "Look where it is. There aren't fifty meters from the outer wall of the city to the first set of doors. I can't strike that without endangering whoever might be living nearby. Those are chemical rockets with a large warhead; if we hit them, we'll get one helluva bonfire."

"*If*, that is, sir, *if* anyone is living nearby." Jack Ballard replied. "We're supposed to see Asoon again in a few days, right? Can we ask them?"

"We can try. If one of the others is military, they might understand. But, I don't see how we get an image like this to them."

David turned away from the display. "Unless we meet them in person, on the surface."

"How, exactly, would you propose to do that, Lieutenant?" Hess pointedly asked.

"We've mapped the planet, sir. The enemy cities are all in the northern hemisphere, but there's plenty of space down south we might be able to use. "

"I don't think so. We'll meet them when we land on Main Street."

David saw that Hess had not considered seeing the Preeminent in person on the surface. Time to pull back. "As you say, sir."

Hess looked at Powell for a second. "On the other hand, Powell, see if you can find a clearly identifiable location where we *could* meet. I don't think it's necessary, but CINC might, so I'd like to have that in my back pocket just in case."

"Yes, sir. Will do."

David looked from Hess to Evans, waiting to see if there were more questions.

Evans filled the awkward silence. "So, Captain Hess, what now?"

"Now, you take me back to FOB Carpenter. I need to get with Barker and CINC, when he gets here, and see how we put an end to this. I've put Loren Booker in tactical command for now. Drop me there, then come back here and keep watch."

"Sir?" David asked.

"Yes, Powell, what is it?"

"If you'll allow, sir, I would like to continue to work the contacts with the Preeminents. So, I guess I'm asking to stay on *Columbia* for the next meeting with Asoon."

Hess turned to Evans. "Thoughts?"

"It's fine with me, sir. He is a fairly useful pain in the ass, but we'll manage even in his absence."

Hess smiled. "OK, Powell, you're in. For now, that is. If Evans decides *Cobra* will fall apart without you, I'll have to send you back."

"Fine, sir. Thank you." David turned to Evans. "And thank you, sir, for that powerful recommendation. Can I use you as a reference for my next job? You know, the truck driving school?"

Evans laughed and left the Operations Center with Hess, headed for the wardroom, and one final dinner before Hess returned to *Columbia*.

Sigma
Near the Enemy Ship Factory
Sunday, May 7, 2079, 1030 UTC

In the several days since *Sigma* had pulled the plug on the ship factory, they had observed a dozen or so shuttle trips to it from one of the nearby ships. To Carol's eye, someone was trying to save the workers she had left in the dark and cold. That was fine with Carol, as not killing them was an essential part of the plan.

Today, Kieran Barker had tossed her yet another hot potato. The enemy had updated their previously crude CW radar system, creating a powerful frequency-swept version with enough tracking ability to find and strike Fleet ships in orbit.

That could not be permitted, according to Barker.

As they left the factory to return to e-prime, Carol went to the Intel Section so she and Roger Cox could review the images Cobra had obtained a few days earlier. Weapons Chief Guzman joined them there.

"So, Commander," Roger asked, "I'm curious. How is it that we keep getting these fussy, one-off assignments?"

Carol smiled. "Barker just likes us, I guess."

Guzman shook his head. "He might love us, but that's not why."

Roger was surprised at the Chief's certainty. "Oh? Why, then?"

"Well, Ensign, first, thanks to Commander White, we have a TRS, so we can shoot faster and longer than anyone else. Without the need to reload, in a pinch we can really churn out some destruction. But I think the real reason is that we have the latest iteration of the Lance: faster, more accurate, more punch, and a wider set of options. Older Lances could not have been detonated above those solar panel conduits, for example."

"I see. And the upgraded Lance is what we need for this radar job?"

"Yes." Guzman pointed to the photographs on the table. "As you see, there's only thirty meters or so from the edge of the missile storage to the doors over the antennas. We don't want to set off the missiles, so we need the increased accuracy."

Carol nodded her agreement. "That, and we need a contact detonation in order to keep the collateral damage to a minimum."

"Yes, I saw that in the Admiral's order. It's a tight target for sure."

Guzman looked at the images, the distances, the ground-reference points, and turned to Carol. "We can do it, Commander. I'd say we can hit these fake doors *Cobra* located with better than ninety-percent probability."

Carol pointed to the printed images on the table. "I was thinking two shots, maybe a second apart?"

Guzman nodded. "Yes, I agree. The second is likely redundant but if the doors are stronger than we think, it'll make sure. If they aren't, it won't do any more extraneous damage than a single shot."

"OK, Chief, get the weapons programmed and let me know when you're ready."

"How soon does Hess want the strike?"

"Soon as we get back. Say, three hours?"

"OK, will do."

Sigma closed to within two hundred kilometers of the planet's surface, closer than any Fleet ship previously had. Carol wanted to make sure they had solid visual contact with the target and could aim the Lance as precisely as possible. If the enemy saw them and decided to open the doors, that was OK with her, too,

Carol stood in her old spot, just behind the Weapons station. Guzman smiled slightly as he realized she was there, leaning against the back of the Bridge, just like she once did.

"We're ready, Commander," he said.

Carol turned to the Surveillance station. "Any change? Any sign of the radar?"

Jayvon shook his head. "No, ma'am. All quiet here."

Carol nodded her understanding, then paused, looking at the solution on the Weapons display. She looked down for a moment, then back up, "OK, Chief."

Guzman carefully touched the blinking red *Commit* control. "Weapons are away, Commander."

"Nav!" Carol called, "Move us up to five-hundred klicks but keep us in sight of the target!"

Peg White got the ship moving, changing both the altitude and inclination of their orbit, making them much harder to find.

"Fifteen seconds!" Guzman called.

Jayvon put the long-range telescope feed on the main display so Carol could see what was happening. The ground erupted in a double flash and a wide column of dirt and debris. As the wind moved the smoke and fine dust away, they could see the doors, buckled and pushed outwards, and the antenna, twisted and lying on its side.

"Grab that last image, Lieutenant Dean," Carol called. "Ship it over to *Cobra* by laser. Tell them 'you're welcome.'"

Jayvon smiled. "Yes, ma'am, will do."

She walked to Lori Rodgers' Comm station. "Send a SLIP to Barker that the radar has been silenced. He'll get the pictures from *Cobra*, eventually. I don't want to send those all the way out there on VHF."

"Yes, Commander."

Carol looked at the image of the wrecked radar for several seconds. There was no additional smoke, and as she looked at the IR sensor, there was no heat beyond what two Lances detonating would create. The enemy missiles had not been affected, and there was no visible damage to the residences nearby.

Mission accomplished, she thought, *at least, for today.*

Ceres Hospital Deck
FOB Carpenter
Monday, May 8, 2079, 0830 UTC

Mike Clark left the *Columbia* shuttle — the same one Melinda had been wounded in — on one of *Ceres*' secondary airlocks and headed for the hospital. His weekly visits over the last months had made him a familiar face, and the nurses and staff greeted him warmly. Each week he would talk to her, tell her about people she knew, funny and odd things that had happened, but leaving out any news about the war itself. He wasn't sure how much she heard, and if she was hearing him, he didn't want her thinking about that. He would sit by her bed and talk to her for a half-hour or so, then once he was out of ship stories, he would review reports on his NetComp or do some minor paperwork — even in a mostly paperless world, it was still 'paperwork' — and listen to her breathing. He loved that sound, as it meant she was still alive, still able to come back to him.

Melinda had been slowly coming out of her coma, but recently had been more asleep than awake. Mike came in and sat at her side, taking her hand as he usually did. Today, he ran out of material early and turned to his reports.

He looked up as he heard her stir.

"Hello, skinny," she said quietly.

She was looking straight at him, fully awake. He slid closer to her, touching her cheek. "Hello there, blue eyes."

She closed her eyes at his touch, then reached up and held his hand. "I've missed you."

"We've all missed you, too. But especially me."

She smiled at the weak joke and shifted in the bed. "Don't lose your day job, Clark. We'll starve." She reached up again and pulled his face down to hers. "I love you, Mike."

He was muted by the baseball-sized lump in his throat, so he just hung on and held her. Finally, they parted, but she kept an iron-clad grasp on his hand as he sat back in the chair, his face still close to hers.

"So, how do I look?"

"Beautiful, as always. You do have a kinda half-Mohawk thing going where they shaved you for the surgery."

"Half-Mohawk?"

"Yeah, kinda sexy now that I think about it. I never had a punk-rocker in love with me before."

She frowned. "Mike?"

"Yes?"

"What's happened?"

Mike looked at her. "Well, you had a head wound — "

"No, Mike. What's happened with the war?"

"Some of the enemy have reached out to talk. I don't understand it all myself. CINC is due here in a few days."

"Talk? Mike, what day is it? And, if CINC is coming here, where are we?"

He reached out again to touch her cheek. This would be hard for her, but he decided to give it all at once.

"It's May 8th, not quite two months since you were wounded. You're in the *Ceres* hospital, and we're at Alpha Mensae now. We beat them at Beta Hydri, Melinda, and badly. But *Eagle* and *Friendship* were lost, and Hansen had to land *Antares* on the surface. Helluva thing, that. We're here blockading them now, trying to get them to talk."

"I don't remember what happened, Mike."

"What do you remember?"

"Something hazy about going somewhere with Dre Ingram. Not much more."

Mike nodded. "You and Dre did four dustoff trips to *Eagle*. Brought back like half the crew. The ship was hit as you were about to leave after the last trip. You took some shrapnel to your right temple."

She smiled. "Well, at least we got the job done."

"Oh, more than that. You were incredible, Melinda, just incredible."

"Dre OK?"

"Yes. Dre got a minor lac or something from the same hit, but he's fine."

"Good, really good." She was clearly getting tired.

"Go ahead and rest. I'll be here a while."

She seemed to rally slightly as she asked, "How bad is my head?"

"Your head?"

"You said I had surgery. How ugly is it?"

He glanced up at the small, healing incision. "Not at all. Once your hair grows out, you won't even see it."

"But what if I keep the half-Mohawk?"

"Well, then it's going to be a conversation starter for sure."

She closed her eyes and settled back down in the bed. "I love you, Clark. Don't ever forget that."

"I won't. And don't you, either, that I love you."

"OK, I won't." She seemed to be dozing off when she opened her eyes slightly.

"When we get back, can we go out somewhere and get drunk and do stuff we'll never tell the kids about?"

Mike looked at her, carefully stifling a laugh. "Sure, Mel, we'll get the same crew as Kapteyn together and you can invade my hand with your fingers again."

She smiled. "Yeah, that would be nice."

She was asleep again in moments. Mike waited a few minutes, then left to tell the nurses what had happened. It was a very positive sign, he thought, that she was coming to the end of a very long road.

Columbia
FOB Carpenter
Tuesday, May 9, 2079, 0930 UTC

Fiona Collins hadn't been on an extended mission in a long time, and she had forgotten how much she enjoyed the rhythms of ship life. Her term in Plans had started when she was a fresh Lieutenant Commander, just off three years aboard ship, and continued through seven years and two promotions. As she sipped her third coffee, she reflected back to the incredible, utterly insane time right after the attack on Inoria. The days were long, spent huddled with her small staff, with Joanne beside her. And Ben Price, always there, always engaging, and smarter than he wanted you to think. Losing him to Joanne was hard, but losing him forever felt as if she had lost a limb. As she looked back now, those early days seemed decades ago. It was seventeen months.

This morning, her face in the mirror looked different to her: too thin, with unwelcome lines at her eyes. At thirty-seven, she wasn't 'old' by any reasonable measure, but the stress, lost sleep, and days where her rations consisted mostly of crises and caffeine were taking their toll. *After this,* she thought, *after this is done, there will be time. Maybe I'll tag along to Fiji with Joanne.* Her pleasant visions of warm waters and salty breezes were interrupted by the arrival of David Powell. He drew himself a cup and sat across from her.

"Good morning, Captain Collins."

"Hello, Powell. How are you doing, anyway? And how is the lovely Commander Hansen?"

David smiled. He had felt a special connection with Collins ever since he had first met her at Ron Harris' house. She was a professional soldier, for sure, but warm, caring, and comfortable to talk to. "We are both fine, ma'am, and together, we are also fine. And she is indeed lovely." David set down his cup and changed the subject slightly. "Her leg is healing well."

"That's good to hear."

David took another sip, shifting slightly in his chair, then set down his cup.

"Captain, I've never forgotten what you said to me that first evening at the Harrises'. I never thanked you for that."

"Oh?"

"Yes. You gave me some encouragement when I didn't even realize I needed it."

"I vaguely remember saying something about what the next guy would have done. But it might have been the Norton."

"It is an awfully nice red."

"Meredith thinks so. She won't drink anything else." She smiled, spun her coffee cup, then continued. "You, Powell, are not any next guy. Never forget that. So how is Carol enjoying her new command?"

David leaned back and smiled. "She loves old *Sigma,* you know? Funny how all that worked out — she ends up with my old ship."

"Do I hear a little green in that comment, Lieutenant?"

David laughed. "Oh, no, ma'am. I have a great job, and the fact that *Sigma* came back just when the *Antares* crew needed a ship, well, there's divine providence for you."

"Yes, I agree. So, what are we to do about the Preeminent? I see you've been added to the agenda."

"There are too many open questions to answer that yet, Captain. I just think we need to keep the pressure on and see how they react."

"CINC has a list for them."

"Yes, ma'am, I'm aware. I just hope they can accept his terms. The alternative..."

"Is ugly for everyone. I've looked at some of the contingencies for a ground assault. The estimates range from a walkover to complete loss of the landing force."

David grimaced. "Useful."

Fiona laughed. "Yes, not much help at all. Sometimes there are just too many variables with assumed values. Sometimes, we just don't know."

"Right."

They sat quietly for a few minutes, then Fiona excused herself to prepare for a meeting with CINC. David spent a few minutes thinking about the Preeminent, then turned in his cup and headed for the CSTO workspace to find Elias Peña and see what might have happened overnight. Collins was an interesting woman, he thought. He could easily see Carol in that role in another ten years.

Time will tell, he thought; *meanwhile, we fight.*

Columbia
FOB Carpenter
Tuesday, May 9, 2079, 1400 UTC

Admiral Connor Davenport, Noah Peters, and Fiona Collins had transferred to *Columbia* shortly after their arrival. *Bondarenko*'s shuttle was barely back in its hangar when a Type III enemy ship came out of FTL a few thousand kilometers from the planet, apparently looking for them. Anna Nonna took pleasure in slowly maneuvering behind the newcomer, then surprising it with a five-Lance strike on its Drive. When the ship fired back in the direction the Lances had come from, a location *Bondarenko* no longer occupied, she waited for it to be far enough from *Columbia* and then struck it with four Bludgeons. The outcome of this engagement, like the outcome of the war, was never in doubt.

"What a waste!" she said to her XO after it was over.

Scad Nee Wok and Asoon Too Lini remained protected in the SD's enormous Core City Headquarters, well out of the First's murderous reach. Today, they walked carefully to the small spacecraft landing facility on the edge of the site. ThisRot, they would be taking Glur Woe Segt and his maleChild Rmah to meet the humans. The First had been firing at the human ships as they pursued the incoming tribute ships, and he'd clearly done damage to at least one, possibly more. But in their typical manner, the humans had changed their tactics to counter his threat. Scad hoped he would be able to get the small exploration ship away without the First attacking it.

Scad waited until well after dark and then left in a low trajectory that took him far from the defense system before rising into space and turning towards Planet Five. It worked. They arrived several drots later, only to find the wreckage of an Armada cruiser floating nearby.

Scad displayed the ship for Rmah and Glur to see. "This is what happens to ships that challenge the humans. They know their chemistry, sir Segt. They strike the oxygen and hydrogen tanks with weapons that spray small spheres, riddling them with holes. The fuels then react explosively, and the ship is destroyed in the fire."

"I wish we understood their technology better," Glur said. "These small ships are accessing a power source we don't understand."

"Yes, sir."

"But, sir Segt, what will Barker, and the more powerful human just arrived, think of this?" Asoon asked. "The First must have sent it, which means he knows we were here before."

"Your talents are clear, Asoon," Glur answered. "The humans may see this as an insult, that we have somehow deceived them."

"And suddenly, things are much more difficult," Rmah said sadly.

"They have not fired on us," Scad pointed out. "They tend to be patient, sir Segt, slow to strike but overwhelming when they do. This may be to our advantage."

"And theirs," Glur Woe Segt replied. "They defeated this vessel, and yet they wait for us. I hope it means they are still willing to talk." He turned to Asoon. "It is time to find out, Asoon. If they answer, tell them we did not send that vessel."

Asoon called to the humans over the intrusion detector. "This is Asoon. We have returned as you asked. I am calling for Barker. Are you here?"

"Yes, Asoon, this is Barker. I am glad that you have returned safely."

"Barker, we see the ship you defeated. We did not order that action."

"It is hard for us to understand, Asoon, why we are being attacked while trying to settle the conflict. As you can see, such actions do not end well for the attacker. We take no joy in this, Asoon, but we will defend ourselves when it is necessary."

Asoon turned to the males. "He is angry about the cruiser. He believes he has been betrayed by us." After several micRots of debate, they directed Asoon on how to respond.

"There remains division with us, Barker. We know the First has tried to attack your ships in orbit, and it is the First who sent this one here. Again, we had no hand in this. We cannot control what he does."

On *Columbia*, the overall response was surprise.

"The First?" David asked, puzzled. "Who, or what, is that?" No one seemed to understand what the alien meant. Davenport looked to Gabrielle Este, then

Greg Cordero, and neither could offer any help. There wasn't any terrestrial analog for a reptile society.

Connor Davenport decided it was time to introduce himself to the aliens. "Asoon, my name is Connor. I have come here to settle this conflict. The attacks on our ships near your planet and the attempt to strike us here are not helpful. Are you prepared to have a serious discussion of what must be done?"

Asoon looked directly at Glur Woe Segt. "This is a new voice, confident, commanding. He says he is here to settle the war and asks if we are ready to talk. He is angry and skeptical of our real intentions."

Segt shifted uncomfortably. "I can speak for the SD, but the First remains uncontrolled. Tell him we can't suppress the last of the Armada, but we are here to talk."

"Connor, we here are prepared to discuss an end. It is what we most desire. A faction of the military is defiant of our control. It is this faction who has attacked you."

Gabrielle spoke first. "A renegade? And, who is this 'First'?"

Davenport nodded his understanding, thought a moment, then spoke again to the alien. "Asoon, we understand that in times of crisis, divisions may be hard to overcome. Who is the 'First' you refer to?"

Glur and Rmah argued at length whether they should try to explain Preeminent society. In the end, they agreed it was too complex to discuss. They would have to simplify the problem for the humans. It was three minutes before Asoon answered Davenport's question.

"The First rules the military. The scientists among us have been blind to his acts for a long time. They have revoked his power, but he refuses to obey and continues to fight."

"Great," Harry Hess commented, "they have a tyrant locked in a bunker."

Davenport nodded, then spoke again to Asoon. "And this is a faction you cannot subdue? Your government is unable to take charge of its own weapons?"

"We cannot. The First has many loyal Combatants and ship commanders who will follow his orders."

Fiona leaned into the conversation. "I think we need to keep this simple, sir. Our interest is ending the war and preventing any new aggression from their species. That's it."

Davenport agreed, then spoke again. "Asoon, your internal politics are irrelevant. Our only goal is the resolution of the current conflict. But, if you cannot end it, please understand that we will."

Asoon was visibly shaken by Davenport's words. "He says he doesn't care about our politics, only in ending the war. If we cannot agree to a resolution with them, he says they will end it."

Rmah raised his head. "That does not sound good for Home."

Glur Woe Segt answered, "They see us as the aggressor, Rmah, and they're not wrong. They want to be safe from us." He turned to Asoon. "Tell him that we will remain here, but we require a drot to confer."

"Will they understand that?" Scad asked.

"I can translate a drot into the time they understand. " Asoon paused, expressing her frustration with one aspect of human culture. "Their time system is hideous, by the way. Twenty-four divisions of each rot, then each of those has sixty divisions, then those have sixty sub-divisions."

Rmah was surprised. "That is strange for a culture that is so scientifically advanced."

"From what I learned," Asoon answered, "it is a continuation of a much earlier system."

She turned to speak to the humans. "Connor, we require time to confer. We will contact you again in two- and one-half hours."

Davenport was surprised but agreed to the delay.

"Two and a half hours?" David said quietly to himself as he pulled out his NetComp, bells ringing in his head. A few seconds later, he smiled. "Of course. Of course! I should have known!"

Fiona looked at him, "Yes, Lieutenant?"

David put down his tablet and looked down the table at Fiona. "One hundred fifty minutes, Captain, is one-tenth of a day on e-prime. Actually, a tenth is closer to one-fifty-one, but I'll give Asoon credit for rounding it off to something we could easily understand."

"And, why should you have known?" she asked, amused.

"Because that was exactly the delay between the Type V's coming up from the surface and the task groups departing. I missed the significance before."

Peña looked across at David. "Do you think that's a deeper insight, David?"

"I don't know, sir. Maybe. Our system of time suits us, but it isn't all that logical in a rational sense. We use the metric system for almost everything, but not time." He turned to Davenport. "If I may, sir, she said something else that caught my attention."

"Oh?"

"She said the scientists had not controlled the military, implying that this lack was the cause of the trouble. I thought it odd that the scientists would somehow be in charge."

Davenport looked thoughtfully at something on the far bulkhead. "I took it as a missed translation."

"No, sir, I don't think so," Fiona said. "Asoon has shown enormous understanding. I see now how they were able to talk to the Seekers."

"If so, it is an amazing gift," Greg Cordero said, adding sadly, "And one which makes me look like a caveman scribbling on the wall." Gabrielle reached over and gave him a gentle hug. He smiled and said, "But, I would sure like to know more about it when this is all over."

Asoon watched silently as the powerful males argued around her. She was surprised at Scad Nee Wok's willingness to give up his Armada, something he had aspired to almost since egghood. He now saw it for the oppressive force it really was and wanted no more of it. Glur Woe Segt resisted the suggestion that they assist the humans in taking the First by force. It was a betrayal, making himself a traitor of sorts. Rmah argued forcibly that it was the First and his cult of superiority, which were the real traitors. To remove the First by force, including with help from the humans, would fulfill the will of the Conclave. It had to be done.

Rmah stood looking out the view window. "Where are they?" he asked himself. "I can't see them at all."

He turned back to rejoin the conversation,

"It has been a hundred revs, maleParent, since the SD properly controlled the military. In that time, they've conquered six species, lying to the citizens of Home about what they were doing and what the returning tribute ships really contained. They tried to wipe out an entire race at System 849, then attacked the so-called Deists for no reason but pride."

"We have always been the highest form, Rmah," Glur answered. "Even the Guardians said the same of our true home planet. The conceit you so easily condemn is part of our makeup from long past. It is part of our natural, instinctive thinking."

Rmah's tail stump expressed his frustration at his maleParent's answer. "Is it not the goal of science to overcome such basic instincts, and replace them with rational, objectively measurable knowledge and decisions? Is that not what you have been teaching me my entire life?"

Glur looked at his maleChild, trying to conceal the pride he felt. It was unusual to know one's production once they were matured, but Glur saw the potential in this maleChild of his from very early on and pressed the Vocations Director to assign him to the SD. There, Glur could guide Rmah in his advanced education and navigate the sometimes tricky priorities that controlled the Directorate's actions. Rmah had flourished in this environment, and Glur was now seeing the confirmation of his choices.

"Yes, Rmah," he finally said, "it is."

"So," Scad began, "if we are to overcome the First, we must isolate him."

"Isolate him?" Asoon asked, speaking for the first time.

"To have any power, he must communicate. He has to give orders."

"So, how do we cut him off?" Rmah asked, intrigued.

"There is a communications station just outside the Armada central facility. If the humans can strike that — "

"He's mute," Glur finished.

"Yes, sir. Mute and impotent."

While the Preeminent were debating treason versus reason, David Powell and Elias Peña were going over the imagery they had collected of the Preeminent's central city. Displayed on the floor-to-ceiling monitor in Peña's work area was the last frame they had taken when the missile and radar doors were open.

"Here," David pointed out, "next to the fake forest, there's a reinforced structure." The structure was on the opposite side of the missile forest from the main wall of the city. The shadows indicated a thick wall with a hard, flat roof. An entrance could be seen on the side facing the missiles.

"So, if this is an entrance, where does it go?"

"That's what I'd like to ask Asoon, sir. The reinforced structure is round but smaller than anything else we've seen in their cities, maybe a hundred meters across. The location, the materials, the access to the missile battery, it just smells military to me."

Peña slid the image slightly to reveal the center of the city. "I'm actually more interested in *this* complex. It's larger than the other you mentioned, and it's not round except here," he pointed to a lone tower. "And that tower is fifty meters high, dead center in the Preem central city." Peña moved his hands around the frame. "Nothing else nearby is even close in height. This is a very important structure, Powell. It would be an imposing sight from the ground. We need to know what it is."

Barker watched them argue, seeing the validity of both points of view. "If we have to take either of those structures, gentlemen, we're going to need help. Asoon said that there are 'combatants' obedient to the First. I take it these are ground troops like we faced at Beta Hydri?"

Peña answered, "Yes, sir. Asoon used that term only once, but that is our interpretation as well."

David frowned. "We need to know how many, where they are, and if there are any loyal to the faction Asoon represents."

Barker nodded his agreement. "I'm worried about the general population, too. Those of us in the West once thought we could march into certain countries and be welcomed as liberators. Those soldiers were not prepared to be shot in the back by those they had just freed from dictatorship. I can't repeat that here."

David stood. "I understand, sir, and I agree. But I'd also argue that the Pottery Barn Rule does not apply here."

"Oh? We break it, but we don't have to buy it?"

"We go in, we neutralize this 'First,' either by death or imprisonment and then we freaking go home and let Asoon's group take over."

"They do claim to be the true government. They make the First out to be a renegade."

Peña smiled. "Which means, from our point of view, we're assisting in the restoration of legitimate rule, not taking down the existing power structure."

David was not convinced. Flopping back into a chair, he looked at Peña. "In the immortal words of the great philosopher Mister Spock, sir, I think that's a distinction without a difference."

Barker nodded, smiling slightly. "Possibly, Powell, but it's one I can live with." He stood. "I'll talk to CINC."

Almost one hundred and fifty-one minutes after requesting a delay, Asoon returned to the radio.

"Connor, this is Asoon."

"Yes, Asoon, we are here."

"I am to tell you that with me here is the Principal Scientist of our Science Directorate. He is the true head of our society. He and his advisors have decided that the First must be removed by force. We cannot accomplish this ourselves, and so we ask your help and offer any assistance we can give you."

Connor looked around the wardroom table, seeing no dispute, he answered, "That is a good first step, Asoon. But there are other issues we must settle."

"He accepts our offer, Glur Woe Segt, but says there are other questions."

"Ask him, Asoon, to say what those are. I am here to listen."

Asoon thought for a micRot, then spoke to the humans. "Connor, the Principal Scientist is here to listen. Please tell us of these other issues."

"There are several. First, the safety of the species recently attacked must be guaranteed. The Seekers, which you tried to exterminate perhaps fifty revolutions of your planet ago, must be returned to their homes and left alone."

After a moment, Asoon's answer was clear. "These actions are regrettable. We can easily agree with this. Additionally, the Principal Scientist offers to provide any assistance to these species that we can, to the extent they are willing to accept it."

Peña looked at Davenport skeptically. "That's almost too good an answer to be true, sir."

"Still, Elias, let's not fail to take yes for an answer." He continued with Asoon, "We must have an accounting of the star systems you have conquered, the species there, and how they can best be freed from Preeminent rule."

"The First would have killed him by now if he could," Scad commented.

"They see us as vicious predators, Scad," Asoon told him. "For them, we are something to be defeated and then controlled."

Segt said simply, "Tell him we agree to all."

"This is too easy," Peña repeated.

Gabrielle spoke up. "No, Commander. This is the rational part of their society, as Asoon said, *the principal scientist*, agreeing to help clean up a mess he didn't make and didn't want. If I'm hearing them right, you'll get everything you ask."

"Asoon, we must have your commitment to never again expand your rule beyond your own star. The Preeminent must never commit such acts of agression, ever again."

"Forever is a long time," Rmah said. "I am not sure we can truthfully say that."

Segt dismissed his maleChild. "What happens in the distant future is beyond our control, Rmah. The humans could suddenly become evil themselves. Asoon, tell him we here agree, but the distant future can't be known or predicted."

"That's a fair answer," David said after Asoon answered. "I'd take it, sir."

Davenport nodded and told Asoon that this answer was sufficient, then asked for a short break.

"So," he asked, "Where do we go from here?"

Elias Peña answered quickly. "We need some answers about what and where, sir. We need to get some hard information from them."

"And," Dan Smith pointed out, "We need to get the Marine commanders back here to plan this assault."

CINC agreed. After some discussion, he decided who would do the talking.

"OK, fine. Powell, get back with Asoon and ask whatever questions you have. You'll be the tactical and intelligence contact, understand? Yours is the only voice they will hear."

"Are you sure, sir? Surely Commander Peña would be — "

"Did I stutter or something, Lieutenant?"

David's eye went to Elias Peña as he answered, "No, sir. You were quite clear."

"I need Commander Peña here, Lieutenant. And I want them working with a single voice, a single name."

As the room began to clear of those not involved in the tactical side of the question, Peña moved to sit next to David.

"Don't sweat it, Powell. I agree with CINC. You'll be fine."

"Asoon, are you still there?" David called.

"Yes, we are here. I hear a new voice. May I have your name?"

"I am David, Asoon, and I will be asking you and the others for some specific planning information we need. Are you prepared to talk to us about this?"

Scad and Rmah were ready.

"Very good. I want you to understand, Asoon, that we have high-resolution photographs of your cities that we have taken from orbit. I will be asking you questions based on these images. Do you understand what that means?"

"Yes, David, we understand."

Asoon was puzzled as she explained to the males. "This new voice, David, is young, I think, more of a technician than a senior officer."

Wok was amused. "So, he's a human Rmah?"

"He says they have detailed images of the cities and they will be asking their questions from those. Does this make sense to you?"

"Yes," Scad answered, "It is a simple technique. Tell him we are ready."

David began by asking about the missile batteries, and mainly what the nearby structure meant. He also tried to confirm Harry Hess' concerns about non-combatants living nearby. There were indeed many personal residences just inside the outer wall of the city. Hess was correct: a strike on the missiles would have killed many. Glur Woe Segt, listening carefully to the conversation, was impressed with the humans' concern for unnecessary death. It further confirmed his belief that this was the right course.

Elias had David ask about the large building in the center of the city and was relieved to learn that it was the headquarters of the Science Directorate, and therefore no threat to the Marines.

Finally, David pushed for information on how to access the First's headquarters, how many guards, what their habits were, shift changes, and weapons. He took notes as he talked, sometimes asking Asoon to clarify or correct his understanding.

After two hours of this, both sides were clearly tiring.

"Asoon, I think we should take a pause now. We have to organize what you have already given us, and consider what other information we require."

"David, we have a request for you as well."

David, surprised, looked at Elias, who simply nodded. "Go ahead."

"The First must be isolated. We can tell you where his communications complex is located. If you can strike it, we will all be safer."

Peña nodded and reached for the ship phone. "I'll call CINC."

"Please wait, Asoon; I am calling Connor back."

CINC and Fiona Collins hurried back into the wardroom, sitting across from David and Elias.

"They're asking us to strike the First's communications complex to cut him off."

Davenport shrugged. "Makes sense. What's the problem?"

Peña answered. "We didn't think we should agree to that without your word, sir."

"Hit whatever they ask. They need to know we're on their side, too."

After telling Asoon they would do as asked, it took a few more minutes before Peña had the location pinpointed and confirmed with Asoon.

They called CINC and Fiona back to show them where the strike would fall.

As they talked, a sly smile spread across his face. "You know, Captain Nonna grumbled all the way out here about taking damage and not being able to hit anything back at Earth."

"So?"

"Laser this over to her and ask her to take it out as soon as possible. It's not too near any residences, but tell her I'd suggest multiple Lances over a Bludgeon."

"Yes, sir," Peña responded. "We'll send it over."

"Then ask her to bring back the Marine officers from *Intrepid* and *Canberra*. We need to plan an assault."

"Yes, Admiral. Right away."

As Elias left to transmit the photographs and orders, Fiona turned to Connor Davenport.

"This military complex, sir, it's seven levels down from the surface to get to the First. It could be a costly victory."

"I know, Fiona, I know," he said, shaking his head sadly. "But no war really ends until some kid from Nebraska who's never been so far from home stands on some shitty little hill and says 'this is mine and you can't have it.' Removing the First will put the final nail in the coffin of this war, and we can all get back to our lives."

"This won't be the end, sir," David pointed out. "There are the conquered worlds to relieve."

"Yes, but that will take time and care to do properly. Our esteemed doctors Este and Cordero will have new and more interesting projects, don't you think?"

"Yes, I do."

They talked quietly until Peña returned to tell them that *Bondarenko* was leaving for e-prime within the hour. The SD Exploration Vessel had already left, so CINC instructed Anna Nonna to wait to strike until Asoon and her party were safely on the ground.

Central Council Chambers
The Preeminent Home World
Earth Equivalent Date: Thursday, May 11, 2079

The Revered First remained cloistered in his chamber for several rots, eating the small meals his assistant brought, but otherwise isolating himself. He had come out only when the Tenth-Commander in charge of the Combatants came to report the loss of communications. He was sent by one of the Counselors because they believed the First would not execute him, despite the news. The news that his communication links had been severed by a direct Vermin attack left him in futile anger.

"Revered First, we are cut off from the Armada, but we retain the half-cohort of Combatants here in headquarters. What are your orders for us, Revered First?"

"The SD has betrayed us, Wodf. I should order you to remove them, to destroy them entirely." The First pounded the council table. "We are the Preeminent, Wodf, you understand this?"

"Yes, Revered First, I do."

"Then defend us against the SD. They are not to enter here again. And, set your technicians to restoring my communications."

Tenth-Commander Wodf knew full well that the Vermin attack had left the

SLIP and radio facility in ruin. It could not be repaired but would need to be rebuilt from scratch. It would take many rots to complete, perhaps as long as a deciRev. If not attacked during the rebuild, once completed, the Vermin would surely destroy it again. He wisely chose to omit those facts from his response.

"I will send what resources I have to begin the process, Revered First."

After Wodf left, the First had few victims left to lash out at, only his last three Counselors, should he choose to summon them. There was no compromise in the First, not a shred of doubt that he was what he was: the highest form of life in the Universe, entitled to rule, even obligated to do so. This was how his maleParent had instructed him, instilling a foundational belief in him that his teachers and mentors had confirmed and amplified until he fulfilled their ambitions and became The Revered First, the ultimate exemplar of the ultimate species. He thought nothing of the bloody trail his ascent had left behind. They were not genuinely Preeminent, he believed, or they would have defeated him instead. But treachery, he thought, the treachery of the SD had now left him alone in his predicament, perhaps the last truly superior being.

His Combatants would fight to defend him. They would prevail, he thought, and when they did, the lies of the SD would be revealed, and he would again direct conquests and accumulate even more glory and tribute. His council could be rebuilt, avoiding the weak-minded like Kiker and Tolf, and young Nowl. Nowl, in particular, would be a flavorful victory for him.

The Vermin. So appropriately named, he thought, for something so troublesome. That they had come from the planet in the Ultimate Origin legend only compounded his disgust. The old stories were irrelevant to the First, his only concern was the present and the future. The stories of the Guardians were fantasy, he was sure. Even if partially true, they could not have been superior to his own species, or they would still be here. They were a lower race, deserving of whatever fate the Preeminent decided for them.

He tried to consider what the Vermin would do next. Likely they would continue their blockade his incompetent subordinates had been unable to break. They would hesitate to strike, as they always did. This hesitation, this patience, he decided, would leave him the opportunity to defeat them. Once his communications were restored, he would order his hidden ships to strike, and the Vermin would be driven off.

Yes, yes, he thought, *they will wait, as if forbearance in war was a strength!* No, he knew, it reflected a lack of confidence, a faulty understanding of how a victor should act. Had the positions been reversed, and he held the power the Vermin did, the city would already be in ruins, the citizens bowing to his rule or dying at his word.

Someday, he convinced himself, he would stand on the Vermin homeworld and confirm for all his place among the intelligent species.

That, he thought proudly, would be a victory worthy of a Preeminent.

Sigma
E-Prime
Monday, May 15, 2079, 2000 UTC

As the news about the impending landing swirled around the ship, Carol called Peg White and XO Alex Williams into her duty cabin. They were surprised to find her in field colors, her personal sidearm holstered at her side.

Alex spoke first. "Going somewhere, Carol?"

She looked back at him with a hard determination he'd not often seen in her. She commanded more softly than that, more out of support and enabling success, less from giving direction. Something had changed.

"My Marines, that is, our Marines, are on *Canberra,* and they're going to the surface. Barker has asked us for a shuttle, and I'm going to fly them down."

Peg looked back at her with equal determination. "You are the captain of this ship, Carol. I don't recommend this."

"I'm not sure I would, either, in your place. But I was there at the start, and now I need to be there at the end. I saw Captain Michael die. I saw her face when she was hit. I watched her fall. I watched the life drain out of Marty Baker's eyes while I knelt over him, helpless to do anything about it." She was quiet for a few seconds; the anger dampening her eyes and reddening her cheeks. "I need to finish it for *them.* And, for Cornell." She paused, then said "But I can't do it without your help."

Peg thought about arguing the point further, but she hadn't been in Inoria. Or, on Beta Hydri. She'd grown quite fond of Carol in their time together and admired her abilities as a leader. "So, what is it you need, exactly?"

Carol turned to her XO. "Alex, you are my friend, as XO you've been my dependable right arm, and I would not have wanted to go through this without you."

Alex smiled. "But you're leaving Commander White in charge while you go running through the enemy capital with the Marines."

She ignored the last part. "Yes."

"Oh, good," he answered, surprising them both. "That's a relief. I'm happy to stay XO and keep things running without actually being responsible."

"Smartass." Carol responded.

"Guilty."

"Peg?" Carol asked.

"I'll accept, Carol, if only to see you able to complete this task that you seem so intent on. Which, I must confess, I see as unwise." Peg decided she had to confront Carol with her reservations. "You asked us to be your personal guard-rails. Well, *this* guardrail is calling your bluff."

Carol didn't respond.

"This choice could have severe consequences you haven't considered."

"Such as?"

"Well, beyond, you know, getting killed down there, you might well lose command of this ship and never get another one. Neither Barker nor Davenport will appreciate such an impulsive, selfish act by a Captain."

"I know. I'm willing to take that chance."

Peg sat and leaned forward, just inches from the desk. "The Carol Hansen as heroine stuff only goes so far. There are limits to what they'll let you get away with."

"I don't think about myself that way, Peg, and I think you know that. If CINC fires me over this, fine. I can live with it. But I can't live with sitting on my ass up here while my Marines go into combat."

"Try to remember, Carol," Alex said quietly, "that they are Barnes' Marines, not yours."

Carol looked up at Alex, undeterred. "They walked Beta Hydri with us, Alex. They saw with us what happened there."

"Yes, I know. I was there, too."

Peg leaned back, resigned that Carol was not to be swayed from what she considered a foolhardy career move. "If you're absolutely sure about this, then yes, I'll take over temporarily. But understand if I do that, Davenport may not give her back to you."

Carol looked from one officer to the other, then said quietly, "That's all. Thank you."

Alex and Peg looked at each other, shared a tiny shrug of resignation, and left the Duty Cabin.

Carol sent a message to her crew, explaining that she was going to the surface and that Lieutenant Commander White would take over until she returned. The whole thing was irregular, and Carol knew Davenport would likely veto it if he could, but by the time he found out, she'd probably be on the surface and not easily recalled.

She took *Sigma*'s shuttle to *Canberra*, ready to take back her Marines. She'd already sent Loren Booker a private message with her plan. As she stepped through *Canberra* port airlock, Booker was waiting with her Marines.

"Welcome aboard, Commander! Playing hooky, are we?"

"Yes, sir, a little. I couldn't let them go down there without me."

"I understand, Commander Hansen."

Carol looked past Booker at the Marines. "Where's Sergeant Jackson?"

A young corporal answered, "Already gone, ma'am. He and Major Barnes took the pathfinder squad down with Lieutenant Powell."

Carol looked at the man for a second. "Lieutenant Powell?"

"Yes, ma'am. I guess he's the ground controller for this junket."

Carol stepped aside as the Marines loaded themselves into the shuttle. It was a full load, commanded by a sergeant she had not met before, likely a replacement from *Canberra*. She closed the hatch, disconnected from *Canberra*, and headed for the rally point they had chosen: *Intrepid*.

Science Directorate Headquarters Landing Site
The Preeminent Home World
Monday, May 15, 2079, 2200 UTC

David watched out the right-side cockpit window with apprehension as the *Cobra* shuttle approached the SD landing site. He and his small group would be the first on the enemy homeworld, and he would be the first to speak to Asoon face-to-face. He knew what a Preeminent looked like, so that part didn't concern him. She knew how humans appeared, too, so, again, that should not be a surprise. Still, face to face with a living alien would be orders of magnitude stranger than picking over remains or talking on the radio.

He also knew that there were others with Asoon that she had not named, including someone very senior. David was concerned about security. He could not help wondering how many Preeminent knew of their plan and were on board. He could be walking into a trap.

He also fretted about the timing. It was several hours before dawn on Alpha Mensae (c), but already late evening for the humans. Their bodies would be fighting through the night even as the star came over the horizon. The adrenaline would probably cure most of that, he thought. In any case, this was the place, and this was the time. They would make it work.

The flight down added to the surreal nature of the whole operation: the shuttle cabin in night mode with only dim, red lighting. After a long, low approach, they settled silently to the surface of the SD Landing Facility. David moved quickly to the hatch and opened it. As he stepped down from the shuttle, he was struck by the cool, dry air of pre-dawn, and the faint but unmistakable smell of decomposition. He fought off his unpleasant reaction, turning around to look at the city around him, tall metallic buildings shadowed the sky, the largest of all just a few dozen meters away. They had done simulations of what it would look like based on their overhead photography, but David was still surprised at how coldly functional it all looked. Alpha Mensae (c) had no visible moons, so the landing site, with three-meter-high walls all around, was quite dark. The sky in the east was still full of stars. Movement nearby caught his eye, and he instinctively placed his hand on his weapon. He'd deliberately left his night-vision glasses in his pocket. He did not want to reveal anything too soon. Better to meet the aliens first on equal ground.

"Are you David?" a familiar voice asked quietly.

As his eyes adjusted further, he saw four Preeminent, the smallest standing closest to him. He had never encountered a living Preeminent before, and they were much larger in life than they looked on an autopsy table. David focused on the smaller one nearest him.

"Good morning, Asoon. Who is with you?" He heard her speak in a combination of tones, clicks, and what sounded like grunts. There were more of the same in response but in an obviously lower register.

"There are three here, David, the same that came with me to Planet Five. Scad is a ship commander. Rmah is a young scientist, and Glur is the Principal Scientist. He is now the head of our society."

"I had only planned to take you with us, Asoon, to translate. I don't have room for four."

He heard more tones and clicks. Then, Asoon turned back to him,

"Scad is my malePair, and his military knowledge will be helpful. The others will come later."

David turned to see Wayne Barnes standing on the top step of the shuttle.

"Two," David said quietly, and Barnes disappeared back inside.

David turned back to Asoon. "MalePair?"

"We are what you would think of as mates, or, perhaps, married, but it is very different with us."

"OK, then. Let's go. Does it always smell like this?"

Asoon looked at him before stepping on the ladder. "Smell like what?"

David started to explain but decided to let it go. This was no time for sociological discussions or questions of hygiene. The Preeminents sat uncomfortably next to the hatch on seats not designed for their anatomy, every Marine eye on them. Becker flew the shuttle from the SD landing zone to the entry point Asoon had given them. Scad had chosen a location within the boundaries of the Armada HQ, an open area inside the compound and not well guarded from the outside.

David watched the approach, again from the right seat, looking for any sign of a response, any indication they had been seen. All was still quiet as Becker set the shuttle down lightly. David, Asoon, and Scad were the first out, moving to the entry doors. A step behind was Barnes with his breaching team, four Marines with shaped charges. As they worked to set the explosives, the other dozen

Marines moved out of the shuttle to form a perimeter around the door. They knelt down, night vision glasses making the pre-dawn darkness seem like day.

In five minutes, the breaching team reported ready. David looked at his watch, then waved to Becker, who silently lifted off, moving low and fast away from the Armada headquarters. As he scanned the sky to the south, he heard Scad talking to Asoon.

"What are they doing?"

"I don't know, malePair, but something to get us inside."

"They scare me more in person than they did in space, Asoon. So fast, so confident."

"I am relieved that they are with us now."

"They are not with us, Asoon. We are with them. And they smell like prey. It makes me hungry just — "

"Be quiet, Scad. They are not prey. Just keep telling yourself that."

"What now?" Asoon finally asked David.

"It won't be long."

"What?"

"Just wait quietly, Asoon. Just wait. They're coming."

"Who is coming?"

"Just wait, please." A minute later, David's earpiece came alive.

"Marco."

He smiled as he keyed his microphone, "Polo." David turned to Asoon. "Five minutes, Asoon. Do you understand what that means?"

"Yes, I do." She turned and spoke again to Scad.

"Someone is coming, malePair. About five cenmilrots from now."

"I will be glad when this is over, Asoon. I do much better on my ship than here on the ground."

"So, Asoon," David asked casually, "how many languages do you speak?"

"Just yours, and my own, of course. I can only learn one alien language."

David watched the sky as he continued the conversation. "Only one?"

"Yes, it is a skill born in me. I am what is called a 'Speaker,' but once trained, it cannot be changed."

"How long did it take you? You speak very well."

"A few months, in human terms."

"That is amazing. I know humans who can't speak as well." David turned to look at Barnes. "There they are."

Six shuttles were just appearing over the south wall of the Armada head-quarters. Their silent approach ended as they set down in the broad area just outside the entry doors. As the hatches opened, David pushed Asoon and Scad back along the wall, and with a flash, the door was gone.

Facility Maintenance Entrance
The Preeminent Home World
Monday, May 15, 2079, 2220 UTC

Asoon was shocked and disoriented, thrown back by the detonation of the breaching charges that shattered the access doors. Scad, standing in front of her, was also knocked off his feet. As they rose, dozens of helmeted, armored humans were rushing through the shattered entrance, David standing to one side.

"Are you hurt, Asoon?" he asked her.

"No, only surprised."

"Sorry. I couldn't really warn you any better."

As they spoke, the final shuttle settled onto the ground and disgorged its load. David was about to enter the enemy headquarters when someone caught his eye. Carol was running behind her group of Marines, her weapon in her hand. She stopped when she saw David, then ran directly over to him.

"What have I missed?" she asked breathlessly.

David smiled. "Just the overture."

"Cool. Let's get going."

As David and Asoon began moving towards the front of the company, the first shots rang out, and the Marines went to the floor or found cover in one of the many doorways along the walls. Barnes, in the lead, could hear agitated voices ahead of him. Asoon and David were soon beside him.

Barnes looked at Asoon and pointed down the curved ramp. "What are they saying?"

Asoon listened for a moment. "They are confused, afraid, but gathering weapons."

He ordered Asoon to move back. As Carol took her and Scad back ten meters, she ran across another familiar face.

"Commander Hayden!"

"Hello Commander Hansen," she said, slyly. "Nice to see you."

Carol smiled. "Quite the reunion tonight." She pointed Asoon to an empty spot near Natalie. "Meet Asoon. She's with us."

Natalie looked at the Preeminents with instinctive distrust. "If you say so. But yeah, Liwanu is here, too, over there." She pointed to the young lieutenant, kneeling with his Marines, his head swiveling to watch ahead and behind.

"So," Natalie asked slyly, "does CINC know you're here?"

"Dunno. Probably does by now."

"This little caper might cost you, Carol, you know that, right?"

Carol nodded. "Yeah, I suppose. But I just need to see this thing right to the end."

Natalie looked down the passageway, then back at Carol, her face hard and determined. "Me, too. All the way to the end."

After a moment, Carol asked her, "Can you cover Asoon for now?"

"Sure. But, Carol, why is she grey? All the others we've seen are purple."

"She's a female, Nat. The purples are males."

"Oh, yeah, right. Bird female."

"Right. So, expect someone to come to fetch her before long."

Natalie nodded her understanding, and Carol worked her way back to the front, finally kneeling beside the large, familiar, comforting figure of Leon Jackson.

"Hello, Commander," he said, smiling. "Caught another case of the promotion plague, did you?"

"Yeah, just can't seem to shake it," she responded quietly as she retrieved her sidearm from its holster and chambered a round.

Barnes had crawled forward to see what was around the curve of the hall. Now back, he called Jackson to his side.

"Take four men, stay low. The voices are coming from an opening on the right. It's not far. Get close and roll a grenade through the opening. Set it for a decent delay and get back, understand? If you're quiet enough, they won't even know what happened."

Jackson picked his volunteers and began to work his way along the cold metallic floor of the dimly lit passage. Apparently, it was still early morning for the Preeminents. He crawled to where he could just see the door Barnes had identified. He turned and gave the Major a thumbs up, and Barnes signaled to everyone to get ready.

Natalie looked at Asoon. "You speak English, right?"

"Yes."

"Get as low as you can, and cover your ears. Now." Asoon motioned to Scad, and they joined the humans on the floor just as the grenade went off thirty meters ahead.

Jackson and his men were up a fraction of a second later, first firing blindly into the opening. As the smoke dissipated, they eliminated one-by-one the Combatants in that compartment.

Barnes looked at the squad corporal next to him. "Lather, rinse, repeat."

The corporal took his foursome around the descending right turn, watching for more doors and more enemy soldiers. About halfway around, they encountered a similar door on the left and gave it the same treatment. That done, they fell back to rejoin the main force.

Barnes was pleased but getting impatient. "This won't be this easy for very long, but we'll keep pushing, OK? We keep moving down. Our target is on the seventh level." As twelve Marines moved ahead, he turned back to David.

"Where's Asoon?"

David looked back and motioned to Natalie to send Asoon and Scad forward. Barnes looked at her. "Ask Scad how quickly they'll get organized."

"He asks how long they will take to get organized."

"It should not take very long. a cenrot at most. But, Asoon, Combatants are trained to attack and subdue, not defend. I don't know how they will react."

"Anything else?"

"There is a side entrance just inside the door they blew up. We could be attacked from behind if they are not careful."

"They're careful, malePair, but I will tell them."

Asoon turned back to David. "Not very long. Perhaps fifteen minutes, in your terms. Scad is also worried about what is behind us. There is a side entrance near where we came through."

"Allen!" Barnes called.

The young second lieutenant trotted up from her position. "Sir?"

"Take a squad and set up a blocking position in the rear. Call for help if you need it. Go!" He turned back to Asoon. "What about all these compartments?"

After another sharp exchange with Scad, she replied: "Some have other exits, so yes, there is the potential that Combatants could come through. But Scad is skeptical that they will."

"Skeptical, eh? I guess I'll just have to accept that."

Shots rang out ahead, and the first pops of Preeminent weapons fire were heard.

They moved ahead carefully, pinned against the walls of the four-meter-wide hallway. As the enemy fire continued, a flash and loud explosion signaled the delivery of another grenade. The enemy fire stopped, and the Marines in front moved in and cleared the compartment.

At the next turn, the Combatants were more ready. Leon Jackson was nearly killed by a plasma bolt but returned fire to push the Preeminent back out of the passage while a PFC rolled two grenades. They went off a second apart, but the enemy was learning, and several survived the initial attack and continued firing. Jackson's group carefully worked their way forward, eventually suppressing the Combatants.

"They're getting better at this," a sweaty Jackson said to Barnes as he moved up. "We need to keep moving."

They did just that, descending again as quietly as possible, listening to the loud voices ahead of them. There seemed to be an opening about every ninety degrees, four per complete turn of the spiral. The passage descended at a shallow angle, perhaps one to twenty.

After the second level, Barnes again summoned Asoon. "If we offer them a chance, will they surrender?"

Asoon and Scad discussed it briefly. "Scad says it is not in their nature. They cannot."

"He understands they will all die?"

"He does. But the way the Combatants are raised and indoctrinated, he sees little option."

As they continued, there was a series of pops followed by gunshots. Shortly David saw two Marines dragging a third back from the leading edge of the engagement. The smoking hole in his chest told the story. His young corporal swore softly as he spoke to Barnes. "He took one step too many, sir, looking back instead of ahead. They were ready."

Three more engagements, and two more deaths, and they arrived at the fourth level. They were now finding offices with desks and chairs, a surprise to David since he'd seen no such furnishings on the wreck at GL 674. As he was looking around an office just after the Marines had cleared it, a Preeminent appeared out of an inner office. David, surprised, stepped back, drew his weapon, and shot the alien in the head. His quick examination afterward revealed no weapon, but David knew the Preeminent's talons and incisors were all the weapons it would have needed to kill him. He moved back into the central passage and quickly caught up with Carol and Wayne Barnes.

"I found a straggler in an office."

"Oh?" Carol asked.

"Don't worry, he's down."

Barnes, hearing this, called to David. "Tell Scad to go see what that was. I don't like that there are any behind us."

David worked his way back a half-turn to Asoon and Scad and motioned them to follow him. He took them to the office and pointed to the remains on the floor.

"Asoon, does Scad know this individual?"

"Who is this?"

"This is bad, Asoon. He's killed Tenth-Commander Wodf, the commander of the headquarters guard. What was he doing here and not with the First?"

"You killed the commander of the Revered First's personal guard. Scad is surprised he is here."

"Cool, thanks."

"Sometime, David, you must explain 'cool' to me. It seems to have no end of meanings."

274

David smiled. "Yes, it does. For now, think of it as 'really good.'"
As they moved back to Barnes, he had more questions for Scad.

The First awoke to the alarms and the distant sound of explosions. He summoned his personal guard to block the last level from the spiral passageway. As the sounds grew louder, he called Tenth Commander Wodf to report to him. He never arrived.

"Fools!" he yelled at his defenders. "Fools and traitors!"

His three remaining Counselors answered his summons, their quarters only one level above. They were clearly afraid, shaking at every explosion, each one louder than the last. The First stepped into the outer room, ordering half the remaining Combatants to hold the outside of the door, the other half to remain inside and prepare to strike out at the Vermin.

They did not wait, he thought to himself. *They lulled me into thinking they would hesitate. No matter,* he thought, *we will prevail.*

He would have preferred to have a weapon, but to wield one was to admit he needed one, or that the Vermin could get to him. He placed his guards and went inside the Central Council chamber with his three frightened advisors.

Lieutenant Kamaria Allen had a political science degree from UCLA. Sometimes she could not quite recall why she chose to pursue OCS and join the US Marines. It was something about the challenge, Kamaria was sure. As she now sat holding the rear of the Fleet Marines, on a hostile, alien planet full of living dinosaurs, she was even less confident if moving over to the Fleet had been such a stroke of genius. But, somewhere down inside, she was happy it had worked out this way. Her Marines were the best, this squad drawn from a half-dozen countries, but all warriors to the core.

Something was happening ahead of her; Kamaria could hear the pounding of feet on the hard surface of the passage. She heard her forward lookouts shoulder their weapons, and she and the rest of the squad did the same. In her night vision glasses, Kamaria saw four aliens approaching, slowly but right down the center of the passage. She waited for them to be ten meters away and fired. All four fell quickly. As she lowered her weapon, she heard the sound of footsteps, and the lookouts started firing. Kamaria dropped back down and waited for a target. At least twenty aliens were running towards them, firing their plasma bolts at the floor. She took out two herself, then stopped long enough to radio Barnes.

"Getting heavy fire back here, sir. Holding for now, but we need help." The lookouts were both dead, so she tossed a grenade in the direction of the approaching aliens and ordered her squad to pull back. They found a spot where there were two openings, one on either side of the passage. They ducked into the doors and waited for the aliens to come on.

As they heard the footsteps again, Kamaria had them toss their last four grenades, which stopped the enemy advance. When she heard nothing for a few seconds, she pulled her squad out and moved back up to engage whatever enemy was there. They killed six more and dispatched three suffering wounded that could not be attended to. Barnes had given them the same speech he had on *Antares*: No Geneva Convention, no second-guessing, just trust your common sense to keep you and your people safe.

It made no sense to anyone to see these creatures suffer when they could not be saved. It had been close, the aliens had almost overcome them, but Kamaria's small band had held.

Barnes dispatched eight more Marines to her, and as they came trotting up the passage, she sent them to recon all the way back to the doors. Their only report was that it was getting light outside.

Kamaria appreciated that detail.

As Barnes was talking to Sergeant Jackson about their next move, David looked at Asoon.

"What the hell is it about seven?"

"Seven?" she asked.

"The First is on level seven, correct?"

"Yes, so Scad has told me."

"Seven in human superstition is lucky. There was a famous book with seven circles of hell."

"Seven is rather unusual, you know."

"Oh?"

"Not very easy to factor, no pattern in its multiples, things like that. It is not on the natural series I read to you."

"OK, we'll just call it weird and leave it at that."

"David, I get the feeling that 'weird' is in the same class as 'cool.'"

"Yeah, maybe."

Barnes finished his conversation with Jackson and turned to Asoon.

"Is there no way we can get them to give up? No way?"

Asoon turned to Scad. *"He asks again if the Combatants can be made to surrender."*

"The Verm-, uh, the humans have not previously shown so much consideration."

"You would, of course, know better than I about that. But did they not refrain

from destroying you when you were at their home planet? They could have, yes?"

"Yes, they could. I suspect their motives were their own and less about our lives."

Barnes was still impatient. "Asoon, is there or is there not a way? I would save every life on both sides if I could."

"He asks again, and he will not wait much longer."

"I can try. We need to go back to the tenth-commander's spaces. From there, I can call the master of the guard."

"Scad says he will try. We need to go back to the tenth-commander's compartment."

Barnes nodded. "Powell, take them back. Meanwhile, we will keep moving forward."

As he turned to take the Preeminents back up the passage, David noticed a tall, athletic-looking Lieutenant Commander moving up with her Marines, preparing to take their turn at the point. *Hayden,* her uniform said. He caught her eye briefly as they passed in opposite directions. *Hayden,* he thought a second later. *Carol talked about a Hayden that was with her on Big Blue.* He'd have to find her again later.

David caught himself: he was no longer wondering *if* there would be a later. *Dangerous,* he thought. *Overconfidence will kill us.*

They found the compartment, and Scad stepped over the tenth-commander and his widening blood pool to get to the inner office. He sat at the desk and called the hundredth-commander of the First's guards.

"Donh, you must relent. The Vermin are here in force. They have taken half the headquarters already."

"I am Preeminent, Wok, and you sound like a traitor."

"Donh, if you persist, you and all your Combatants will die. That is not victory. Think, Donh, think!"

"Wok, the Vermin have killed thousands of Combatants, why should they stop now?"

"Because it is not necessary." He turned and looked at Asoon, remembering what she had said to him.

"They did not kill me when they could, Donh. I believe they will not kill you, either."

"We are the Preeminent, Wok."

"We are not, Donh. Here on Home, yes, but not out there. It is a bitter lesson I have learned. Relent, Donh. Relent, and live."

"I do not care to be a meal for the First, Wok."

"The First is powerless. The SD revoked his authority. You know this! Why

do you follow his orders?"

"Because he is the First. If I order them to surrender, what then, Wok? Slave labor?"

"No. I don't know what will happen, but not that."

"What shall we do?"

Scad turned to Asoon. *"How are they to surrender?"*

After Asoon translated, David called Barnes on the radio.

"We may have made some progress here, sir. What would you have them do?"

"Keep it simple. They should just leave their arms behind and walk up the passage. We will not fire on an unarmed Combatant."

David turned to Asoon. "They should drop their weapons and walk up the passageway. They will not be harmed. They will, however, be restrained for our safety. They can kill us without weapons."

As David spoke, they heard shots in the distance, both human and Preeminent weapons. There was a firefight somewhere below.

"Stay here!" Liwanu Harry had said to Natalie, his face inches from hers.

"Go to Hell, Liwanu," she replied. "I'm coming."

He leaned in even closer. "Natalie, *please* stay here."

Her unchanging expression told him there was no changing her mind. Liwanu gave up. Leaning back, he said in a clear voice, "Stay low, Commander, and please don't get killed on my watch. Henderson will chew my ass for a month."

Now, as she moved forward with the Marines, she was wondering if maybe Liwanu was right after all. The Preeminents had set up a good defensive position where the passage widened and met another, perpendicular, passage. They had pulled furniture and other equipment together and managed a decent barricade. Two of Liwanu's Marines were wounded right away, and they pulled back to a doorway to regroup. From across the passage, three Marines kept up the pressure on the Preeminents, trying to pick a few off and discourage their comrades. Natalie was prone on the floor in front of them, firing at the opening on the opposite wall.

"Get her back!" Liwanu yelled to his corporal.

"You get her back, Lieutenant. I'm afraid she'll shoot me if I tried."

"Dammit. I was afraid of this." Harry looked at her, her focus entirely on her target, and decided to leave her there for now. If something happened, he'd regret it, but for the moment there wasn't much he could do about it.

Barnes hustled down the passage, settling as close as he could safely to the battle below. He sent a runner to fetch Harry, who sent him back.

"The Lieutenant respectfully declines your offer to abandon his Marines. Sir."

Barnes looked at the runner. "That what he said?"

"Not really, sir. What he actually suggested was sexual in nature, sir, and I think anatomically impossible."

Barnes smiled. "That kid will be a general someday."

Carol pulled her group up behind Barnes, then carefully crawled over to the Marine Major. "So, what now?"

"Well, Commander Hansen, we didn't bring any mortars."

"Those would seem unhelpful down here."

"Yeah, unhelpful."

"Any more grenades?"

"A few. I was hoping Lieutenant Powell would make all this moot, but the longer we're stuck in front of this barricade, the longer the enemy has to reorganize."

They heard shouts from further down, voices punctuating the sounds of weapons fire. As the shouts increased, so did the volume of fire.

Natalie kept her eye on the wide opening to her right, firing at anything that moved. The enemy behind the barricade saw she was there, and several plasma rounds struck above and beside her. Just after the third near-miss, Liwanu had had enough. His Marines began firing heavily, driving the Preeminents back as he dropped to the floor, pulling Natalie physically back as a plasma round exploded at his feet.

"Shit!" he yelled as he went down. Natalie, now back on the floor, slapped out the small fires on her uniform and then grabbed Liwanu by the collar and dragged him back, out of sight of the enemy. She rolled him over.

"What the hell was that?" she yelled at him.

"Another minute, Commander, and you'd be dead."

"I don't need to be rescued, Lieutenant." She was suddenly aware that other Marines were pushing her down and pounding small fires out on her back.

"You sure of that?" Liwanu shot back at her.

"How's the foot?" she asked, still angry, but just a little chastened.

"It stings. Thanks for asking."

The squad sergeant had called for a medic, who was now examining Harry's foot. One side of his boot was mostly gone, but the burns were superficial. The medic sprayed it with antiseptic/anesthetic and wrapped the foot in camo tape.

"Sorry, Lieutenant," he said, "not enough to pull you out of the fight." With that, he moved back a few meters, repacking his medical bag.

"Sorry?" he said to no one in particular. "I ain't leaving no how."

Natalie looked at him and smiled slightly, "OK, cowboy. Thanks."

Liwanu looked over at her. "I don't need Henderson six feet up my rear end, Commander."

"Mine, either, Lieutenant," Major Barnes said as he slid in next to them. "You're OK?"

"Superficial, sir, no problem."

"What's your status?"

"Well, besides not letting Commander Hayden get killed, we've reduced them by maybe a half, but there are more coming in. I think, anyway. The crossing just hides too much, sir."

As he spoke, a plasma round struck a few meters away, leaving a melted defect in the wall and spraying bits of hot metal on them.

"OK, I was hoping Scad would fix this for us, but I guess not." He looked around once more, then his face became set. He turned to the platoon sergeant. "Get whatever charges we have left up here."

Asoon stood over Scad as he argued with the remaining guard officer. Scad thought they were making progress, but Donh had turned resistant.

"I wonder if someone is pushing him to resist."

"Is he not in command?"

"Yes, but there is much confusion. To lose an engagement is unthinkable for the Combatants. They would fight to the death trying to advance. Telling them to quit is not so simple."

David watched this exchange. "Asoon?"

"Scad thinks they're pressuring Donh to resist."

He keyed his radio. "Major Barnes, this is Powell. Not so hopeful back here."

"Roger that. They have five minutes, Powell, and then we're done talking. Clear?"

David looked over at Asoon. "They have five minutes to decide, Asoon. After that, we're done."

Asoon passed the deadline to Scad.

"Donh, you must decide. Their patience is running out."

"Then let it run out, Wok. I am told we are holding them. Soon we will be pushing them back. And then, we will win."

"Donh do not forget what I have said."

"I will not forget you, traitor Wok. I will never forget."

Asoon turned to David, sadness on her face that he could not recognize. "They will fight on. Scad says they're planning to push you back."

David keyed the radio again. "They told Scad that they're going to push us back. I don't think we should consider that an empty threat."

"Understood. Get down here as soon as you can. I may need Asoon."

Barnes turned to Liwanu. "Powell says they're planning to push us out. Too bad." He peeked around the corner, just enough to see the barricade, then turned back to his sergeant. "We'll hit them on three sides at once. I want a breaching charge to go into the middle of the barricade, then grenades in the left and right entrances. Lieutenant Harry here will give you suppression. Clear?"

As Liwanu worked his way back to his squad, he was suddenly aware of someone right behind him.

"Will you never learn?" he asked Natalie.

"Will you?"

Carol was relieved by David's reappearance in Barnes' informal forward command post, grabbing his hand briefly as they settled in along the high, cold wall. She quickly explained the plan to David, who turned to Asoon.

"There will be gunfire, then more explosions. It will be deafening."

"Yes, David, we will be ready." She turned and translated for Scad.

There was no mistaking the suppression fire, as Liwanu's squad, reinforced with some of Carol's former *Antares* Marines, opened up on the barricade, picking off several Combatants and sending the rest to cover. Fifteen seconds later, the breaching charge went off, blowing a two-meter-wide hole in the barricade and revealing a large number of combatants hiding behind it. They were thrown back and disoriented by the flash and deafening sound of the explosion. Liwanu saw this opening for what it was and ran to the barricade, firing into the mass that had snuck up behind it while Powell was trying to get them to give up. The *Antares* Marines moved into the open intersection, pushing left and right until there was no more opposition.

Back in the center passage, Barnes had called for an all-out assault of the barricade. Some of the Combatants were still resisting, and their volume of fire increased rapidly with their desperation. Carol worked her way down to the wrecked barricade, Leon Jackson beside her, and as she turned to go through the gap, a body suddenly fell on her as a plasma bolt flashed out from the mass of bodies behind. As she looked up, she realized Leon was lying on top of her, smoke rising from his body. She pushed with all her strength to move him off and, with a Marine, pulled him away from the gap.

"Leon! Oh my God, Leon! What have you done?"

He looked up at her, the pain evident in his eyes. "Totally worth it, ma'am."

He smiled slightly. "I'd do it again."

She grasped his hands, which were softer than she expected. "You can't die, Leon. You can't."

"Miss Carol, ma'am, if I might call you that, it's no longer in your hands."

Leon's corporal had already yelled for a medic, who arrived and pushed the heavy sergeant back on his side. "Sergeant, can you feel your feet?" she yelled at him over the sound of gunfire.

"Yeah, some. Feet hurt."

"You are one lucky son-of-a-bitch, Sergeant. You're gonna live." She looked up at Carol's frightened face. "He's got some bad burns across his back, ma'am, but nothing fatal."

Carol leaned over the big man. "Told you."

Jackson winced in pain as he turned his head slightly to look at her. "Excuse me, Commander, but don't you have a war to win or something?"

The carnage behind the barricade was something Carol had never seen before. Even on Big Blue, it had not been so bad. There were a hundred dead Combatants scattered along thirty meters of passage. The floor was slick with blood, but the humans got by on the inside of the curve. The main force was now past her, so Carol trotted downhill until she rejoined her *Antares* Marines. She reassured them about Jackson, then moved forward, looking for Barnes. And, David.

She found them just below the intersection at the sixth level. Their numbers had been reduced both by casualties and the need to leave a small rearguard on each level. They could not afford to be surprised from behind, should the Preeminents figure out how far they were from any help.

Asoon and her malePair Scad Nee Wok were in conversation with Wayne Barnes about what to do with the last company of Combatants just around the turn to level seven. Liwanu Harry had managed a quick look, and they were standing in a group, talking. Asoon listened for a minute and reported that they were arguing over what to do and whether certain death was their only choice.

Barnes pointed to a photograph Harry had been able to snap. "Asoon, what's behind these doors?"

"Scad, look at the image. He asks what is behind the doors."

"There is a small intermediate room, then the second set of doors that lead to the council chamber. The First's private chamber is beyond that."

"Will there be more Combatants behind the doors?"

She asked Scad again. "Almost certainly, yes," she reported.

"Asoon," Barnes said to her, "can Scad order them to stand down? Does he have sufficient rank?"

282

They talked quietly for a minute before she responded.

"He says he does not. He is a ship commander, not a Combatant officer. But he is willing to try to talk to them, convince them."

Scad Nee Wok made his way carefully, several Marines escorting him as far as they could without being seen. From there, he walked down the center of the passage. The Combatants stopped their arguments and drew their weapons as he approached.

"Who is in command here?" he asked.

An older Combatant came forward. "I am Combatant 32581. I am the eldest here."

"You have no officer?"

"We do not. The Hundredth-Commander is inside, with the rest. Who are you?"

"Ship Commander Scad Nee Wok."

"Ah, the traitor. Donh said you would come. He said we should drop you where you stand."

Wok turned and looked in the direction of the human force hiding behind him. "That would be unwise." He turned back to the Combatant. "Who, 32581, is the real traitor here? The one who throws your lives away for nothing, or the one who begs you to save them? The one who defies the rule of the Conclave, or the one who comes to enforce it?"

"I have my orders. I am to hold this position."

"Since when do Combatants 'hold' a position? You were trained to strike, to conquer, not to stand and await certain death."

They again argued among themselves, some fiercely loyal to the First, others questioning why they were here at all.

"We have our orders."

"I am giving you a new order, 32581, to set down your arms and leave."

"The Vermin will murder us."

"They will not."

"And you know this, how?" 32581 was not a Combatant to be easily swayed.

"They are just out of sight, around this curve. If they wanted to kill you all, you would already be dead."

"Prove it."

Scad turned his head slightly. "Asoon, do you hear?"

"Yes," she answered.

"They need to see. Perhaps four, just so they understand?"

Asoon turned back to Barnes. "The Combatants don't believe you're here."

"What, are they deaf?"

"No, but the noise of battle does not always tell the outcome. Can you send four ahead, so they might see?"

Barnes turned to Liwanu. "They want a show, we'll give them one. Here's what I want..."

Liwanu moved down the outer side of the passage, weapon ready but not aimed, until he could just see the Combatants. Natalie remained a few meters back, ready if needed. Liwanu's Sergeant Barczak moved down the inner side of the passage, again stopping just where she could see the Combatants, with three more just behind her along the wall. This cover in place, four Marines walked down the center of the passage, stopping once in full view of the aliens standing in front of the massive Council door. David stood behind them, watching, his hand on his sidearm.

Wok looked at the Marines, then back at the eldest Combatant. "They have fought their way down seven levels, 32581. Do you really believe you can stop them here?"

Intimidated, perhaps sobered by the realization of imminent but optional death, 32581 gained control of his small detachment. As they came in line, he turned back to Scad.

"Very well, ship commander. What now?"

"Set your weapons aside and walk up the passageway. I will come with you. Just do as you are told."

Barnes told Asoon what the Combatants should do, and she translated for Wok, who took them through the massed Marines to a quieter place just above. Barnes left a half dozen Marines to guard the captives and turned back to the doors. As he did, his radio crackled.

"Major Barnes, this is Allen. Three aliens here want to come forward."

Wayne turned to Asoon. "There are three aliens back up top that want to come down here?"

"But, how do you know that's what they want? Is there a Speaker with them?"

"Allen, is there an English speaker there?"

"Yes, sir. Still severely weird to hear, but yes."

Barnes nodded to Asoon.

"It is probably the Principal Scientist and his maleChild. Ask that."

It was indeed Glur Woe Segt. Barnes ordered them admitted and two Marines to escort them down the long, ugly passage to where he and Asoon stood.

A few minutes later, the three stood with Wayne Barnes. The second speaker, Asoon's teacher, spoke for Segt.

"The Principal Scientist asks if you are the authority he spoke with at Planet Five."

"I am not. Connor is still on board *Columbia* with Barker. I command these Marines."

"*Columbia*?" Asoon asked.

"Ship name," David answered.

The tall alien in the black robe spoke again after hearing the translation.

"He thanks you for saving the lives you could. We saw the Combatants above."

"Well, that was more Scad than me. He convinced them. Tell me, why is the Principal Scientist here?"

"The First is a renegade. Sir Segt is here to take him under control."

Barnes looked at her with skepticism. "Assuming we get him alive, I will be delighted to turn him over. Meantime, we are in control here. Is that clear?"

Glur Woe Segt was content to let the humans take charge for now. Once the First was under control, he would take him back to the Conclave. His fate would rest with them.

David and Carol met up a few meters behind Barnes as he and Liwanu Harry were discussing what to do about the doors. She had just finished checking her people.

"Nice move, standing there with the Marines," she said quietly, her worry plain in her voice.

"Gotta do something to tell the children about, right?" he responded, smiling. "I can't let you tell *all* the good war stories."

Carol grabbed his armor vest and leaned in closer. "I really do love you."

David smiled again and winked. "Gonna hold you to that, *Commander*."

"Powell!" Barnes called. David hustled back up to where Barnes and Lt. Harry sat along the wall of the passageway with Segt and the Speaker.

"Yes, Major?"

"Asoon seems to think you have a handle on this. The Principal wants to talk the last Combatants out. This speaker — "

"Egieh Soo Neso," she said, finishing for him.

"Yes, Neso, wants you to escort him there."

"Me, sir?"

"Yeah, you. Danka here will go with you, and her squad will be covering you."

"OK, Major."

"One more thing. Principal Segt says that there are counselors in there with the First. They will be wearing grey. He will be in silver."

"Yes, sir."

"Powell, I don't know how fast this evolution will go, understand? It would be best to get that son of a bitch alive, if at all possible. Are we clear on that?"

"We are, sir, but if he strikes out at us —"

"If he threatens anyone, Lieutenant Powell, *anyone,* you are to blow his god-damn brains out."

"Yes, sir, will do."

After Asoon and Egieh completed translating the conversation for Glur and Rmah, David stood and looked directly at the older female.

"You are Neso?"

"Yes."

"Asoon says you were her teacher."

"I was."

"You did very well, Neso. She speaks well. Can I count on you as I have her?"

Barnes stood quickly. "No, Powell, you can't — "

"Oh, sir, yes, I can," he responded without looking away from Egieh. "I am betting my life on her. I can ask."

Egieh Neso could tell a tense moment when she saw it, even with someone as alien to her as Powell.

"I will be a faithful translator, David. This is all I can offer."

David set aside his doubts. "OK, then, let's go."

Just outside the Central Council Chamber
The Preeminent Home World
Tuesday, May 16, 2079, 0115 UTC

As they gathered themselves to move down to the Council doors, Danka Barczak leaned over to David and asked, "So, what happens now?"

David leaned back towards her. "Beats me, Sergeant. I was just sitting there with this pretty girl I know, next thing I'm walking into hell with the aliens." Barczak laughed slightly and stuck David with a gentle left elbow. More seriously, he answered, "Keep alert, just play it where it lies, and I think we'll be OK."

She nodded and passed the word to her squad.

As the small group approached the doors, David noticed the details: they were heavy and thick, likely steel, with large, crude-looking hinges and a similarly heavy latch holding the two sides together. There was more ambient light here than they had seen higher up. In the center of the door was a panel that looked to David like access controls. The whole thing reminded him of a gigantic, but comically ugly, bank vault.

The Preeminents placed themselves in the center of the door, with armed humans on either side, weapons ready. More Marines were just up the passage, out of sight, but ready to surge forward if necessary.

Glur Woe Segt worked the access panel for a second or two, and the doors swung open. The Combatants inside, including Donh, who Wok had tried to convince to surrender, reflexively raised their weapons in response, but quickly shrank back in fear once they saw Segt. David watched in wonder as Segt spoke again, and the Combatants moved aside, then filed meekly out to be taken captive.

Segt walked through the anteroom and opened the inner doors to the Central Council Chamber. David holstered his weapon as they moved inside, motioning to the Marines to lower their rifles. David placed himself in the center, next to Asoon.

"Segt!" the First yelled at him disparagingly as they entered. *"Again, the great traitor comes to my chamber. I should have you killed!"*

"There is no one left to carry out your will, First. Your power was revoked. It is nonexistent."

"Nonexistent? You fool, I am the First." But even as he spoke, the First was moving back, away from Segt as if cautiously avoiding a dangerous animal.

Neso kept up a quiet translation for David, and other humans began to slowly make their way in from the anteroom. David quickly assessed the situation in the council room: three counselors cowering on his left, a larger, older male now staring back at David, framed by a dark curtained entrance. There could be no doubt who he stood staring eye-to-eye with; his ugliness now so menacingly obvious. It was like staring at a rattlesnake, David thought, but this predator was intelligent, fast on his feet, and far more dangerous than even the worst Terran reptile. The First seemed to be sizing up his opposition, tightening his posture for a strike which David knew he could not allow.

It was time to take control. David drew his weapon and stepped towards the First.

"Stay back!" David shouted. Then, quieter, he repeated: "Stay where you are." David's focus was entirely on the enormous old alien, dressed in a long silver tunic with black lettering at the neck, his face leathery and dark. He saw the alien's eyes move slightly away. With part of his brain, he heard Asoon translating for the First.

David took another half step forward. "No!" he shouted, "Eyes on me, asshole. Are you ready to surrender? You don't have a lot of other good choices right now."

The First seemed to ignore David. Instead, he turned to Asoon. "I HAVE NO NEED OF YOUR TRAITOROUS SPEECH, WORTHLESS FEMALE!" he thundered in clear English. The sound shocked everyone as it carried two levels up the passageway.

The First looked at Asoon and her teacher, his pitted teeth bared in anger and conceit. "You thought only females can learn? No, exceptional males can, too. The kind of exceptional male who is a true Preeminent. The kind of exceptional male who can become the Revered First."

"Preeminent?" David said, almost laughing, "How dare you make such a claim?"

"I am the Preeminent, vermin. You should be on your knees before me!"

David's weapon never wavered as the First paced in front of him, threatening, seemingly looking for an opening to get past him. The weapon was his great-grandfather's prized .45 caliber M1911A1 hand cannon. The first David Powell had been a two-star general of some renown, but David felt his father had disgraced the weapon by his choice of suicide methods. It had taken David hours to properly clean it. This would be a good time to redeem it, he thought.

The First surprised David when he took a half step back. "I speak the languages of every obsequient culture." His eyes came back to David. "Yours should be the next, milk sucker."

"Whatever, but I think not. Since you understand so well, give it up, asshole, before I blow your twisted brains out."

"I am *the* Preeminent, Vermin. You should be on your knees!"

David smiled, his hand firmly on his sidearm, a round chambered, safety off. "Yes, so I've heard. But I am not, and you can't compel me, can you? Not without dying, anyway. My very presence here exposes you as the obscene lie you are."

"Kneel, or die, vermin!" the First threatened again, leaning forward. David saw the nostrils flare, and he could hear the movement of weapons behind him. There was no reason to stop now.

"Take your own advice, First. It's your only chance to get out of this alive. Give up and we'll see what Segt and the Conclave has in mind for you."

"Why would I? What power have *you* to compel *me*?"

"Besides the gun, you mean? The power of the truth, First. The voices of the innocent dead. You murdered a whole culture because they didn't understand what it meant to worship you."

"The ignorant Scholars? They deserved their fate."

"Deserved? They were just living their lives, threatening no one. I've seen the battlefield, First, I know the crime you committed there. Children, infants murdered in their mothers' arms."

"They failed to understand. They deserved no better."

"And what of the Inori? What crime did they commit?"

"The Deists? Despicable, credulous simpletons, too in love with their fantasies to be useful."

Even when faced with his crimes, David could see the First was unrepentant, proud, even. Time to change direction.

"Speaking of death, how many, First, how many did Dean Carpenter's crew kill that day at Inor? How many?"

As the First stared at him, he heard Scad speak quickly to Asoon.

"Ten thousand!" came her voice from behind him.

David smiled. "*Ten thousand!* You caught him by surprise, First, with much of his crew down on the planet, and still, still he beat you. How did you not understand what that meant, if you personally are the highest intelligence in the Universe? How?"

David heard Asoon translating quietly behind him for Segt and Wok. He half expected the First to attack him, but instead, he again turned to Asoon and snarled in his tone-rich, grunt-filled language.

"Stop talking, worthless female."

"I will not. As the human has said, you cannot control me."

"Do as I say or I will have your life."

"I will not," she replied dismissively,

As this exchange began escalating, Naso continued translating for the humans, which seemed to distract the First. He turned away from Asoon.

"And you, traitorous old female. I should feast on you as well."

"You will not," she responded defiantly. *"My duty as a Preeminent no longer includes obedience to you."*

The First became silent, moving again towards the center of the room. David felt he was maneuvering for some advantage, but he couldn't tell what it was yet. Meantime, he would keep countering the First's moves, remaining the center of his attention.

"Are you ready, First, finally ready?" David challenged. "Are you ready to face the truth of your condition? You are the vermin here, First, not us. You are the pestilence. Not Segt, not Asoon, not even Wok. *You.*"

"I will have your life, small —"

"You will have nothing." David cut him off. "It is you who is drenched in blood, First, not us. It is you who deserves death, not us, not the Scholars, not the Inori. *You.*"

"Young Vermin, you are so insolent I should crush your skull."

David shrugged. "Fine. Go ahead. You are the First, are you not? The finest of the Preeminent? Go ahead."

"I am the First. Yes, I am the most Preeminent, and you —"

"And yet, here you stand, alone and powerless to strike me and live. And *you* lecture *me*?" David kept up his pressure, interrupting, controlling the conversation, hoping to keep the First off guard and unable to strike.

"We are the highest form in the universe!"

"No, you're not. You and your Armada are a perversion of that idea. The fact is, you're ignorant, First, consumed with a towering ignorance wrapped in unbounded conceit. You're too ignorant and narrow-minded to understand the true meaning of the universe around you. You would be pitiful if you weren't so malignant."

"Malignant? We are the Preeminent!"

"Do you not understand how circular your argument is? How blinded by your own arrogance your thinking is? It's all bullshit."

"I am the First, we are —"

David had finally had enough. "So, what will it be for you. First? What will it be? Death or humiliation? Life in chains or a bullet in your brain? Time is running out, First. We won't wait forever."

"Impudence!" The First began moving again, still preoccupied with the Speakers quietly translating behind David: Asoon for the Preeminents, Naso for the humans. David kept moving as well, trying to keep himself between them and the First.

"The truth cannot be impudent, First. It can only be true. It is you who has lived his whole life in a malignant delusion."

The First came to a stop, staring at David. He thought briefly he might even be ready to surrender. Instead, he raised his talons and lunged towards Asoon.

David fired. The noise in the small space was deafening.

Asoon initially shrunk back from the First's assault, but was even more frightened by the blast that threw him back three steps, falling first into the heavy drapes that covered the entrance to his inner chamber, then to the floor, his breathing noisily liquid as he struggled for air.

David, as surprised at the sound as Asoon, holstered his weapon. He looked around to see Liwanu and Carol doing the same. Natalie, her sidearm still smoking, moved unhurriedly to stand over the gasping alien on the floor, four bubbling holes in his chest.

The alien's eyes widened as he saw her towering over him. "I... am... the... FIRST!" he hissed at her in defiance between shallow breaths, dark blood flowing between his teeth, droplets spraying with his desperate words.

Natalie leaned down, her impassive face just inches from his.

"And, the last. This one is for Ben."

She raised herself upright, squeezed off a single round into his forehead, then calmly put the weapon away. The First convulsed twice, then was still.

Major Barnes came forward, looked around briefly, then moved to where the First lay still on the floor.

"Damn," he said quietly after a few seconds.

"What is it, Wayne?" Carol asked.

"Four in the chest. Nice work, people."

"I know you hoped to get him alive, sir," David said. "I was hoping he'd give up when he had no choice."

"No, Powell, he wasn't going to be taken. He was a cornered predator, and he'd rather die than face the truth. You did fine."

The three remaining counselors were lying on the floor, stiff with fear. Barnes looked at them and then at Asoon. "Those are your problem, Asoon. Tell Segt."

"Yes, I will."

Barnes let out a deep sigh of relief. "Actually, Asoon, tell him everything is now his problem. We're leaving."

The tall Preeminent in black spoke to Asoon after hearing her translation.

"Sir Segt would meet with Connor and Barker if that is possible."

Barnes nodded. "It's not just possible, Asoon, it's required. You know the terms for ending this conflict, and you must comply with them. All of them. But, right now, we're leaving. This facility is yours."

"I guess we should thank you."

Wayne turned to her. "Yes, Asoon, you should."

He looked at the other Preeminent standing nearby.

"All of you should. We have other weapons, immensely powerful weapons, that we have refrained from using on you. We could have leveled this city in an instant had we desired to do so. One bright flash of light and heat, and it would have been gone, and all of you with it, leaving a desert uninhabitable for thousands of years. Instead, we spared the innocent and killed only those who left us no choice, and we did that at great loss of life to ourselves. Try to remember that, Asoon. Try to remember what we didn't do here, and what *we* sacrificed here."

"I will inform the Principal Scientist," she replied.

Barnes' expression softened, and he lowered his voice as he continued. "But, Asoon, also know that this victory is yours, too. Your outreach to us, your courage, and that of Scad and the others saved many lives on both your world and mine. So, you are deserving of our thanks, too."

She looked at the Principal Scientist, who was following the conversation with obvious curiosity. "I will tell Segt this as well."

"Good, you do that, Asoon. But, for now, goodbye." Barnes turned and headed up the passageway without waiting for a response. It would be a long, tiresome walk back to the top.

As the rest of the humans moved to follow him, there were no handshakes, no high-fives, no celebration. The cost of this victory had been too high for all of them. There were too many friends they would never again share a meal with, too many mentors whose wisdom was gone forever.

But it was over, and finally, *finally,* they could awaken from the nightmare that had started seventeen months earlier in Inoria.

Liwanu looked at Natalie. "Mine was for Ben, too." She didn't smile but simply nodded as they walked through the anteroom and started up towards the sunlight. "Nice shot, though. For a Fleetie."

Natalie relented with a small smile. "Thanks, Liwanu."

David and Carol were the last out of the Council Chamber. Carol took one final look at the cooling corpse that had started it all. David slipped his arm around her waist, and she pulled him close, kissing his cheek and holding him for a long moment.

As they turned to leave, Asoon, who was still standing at the door watching the humans file out, stopped them.

"You are paired?"

Carol looked with surprise at her. "We're engaged, if that's what you mean."

Scad's voice crackled for a few seconds.

"They're what?" he asked.

"I will explain later," Asoon answered. *"They are agreed to be paired, but with them it is insufferably complicated."*

Carol looked at Asoon for a moment, waiting for a translation. When it didn't come, she turned David towards the door, and they began the long uphill trek to the shuttles, tightly arm in arm.

"Goodbye, Asoon."

Asoon said nothing, responding with just a slight bow of her head.

Once outside the Council Chamber, she looked up at him. "I had a message from home a couple weeks ago. We need to talk."

"Really? What about?"

"Grandchildren."

Silver Victory

Rock Whitehouse

Epilogue – June 2079

With the death of the Revered First and the collapse of his cult of Preeminence, Principal Scientist Glur Woe Segt took full control of the Armada and assigned Sdom Roi Gotk, who had decisively held back the Preeminents' remaining warships during the crisis, to command them. Gotk's first assignment was to return promptly to Beta Hydri, retrieve the 'leftovers' that Liwanu Harry had declined to kill and remove the crashed shuttles from the planet. That project would take several months, all done under the watchful eye of the Seekers.

Asoon Too Lini had completed her immediate translation task, but there was more for her to do. At Glur Woe Segt's direction, Asoon and Scad Nee Wok established a liaison office with the humans. They would be the contact for those who would oversee the relief of the enslaved systems. When her fertility arrived, she and Scad Nee Wok produced four eggs, all of which were viable and returned to them.

Fleet Marine Sergeant Leon Jackson, who as a new corporal, had backed up Carol Hansen in Inoria, and then saved her life on the descent to the First's chambers, died the next day on *Ceres*. He contracted a fast-moving infection that started on his burns but quickly engulfed his entire system. He was twenty-five years old. Days later, they would discover that a previously unknown, extremely motile and toxic strain of the Terran bacteria *Proteus* had overwhelmed him. Theories about the source were legion, but an antibiotic cocktail was found in laboratory testing that eventually defeated the bug in later patients.

Carol would learn of his loss only after she was back on Earth. Devastated, she wrote long letters of gratitude to his wife and parents.

Eaagher never revealed the secret of their evacuation to his new friends. The submarine they had been hiding since it left their secret underwater port, a port whose entrance the humans had found but not understood, was brought up from the ocean floor. Once the Preeminent had evacuated their survivors, the sub carried the Seekers back to their cities in a few Big Blue days. Soon the skeletons were removed and properly disposed of in the sea. Then, the Seekers could begin rebuilding their lives and again spend time in the priceless accumulation of knowledge, the foundation of the pursuit of wisdom.

Professors Gabrielle Este and Greg Cordero worked with Elias Peña to understand the societies the Preeminent had conquered, and how they might be

295

brought back to their previous free state. It would take years, they decided, to unwind the situation. They were now an inseparable team, both on-duty and off. After a trip home with Alona Melville aboard *Jarvis* to prepare, they would return to Alpha Mensae several months later to begin the work.

Mark Rhodes' *Chaffee* was, indeed, fatally broken. Without FTL capability, she was no longer of any use, and CINC ordered Mark to remove everything useful onto *Ceres* and then scuttle her into Alpha Mensae. CINC could not permit a Forstmann Drive, or a nuclear fission reactor, to be simply left behind. *Sigma* stood by as Mark set *Chaffee's* final course and was the last person off the ship. He and his crew had a long, sad ride home in the new Marine bunk space aboard *Sigma*.

Melinda Hughes returned home in the hospital on *Ceres*. Her condition improved rapidly with therapy, and by mid-July, she was fully recovered and ready to resume her duties aboard *Columbia*. She and Mike Clark were married in August in Newport News. She did not keep the faux-hawk.

Liwanu Harry came home on *Intrepid*, spending time with Natalie Hayden and writing the letters officers are required to write. Even with the losses, he was grateful that most of his Marines had survived. Sergeant Danka Barczak helped him with details, gathering personal effects, and keeping the letters brief and to the point.

Dan Smith kept *Columbia* in orbit at Alpha Mensae for another two weeks while Powell worked with Rmah Teo Segt to identify the subject systems the Preeminent had conquered. There were six, all on the opposite side of Alpha Mensae, so every system would be a long trip from Earth. Davenport decided that the Preeminent would be allowed to keep what they had built on three other uninhabited planets, once Fleet had inspected them and confirmed their status. Rmah did not argue.

Rich Evans retained command of *Cobra*. After a month's respite home in New Zealand, he returned in early July to begin preparations for the extended trips to recon the slave systems. He trusted Rmah, but trust was one thing, seeing with your own eyes was something else.

"In God we trust;" he told Rmah, "All else we verify."

After his return in *Columbia*, Elias Peña passed on CINC's offer of an assignment to FleetIntel, and instead requested a ship of his own. He took command of *Resnik* as she came out of the ship factory. The less time on Earth, the better, as far as Elias was concerned.

Ron Harris took the end of the war as an opportunity to call an end to his Fleet career. Late in July, once nearly everyone was home, he and Meredith held their last enormous cookout, an extended affair visited several times by base security, who left each time with full plates. They returned to her small home town in Ohio, and Ron took a part-time position teaching *Current Intelligence Systems and Methods* at SFU. Meredith, her family finally at peace, slept every night like she never had before. Their fourth child, a son, Benjamin Dean Harris, was born the next spring.

Fiona Collins hitched a ride home on *Intrepid*, then took a leisurely three week leave in Fiji with Joanne. Afterwards, she accepted CINC's offer of a star and command of FleetIntel, following in her classmate Ron Harris' footsteps. She thought about following Ron into retirement, but the Fleet was still her life, and she just wasn't quite ready to leave it all behind. No one applauded louder at her promotion announcement than Rich Evans, who was quite sure he had just dodged a serious bullet.

Natalie Hayden enjoyed sharing her *Intrepid* cabin with Fiona on the trip back to Earth. Fiona had known Ben very well, and they talked about him almost every day. It helped Natalie to hear someone else's experiences with him. Once off the ship, she stopped at Sugarloaf Mountain for a solitary sunset, then visited Ben's parents before heading home to Bozeman for an extended leave. Natalie politely, but firmly, declined Joanne and Fiona's repeated invitations to join them on their warm South Pacific beach. She needed her mountains, she told them; cool, thin air suited her best. A bit of Ben would always live in her heart, and as she walked familiar trails in Custer-Gallatin National Forest, she felt him nearby. She would not return to *Intrepid*, but instead took a teaching position at SFU, starting after the New Year.

Joanne Henderson, freshly tanned and well-rested after three weeks on the beach with Fiona, passed on CINC's offer to command Plans, choosing instead to return to *Intrepid* and the opportunity to find new inhabited worlds. Now that she was out of HQ, she made it clear they would play hell getting her back there. Joanne begged Natalie to come back to *Intrepid* with her, but she was adamant that she'd had her fill of deep space for now. *Maybe later*, Natalie told her, but for now, she needed peace and quiet and time to heal. Joanne understood that completely, she just found her comfort in a different place.

Carol Hansen took *Sigma* back to Big Blue to personally deliver the news of the Preeminent defeat to Eaagher and the rest of the surviving Seekers. It would take time, she told them, for the Preeminent to remove their survivors and wreckage from the old settlement, but they were safe and free to return. Ullnii learned a new word in English: Peace.

Once back home, CINC had some very loud and direct words for her about leaving her command. But, he also congratulated her on *Sigma*'s performance at e-prime. Still, she was relieved of her command and reassigned to Plans, both to give her some HQ experience and permit her to attend the six-month-long Deep-Space Command School. Peg White took over as *Sigma's* XO. *Intrepid's* Alonzo Bass took command after his promotion to full Commander.

David Powell thought about hitching a ride back to Earth on *Sigma*, but instead he dutifully remained on *Cobra*. His time with Carol would have to wait just a little while longer. He worked with Asoon and Rmah to locate the slave systems, and on the long trip home, he and Rich Evans studied how they would approach, from a military viewpoint, the relief of those cultures. *Cobra* was the last ISC Fleet ship to leave Alpha Mensae. With Carol assigned to Plans and the command school, David requested FleetIntel and was granted a long-term assignment. Fiona's first task for him was a year as Frances Wilson's understudy, with occasional trips to Alpha Mensae to work with Asoon and the other Preeminent.

David and Carol were married on the Hansen farm in September. It was a small affair, but several of their fellow officers from *Antares, Columbia, Cobra,* and *Sigma* attended. Fiona Collins was there. Natalie Hayden was there. Terri Michael's husband and three daughters were there. And, perhaps most importantly, Grandma Virginia was there.

It was quite the party.

Silver Victory

Appendix A: Preeminent Time

Alpha Mensae (c), which the Fleet labeled 'e-prime' and the Preeminent refer to as 'Home,' is the third of the eleven planets that revolve around that star. 'Home' turns on its axis in 25 hours and 8 minutes. The Preeminent developed their time-keeping method using successive factors of 10, unlike human time which uses 24 hours per day, each consisting of 60 minutes of 60 seconds each.

For the Preeminent, each rotation of their planet is divided into ten 'deciRotations,' colloquially called a 'drot.' A drot is roughly analogous to a human hour, but is much longer – almost 151 human minutes. Each drot is further divided into decimal-derived subdivisions, as shown in the following table:

Term	Slang	Fraction	Human Equivalent
Rotation	Rot	1	25 hours, 8 minutes
Deci-Rotation	Drot	1/10	150 minutes, 48 seconds
Centi-Rotation	Cenrot	1/100	15 minutes, five seconds
Milli-Rotation	Milrot	1/1,000	91 seconds
Centi-Milli-Rotation	CenMilRot	1/100,000	0.9 second
Micro-Rotation	MicRot	1/1,000,000	0.01 second

For the cardinal times of the day, like sunrise, noon, and sunset, the Preeminent use more technical terminology: StarRise, StarZenith, and StarSet. Similarly, 'lastRot' is equivalent to 'yesterday,' 'thisRot' is 'today,' and, of course, 'nextRot' is 'tomorrow.'

As to 'years,' the Preeminents' Home revolves around Alpha Mensae in 320 rotations, plus a small fraction. What we call a 'year' they refer as a 'rev,' short for 'revolution.' Each rev is divided into ten decirevs, or 'drev,' which are analogous to our months.

There is no concept of a 'week' in Preeminent time, but with 32 rots in a decirev, there is a universal day of rest every fifteen days. Dates are similarly technical, based on which rotation it is within which deci-revolution. The idea of repeating day names as humans use never occurred to the Preeminent.

Revs are numbered, and are believed to be counted from the beginning of Preeminent society, although there is no extant documentation of how the numbering began, or who defined it. Some in the SD believe the system dates to the founding of that institution, but there is no contemporary record to support that idea, either.

They do recognize the concept of a 'decade' and a 'century' and, similar to human calendars, revs are counted by which rev within which century it occurs. For example, the war ended in the 45th rev of the 9155th century of the Preeminent.

Appendix B: Dramatis Personae

Name	Rank	Description
Alex Williams	SLT	Navigator, then XO on *Antares*
Alonzo Bass	LCDR	*Intrepid's* XO
Andy Martin	CPT	Fleet Marine Captain
Ann Cooper	LT	HQ Intel Analyst.
Anna Nonna	CDR	*Bondarenko's* Captain
Ashil Kiker		Preeminent Third Counselor
Asoon Too Lini		Preeminent Speaker
Ben Price	WO4	Intel Chief on *Intrepid*. Shortly after becoming engaged to Natalie Hayden, Ben was killed in the first battle on Big Blue.
Carol Hansen	SLT	Our Heroine
Chuck Anderson	SLT	Intel Officer on *Intrepid* after Ben Price's death
Connor Davenport	ADM	Fleet Commander (aka CINC)
Dagny Forstmann Carpenter		Randy's sister and Dean Carpenter's wife.
Dan Smith	LCDR	SFU classmate of Carol and David, Captain of *Columbia*
Danka Barczak	SGT	Marine Sergeant
David Powell	SLT	Our Hero
Dean Carpenter	CPT	*Liberty's* Captain when she was destroyed above Inoria. Carpenter was an early pioneer in Drive ship handling before joining the Fleet at its inception.
Denise Long	WO4	Inoria survivor, Reactor Officer on *Antares*
Dremonte Ingram	ENS	Nurse on *Columbia*
Eaagher Fita		Leader of the Seeker survivors
Elias Peña	LCDR	Deputy to Ron Harris in FleetIntel, then CSTO's Chief of Intel
Emilio Guzman	Chief	Chief Weapons Tech on *Antares*

Name	Rank	Description
Fiona Collins	CPT	Chief of Plans Division.
Frances Wilson		HQ Intel Analyst
Gabrielle Este		Archeologist
Glur Woe Segt		Preeminent, Second Principal Scientist,
Greg Cordero		Linguist who broke the Seeker language.
Jack Ballard	SLT	Intel Analyst on *Cobra,* previously Intel Officer on *Antares.*
Jayvon Dean	LT	Surveillance Officer on *Antares*
Joanne Henderson	CDR	*Intrepid's* Captain
Jon Swenson	CW3	Weapons Maintenance Officer on *Antares*
Kamaria Allen	2LT	New Marine Lieutenant
Kieran Barker	RADM	CSTO (Commander, South Theater of Operations)
Leon Jackson	SGT	Inoria survivor, Marine sergeant on *Antares.*
Liwanu Harry	1LT	Young Marine officer; he was with Ben when he was killed at first battle on Big Blue.
Lori Rodgers	SLT	Communications Officer on *Antares*
Marcia Soto, MD	SLT	Carol's roommate, Medical Officer on *Antares*
Marco Gonzales	LT	*Intrepid's* Surveillance Officer
Mazablaska Dawes	SLT	*Columbia's* XO
Melinda Hughes	SLT	*Columbia's* Surveillance Officer
Meredith Harris		Ron's wife
Mike Clark	LT	Weapons Maintenance Officer on *Columbia*
Natalie Hayden	SLT	Weapons Maintenance Officer on *Intrepid*
Nobuyuki Kawaguchi	CPT	Captain of *Nippon*
Patricia Cook	RADM	Chief of Fleet Operations
Peg White	LCDR	Chief Engineer at Tranquility II
Randy Forstmann		Inventor of the Faster-than-Light drive.

Name	Rank	Description
Rich Evans	LCDR	Rich was the Intel Officer on *Liberty*, and survived the attack on Inoria. After a stint in FleetIntel, he was placed in command of *Cobra*.
Rmah Teo Segt		Glur's maleChild, student, and co-conspirator
Roger Cox	LT	Ballard's replacement on *Intrepid*
Ron Harris	RADM	Chief of Fleet Intelligence.
Scad Nee Wok		Preeminent Ship Commander who took Kiker to Earth. Later, malePair of Asoon Too Lini.
Stanimir Arkadiy Yakovlev	VADM	Deputy Fleet Commander
Susan Scranton, MD	CDR	Exobiologist
Terri Michael	CPT	Captain of *Antares*
Wayne Barnes	MAJ	Commander of the Fleet Marines at Beta Hydri and e-prime

Acknowledgements

Thanks for reading *Silver Victory*. Please leave a review at the vendor where you purchased it. If you have questions or comments, feel free to email me at rock@iscfleet.com. I'd be glad to hear from you.

This book completes the story of 'Carol and David and The War' I originally wanted to tell. I hope you found it entertaining. But there is certainly more in this universe that we could explore. Maybe we need a prequel about Forstmann's invention of The Drive, or some additional stories during the war that we didn't have space to include. The six enslaved cultures also seem like fertile ground for David and Carol to explore.

Time to acknowledge (admit?) our sources and methods...

As usual, solstation.com and wikipedia.com were frequent references, as were nasa.gov and jpl.nasa.gov.

My spelling is now utterly dependent on dictionary.com. I send my gravest apologies to my high school college-prep English teacher, the one who believed I could be a success 'at whatever he decides to do.' I've never forgotten those words. I still have the yearbook to prove it.

Likewise, thesaurus.com saved me when I was struggling to find that word, kinda like that other word, but with a different implication, you know, the one that starts with, um, you know, that other letter? True story: I could not recall that word that's like determination but is more personal, and, I think it starts with p. I kept at it until I finally came up with 'persistent.' I then had a good laugh at myself that I had been persistent in my search for 'persistent.'

I used the site www.philipmetzger.com/type-of-asteroid-to-mine-part-3 when trying to figure out what type of asteroid I would choose for a space ship factory. I then used the resources at Wikipedia's 'List of exceptional asteroids' and JPL's search at ssd.jpl.nasa.gov to find just the right one. These were very useful in telling me that the asteroid I really wanted doesn't actually exist. I had to settle for 1235 Schorria, which was close enough, and has the advantage of being real.

I thought the Preeminent's use of decimal time would be a unique and interesting diversion from our fairly weird clock system. But in researching it I found at www.mentalfloss.com/article/32127/decimal-time-how-french-made-10-hour-day that this had already been tried during the French Revolution. There were (and perhaps still are?) clocks in decimal time. Who knew?

New character names were again generated in Excel from lists of common first and last names, with several specialized (i.e., non-US) names coming from www.namegeneratorfun.com and behindthename.com. Preeminent and Seeker names were generated programmatically with Perl, using a predefined vowel/consonant pattern and a randomly sampled seed phrase. That was the really fun part.

I am again indebted to the friends and beta-readers who have supported me and contributed so unselfishly to this process. Their comments and corrections are vitally important to me and to the quality of the work.

My editor, Kimberly Greenfield-Karshner, does an excellent job of keeping me honest and coloring inside the grammatical lines.

My wife Carey has been very tolerant of my long days in the office and is an excellent proof-reader as well. Her support, and that of my immediate and extended family, is priceless.

Made in the USA
Columbia, SC
17 October 2021